Star-Dust

Fannie Hurst

Contents

STAR-DUST

BY

Fannie Hurst

Book One
THE VINE

Oh, the little more and how much it is:
And the little less, and what worlds away.
--BROWNING.

CHAPTER I

When Lilly Becker eked out with one hand that most indomitable of pianoforte selections, Rubinstein's "Melody in F," her young mind had a habit of transcending itself into some such illusory realm as this: Springtime seen lacily through a phantasmagoria of song. A very floral sward. Fountains that tossed up coloratura bubbles of sheerest aria and a sort of Greek frieze of youth attitudinized toward herself.

This frieze was almost invariably composed of Estelle Foote, a successful rival in a class candidacy for the sponge-and-basin monitorship; Sydney Prothero, infallible of spitball aim; Miss Lare with her spectacles very low on her nose and a powdering of chalk dust down her black alpaca; Flora Kemble with infinitely fewer friendship bangles on her silver link bracelet; Roy Kemble, kissing her yellow, rather than yanking her brown, braids.

And then suddenly, apropos of nothing except the sweet ache of Lilly's little soul, the second movement would freeze itself into a proscenium arch of music, herself, like a stalagmite, its slim center.

At this point, "Melody in F" veils itself in a mist of arpeggios, and Mrs. Becker, who invariably, during the after-school practice hour, sat upstairs with Mrs. Kemble in her sunny second-story back, would call down through the purposely opened floor register.

"Lilly, not so fast on that part."

"Yes'm."

Were it not that the salient spots, the platform places in experience, are floored over in little more or less identical mosaics of all the commonplace day by days, Lilly Becker, at the rented-by-the-month piano in her parents' back parlor in Mrs. Schum's boarding house, her two chestnut braids rather precociously long and thick down her back, her mother rocking rhythmically overhead, were spurious to this narrative.

Yet how much more potently than by the mere exposition of it and because you have looked in on the nine-year-old chemistry of a vocal and blond dream in the dreaming, are you to know the Lilly of seventeen, who secretly and unsuccessfully washed her hair in a solution of peroxide, and at eighteen, through the patent device of a megaphone inserted through a plate-glass window, was singing to--But anon.

There was a game Lilly used to play on the front stairs of Mrs. Schum's boarding house, winter evenings after dinner. She and Lester Eli, who, at seventeen, was to drown in a pleasure canoe; Snow Horton--clandestinely present--daughter of a neighborhood dentist and forbidden to play with the "boarding-house children"; Flora and Roy Kemble, twins; and little Harry Calvert, who would creep up like a dirty little white mouse from the basement kitchen.

"C"--hissed sibilantly.

"Can't carry cranky cats!"

"No fair, Snow; that doesn't make sense."

"Does."

"Your turn, Roy."

"Z."

"No fair. Nothing begins with 'Z.'"

LILLY: "Does so. Z! Z--zounds--zippy--zingorella--zoe! Zoe!"

By similar strain of alliterative classification, Mrs. Schum's boarding house might have been indexed as Middle West, middle class, medium price, and meager of meal.

Poor, callous-footed Mrs. Schum, with her spotted bombazine bosom and her loosely anchored knob of gray hair! She was the color of cold dish water at that horrid moment when the grease begins to float, her hands were corroded with it, and her smile somehow could catch you by the heartstrings, which smiles have no right to do. How patiently and how drearily she padded through these early years of Lilly's existence. There were rubber insets in her shoes which sagged so that her ankles seemed actually to touch the floor from the climbing upstairs and downstairs on her missionary treadmill of the cracked slop jar; the fly in the milk; the too-tepid shaving water; the bathroom monopoly; the infant cacophony of midnight colic; salt on the sleety sidewalk, the pasted handkerchief against a front window pane; ice water. Towels. Towels. Towels.

And how saucily after school would Lilly plant herself down in the subterranean depths of the kitchen.

"Mrs. Schum, mamma says to give me a piece of bread and butter."

With her worried eyes Mrs. Schum would smile and invariably hand out a thick slice, thinly buttered.

"More butter, mamma said."

"That's plenty, dearie; too much isn't good for little girls' complexions."

"More but-ter!"

"Here, then."

Scalloping the air with it before little Harry's meek eyes: "You can't have any. You don't pay board. We do!"

"My Mamma-Annie she paid board once. Uh-huh! my Mamma-Annie she's an angel in heaven and you aren't. Uh-huh!" This from little Harry, who was far too pale and wore furiously stained blouses.

"But your mamma-Annie's dead now. You can't be a real live angel without being dead first, and I'd rather be me."

"Lilly, aren't you ashamed? You run on now, or I'll tell your mamma. Poor little Harry can't help it he's an orphan with only his old gramaw to look after him. You a great big girl with your mother and father to do for you. It's not nice to be against Harry."

"Well, what was I saying so much, Mrs. Schum? Can I help it he says she's an angel? Here, Harry, you can have it. Mamma's got a whole basket of apples in the closet and a dozen oranges. Honest, take it, I'm not hungry."

He would mouth into it, round eyes gazing at her above the rim of crust.

There were times again when Lilly would bare her teeth and crunch them in a paroxysm of rage and tyranny over little Harry. She would delight in making herself terrible to him, pinch and tower over the huddle of him with her hands hooked inward like talons. His meekness hurt her to frenzy, and because she was ashamed of tears she clawed.

"Oh, you! You! You just make me feel like--I don't know what."

"Ouch! Lilly, you pinch!"

"Well, then, don't always hold your head off to one side like somebody was going to hit you. I hate it. It makes me feel like wanting to hit you."

"I won't."

"You aren't such a goody-goody. You steal. You stole some balls of twine my papa brought home from his factory. Mamma says you got it behind your ears."

"I haven't anything behind my ears."

"Oh, silly! Everything isn't there just because you say it's there. If I close my eyes just a little eeny, I can see birds and fountains and a beautiful stage, and me with my hair all gold, and a blue satin train that kicks back when I walk, and all the music in the world winding around me like--like everything--like smoke. But it isn't truly there, silly, except inside of me."

"Haw."

"I'm going to be the beautifulest singer in the world some day, with a voice that goes as high as anything, and be on the stage, and you can't even be on it with me."

"'N' I'm going to work in a butcher shop and give gramaw all the meat she wants without even putting it down in the book."

"You steal."

"Don't."

"Do."

"And I won't ever have to touch the meat if it's got blood on."

"Fraidy, scared of a little blood." Then with not a great deal of relevance, "I could have the yellowest hair in the world if I wanted to."

"How?"

"Oh, by just wanting to."

"Nit."

"Could."

"Your mamma's calling you."

"Lil-ly, come practice."

"I'm coming." To Harry, "I can do something you can't do."

"What?"

"Hop up six stairs on one foot."

"Dare you."

Ankle cupped in her hand, brown braids bobbing, she would thus essay two, three, even four steps of staggering ascent, collapsing then against the banister.

"Ouch!"

"Told you so."

"Well, I nearly did."

"Oh, you *nearly* do everything."

"I can't help it if my foot isn't strong enough to hold me."

"Lil-ly, don't let me have to call you again."

"I'm coming, mamma." And then for a final tantalizing gleam of her little self across the banister, "Last tag."

CHAPTER II

One wall of the Becker back parlor was darkly composed of walnut folding doors dividing it from the front-parlor bachelor apartment of Mr. Hazzard, city salesman for the J.D. Nichols Fancy Grocery Supply Company, his own horse and buggy furnished by the firm.

It was Mrs. Becker's habit during his day-long absence, in fact just as soon as her acute ear detected the scraping departure of his tin-tired wheels from the curb, to fling back these folding doors for the rush of daylight and sense of space, often venturing in beside the front window with a bit of sewing and pottering ever so discreetly at the sample packages of fine teas, jars of perfectly conserved asparagus, peas, and olives spread out on his mantelpiece and fingering, again ever so discreetly, the neatly ripped stack of letters on the dresser. Once, and despite Mrs. Becker's frantic swoop to save it, a piece of pressed flower fell out from one of these envelopes in the handling, crumbling to bits as it fluttered to the floor.

Next morning the folding doors refused to part to touch, an eye to the keyhole discovering it clogged with key. Then Lilly began music lessons and the newly rented upright piano was drawn up against these doors.

Never were fingers more recalcitrant at musical chores. The Bach "Inventions" were weary digital gyrations against the slow-moving hands of the alarm clock perched directly in her line of vision. Czerny, too, was punctuated with quick little forays between notes, into a paper bag of "baby pretzels" at the treble end of the piano, often as not lopping over on the keyboard.

But with the plunge into brilliant but faulty execution of one of her "pieces," her little face would flood over and tighten up into the glyptic immobility of a cameo and her toes curl as they pressed the pedals.

"The Storm King" of the Parlor Pianoforte Series was a favorite. Dashing her quickly memorized way through it, she would follow closely the brief printed synopsis on the cover page ... suddenly the clouds gather, a bird carols, a faint rumble is heard in the distance (it is important that the student practice this base tremolo with left hand only), the rush of approaching wind mingles with the nearing roll of thunder, accompanied by occasional flashes of lightning....

The red would run up into Lilly's face and her hands churn the white keys into a curdled froth of dissonance.

"Lil-ly, not so fast. Play 'Selections from Faust' now, slowly, and count, the way Miss Lee said you should."

Another favorite was the just published "Narcissus" of Nevin. Its cross-hand movement was a phillipic to her ever-ready-to-ferment fancy. Head back and gaze into the scroll-and-silk front of the piano, the melody would again, like a curve of gold, shape itself into the lovely form of a proscenium arch.

"Lilly, that is beautiful. Play the tune part over again."

The tingling that would actually gooseflesh her would die down as surely as a ringing crystal tumbler, had she closed her warm little hand over it.

"Mamma," her voice directed upward toward the open register, "can I--may I go out on my tricycle?"

"No."

"I've only ten minutes yet, mamma. I'll make them up to-morrow."

"No, I don't intend to pay Miss Lee fifty cents a lesson so you can go out and ride on your tricycle. You bothered me for the lessons, so now you practice. Work on 'Narcissus' so you can play it for your father to-night."

"Oh, mom, please."

"I don't care. Go! Only put on your hat and don't let me see you riding around on Taylor Avenue."

"No'm."

CHAPTER III

The St. Louis of Lilly's little girlhood, sprung so thrivingly from the left bank of the Mississippi and builded on the dead mounds of a dead past, was even then inexplicably turning its back to its fine river frontage; stretching in the form of a great adolescent giant, prone, legs flung to the west and full of growing pains, arms outstretched and curving downward in a great north-and-south yawn.

Taylor Avenue (then almost the city's edge, and which now is a girdle worn high about its gigantic middle) petered out into violently muddy and unmade streets and great patches of unimproved vacant lots that in winter were gaunt with husks.

A pantechnicon procession of the more daring, shot with the growing pains, was grading and building into the vast clayey seas west of Kings-highway, but for the most part St. Louis contained herself gregariously enough within her limits, content in those years when the country rang hollowly to the cracked ring of free silver to huddle under the same blanket with her smoke-belching industries.

A picture postcard of a brewery, piled high like a castle and with stables of Augean collosity, rose from the south tip of the city to the sour-malt supremacy of the world; boots, shoes, tobacco, and street cars bringing up by a nose, Eads Bridge, across the strong breast of the Mississippi, flinging roads of commerce westward ho.

For one rapidly transitional moment street-car traffic in St. Louis stood in three simultaneous stages of its lepidopterous development: a caterpillar horse-car system crawled north and south along Jefferson Avenue, glass coin box and the backward glance of the driver, in lieu of conductor. A cable-car system ready to burst its chrysalis purred the length of Olive Street, and a first electric car, brightly painted, and with a proud antenna of trolley, had already whizzed out Washington Avenue.

When Lilly was twelve years old her walk to school was across quite an intricacy of electric-car tracks, and on rainy days, out of a small fund of children's car tickets laid by in Mrs. Becker's glove box for just that contingency, she would ride to and from school, changing cars with a drilled precision at Vandaventer and Finney Avenues.

For the first few of these adventures Mrs. Becker wrote tiny notes, to be handed out by Lilly along with her street-car ticket:

Conductor, please let this little girl off at Jefferson Avenue: she wants to change cars for the Pope School.

One day by some mischievous mischance Mrs. Schum's board receipt found its way into Lilly's little pocketbook:

Received of Mrs. Ben Becker, forty-five dollars for one month's board for three.

"Aw," said the conductor, thrusting it back at her, "ask your mamma to tell her troubles to a policeman, little girl."

From that day Lilly rebelled.

"Guess I can find my way to school without having to carry a note like a baby."

"But, Lilly, you might get mixed up."

"Nit."

"Don't sass me that way or I'll tell your father when he comes home to-night."

A never quite bursting cloud which hung over the entire of Lilly's girlhood was this ever-impending threat which even in its rare execution brought forth no more than a mild and rather sad rebuke from a mild and rather sad father, and yet which was certain to quell any rising rebellion.

"I notice you never get sassy or ugly to your father, Lilly. I do all the stinting and make all the sacrifices and your father gets all the respect."

"Mamma, how can you say that!"

"Because it's a fact. To him it is always, 'Yes, sir, no, sir.' I'm going to tell him a few things when he comes home to-night of what I go through with all day in his absence. Elocution lessons! Just you ask him for them yourself."

"Oh, mamma, you promised!"

"Well, I will, but I oughtn't."

Every evening until long after Lilly's dresses had descended to her shoe tops and until the ritual came to have a distinctly ridiculous aspect, there took place the one pleasantry in which Lilly and her father ever indulged.

About fifteen minutes before seven, three staccato rings would come at the front-door bell. At her sewing or what not, Mrs. Becker would glance up with bird-like quickness.

"That's papa!" And Lilly, almost invariably curled over a book, would jump up and take stand tensely against the wall so that when the room door opened it would swing back, concealing her.

In the frame of that open doorway Mrs. Becker and her husband would kiss, the unexcited matrimonial peck of the taken-for-granted which is as sane to the taste as egg, and as flat, and then the night-in-and-night-out question that for Lilly, rigid there behind the door, never failed to thrill through her in little darts.

"Where is Lilly, Carrie?"

MRS. BECKER (assuming an immediate mask of vacuity): "Why, I don't know, Ben. She was here a minute ago."

"Well, well, well!" looking under the bed, under the little cot drawn across its baseboard and into a V of a back space created by a catacorner bureau. "Well, well, well! What could have happened to her?"

At this juncture Lilly, fairly titillating, would burst out and before his carefully averted glance fling wide her arms in self-revelation.

"Here I am, papa!"

"Well, I'll declare, so she is!" lifting her by the armpits for a kiss. "Well, well, well!"

"Papa, I got ninety in arithmetic. I'd have got a hundred, but I got the wrong common denominator."

"That's right, Lilly. Keep up well in your studies. Remember, knowledge is power."

"Get your father's velveteen coat, Lilly."

"Papa, Ella McBride kisses boys."

"Then don't ever let me hear of your associating with her. The little girl that doesn't keep her own self-respect cannot expect others to respect her."

"And you ought to see, papa, she always rides her tricycle down past Eddie Posner's house on Delmar just to show herself off to him."

"Lilly, go wash your hands for supper. How is business, Ben?"

"Nothing extra, Carrie."

"Oh, I get so tired hearing a poor mouth. Sometimes I could just scream for wanting to do things we are not in a position to do. Go housekeeping, for instance, have a little home of my own--"

"Now, now, little woman," at the invariable business of flecking his neat gray business suit with a whisk broom, "you got up on the wrong side of bed this morning. Lilly, suppose you shine papa's spectacles for him."

"There is the supper bell. Quick, Ben and Lilly, before the Kembles."

The dining room, directly over the basement kitchen, jutted in an ell off the rear of the house so that from the back parlor it was not difficult to precede the immediate overhead response to that bell. A black-faced genii of the bowl and weal, in a very dubiously white-duck coat thrust on hurriedly over clothing reminiscent of the day's window washing and furnace cinders, held attitude in among the small tables that littered the room. There were four. A long table seating ten and punctuated by two sets of cruets, two plates of bread, and two white-china water pitchers; Mr. Hazzard's tiny square of individual table, a perpetual bottle of brown medicine beside his place. The Kembles also enjoyed segregation from the mother table, the family invariably straggling in one by one. For the Beckers was reserved the slight bulge of bay window that looked out upon the Suburban street-car tracks and a battalion of unpainted woodsheds. A red geranium, potted and wrapped around in green crepe tissue paper, sprouted center table, a small bottle of jam and two condiments lending further distinction. A napkin with self-invented fasteners dangled from Mr. Becker's chair, and beside Lilly's place a sterling silver and privately owned knife and fork, monogrammed.

To Mr. Becker, the negro race was largely and genetically christened Gawge, to be addressed solely in native patois.

"Evenin', Gawge."

"Evenin', Mistah Beckah."

"George, are you going to take good care of my husband to-night? That piece of steak you served him yesterday wasn't fit to eat."

"Law now, Mis' Beckah, kin I help it if de best de kitchen has ain't none too good?"

"Don't tell me! I saw the piece you brought Mr. Kemble."

"Now, Carrie ..."

"What have we to-night, George?"

"Fried steak, lamb, or corn'-beef hash."

"Bring us steak, and if it isn't tender, tell Mrs. Schum for me that right back downstairs it goes! A little piece of lamb on the side in case Miss Lilly don't like the steak, and bring up a dish of those sweet pickles. You know, under the tray the way you always do. There's a pair of Mr. Becker's old shoes, good as new, waiting to be given away."

"Carrie!"

"Miss Lilly loves pickles. George, do as I say."

"Carrie!"

"Law! Mistah Beckah, I knows Mis' Beckah and her ways. Law! I doan take no offense."

"I wish if you want extras, Carrie, you would buy them. It is a darn shame to make yourself so small before the other boarders."

"I haven't as much money as you have, Ben Becker. I'm not ashamed to ask for my money's worth. Lilly, haven't I told you not to talk on your fingers at meals?"

This form of digital communication between the children of the boarding house seemed to break out in its most virulent form at dinner. In spite of a sharp consensus of parental disapproval, there was a continual flashing of code between Lilly, the Kemble twins, and Lester Eli at the larger table.

"Ben, will you speak to Lilly? She won't mind me."

"Lilly!"

"Yes, sir," immediately subsiding to a contemplation of the geranium.

Poker played for penny stakes was a favorite after-dinner pastime. A group including Mrs. Eli, the Kembles, and Mr. Hazzard would gather in the Becker back parlor, Mrs. Becker, relieved of corsets and in a dark-blue foulard teagown shotted all over with tiny pink rosebuds, presiding over a folding table with a glass bowl of the "baby pretzels" in its center.

The children meanwhile would forgather on the front hall stairs, the peaked flare of an olive of gaslight that burned through a red glass globe with warts blown into it, bathing the little group in a sort of greasy fluid. Roy and Flora Kemble, Snow Horton, Lester Eli, and Stanley Beinenstock, racked with bronchitis and lending an odor of creosote, Lilly, and even Harry in his poor outlandish blouse.

"Snow, tell us a story; you're the oldest."

Snow was full of lore; would invoke inspiration with a very wide and very blue gaze up to the ceiling, her thin hands clasping her thin neck.

"Once upon a time--once upon a time there was the most beautiful girl in all the world and her name was--"

"Aw, give us one about boys."

LILLY: "You shut up, Roy Kemble. I guess Snow can tell a girl story if she wants to. Go on, Snow, 'once upon a time there was the most beautiful girl in all the world' and she had honey-colored curls and--"

"I didn't say she had honey-colored curls. Honey! Who ever heard of a girl having honey curls?"

"Well, she had."

"Didn't."

"Did."

"--and her name was--was--Gladys."

"Oh no, Snow, call her--"

"I think Gladys is just a beautiful name for a girl," ventured Flora Kemble on this occasion. "I like Elsie, too. I think Elsie Dinsmore is my favorite name."

"Elsie Dinsmore!" flared Lilly. "Girls aren't pokey like her any more."

Thus diverted, there ensued a quick confetti of flung opinions.

"Minn is a pretty name."

"That's because you're stuck on Minnie Duganne in your class. Oh-oh, Roy is stuck on Minnie Duganne!"

"Arabella--I just love that name. Don't you, Lilly?"

"If I was a girl, I would be named Mamma-Annie."

"Shut up, Harry; and, say, you better take back that can opener. You stole it off Mr. Hazzard's dresser."

"What is your favorite name, Lilly?"

Her eyes on the warts blown into the glass globe, hugging her knees in their sturdy ribbed stockings, her smooth brown hair enhancing her clean kind of prettiness, Lilly gazed up roundly.

"I choose," she said, mouthing grandiloquently, her little pink tongue waving like a clapper--"I choose--choose--ah--Zoe!"

"That isn't a name!"

"'Tis so."

"Who ever heard of a girl named Zoe! You never did yourself."

"I know I never did, Roy Kemble, but just the same I think it is the most beautiful name in the world. It isn't so much what it really means; names don't have to mean anything--it's what it feels like it means. To me the name Zoe feels like it means--means--"

CHORUS: "She don't know what it means. She don't know what it means."

"She means doe! The doe in the zoo at Forest Park. Hauh-hauh--her favorite name is Doe."

"Zoe," repeated Lilly, her eyes in a trance and lakes of reflected vision. "Zoe--it means--it means something--something full of life. Life--free--to me Zoe means free! Life!"

CHAPTER IV

When Lilly was fourteen she graduated from grade school, second in her class.

"It's an outrage," said Mrs. Becker. "Miss Lare always did pick on the child."

"I'd rather have been last than second," said Lilly, trying to keep firm a lip that would tremble.

"Never mind, Lilly, you'll have the prettiest graduation dress of them all. I've got Katy Stutz engaged for three days in the house. A girl don't have to be so smart."

"I'd rather have the valedictory address than--clothes," still very uncertain of lip.

"Of course. That is because for a child you certainly have crazy ideas. Why don't you nag your father a little with what you've been nagging me all week?"

"I--Not now, mamma."

"Why not now? All I've got to say about it is, if he is willing, I am."

"What is it?"

"Tell him, Lilly."

"I--You see, papa, I thought if only you would let me begin vocal lessons, now that I am going to High School. Not real singing, papa--I'm too young for that--but just the foundation for voice."

"She wants to study with Max Rinehardt, Ben. I say it can't do any harm for the child to learn parlor singing. I think I can manage it at a dollar and a half a lesson. The elocution I say 'No' to. We don't need any play-acting in the family."

"Why--er--I'm surprised, Lilly, that you should have your heart set on that kind of thing. Seems to me a young girl could find something more worth while than that. Singers never amount to much."

"Oh, papa, it's what I want most in the world."

"Let her have them. A little parlor singing helps any girl with the young men. I notice you courted me from the choir. If she waits for encouragement from you, her accomplishments won't amount to a row of pins."

"You see, papa, I'm going to take the commercial course at High and learn stenography and typewriting, so it will just balance my education fine."

"Well, little woman, whatever you say."

"You know what I say."

"Don't you think she is a bit too young?"

Mimetically: "No, I don't think she's a bit too young. The sooner you wake up to the fact that your daughter is growing up, the better. She's a graduate already from grammar school."

"Papa, I'm on the graduating program."

"For what, daughter?"

"A piano solo. 'Alice,' with variations."

"Well, Carrie, if that is the way you feel about it--if you think those kind of lessons are good for her--"

"That is the way I feel about it."

These little acid places occurring somewhere in almost every day hardly corroded into Lilly's accustomed consciousness. If they etched their way at all into Mr. Becker's patient kind of equanimity, the utter quietude of his personality, which could efface itself behind a newspaper for two or even three hours at a time, never revealed it. His was the stolidity of an oak, tickled rather than assailed by a bright-eyed woodpecker.

"Little woman" he liked to call her in his nearest approach of endearment, although it must have been her petite quickness rather than a diminutive quality that earned the appellation. Even when he had wooed her in Granite City, Missouri, and she had sung down at the quiet-faced youth from a choir loft, she was after the then prevalent form of hourglass girlish loveliness. Now she was rather enormous of bust, proudly so, and wore her waist pulled in so that her hips sprang out roundly. A common gesture was to place her hands on her hips, press down, and breathe sharply inward, thus holding herself for the moment from the steel walls of her corsets. Their removal immediately after dinner was a ritual to be anticipated during the day. She would sit in her underbodice, unhooked of them, sunk softly into herself, her hands stroking her tortured jacket of ribs and her breath flowing deeper.

"I don't believe I'd pull in quite so tight, Carrie, if I were you. It will tell on your health some day."

"You don't catch me with a sloppy figure. I don't give a row of pins for the woman without some curve to her."

To Mrs. Becker a row of pins was the basest coinage of any realm. It ran through her speech in pricking idiom.

She was piquant enough of face, quick-eyed, and with little pointy features enhanced by a psyche worn as emphatically as an exclamation point on the very top of her head. On eucher or matinee days her bangs, at the application of a curling iron, were worn frizzed, but usually they were pinned back beneath the psyche in straight brown wisps.

As she grew older, Lilly came more and more to resemble her father in a certain tight knit of figure, length of limb, and quiet gray eyes that could fill blackly with pupil and in the smooth, straight, always gleaming brown hair growing cleanly and with the merest of widows' peaks off her forehead.

At fourteen she stood shoulder to shoulder with her mother, and their gloves and shirt waists were interchangeable. One really distinguishing loveliness was her complexion. The skin flowed over her body with the cool fleshliness of a pink rose petal. There was a natural shimmer to it, a dewiness and a pollen of youth that enveloped her like a caress.

"Looks more like her father, if she looks like either of them," Mrs. Schum was fond of saying, "and she has his easy disposition. But there is a child who runs deep. If she was mine I'd educate her to be something. Ah me, if only my Annie hadn't lost her head and married, she had the makings, too."

As a matter of fact, Lilly's resemblance to her parents stopped abruptly. Her first year in High School, a course in natural science revealed to her the term "botanical sport."

"That's what I am," she determined, with youth's immediate application of cosmos to self, "a botanical sport." A spontaneous variation from the normal type. "Papa, I learned to-day that I'm a sport."

MRS. BECKER: "A what? That *is* a genteel expression for a young girl to apply to herself! That High School does you more harm than good."

"But, mamma, it's a term used in botany. A term from Darwin."

"Darwin! That's a fine thing to teach children in school--that they come from monkeys! No wonder children haven't any respect for their parents nowadays."

"Well, just the same it is in the biology. We're on frogs now. You ought to see the way frogs get born!"

"In my day children weren't taught such stuff. I'm surprised, Ben, it's allowed."

Across the biology of life, as if to shut out the loathsome facts of an abattoir, a curtain of dreadful portent was drawn before Lilly's clear eyes.

"When baby came," was Mrs. Becker's insinuation for the naked and impolite fact of birth.

In a vague, inchoate sort of way, Lilly at sixteen was visualizing nature procreant as an abominable woman creature standing shank deep in spongy swampland and from behind that portentous curtain moaning in the agonized key of Mrs. Kemble.

About this time Mrs. Kemble's third child was within a few weeks of birth.

"Mamma, what makes Mrs. Kemble look so funny!"

"Hush, Lilly. Don't you ever let me hear you talk like that again. Little girls shouldn't ask such questions."

One night shortly after, a cry that tore like a gash through the sleeping boarding house roused Lilly to a sitting posture on her little cot drawn across the baseboard of her parents' bed.

"Mamma! Papa! What was that?"

There were immediate voices and running up and down stairs and more cries that beat the air and Mrs. Becker already up and clamoring into her kimono.

"Sh-h-h, Lilly! Go back to sleep. It is nothing but Mrs. Kemble not feeling very well. I'll run upstairs a minute, Ben. See that Lilly goes back to sleep."

Until the break of day Lilly lay tense there on her little cot, toes curled in, and still her mother did not return. Time and time again the moans rose to shrieks of dreadful supplication that set her to trembling so that her cot rattled against the baseboard.

"Kill me! God! Put me out of it! Please! I can't suffer any more! Kill me, God! Kill me!"

"Papa, I--I'm scared."

"Go to sleep, Lilly," said her father from the pool of darkness, his voice rather thin and sick. "Go to sleep now, like a good girl."

In a little area of quiet that ensued, she did drop healthily off, wakening to the warmth of sunshine, her father already departed, her mother rocking and sewing beside the window.

"Mamma, why didn't you wake me? I'll be late to school."

"You won't if you hurry and--and, Lilly, what do you think?"

"What, mamma?"

"The stork brought Flora and Roy the dearest little baby sister last night. They're going to call her Evelyn. That's why Roy and Flora went to spend the week with their Aunt Emma, so they wouldn't frighten the stork away when he flew in with it. In a few days you can go up and see it. Isn't that nice, Lilly?"

Still tousled with sleep, but the red rising up out of the yoke of her nightgown, Lilly answered, with averted face, "Yes, mamma."

CHAPTER V

This episode marked the beginning of what was to be a three years' refrain.

"Ben, we must go housekeeping. It's an outrage to board, with a girl Lilly's age. Not as much as a parlor for her to bring her friends, and a great big girl like her without a room to herself! It's not even delicate."

"Well, Carrie, I'm willing."

"I know, until the time comes. I don't forget so easily the way you sighed all night in your sleep that time I came near renting the house on Delmar Avenue. Where is the money coming from! The minute that old business down there earns a penny, right back into it go the earnings, instead of drawing out a few dollars for the comfort of his family, like any other man would."

"But, Carrie--"

"There is not another woman in the world would stand for it but me. A woman that could enjoy a little home of her own as much as I! What do I get out of it, I'd like to know! Stint. Stint. Stint. Shove it all back into that old rope-and-twine business down there that doesn't show a cent of capital when you take stock except in rope, rope, rope, until I'd like to hang myself with some of it."

"Now, little woman, you got up on the wrong side of bed this morning. Just hold your horses. These are tight times, I admit, but we have our health--"

"I've heard that since I'm married. Health! Suppose we have got our health. We can't thank the business for that."

"Lilly, your mother certainly got up on the wrong side of bed this morning, didn't she?"

"Well, it's right discouraging, if you ask me."

"You're all right, little woman."

"Yes, I know," trying not to smile, "I'm all right when it don't cost nothing and when it comes to the dirty work of trying to make two ends meet."

"You're certainly a splendid manager. No one can take that away from you."

"Well, I wish you would both appreciate it a little more."

"We do appreciate it, don't we, Lilly?"

"Yes, papa."

Her second year in High School, Lilly was kept out for five weeks by an attack of typhoid fever.

An aversion for physical shortcoming, from her mother's occasional headaches to the mortally afflicted Mr. Hazzard with the great chronic sore crisscrossed with court plaster at the end of one of his eyes, amounted in Lilly to something actually Indian.

"Oh, mamma, if I had a headache, I wouldn't always be talking about it. People aren't interested."

"I'm going to tell your father when he comes home to-night what a sympathetic daughter I have. If ever I fall sick the City Hospital will be the place for me. When I see the way that Flora Kemble carries her mother around and the way my own daughter sympathizes with me. If I don't tell your father this night!"

It was this queer little congenital urge that kept Lilly on her feet for two weeks after the malady had hold of her. With a stoicism that taxed her cruelly, she would march smilingly off to school, a bombardment of pains shooting through her head, her hands and tongue dry, a ball and chain of inertia dragging at her ankles.

"Lilly, what is the matter? Why don't you eat your bread and butter after school? Has Mrs. Schum said anything?"

"No, no, mamma. I'm not hungry, that's all."

"Funny. Open the closet. There is a basket of oranges behind your father's overcoat, and a bag of baby pretzels, too."

"Goodness! mamma, if I was hungry, I'd eat."

"Don't you feel well, Lilly?"

"Of course I feel well, mamma. Why shouldn't I?"

But next day, at her after-school hour of practice, a small discordant crash broke suddenly in upon "Chaminade's Scarf Dance" and Mrs. Becker's rhythmic rocking above. Lilly had fainted, with her head in her arms and face down among the keys.

Followed two weeks that crowded up the little back parlor with anxiety, the tension of two doctors in consultation, and a sense of hysteria that was always just a scratch beneath the surface of Mrs. Becker. She would break suddenly into loud and unexpected fits of crying, crushing her palms up against her mouth; would waken from a light doze beside the bed, on the shriek of a nightmare, and have literally to be dragged from the room. She harassed the doctors with questions that only the course of the disease could answer.

The crisis came in the watches of the night, Lilly very straight and very white and light of breathing in the center of her parents' bed, her glossy hair in a thick plait over each shoulder, her fine white and developed chest hardly rising.

"O God! help me to live this night! Ben! Ben!"

"Carrie, you're only making yourself sick and not helping the child."

"My baby! My beautiful snow-white baby! The best child that ever lived! Help me to live this night!"

"Carrie, little woman, if only you won't take on so. There's every reason to hope for the best. The doctor assured us."

"How long before we know? Go get Doctor Allison over. Ask Roy Kemble to run over to Horton's and telephone for Doctor Birch. I want them here. My baby!"

"Carrie, Carrie, haven't they told you time and time again there is nothing they can do now? Don't antagonize Doctor Birch by calling him over here again to-night. Everything is being done for the child. Now all we can do is to sit and wait and hope for the best."

"You don't care! You're made of iron. At a time like this you stop to consider the doctors' feelings. Mine don't count. My baby. Get well, Lilly. Mamma's been cross at times, but never again. We'll do everything to make you happy. You can read your eyes out and mamma won't turn out the light on you. Mamma will buy you books and a box of paints and a little bird's-eye-maple room all your own. Lilly, mamma's baby. We're going housekeeping--your own piano--your own room. Aren't we, Ben? Aren't we?"

"Yes, Carrie."

"You can take your choice, baby, of all the things you want to be. Mamma won't oppose any more, or papa. Opera singing if you want it. You come by it naturally from my choir voice. Whatever you say, baby. Even an actress and all the elocution and singing lessons you--"

"Carrie!"

"Oh, you don't care! You're only her father. What does a father know? You don't care."

Against this age-old indictment of paternity, and absolutely without precedent, the patient, the iron-gray head of Mr. Becker fell forward, a fearful and silent storm of sobs beating against his repression.

Full of dumfounded hysteria, walking on her knees around the bed edge to him, Mrs. Becker drew down his head into the wreath of her arms, kissing into it, mingling her tears with his, and tasting their anguish.

"My darling! Ben--please, darling! I say a lot of things I don't mean. You are my husband--and my life. Ben--don't! I can't stand it! Ben!"

At six o'clock Lilly opened her eyes. They were clear and cool and the petal-like quality was out on her skin.

"Sweet Alice," she said, "oh, Sweet Alice, Ben Bolt," a bit of dream floating up with her like seaweed to the surface of consciousness. "Sweet Alice."

She had been reading *Trilby*, surreptitiously filched from Mrs. Kemble's stack of novels.

"Lilly--mamma's Lilly!"

"Where--I--Where--"

"In your own room, sweetheart, and your own mother and father beside you."

"I thought--Sweet Alice--"

"The fever is gone now, Lilly. You won't have any of those thoughts any more. Go to sleep now, papa's girl."

"I must have been singing--'Faust'--what makes you and papa--so angry--with me--dears?"

"We're not, Lilly. Nothing makes us angry any more."

She was too tired to smile.

"I kept dreaming, mamma, that my hair was two big honey-colored braids all wound up with pearls, like Marguerite's picture in *Stories of the Operas*."

"Go to sleep, Lilly, like a good child. Our girl has got too much sense to fill her head up with such nonsense."

"No, no, papa, I won't have common sense. I want to ride up to meet the sun, like the princess in--"

"She wants to what? Are you sure her fever is gone, Carrie?"

"Nonsense! It is stuff she reads in her fairy tales. Yes, darling, anything you want."

"You know, mamma--pearls--in my hair--"

"Yes, yes, darling. Sh-h-h!"

"Mamma?"

"Yes."

"We're middle-class, aren't we?"

"What does she mean?"

"Middle-class people, I mean. You know."

"Why, yes, dear, we're middle-class. I guess that is what you'd call it. What an idea!"

"Help me."

"Yes, yes. How, baby? The doctor will be here any--"

"You don't know what I mean. No matter what I say, you don't know what I mean. Isn't that terrible?"

"Help you to get well, that's what mamma and papa are going to do."

"No, no, no! Help me--out--up!"

Presently Lilly fell asleep. To her watching parents her light and regular breathing took on the meter of a Doxology.

CHAPTER VI

Center High School, the city's only at a time when half a million souls beat up like sea around it, a model and modern institution that was presently and paradoxically to become architectural paragon for what to avoid in future high-school buildings, was again within street-car distance, except on usually bland days, when Lilly and Flora Kemble would walk home through Vandaventer Place, the first of those short, private thoroughfares of pretentious homes that were presently to run through the warp of the city like threads of gold.

On these homeward walks Flora and Lilly, who referred to each other as "my chum," were fond of peripatetically exchanging the views, the consciousness, and the sweetness of sixteen.

"If you had your choice, Lilly, what house would you select for yours in Vandaventer Place?"

"None."

"Why?"

"I don't want to live in between stone gates with 'No Thoroughfare' stuck on each end."

"You're the funniest girl! What do you mean, 'No thoroughfare'? Don't you want to be exclusive and private?"

"Yes, but a person can be private somewhere high--high--not just stuck between gates like everybody else. Sappho always sat on a balcony that overlooked the Aegean Sea."

"Maybe she did, and she jumped off, too, but I'm not talking to-day's Greek history lesson. I'm talking about regular folks. Between the gates of Vandaventer Place would be good enough for me. Wouldn't I just love to be mistress over one of these houses and give parties with an awning stretched out over the sidewalk!"

"What did you get in algebra, Flora?"

"B plus. And you?"

"B minus."

"Lilly Becker, that is the fifth B minus you've had in succession. I'm going to call you Lilly Minus."

"If she hadn't sprung that old oral exam on us--"

"Oh, if ifs and ands were pots and pans!"

Flora, rather freckly, elbowy, and far too tall, was none the less about to be pretty. She was fraily fair, like her mother, and could already throw her blue eyes about their balls, in the Esperanto of coquetry. She had a treacherous little faculty of appearing never to study and yet maintaining an excellent grade of scholarship.

"You get me to do all sorts of things with you, Flora, and then you sneak off and study on the quiet and leave me to flunk because I promised you I wouldn't study, either."

"Why, Lilly Becker, I never studied one minute for that algebra quiz."

"You did so! When I went downstairs to write in my Friendship Book, like you said you were going to do, you worked your algebra instead. Roy told me."

"Well, if I was as pretty as you, Lilly, I wouldn't ever care if I got my lessons or not," said Flora, to palliate.

"Flora Kemble, I'm not pretty!"

"You are, too. Everybody says your complexion is like peaches and cream, and look at mine, all freckles."

"Complexion, huh! If I had your yellow hair, you could have all my complexion."

"Boys hate freckles because so many of them have them themselves."

"Always boys. Honestly, you're boy-crazy, Flora."

"Well, I like that. Can I help it if I got an invitation and you didn't? You sat right next to him in English and I sat two whole seats away."

A cloud no larger and smudgier than a high-school boy's hand had dropped its first shadow between them. Eugene Bankhead, son of the credit man for Slocum-Hines, the city's largest wholesale hardware firm, had suddenly, out of this clear sky, invited Flora to the Thanksgiving Day football game between Center High and an exclusive local academy. A new estate felt, rather than spoken, quickened the eye and authority of Flora. A sense of it rode on the air waves between them.

"I hate boys."

"How do you know? You've never seen any except my brother and sneak-thief Harry."

"Papa says if a girl begins to run around with boys too soon it makes her so forward that by the time she's eighteen she's too old and faded--"

"That's old-fogy talk."

"You mean it's old fogy for girls to let boys jam everything else out of their heads. I'd like to see the boy that could make me forget my--my ambitions."

"If Eugene had asked you instead of me you wouldn't be saying that."

"Anyway, I hate snips. I like men--real men."

"Oh, I know. You're stuck on Lindsley!"

A violent splash of red and a highly superlative denial of word and manner laid hold of Lilly.

"Why, Flora Kemble!"

"Look at her blushing. Oh, what I know about you!"

"You fibber. I think he's the limit. I never saw a fellow so stuck on himself."

"Oh, I know! I know now why you carry home twice as many books as you used to since he got charge of the library."

"I'm reading the *Lady of the Lake* and you know it. That's why I stopped in to-night."

"I know why you're always writing compositions since you have him in English. Lilly's stuck on Lindsley."

Tears were rare with Lilly, but a tremor waved her voice.

"I think you're horrid, Flora Kemble. Anyway, he's more worth while being stuck on than Eugene Bankhead. He's just--just middle-class. His future is to work in Slocum-Hines's hardware store, like his father."

"Well, that's more of a man's job than sitting around in a schoolroom doing lady's work. Papa says Eugene's father is a five-thousand-a-year man. Eugene has all the spending money he wants and they have a conservatory in their house."

"Well, I'd rather be Lindsley than Eugene; besides, he's a kid hardly out of short trousers."

"Silly, you don't think it's Eugene I'm stuck on, do you? His brother Vincent is a big man down at Slocum-Hines's, too, and a catch. I'm going to meet him some day. Lindsley! Ugh! I like a little sponduliks thrown in with a fellow. Lindsley's elbows shine."

For the most part the Board of Education drew upon the offspring of its own system for teaching talent, occasionally letting in an artery of new blood. Lilly's second year in High School such an infusion took place in the form of one H. Horace Lindsley, the young master of arts, his degree rather heavy upon him, dawning blondly and behind high-power pince-nez upon the English department.

Sweet sixteen capitulated to English literature. The double wave of Mr. Lindsley's hair, the intellectual rush of very long, white teeth to the front, somehow mitigating for the sins of a curriculum that could present Gorboduc, and *Friar Bacon* and *Friar Bungay*, to young minds illy furrowed for such seed.

Notwithstanding the literary odor with which Mr. Lindsley sprayed himself as he sprayed his handkerchief with a domestic scent called "Sesame and Lilies," his neoclassic determination to write the American *Iliad* must have died painlessly when his iambically disposed feet ventured too deeply into the quagmire of pedagogy, from which he was not to emerge. But for the first time in her life Lilly was hearing her name pronounced by one who rolled it under his tongue like a lollypop. He rolled all names quite so, but in her beatitude she was only conscious of her own as it candied. Besides, his eyes, through the pince-nez, had a gimlet, goosefleshing quality; he recited "Straits of Dover" to a class of young women with rapt adenoidal expression when he should have been inoculating them with the bitter serum of Burke's Conciliation Speech, and walked to school of wintry mornings without an overcoat; skates and the *Areopagitica* under his arm.

It was undeniable that at this stage Lilly had veered unaccountably to authorship, her after-school practice hour gouged into by a suddenly stimulated pen.

"Papa, I know my ambition!"

Mr. Becker let fall his newspaper to his knee, glancing up over the rim of his reading glasses.

"What's it now, daughter?"

"I want to be a writer. You know, an author of stories. My English teacher says I have talent. I get A minus on all my essays, and to-day he wrote on the edge of one, 'Quite a literary touch.'"

MRS. BECKER (who rocked as she darned): "The trouble with you, Lilly, is that you have it too good. You don't know what you want."

"You don't care if I am a writer, do you, papa?"

"Last week it was the stage, and last month the opera, and now it's writing. What next, I wonder?"

"Your mother's right. There's no stability to this art business, Lilly. They're a loose lot that never come to a good end."

"Well, just the same," cried Lilly, hot with a sense of futility and rebellion, "your own father was the next thing to an actor. Preaching is kin to acting."

"Don't you ever let me hear you talk like that again. Your grandfather was a God-fearing, not a play-acting man." Attacking this subject, a little furrow would invariably appear between Mr. Becker's fine gray eyes and his lips express bitter intolerance for a world that translated itself to him solely in terms of pink tights.

Not that the odor of religion lay any too heavily on Lilly's youth. Sunday school was not enforced, Sabbath ethics were observed loosely, if at all, but a yearly membership in the Garrison Avenue Rock Church was maintained, not without remonstrance from Mrs. Becker.

"I don't see why we belong. If I want to attend church on Easter Sunday or a Christmas, I don't have to pay dues all year for it. A person can pray just as well at home as in church if he's inclined that way."

"Our child doesn't need to be raised like a heathen just because we aren't as regular as we might be about churchgoing. Besides, when trouble comes we don't want to be buried like heathens, either."

"Calamity howler."

"In England, papa, writers get buried in Westminster Abbey. If I lived in England, that would be my ambition."

"The child has ambitions even about funerals. I bought you goods for a navy-blue poplin to-day, Lilly. Gentle's had a sale."

"Oh, mamma, can you get Katy Stutz to come in time to make it for auditorium next Friday? Mr. Lindsley may call on me to read my essay out loud."

"That Mr. Lindsley makes me sick. You're a changed child since he's come to that school. Mrs. Foote said the same thing of Estelle at the euchre yesterday. All the girls want new dresses and to be in his classes."

"Why, mamma!" coloring up.

"Oh, run over to Pirney's and buy me a postal card. I'll write Katy Stutz to take Mrs. Foote's days away from her and give them to me."

By small briberies employed without sense of compromise, Mrs. Becker had a way with those who served her. Katy Stutz, an old soul as lean and as green as a cotton umbrella, had sewed at minimum wage through fourteen years of keeping Lilly daintily and a bit too pretentiously clad. Willie, Mrs. Schum's old negro cook, who wore her feet wrapped in gunny sacking, and every odd and end that came down in the day's waste baskets, from empty spools to nubs of pencil, stored away in the kink of her hair, would somehow invariably send up the giblets along with the Beckers' Sunday allotment of chicken. Mr. Keebil, too, an old Southern relic, his head covered with suds of gray astrakhan and a laugh like the up and down of rusty bedsprings, for ten years had presided over the hirsute destinies of Lilly and her mother. Bi-monthly he arrived on his shampooing mission, often making a day's tour throughout the boarding house.

"Mr. Keebil, don't you do the Kembles' heads first to-day. That's the way with you people. I get you all your customers and then you neglect me for them."

"Law! Mrs. Beckah, how cum you think that? Don't I give you and Miss Lilly shampoos for two bits when I chawges Mrs. Kemble three heads for a dollar?"

"Yes, but what about the underwear and socks of Mr. Becker's that you get?"

"I allas say I 'ain't got no bettah friend than Mrs. Beckah. That was certainly a fine suit you done give me las' time, except for the buttons cut off."

"You should consider yourself lucky to get a head like Miss Lilly's to take care of at any price. Just look at it--like spun silk."

He would fluff out the really beautiful cascade of smooth and highly electric hair, his brown hands, so strangely light pink of palm, full of pride in their task.

"Law! Miss Lilly, if you ain't going to grow up the pick of them all."

"Ouch! Mr. Keebil, you hurt!" cried Lilly, ever tender of scalp.

Nor was Mrs. Becker above a bit of persiflage.

"Mr. Keebil, I hear it is something scandalous the way you and Willie are setting up to each other."

The old shoulders would shake, the face crinkle into a raisin, and the little spade of gray beard heave to the springy laughter.

"Law! Mrs. Beckah. if you ain't the greatest one to joke."

"Joke nothing. It's a fine match. A good upstanding church member like you and a fine-looking woman like Willie."

Lilly would turn a quirking but disapproving eye upon her mother.

"Mamma, haven't you anything better to do?"

"Law! Miss Lilly, me and your ma we understand each other. Me and your papa we know she will have her little joke but the heart is there. That's what counts on the Lord's Judgment Day--the heart."

Lilly's poplin frock was completed for the Friday auditorium exercises. Her two braids, now consolidated into one hempy rope, lay against her back, finishing without completement of hair ribbon into a cylinder of brushed-around-the-finger curl. It was a little mannerism of hers, not entirely unconscious, to fling the heavy coil of hair over one shoulder. It enhanced her face, somehow, the fall of shining plait down over her young bosom. Contrary to her choking expectation, she was not called upon to read, but to sit on the platform in an honorable-mention row of five.

Flora Kemble read a B-plus paper, largely and in immaculate vertical penmanship, entitled "Friendship," Lilly, the tourniquet twist at her heart, sitting by. Her name was read later among the honorable five, true to manner, Mr. Lindsley seeming to caress it with his tongue.

"Miss Halpern. Mr. Prothero. Miss Foote. Miss Deidesheimer. Miss Beck-er."

From where she sat Lilly could see the slightly protuberant shine to his teeth, the intellectual ride of glasses along his thin nose, the long, nervous hand with a little-finger fraternity ring.

Her own hands were very cold, her cheeks very pink. She had a pressing behind the eyes of a not-to-be-endured impulse of wanting to cry. His reading of her name was a hot javelin through the pit of her being.

After the exercises and as school was in dismissal she saw him hurrying out of a side door with a tennis racket. It seemed suddenly intolerable that walk home through Vandaventer Place to her boarding-house world.

Flora's perceptions were small and quick.

"Why, Lilly, your cheeks are as red as anything and you're getting a fever blister. Somebody kissed you!"

Her hand flew to her mouth almost guiltily, as if to the feel of lips slightly protuberant.

"Why--Oh, you horrid girl!"

"It was Lind! Lind!"

"Lind--what--who?"

"Lindsley, of course," dipping with laughter.

"Flora Kemble, I'll never speak to you again. You're stuck on him yourself and trying to put it on to me."

"Me stuck on him, the way his teeth stick out! No poor school-teacher for mine!"

"You're boy-crazy. I'm not."

But that night for the first time in her life Lilly lay through a sleepless hour, staring up into the darkness. The blanket irked her and she plunged it off, burrowing one cheek and then the other into her pillow in search of cool spots. Her mother puffed out slowly into the silence, her father a bit more sonorous and full of rumblings.

Lilly felt herself wound up tightly and needing to be run down. She was taut as a spring. After a while she took to plucking out from the darkness words of sedative quality.

"Dove," she repeated softly to herself, and very, very slowly. "Dove. Beautiful, quiet dove. Saint. Cathedral. Peace. Dell."

But when she finally did drop off to sleep a smile of protuberant teeth was out like a rainbow across her darkness.

CHAPTER VII

Latitudinally speaking, there are about two kinds of Americans--those who live west of Syracuse, and those who do not. An imaginary line separates the tropic of candescence, fast trains, naval reviews, broad a's, Broadway, Beacon Street, Independence Square, and Tammany Hall from the cancer of craps, silver dollars, lynchings, alfalfa, toothpicks, detachable cuffs, napkin rings, and boll weevils.

It is more than probable that Horace Lindsley's and Lilly Becker's lineage were loamy with about the same magnesia of the soil. Generations of each of them had tilled into the more or less contiguous dirt of Teutonic Europe.

Lilly's progenitors had bartered in low Dutch; Horace Lindsley's in high German, which, after all, is more a matter of geography than altitudes.

An oval daguerreotype of a great-grandmother at the harpsichord had hung in Carrie Becker's (*nee* Ploag) home in Granite City.

A Lindsley had once presented an emperor with a hand-illuminated version of the King James Bible, wrought out of peasant patience. Horace Lindsley's mother belonged to a New England suffrage society when ladies still wore silk mitts, and had dared to open a private kindergarten in her back parlor after marriage.

It was this tincture of culture running like a light bluing through Lindsley's heritage that began to set in motion the little sleeping molecules of Lilly's class consciousness.

"Middle class," came to be a term employed always with lips that curled. There were, then, actually men creatures outside the English "Fireside Novels" she was allowed to devour without interruption by parents to whom books were largely objects with which a room was cluttered up, who wore spats, did play tennis in white flannels, turned down the page at a favorite passage of poetry, eschewed suspenders for belts, were guiltless of sleeve garters, and attended Saturday-afternoon symphony concerts, in Lindsley's case, almost a lone male, debonaire and unabashed in a garden of women.

At Lilly's urgent instance she and her mother often attended these subscription concerts, seats for single performances obtainable (in a commendable zeal to promote local music) in exchange for a newspaper coupon and twenty-five cents.

Mrs. Becker frankly yawned through them, nictitating, as it were, during the long narrative passages of the symphony or occupied with the personnel of the audience.

"Look, Lilly," whispering behind her unopened program, "that's a pretty idea over there on that red-haired girl. See the way the baby ribbon is run through the sleeves. Do you want a dress like that?"

"Sh-h-h-h, mamma! No; it's too fussy!"

"Why don't they play something with a tune to it? I wouldn't give a row of pins for music without any air at all."

"Sh-h-h-h, mamma. There isn't much tune to classical music."

"I wish the first violinist would play a solo. 'Warum,' like last time. I've some baby ribbon just like that, Lilly. I picked it up on sale in Gentle's basement bins--"

"Mamma, don't stare so."

"Don't criticize everything I do."

At one of these concerts Lilly shot out her hand suddenly, closing it over her mother's wrist.

"Mamma, there's Lindsley. See, down there in the fourth row."

"Who?"

"My English teacher. See, polishing his eyeglasses."

Mrs. Becker sat straight, chin out like an antenna.

"Is that him?"

"Yes, that's he."

"I don't see anything so wonderful about him. He needs a haircut."

"Oh, mamma, you think all men have to wear their hair short and ugly like papa and Uncle Buck. In the East men look like that."

"The idea! A man calls himself a man coming to a matinee like this. Your papa ought to know that you have a sissy like him on your mind. Such a looking thing!

Ugh!"

These recurring intimations could sting Lilly almost to tears.

"Oh, mamma, that's just the--the meanest thing to say. Can't I show you my English teacher without having him on my mind?"

"I never could stand a man whose teeth stick out. He looks like a horse."

"Papa's teeth stick out."

"Yes, but just one, and his mustache hides that. I only hope for you, Lilly, that some day you get a man as good as your father."

"How did papa propose to you, mamma? What did he say?"

Even Mrs. Becker could flush, quite prettily, too, her lids dropping at this not infrequent query of Lilly's.

"It's not nice for young girls to ask such questions."

"Go on, mamma, what did he say?"

"I don't remember."

The overture broke in upon them then, a brilliantly noisy one from Tschaikowsky that bathed them in a vichy of excited surf.

Settling with her head snuggled against her fur tippet, the back of her neck against the chair top, Lilly could feel herself recede, as it were, into a sort of anagogical half consciousness, laved and carried along on currents of melody that were as sensually delicious as a warm bath. Her awareness of Lindsley on a diagonal from her so that she could see his profile hook into the music-scented dimness, ran under her skin like a quick shimmer.

The proscenium arch curved again into her consciousness, herself its center and vocal beyond the powers of the human organ.

The slamming up of chairs and mussy shuffling into wraps recalled her. It was indescribably sad, this swimming up to reality. The buttoning of her little tippet. The smell of damp umbrellas. Then the jamming down the aisle toward the late and rainy afternoon. At the door they were suddenly crushed up against Horace Lindsley, his coat collar turned up about his ears.

"Miss Becker," he said, by way of greeting, nodding and showing his teeth.

Her heart became a little elevator dropping in sheer descent.

"Oh--how--do--you--do?" They were pushed shoulder to shoulder, and, to Lilly's agony, her mother's voice lifted itself in loud concern.

"For pity's sake, look at that downpour, will you? I hope your father has the good sense to wear his rubbers. Ouch! Don't knock me down, please."

"Mamma--please. Mr. Lindsley, I want you to meet my mother."

"Pleased to meet you. Lilly certainly has talked of her English teacher a lot."

"She is a very interesting little student, Mrs. Becker. Quite a quality to her work."

"Well, I am certainly pleased to hear that. She's our only one, you know."

"Lilly has a tendency to let her imagination run away with her. A good fault if she controls it."

"That's what her father and I always tell her. The child has too many talents to settle down to any one. She gets her music from my side of the house, but she quits practicing to write and she quits writing to practice. It's not that we want our little girl ever to make her own living, but her father and I believe in a girl being prepared, even if she never has to use it. That's why we are having her take the commercial course. We don't pretend to be swells, but at least we plan to do as well for our child as the next."

"Exactly."

LILLY (in her agony): "Come, mamma."

"I wish you could read the poem she wrote last night, Mr. Lindsley. Not that I give a row of pins for poetry, as a rule, but I told her she ought to take this one to school."

"Please, mamma, please!"

"If I do say it myself, it was grand. Mr. Hazzard, quite an educated gentleman who boards where we do, thought so, too. Lilly, why don't you show Mr. Lindsley that poem? He's authority."

"Mamma, if only you won't talk about it."

"You must bring it to class, Miss Becker."

"No, no! I've--I've torn it up."

"I don't remember all of it, but everybody considered it a grand thought for such a young girl; it goes--"

"Mamma! Mamma--not here--now!"

"I would not have the restless soul   That sees not beauty everywhere.   I see it glint on ocean waves,   Dance through a youth's or maiden's hair."

"Mamma, they're pushing so! Good night, Mr. Lindsley. Mamma, come!"

Outside in the wet dusk they boarded an electric car, Lilly and her mother crammed on a rear platform of the wet overcoats, leaking umbrellas, and wet-smelling mackintoshes of dinner-bound St. Louis.

"He's a right nice young man, intelligent--but if ever a person looked like a horse! You see, he agrees with your papa and me. You don't apply yourself to any one thing."

Lilly turned her inflamed, quivering face upon her mother, trying to speak through a violent aching of tonsils.

"Oh," she cried, "how could you? I'll never look him in the face again! Oh--oh--how could you?"

"Are you crazy? How could I what?"

"The poem. The--the glint in--his hair. He'll think it was his hair I meant. Oh! Oh!"

The ready ire which could flame up in Mrs. Becker leaped out then.

"If you are ashamed of your mother, maybe you had better not be seen out with her again. All I am good for is to stint and manage to get you pretty clothes."

"No, n-no, mamma, I didn't mean that, dear."

"For a horse-face like him I won't be made little."

"Sh-h-h-h, dear! The whole street car doesn't need to hear."

"I wouldn't give a row of pins for ten like him."

"Mamma, the way you--talked."

"The way I talked, what? I suppose hereafter when I go out with my educated daughter I will have to wear a muzzle."

"I--Oh, it wasn't what you said, mamma; it was--the way you said it."

"The way I said it? That's a rich one. If I don't tell your father! My own child is ashamed of her mother. Well, let me tell you I--"

"No, mamma, you don't understand. Take that word 'swells,' for instance. Oh, I know I've used it myself, but all of a sudden, to-day, it--it sounded so ordinary."

"For a hundred-dollar-a-month school-teacher that your papa has to pay taxes to support, I'm not afraid of my p's and q's."

"And, mamma," suddenly and acutely sensitive to pleonasm, "you begin every sentence with 'say' and you say 'certainly' so often."

"If I don't have a talk with your father when he comes home this night! That's the thanks I get for sitting through a concert with you when I might have been enjoying myself at my euchre club. Just get those high-tone notions out of your head. We're simple people, not swells. You're a changed child these days."

It was true. An ineffable ache, a darting neuralgia of spirit, too cunning and quick for diagnosis, was shooting through Lilly her last two years at High School.

That Horace Lindsley, who was hardly to indent her life and whose interest in the clean-eyed girl was little more than a leaf upon his consciousness, and whose feet were already feeling the tug of the quicksands of mediocrity which were to suck him out of her reckoning, should have been the innocent source of this neurosis, is hardly remarkable.

Lilly, with the mysterious tenacity of a crannied flower, was pulling from her soil toward the light. And light in all its chiaroscuras rules the *se leve, couche*, complexion, and humors of the world. Lindsley was a ray.

And so her adolescence came in suddenly, almost stormlike, uprooting little forests of sapling traditions.

At sixteen she still slept on the cot drawn across the bed end and rode her bicycle up and down the sidewalks, holding her skirts down against the wind, but also she had ransacked the boarding-house shelves and High School library, reading her uncensored way through *Lady Audrey's Secret, Canterbury Tales, Five Little Peppers and How They Grew, Plain Facts About Life, Arabian Nights, Golden Treasury, Childe Harold, To Have and to Hold, Tales from Shakespeare, Pilgrim's Progress, Old Curiosity Shop, Diary of Marie Baschkertcheff, Pride and Prejudice, Vanity Fair, Les Miserables, Stories of the Operas*, and a red volume rescued from propping up the hall hatrack, *Great Lovers*.

Within that same year Katy Stutz twice lowered her skirt hems.

"Mamma, I think it is terrible I haven't a room to myself."

The entire surface of Mrs. Becker seemed to coat over with sensitiveness to this frequently discussed issue.

"Why," her lips writhing with an excoriating brand of self-pity, "who am I that I should want a home for my daughter, now that she is grown? Mr. Kemble can treat his wife like a queen, but me--why, I'm mud under my husband's feet."

The Kemble family, on a wave of putative prosperity, had eight months since gone to housekeeping in a rather pretentious rock-fronted house on one of the many newly graded streets west of Kingshighway. Every Friday night Lilly slept with Flora, the two side by side in Flora's pretty new bird's-eye-maple bed, exchanging unextinguishable confidences well through nights wakeful with their dreams.

"Flora has her own parlor to practice in, and here I can't even sing a little without the entire boarding house rapping on the wall."

"It's a shame. Watch me talk to your father to-night."

"Mamma, can't I please take elocution?"

"I should say not. Aren't piano and voice sufficient? The idea! I wouldn't give a row of pins for all the elocution in the world. Reciting is out of date."

"Mamma, it isn't. Mr. Lindsley says the modern woman of culture should cultivate her speaking voice the same as she learns to use her singing voice. Please, mamma; only a dollar a lesson."

"Oh, I don't care! Goodness knows where the money is coming from, with flax twine where it is; but anything for peace."

And so when Lilly graduated from High School, third in her class, and again slightly to the rear of Estelle Foote, who read the valedictory, she was executing excitedly, if sloppily, "The Turkish Patrol," was singing in an abominably trained but elastic enough soprano, the "Jewel Song" from "Faust," and "Jocelyn," a lullaby, and at a private recital of the Alden School of Dramatic Expression had recited "A Set of Turquoise" to incidental music.

Mrs. Schum's boarding house, to the man, turned out to Lilly's High School graduation, Katy Stutz and Willie standing in the wings and all unwittingly visible from the house. A German-silver manicure set, handsomely embossed, bore the somewhat cryptic card, "To Lilly Becker, as she stands on the threshold of life, from her friends in the house." There were a Honiton-lace fan with mother-of-pearl sticks, with the best wishes of her mother's euchre club, and from her parents a tiny diamond ring set high in gold facets, "To Lilly, from her parents, June, 1901," engraved in the hoop.

That night, still in her white organdie frock, with its whirligig design of too much Valenciennes lace, her hair worn high and revealing an unsuspectedly white nape of neck, Lilly regarded her parents across a little table-display of gifts.

"I feel so queer," she said, looking off through the chocolate-ochre wall paper, the reaction already set in. "So sort of--finished. Nothing to do."

MR. BECKER: "That was certainly a fine speech the president of the Board of Education made. You've something now that no one can take away from you. Knowledge is power."

"Two girls in our class are going to the University of Missouri, papa. That's what I'd like to do--go to college."

"Don't spoil a good thing by trying to overdo it, Lilly. It is as bad for a young girl to permit herself to be educated into one of those bold, unwomanly woman's-rights girls as it is for her to be frivolous and empty-headed. When women get too smart they get unattractive."

"But, papa, girls are beginning more and more to go to college, and all women will be--suffrage--some day."

"Not womanly girls, Lilly."

"I always said that High School would be her ruination."

"I didn't learn it there, mamma. I always wanted to be something--"

"Well, you're a finished stenographer, aren't you? Why not go down to your father's office a couple of mornings a week?"

"I don't mean stenography. I hated learning it. I mean something--something--beyond--"

Suddenly Mrs. Becker, quiet at the business of wrapping away some of the gifts, glanced up, two round spots of color on her cheeks.

"You *are* going to do something, Lilly. Have a home and entertain in it like other girls."

"But--"

"I've a piece of news for you and your father. If I waited for him to take the initiative I'd wait until the crack of doom."

"What is it, little woman?"

"I signed a lease yesterday for one of those yellow-brick houses--seven rooms, bath, furnace heat, and privilege of buying. Twenty-eight dollars, out on Page Avenue near Union. We move in two weeks from to-day."

CHAPTER VIII

There followed one of those years which come and go even in the small affairs of small men, when for Ben Becker swift waters flowed under the bridge. He was just that, a small man, prided himself upon it and was frequent in his boast: "I'm a small man, Carrie. I don't hope to make a big or showy success of it. Just a comfortable and unassuming living is about all I expect to get out of it, and that's a pretty good deal."

The Spanish-American War, something of musical comedy in its setting, had run its brief malarial engagement, netting Ben Becker, in one order of hemp rope alone, a cleanly realized profit of forty-two hundred dollars.

On a new and gradually attained bank credit the B. T. Becker Hemp, Rope, and Twine Company bought out the about-to-be-insolvent Mound City Flax Twine Company, the consolidated interests moving into a two-story brick building on South Seventh Street.

The firm took on the subtle and psychological proportions that go with incorporation, however unassuming, capitalizing at fifteen thousand dollars, B. T. Becker, president; Jerry Hensel, trusted foreman of years, vice president and holder of ten shares; Carrie Becker, secretary and treasurer and, to propitiate the law, holder of one share.

The little house on Page Avenue, too new for wall paper, still exuding the indescribable cold, white smell of mortar in the drying, was none the less---and with the flexible personality of houses--taking on the print of the family. A mission dining-room set, ordered wholesale through the machinations of one of Mrs. Becker's euchre friends, arriving from Grand Rapids two months late, completed a careful and thrifty period of housefurnishing. There were an upright piano, still rented, but, like the house, payments to apply to a possible future purchase, in the square of "reception hall"; a double brass bedstead in the second-story front; and tucked away in the back of the tiny house, overlooking, through sheerest of dimity curtains, a rolling ocean of empty lots, the German-silver manicure set spread out on the dressing table, Lilly's bird's-eye-maple bedroom come true.

Followed even then a long and uneasy period of adjustment. The up and down stairs tugged at the rear muscles of Mrs. Becker's legs, compelling evening foot baths. Mr. Becker chafed under the twenty minutes additional street-car ride, eating his dinner by gaslight even in August. The bed making and her allotment of the upstairs work irked Lilly, even though Willie's stepniece, Georgia, came to help out once a week, and evenings the little house could seem very still and untenanted.

But after the arrival of the mahogany-and-velours parlor set, the music cabinet, and the hanging of crispy lace curtains, Lilly standing on the ladder, her mother steadying from below, and finally the laying of a well-padded strip of stair carpet to eat in the hollow noises of new tenancy, the house began to settle, so to speak.

Something latent, something congenital, even malignant, however, had developed in Mrs. Becker. She took a fierce kind of joy, not untinged with the mongrel emotion of self-pity, in scrubbing, on hands and knees, the entire flight of back stairs at the black six-o'clock hour of wintry mornings, her voice tickling up like a feather duster to Lilly's reluctantly awakening senses.

"Lil-ly! Get up! I've done a day's work already. If I was a girl I wouldn't want to sleep while my mother slaves."

But let Lilly so much as venture down into the wintry gaslight of the bacon-fragrant kitchen, proffering her drowsy aid, a new flow, still in the key of termagency, would greet her.

"Go right back to bed, Lilly. You want to catch your death of cold?"

"But, mamma, you fuss so. I'd rather help than listen. Here, let me stir the oatmeal."

"Go back to bed, I say. I don't intend to have you spoil your hands with kitchen work. Maybe some day your father will feel in a position to give his wife a permanent servant girl like any other woman has."

"Mamma, he's always begging you to get one,"

"I know. Talk is cheap. Did you hear what I said, Lilly? Stop that stirring and go back to bed! I'll bring up your breakfast after a while. I'll fix your sandwiches for the sewing circle this afternoon."

"Oh, mamma, I just hate that circle! I wish to goodness you would let me resign."

"I have a grateful daughter, I have. Any other child with your advantages would think she had heaven on earth."

"I hate it, I tell you. Flora and Snow and all those girls, with nothing on their brains except fellows and fancy work, make me positively sick."

"I notice Flora had enough brains to become engaged to a fine young fellow with prospects like Vincent Bankhead."

"Every time I sit down at that circle I think I'm going to scream. I just can't rake up enthusiasm over French knots. Something in me begins to suffocate and I can't get out from under. I hate it."

Regarding her daughter through the bluish aroma of bacon in the frying, her early-morning coiffure and wrapper not lenient with her, a bitterness pulled at the lips of Mrs. Becker.

"That settles it. I'm going to have a talk with your father this morning."

"Oh, mamma, please don't begin a scene!"

"Ben, are you ready for breakfast? Come down. What do you do up there so long? You've been one solid hour splashing around the bathroom, as if I didn't have to get down on my hands and knees to wipe up the flood around the bathtub. Hurry! Your daughter has something to say to you."

"Coming, Carrie. Don't get excited."

"Don't get excited! I think your father would ram that down my throat if this house was tumbling around our heads."

It was true that Mr. Becker's imperturbability incased him like a kindly coating of tallow. His daily and peremptory call to breakfast brought him down only after the last satisfactory application of whisk, tooth, hand, shoe, bath, and hair brush, his invariable white-linen string tie adjusted to a nicety, his neat gray business suit buttoned over a gradual embonpoint.

"If I took as good care of myself as my husband does, I'd live to be a thousand."

"Now, little woman, you got up on the wrong side of bed to-day."

On this particular morning he descended genial, rubbing cold, soap-exuding hands together.

"Well, little woman! Good morning, daughter."

"Ben, I'm at my row's end with Lilly. Something has got to be done or I can't stand it."

He sat down, an immediate tiredness out in his face, adjusting his napkin by the patent fasteners to each coat lapel.

"Now, Carrie, have you and Lilly been quarreling again? Doesn't it seem too bad, Lilly, that you and your mother cannot get on without these disturbances? Your mother may have her peculiarities, but she means well."

A ready wave of red self-commiseration dashed itself across Mrs. Becker's face.

"I can't stand it, Ben. I don't know what she wants. Maybe you can please her. I can't. Everything I do is wrong. Everything."

In her little blue-gingham morning dress, out of which her neck flowered white and ever beautiful of nape, Lilly crumbled up her biscuit, eyes miserably down, the red-hot pricklings which invariably accompanied these scenes flashing over her and a crowding in her throat as if she must tear it open for language to make them understand.

"Talk to your father, now! Tell him some of the things you hound me with."

"Lilly, what seems to be the trouble?"

"I--I don't know. Mamma gets so excited right away. I just happened to mention that--I don't know what to do with myself."

"Do with yourself! Help me in the house. I can give you enough to do with yourself. I don't get lonesome."

"Carrie, now, don't holler."

"That's the way she is, papa. She gets excited and hollers at me because I can't get interested in sewing clubs and housework."

"It's because you've got it too good that you're not satisfied. That Flora Kemble, that never has a decent thing to wear, gets engaged to a--"

"Now, Carrie, that's no way to talk."

"Mamma always makes me feel uncomfortable because I'm not married yet."

"Now do you believe what I go through with, Ben?"

"You haven't any faith in me, but--somewhere--destiny, or whatever you want to call it, has a job waiting for me!"

"That's too poetical for me to keep up with. Thank goodness I'm a plain woman who knows her place in life."

"Exactly, mamma. It isn't that I consider myself above Flora's party to-morrow night. It's not my place. I don't belong there. I hate it, I tell you."

"You hear that, Ben? That's the thanks I get. You know the way I've tried to make this little home one a child could be proud of. Take the time that fine young Bryant fellow came to call. Why, that little parlor of ours was fit for a princess. His knuckles didn't suit her! They cracked, she said. I've heard of lots of excuses for not taking to boys, but that beats all. Three girls out of the sewing club already married and Flora engaged to that well-to-do Bankhead boy, and mine holds herself above them all."

"Your mother isn't all wrong, Lilly."

"I've run my legs off for the white organdie so Katy Stutz could make it up for Flora's engagement party to-morrow night. Does she appreciate it? Oh yes, long face is the kind of appreciation I get."

"I'd rather stay home, mamma, and practice my singing or read--anything--"

"You'll sing *there*. Mrs. Kemble has it all fixed for Flora to call on you just before the refreshments. If you begin to pout about this party, Lilly, I--"

"Oh," cried Lilly, turning her face away to hide the embitterment of lip and still crumbling up her biscuit, "don't worry. I'm going if--if it kills me."

Suddenly Mrs. Becker's face quivered ominously, the impending storm-cloud bursting.

"I wish I was dead. What do I get out of it? Struggle and sacrifice, and all for an ungrateful daughter that isn't happy in her home."

"It isn't that. Just let me be--myself!"

"Then what is yourself? For God's sake tell us what? Anything to end this state of affairs."

"I'm suffocating here. Let me make something out of myself."

"Listen to her, Ben. Make something. Her stories come back from the editors. Her teacher keeps telling me her voice isn't ready yet. Miss Lee says her piano technique is lazy--"

"Then let me travel--college--anything."

"She thinks we're millionaires, Ben."

"Lilly, Lilly! What is the young generation coming to?"

"I wish I was dead. Dead," cried Mrs. Becker, beating at the table until the dishes shivered. Danger lights sprang out in little green signals around about the flanges of her nose. She was mounting to hysteria.

"Lilly, aren't you ashamed to torture your mother like this?" cried Mr. Becker, his voice shot through with what for him amounted to a pistol report. "Comfort your mother. Apologize at once!"

"Mamma, I'm sorry! I am, dear."

"You would think we were plotting against her."

"Now, now, Carrie, Lilly doesn't mean all she says."

"But she eats my life out."

"She wants to please us. Don't you, Lilly?"

"Y-yes, papa--"

"Now let us see if things can't run smoother in our little home, eh, Lilly? We'll all try and do each his part, eh, Lilly?"

"Y-yes, papa."

"It's late," cried Mrs. Becker, suddenly, on the single gong of half after seven, and, ever quick and kaleidoscopic of mood: "Katy Stutz will be here any minute. That's her now. Run upstairs, Lilly, and take the top off the sewing machine and lay out the white organdie. Quick, Lilly. I want you to have it without fail for to-morrow night."

CHAPTER IX

It was at this controversial gathering of young people at the home of Flora Kemble that Lilly met, for the first time, Albert Penny.

The Kemble home lent itself gracefully to occasions of this kind, the parlor and reception hall opening into one, and the impending refreshments in the dining room shut off with folding doors. There was more of ostentation in the Kemble home. More festooning of fringed scarfs, gilt chairs, and a glass curio cabinet crammed with knickknacks.

"Dutch as sauerkraut," was Mrs. Becker's indictment; and Flora Kemble came under the gaucherie of the impeachment, too.

She had attained tall and exceedingly supine proportions, wore pinks and blues and an invariable necklace of pink paste pearls to fine advantage, and a fuzz of yellow bangs that fell down over her eyes, only to be repeatedly flung back again.

Again MRS. BECKER (who could be caustic): "She makes me so nervous, with her hair down over her eyes like a poodle dog, that I could scream."

Nevertheless, at eighteen Flora's neat spiritous air lay calm as a wimple over her keenly motivated little self. The same apparently guileless exterior that had concealed her struggle along a road lit with midnight oil toward her graduation, enveloped the campaign of strategy and minutiae that had resulted victoriously in her engagement to Vincent Bankhead, assistant credit man to his father.

Albert Penny at this time was second-assistant buyer for Slocum-Hines, and, at the instance of his friend Vincent, somewhat reluctantly present.

"Al, what are you doing to-night?"

"Oh, about the same old thing! Take a stroll and turn in, I guess. Why?"

"There is a little gathering up at the Kembles' this evening. Thought maybe you'd like to meet the girl. Nothing formal, just a few of the girls and boys over to celebrate."

"I'm not much on that kind of thing, Bankhead. Guess you'd better count me out."

"Come along. Want to show you the kind of little peach I've picked."

"Ask me out some night to a quiet little supper, Bankhead. I feel a cold coming on."

"Quiet little supper, nothing. That's your trouble now, too much quiet. Nice people, her folks. It'll do you good."

And so it came that when the folding doors between the Kemble dining room and parlor were thrown open, Lilly Becker, still flushed from a self-accompanied rendition of "Angels' Serenade" and an encore, "Jocelyn," and Albert Penny, in a neat business suit and plaid four-in-hand, found themselves side by side, napkin and dish of ice cream on each of their laps, gay little bubbles of conversation, that were constantly exploding into laughter, floating up from off the gathering.

There is a photograph somewhere in an album of Lilly much as she must have looked that night. Her white organdie frock out charmingly around her, a fluted ruffle at the low neck forming fitting calyx for the fine upward flow of her high white chest into firm, smooth throat; the enormous puff sleeves of the period ending above the elbow where her arm was roundest; the ardent, rather upward thrust of face as if the stars were fragrant; the little lilt to the eyebrows; the straight gray eyes; the complexion smooth as double cream, flowing in cleanest jointure into the shining brown hair, worn in an age of Psyche or Pompadour, so swiftly and shiningly drawn back that it might have been painted there.

That was the Lilly Becker upon whom Albert Penny cast the first second glance he had ever spared her sex.

"Miss Becker, we certainly did enjoy your solo."

She was still warmed from the effort, the tingling nervousness of the moment not yet died down, and she was eager and grateful.

"Oh, Mr. Penny, did you really? I was so afraid I flatted there at the end."

"I had to laugh the way they broke in with clapping before you were finished. I knew you weren't done."

"Oh, then you're musical, too?"

"No, but I could see there was one more page you hadn't turned."

"Oh!"

"My! but you can go high! Like a regular opera singer."

"Oh, if I thought you meant that! It's my ambition to sing--real big opera, you know."

"It certainly was a pretty song, not so much the song as the way you sang it. I could understand every word."

"If only my parents could hear you say that. You see, they don't approve. They think it's all right for a girl to have a parlor voice, but it must stop right there, otherwise it becomes a liability instead of an asset."

At this little conceit of speech he turned delighted eyes upon her.

"Why, you're a regular little business woman!" he cried.

"Yes," she sighed out at him through a smile, "I took the commercial course at High."

Inhibitions induce callosities, and Albert Penny's inhibitions, incased within the shell of himself, were as catalogic as Homer's list of ships. First, like Tithonus, he had no youth. Persiflage, which he secretly envied in others, on his own lips went off like damp fireworks. He loved order and his mind easily took in statistics. He had invented a wire kind of dish for utilizing the left-over blobs of soap. He never received so much as a street-car transfer without reading its entire face contents. In seven years he had not availed himself of the annual two weeks' vacation offered him by his firm, and, conspire as he would against it, Sunday continued to represent to him a hebdomadal vacuity of morning paper, afternoon nap and walk, unsatisfactory cold supper, and early to bed. His very capacity for monotony seemed to engender it. He could sit in Forest Park the whole of a Sunday afternoon, poring over a chance railroad time-table picked up on the bench; paring his straight, clean finger nails with a penknife; observing the carriages go by; or sit beside the lake, watching the skiffs glide about at twenty-five cents the hour; and finally, hat brim down over his eyes, doze until twilight seeped damply into his consciousness.

This same unsensitiveness to routine had enhanced his value with Slocum-Hines from delivery boy at fifteen to second-assistant buyer at twenty-five, an amenability, however, that threatened to pauperize him of any capacity for play. Under the well-meant banterings of friends he became conscious of it, but to cast it off was to cast off the thing he was. He tried to learn to recreate, and took Saturday-evening street-car rides to Forest Park Highlands and joined a bowling club. He paid ten dollars in advance for a course of six dancing lessons, too, and only took four of them.

There had never been a woman, a perfume, or a regret in his life. In the period of ten years since his migration from the paternal farm ten miles outside of Sparta, Missouri, he had worked for one firm, boarded with one landlady, and eaten about three thousand quick lunches in the Old Rock Bakery at Lucas Avenue and Broadway. To further account for the state of existing hiatus in Mr. Penny's scheme of things would be tautology.

A short femur line gave him an entirely false appearance of stockiness. On the contrary, he stood a full five feet ten, was thewed with fine compactness and solid with clean living and clean with solid living. Even the fiber of his remarkably fine hair was strong. It was the brilliant honey color of full-moon shine, lay off his brow, but not down, lending him a look of distinction to which he was hardly entitled.

He regarded Lilly with a furtiveness prompted solely by a desire not to appear audacious. Her softly rising throat just recovering its normal beat reminded him of the sweet agitation of pigeons in the park. He was close enough to be conscious of an amazing impulse on his part to reach over and touch the soft white flesh above the cove of her elbow. A little blue thread of a vein showed there, maddeningly. A sense of inner pounding suffocated him. He felt as if he had suddenly stepped into a bath of charged waters, little explosions all over the surface of him. Then a numbness so that, when he placed his tongue to the roof of his mouth, it was insensate, and, somewhat frightened, he pinched the back of his hand, relieved by the stab of pain.

"Do you dance, Mr. Penny?"

"Me? I--No, I guess I'm what you would call temperance when it comes to frolics."

A little clearing had been made in the parlor, a music box pricking out the "Blue Danube." From the dining room they sat regarding the three or four couples, Lilly marking time with the toe of her white-kid slipper. The elixir of the dance could rush to her head like wine, but she was not sought after as a partner, due to her reserve against a too locked embrace and a curious tendency to lead.

"To me, dancing is poetry as written by the feet."

He relieved her of her napkin and ice-cream dish, eager for suitable reply to this syrupy observation.

"Speaking of feet, have you seen the show at Forest Park Highlands this week?"

"No."

"Well, really remarkable. There is an armless fellow there who eats and juggles, even writes, with his toes."

"Indeed!"

"Sometime if you would honor me by--by accompanying--I--er--Becker, did I understand the name to be? I wonder if by any chance you are related to Ben Becker."

She turned upon him with the immemorial sense of a point about to be scored, her eyes full of relish.

"Why, I think I'm slightly related, Mr. Penny. He happens to be my father."

He whacked his thigh.

"You don't tell me! Why, I've bought rope and twine from your father for three years! A mighty fine gentleman, there. Well, well, this is a small world, after all."

She noticed his large, protuberant Adam's apple throbbing with the accelerando of pleasure, and a thaw set in between them. He let his arm drape over the back of her chair, a stolen sense of her nearness dizzying him. He was like a man with a suddenly developed new sense, which he could not tickle enough.

"Well, well!" he said. "Well, well, well!" And she sighed out again through her smile that he could fall so short of what he looked to be.

"I used to say, when I was a little girl, Mr. Penny, that I wished my father were in a more romantic business than rope and twine. I wanted him to be a florist or a wood carver or a music publisher or some of the perfectly silly things that girls get into their heads."

"I always say of myself that I must have been born with a wooden spoon in my mouth. Took to hardware from the very start. Left my stepfather's farm and general store at fifteen and made a bee line for the hardware business before I hardly knew what hardware meant. I suppose I'll die with my nose to one of those very grindstones we carry in stock and be buried with one of those same wooden spoons in my mouth. Although I always say, no burial for mine. Burn me up--cremate me when I'm finished here."

"Papa is that way, too, about his business, I mean. Tied up in twine, I tell him."

"Just ask your father if he knows Albert Penny, Miss Becker. Queer how things happen. This very day I turned over a memorandum to the head of my department, advising a certain buy in hemp rope, Becker and Co. in the back of my head all the time."

At eleven o'clock the first guest rose to go, Lilly following immediate suit.

His state of eagerness rose redly to his ears.

"Will you permit me to escort you home, Miss Becker?"

"Why, yes, if it won't upset Flora's plans for me. I only live two blocks over on Page."

"I wish you lived as far as Carondalet," he said, choking over words too strange to be his.

They walked home through quiet streets that smelled sweetly and moistly.

He was scrupulously careful of her at crossings, his tingling fingers closing over the roundest part of her arm, the warmth of her shining through to the fabric of her eider-down-bordered cape, lending it a vibrant living quality that thrilled him.

"I certainly have enjoyed a perfect evening, Miss Becker."

The magic of youth stole out of the citified night upon her.

"See!" she cried, her arm darting out of her cape, "that's Taurus up there. I can always tell him. He's green. See how he glitters to-night. Sometimes I feel sorry for Taurus. It's as if his little emerald soul is bursting to twinkle itself out of the monotony of all the white ones. That's what they were at the party to-night, all white. All of a color."

"Except you."

"Oh! Do you know the names of the stars, Mr. Penny?"

"I know the Dipper. It's our trade-mark, you know. That's how I happened to work out our nest of aluminum dippers. Wonder if you wouldn't permit me to bring you out a set of those dippers, Miss Becker. All sizes fitted into one another. Just a little kitchen novelty you might enjoy."

They were at her front steps now, the hall light flickering out over them.

"I just certainly have enjoyed this evening, Miss Becker."

"Nice of you to put it that way, Mr. Penny," she said, trying to appear unconscious of the unmistakable suns in his eyes.

"I--I'm not much of a fellow for this kind of thing, but I see I've been making a mistake. A fellow like myself ought to get about more. But most of the--er--er--ladies--young ladies--I have met, if you will pardon my saying it, haven't been the sensible kind like yourself that a fellow could sit down and have a talk with."

"I'm not very congenial, either, Mr. Penny, with the boys and girls I am thrown in with. Flora's all right, and Vincent, but I'd rather stay at home with my music or a good book than waste my time with social life. I just ache sometimes for something better."

"Well, well," he said, "we certainly agree in a lot of ways. I thought I was the only home body."

She was inside the door now, bare arm escaping the cape and out toward him.

"Good night, Miss Becker. I--I hope I may be permitted to bring over those dippers some evening."

"Why--er--yes, thank you."

"Good night."

Turning out the hall light, Lilly felt her way carefully upstairs to save creaks.

"Lilly, that you?"

"Yes."

"Tear your dress?"

"No."

"Turn out the hall light?"

"Yes."

"Tight? Wait. I'm getting up."

"Never mind."

But during the process of Lilly's undressing, huddled on the bed edge, arms hugging herself, Mrs. Becker held midnight commune.

"Who was there?"

"Oh, the usual crowd."

"Refreshments?"

"The usual."

"Anybody admire your dress?"

"No."

"Don't tell me too much, Lilly. I might enjoy hearing it."

"But, mamma, won't it keep until to-morrow? I'm sleepy now, dear."

"Who brought you home--Roy?"

"A Mr. Penny."

"Who? I thought you said only the old crowd was there. It's like pulling teeth to get a word out of you."

"A friend of Vincent's. Works at Slocum-Hines's."

"Seems to me I've heard your father mention that name. Penny--familiar. Is he nice?"

Lilly shuddered into a yawn. In the long drop of nightdress from shoulder to peeping toes, her hair cascading straight but full of electric fluff to her waist, she was as vibrant and as eupeptic as Diana, and as aloof from desire.

"Yes, he's nice enough--"

"Penny--certainly--familiar name."

"--if you like him."

"What?"

"I say he's nice enough if you like his kind."

"Well, Miss Fastidious, I wish I knew who your kind is."

"I wish I did too, mamma."

Suddenly Mrs. Becker leaned to the door, her voice lifted.

"Ben!"

"Oh, mamma, he's asleep!"

"Oh, Ben!"

"Mamma, how can you?"

"Y-yes, Carrie."

"Isn't that assistant buyer down at Slocum-Hines's, the one you say has thrown some orders in your way, named Penny?"

"Mamma, surely that will keep until morning."

"Isn't it, Ben?"

"Yes, Carrie; but come back to bed."

"I knew it! He's one of the coming young men at Slocum-Hines's. Vincent Bankhead swears by him. He throws some fine orders in your papa's way. I knew the name had a ring. Lilly, did he ask to--call?"

"Mamma, I'm sleepy."

"Did he?"

"Yes--maybe--sometime."

Then Mrs. Becker, full of small, eager ways, insisted upon tucking her daughter into bed, patting the light coverlet well up under her chin and opening the windows.

"Good night, baby," she said, giving the covers a final pat. "Sleep tight and don't get up for breakfast. I want to bring it up to you."

But, contrary to the blandishment, Lilly lay awake, open-eyed, for quite a round hour after her mother's voice, broken into occasionally by the patient but sleepy tones of her father, had died down.

From her window she could see quite a patch of sky, finely powdered with stars, the Dipper pricked out boldly.

For some reason, regarding it, a layer of tears formed on her eyes and dried over her hot stare.

CHAPTER X

On the 6th of the following July, Lilly Becker and Albert Penny were married.

The day dawned one of those imperturbable blues that hang over that latitude of the country like a hot wet blanket steaming down. The corn belt shriveled of thirst. The automobile had not yet bitten so deeply into the country roads, but even a light horse and buggy traveled in a whirligig of its own dust. St. Louis lay stark as if riveted there by the Cyclopean eye of the sun. For twenty-four hours the weather vanes of the great Middle West stood stock-still while July came in like a lion. The city slept in strange, improvised beds drawn up beside windows or made up on floors, and awoke enervated and damp at the back of the neck.

Throughout the Becker household, however, the morning moved with a whir, the newly installed telephone lifting its shrill scream, delivery wagons at the door, the horses panting under wet sponges and awning hats, Georgia wide-eyed at the concurrence of events.

For the half-dozenth time that morning Mrs. Becker suffered a little collapse, dropping down to the kitchen chair or hall bench, fanning herself with the end of her apron.

"I'm dead! Another day like this will finish me. Georgia, have you polished the door bell? Those delivery boys finger it up so. I'm wringing wet with ***prespiration***. If only there is a breeze in the church to-night. Georgia, if that is Mr. Albert on the telephone, tell him Miss Lilly isn't going to leave her room until noon. No, wait. I want to speak to him myself. Hello, Albert? Well, bridegroom, good morning!... What's left of me is fine.... I'm making her stay in her room. Poor child, she's all nerves. Don't be late. I hate last-minute weddings. Did you see the item in the morning ***Globe***?... Yes, the name is spelled wrong, Pen-nie, but there's quite a few lines. 'In lieu of a honeymoon,' it goes on to say, 'the young couple will go to housekeeping at once in their new home, 5199 Page Avenue, directly across from the parents of the bride.' I'm sending over now to have all the windows opened so it won't be stuffy for you to-night. Wait until you see the presents, Albert, that came this morning. A check for five hundred dollars all the way from her uncle Buck in Alaska. That makes six hundred in checks. Three beautiful clocks, a dozen berry spoons from my euchre club, and an invitation in poetry for her to become a member of the Junior Matron Friday Club. If I wasn't so rushed I think I--I could just sit down and have a good cry. Albert, be careful of those silk sleeve garters I sent you for your wedding shirt, don't adjust them too tight; and you know how you catch cold. Don't perspire and go in a draught. And--and Albert, I see I have to remind you of little things the way I do Ben. You men with your heads so chock full of business!" (Very *sotto voce*.) "Send Lilly flowers this afternoon. Lilies-of-the-valley and white rosebuds. Remley's on your corner is a good place. Tell them your mother-in-law is a good customer and they'll give you a little discount.... Yes, she's upset, poor child. I was the same way. My mother almost had to shove me into the carriage. Well, Albert, call up again about noon. She'll be up by then. Good-by--son."

A pox of perspiration was out over her face, sparkling forth again after each mopping. A box arrived from a jeweler's and one from a department store. They were a pie knife and a table crumber in the form of a miniature carpet sweeper. The usual futilities with which such occasions can be cluttered and which have shaped the destinies of immemorial women into a tyranny of petty things.

Then Mrs. Becker hurried upstairs, her white wrapper floating after.

In the bathroom her husband leaned to a mirror, his jaw line thrust to the cleave of a razor.

"I really envy you, Ben. Not even your daughter's wedding day can disturb you. For a cent I could cry my eyes out. It's only excitement keeps me going. I--could--c-c-cry."

"Now, now, little woman."

She sat down on a hall chair, regarding him through the open bathroom door.

"Has she said anything to you, Ben, since yesterday? It's made me so upset."

"Now, now, little woman, you must make allowances for a young girl's nervousness."

"I know, Ben, but it worries me so. It's not natural for her to have crying spells like that one yesterday."

"Nonsense! I'm not so sure you weren't a red-eyed bride."

"My nervousness wasn't anything like hers. She'll make herself sick."

"You mean you will."

"Have you heard her moving about her room yet?"

"No."

"Shall I knock?"

"No, Carrie; now let the child alone this morning."

"I never knew her to stay in bed so long. It's after eleven, and the hair dresser coming at twelve. It will seem funny, won't it, Ben, her--little room empty to-night."

"Now, now, no waterworks. What if she was moving away to another city instead of just settling down across the street? You worked this thing your way, and even now you don't feel satisfied."

"I do feel satisfied, Ben, but I want her to be, too."

"Now, little woman, mark my word, Lilly may feel that she is doing this thing in more or less of a spirit of sacrifice to our pleasure, but inside of a week she'll be as busy and happy a little housekeeper as her mother."

"Is that her calling?"

"Yes. Go to her, Carrie."

Out in the little upper square of hallway Lilly appeared suddenly; her hair still down in the beautiful way she let it toss about her in sleep, and her body boldly outlined in a Japanese kimono she held tightly about her.

"Mamma, will you and papa please come to my room? I want to talk to you."

"Your father is shaving, Lilly. Can't you talk to us out here? How is our girl on her wedding day? Frightened? You're me all over again. Ask your father if I wasn't as pale as you are." She kissed her daughter on lips that were cold, brushing back the shower of hair from her shoulders. "You ought to see the presents, Lilly, that just--"

"Mamma--papa--you must listen."

"Yes, Lilly."

"Please, won't you let me off? Please!"

Her father regarded her from behind the white mud of lather, his eyes darkening up.

"Now, now, sweetheart," he said, using one of his rarest words of endearment, "this won't do at all."

"But I can't, papa. I just can't. I know it's terrible, this last minute, but--but--I tell you--I can't."

"My God, Ben!"

"Can't what, Lilly?"

"Can't! I never had such a funny--a terrible feeling. I can't explain it, only let me off. Please! It's not too late. Lots of girls have done it--found out at the last minute they couldn't--"

"My God! What are we to do, Ben? Ben!"

"Carrie, if only you will hold your horses I'll handle this." He mopped off his face hurriedly, sliding into a dressing gown.

"Come now, Lilly, into the front room. Sit down."

She moved after him with the rather groping look of the blind.

"Now what is this nonsense, Lilly, you've been hinting these last few days?"

"I've made a mistake, papa. I should have said so weeks--ago--from the start. It isn't Albert's fault. It isn't anybody's fault. I've had it all along, this queer feeling all through the engagement and parties, but I kept hoping for your sakes I'd get over it--hoping--in vain--"

"Why, of course, Lilly, you'll get over it! It's natural for a young girl to feel--"

"No! No! My feeling won't lift! If only I had said nothing the night he--proposed. But mamma was waiting up. She--she pressed me so. It was so hard the way you put it. I know he's a fine fellow. I know, papa, he's thrown big orders in your way. But I can't help being what I am. Please, papa, let me off! Please!"

An actual shrinkage of face seemed to have taken place in Mrs. Becker.

"What'll we do? What'll we do, Ben?" she kept repeating, rocking herself back and forth in what seemed to border on dementia.

"You see, papa, it's only to be a small wedding. We could so easily call things off. I'll take all the blame--"

"No! No! No!"

"Mamma dear, I'm as sorry--about it as you are, but--"

"No! No! She's ruining our lives, Ben--disgracing--"

"Lilly, are you sure that you are telling us everything?"

"I swear it, papa. I know I'm inarticulate, I don't seem able to explain the terrible state I've been in for days--"

"It's nervousness, Lilly."

"I tell you, no! I can't make you understand. But I'm not cut out, papa, for what I'm going to settle down to. I'm something else than what you think I am. I guess I--I am a sort of botanical sport, papa, off our family tree. I know what you're going to say, and maybe you're right. I may have more ideas than I have talent, but let me go my way. Let me be what I am."

"Lilly, Lilly, let us take this thing step by step, quietly. Surely, daughter, you appreciate the enormity of the situation!"

"I do. I do."

"Now to go back to the beginning. Did you consent to this engagement of your own free will?"

"I did and I didn't."

"You didn't?"

"Oh, I know you let me decide for myself, but don't you think I felt the undercurrent of your attitudes? All the other girls settling down, as you put it. You and Albert such good friends, and then Albert himself so--so what he should be."

"Now you are talking. If your mother and I hadn't felt that Albert was the fine and upright man for their little girl to marry, do you think they would have--"

"I know! There we go around in the circle again. Everything is perfect. The little house, Albert's promotion to first assistant. Everything perfect, but me. I don't want it. I don't love him. You hear me! There is something in me he hasn't touched. Respect him? Yes, but respect is only a poor relation to love and comes in for the left-over and the cast-off emotions."

"Her head is full of the novels she reads!"

"You can't keep me from thinking like a woman. Feeling like one. Is it shameful to want to love? Is it wrong to desire in the man you are to marry that fundamental passion that makes the world go around? I'm not supposed to know any thing about the thing I'm plunging into until after I've plunged! I'm afraid, papa. Save me!"

"Ben, I could swear who is at the bottom of this indecent talk of hers. I found his picture cut out of the school magazine and pasted in her diary. She's a changed child since that Lindsley came to the High School the year before she graduated."

"Mamma! Mamma!" fairly exploded to her feet by the potency of her sense of outrage. "Oh, you--you--"

"I know I'm right."

"Why, I haven't even seen him since I graduated! I've never talked ten words to the man in my life! Oh--oh--how can you?"

"Just the same, he's been your ruination. Since you got him into your head not one of the boys you met has been good enough. I knew you had him in mind the day you told me you wished Albert was a little more bookish and musical. I know why you wanted him to subscribe to the Symphony. The spats you made him buy. Poor boy! and his ankles aren't cut for them. Love! Your father and I weren't so much in love, let me tell you. Only I knew my parents wanted it and that was enough. I wish to God I'd never lived to see this day--"

"Carrie!"

"I do. Noon of my daughter's wedding day, and she can't make up her mind whether she'll be married or not. O God! it's funny--love, now at the last minute--oh--oh--" A geyser of hysteria shot up, raining down in a glassy kind of laugh. "Oh--oh, it's funny!--love--"

"Carrie, you're hysterical. Here, smell this ammonia."

"The little house--my heart's blood in it. A doll's house, ready for her to walk into. Membership in the Junior Matrons--trousseau--oh, it's funny--funny--"

"For God's sake, papa, try to calm her!"

"Funny--funny--funny."

With a wave of sobs that broke over her, she went down, then, literally to her knees, her back heaving and shuddering.

"Her wedding day--O God--funny--"

"Mamma! Mamma! It's all right, dear. Don't--holler like that. I just got upset, that's all. Frightened like--like any other girl would. I'm all right now, mamma. I'm sorry."

"We want to see you happy, baby. It's for your good."

"Of course you do. I know it. I'm all right now, mamma."

"We're your best friends, Lilly. We would go through fire for you."

"Of course, mamma. I--I was nervous, that's all."

"There's no finer boy breathes than Albert."

"You're right."

"He's sending you lilies-of-the-valley, baby. He's ordered himself some white-flannel tennis pants, too--the kind you admired. He got his report from the life-insurance people and he's a grand risk, Lilly. In as fine a condition to marry as a man could be. Baby, tell me--tell papa--aren't you happy?"

"I am--I--oh, I am, dear! Why, here is Elsa ready to dress my hair! Mamma--dear--I'm all right now. Fine."

*   *   *   *   *

At eight o'clock that evening, in the Garrison Avenue Rock Church, little Evelyn Kemble, in the bushiest of white skirts and to the accompaniment of organ music rolling over her, placed a white-satin cushion before the smilax-banked altar.

Kneeling on it, and to the antiphonal beat of the Reverend Stickney's voice, Lilly Becker and Albert Penny became as one.

CHAPTER XI

By a strange conspiracy of middle-class morality, which clothes the white nude of life in suggestive factory-made garments, and by her own sheer sappiness, which vitalized her, but with the sexlessness of a young tree, Lilly, with all her rather puerile innocence left her, walked into her marriage like a blind Nydia, hands out and groping sensitively.

The same, in a measure, was true of Albert, who came into his immaculate inheritance, himself immaculate, but with a nervous system well insulated by a great cautiousness of life.

He was highly subject to head colds and occasional attacks of dyspepsia, due to his inability to abstain from certain foods. He was, therefore, sensitive to draughts and would not eat hot bread. He carried an umbrella absolutely upon all occasions and a celluloid toothpick in his waistcoat pocket.

Then, too, he gargled. To chronicle the heroic emotions that motivate men is a fine task. Love and hate and all the chemistry of their mingling that go to form the plasma of human experience. It is a lesser, even an ignominious one to narrate Lilly's kind of anguish during this matinal performance of her husband. She suffered a tight-throated sort of anguish that could have been no keener had it been of larger provocation. Her toes and her fingers would curl and a quick ripple of flesh rush over her.

Mornings, when he departed, his kiss, which smelled of mouth wash, would remain coldly against her lips with the peculiar burn of camphor ice. All her sensibilities seemed suddenly to fester.

On a week day of the third week of her marriage, in her little canary cage of a yellow bedroom dominated with the monstrous brass bedstead of the period and a swell-front dresser elaborate in Honiton and flat silver, she endured, with her head crushed into the chair back, those noisome ablutions from across the hallway. She was wearing, these first mornings, a rose-colored negligee, foamy with lace and still violet scented from the trousseau chest, and especially designed to pink this early hour.

It lay light to a skin that, strangely enough, did not covet its sensual touch. She craved back to the starchy blue-gingham morning dresses. It was as if she sat among the ruins of those crispy potential yesterdays, all her to-morrows ruthlessly and terribly solved.

Something swift and eager had died within her. She was herself gone flabby. A wife, with a sudden and, to her, horrid new consciousness that had twisted every ligament of life.

Her husband's collar so intimately there on the dresser top. His shirt, awaiting studs, spread out on the bed--their bed. His suspenders straddling the chair back. The ordering of the evening beefsteak lurking back in her consciousness. He liked sirloin, stabbing it vertically (he had a way of holding his fork upright between first and third fingers) when he carved, and cutting it skillfully away from the T bone. After the first week, he liked the bone, too, gnawing it, not mussily, but with his broad white teeth predatory and his temples working. She was a veritable bundle of these petty accumulated concepts, harrowed to their quick.

She knew that presently he would enter the room in his trousers and under-shirt, which he did upon the very minute, the little purple circle, like a stamp mark on the rind of a bacon, showing just beneath his Adam's apple, the shag of his yellow hair wetly curly from dousing, like a spaniel's.

"Certainly fine water pressure we have in the bathroom, Lilly. I am going to bring home some tubing from the store and attach a spray."

She looked out of the window over the languid little patch of front lawn, more gray than green from the scourge of heat. Insect life hung midair like a curtain of buzzings. Directly opposite the dusty, unmade street, she could see her parents' home standing unprotected except for one sapling maple, the sun already pressing against the drawn shades. There was a slight breeze through this morning that turned the sapling leaves and even lifted the little twist of tendril at the nape of Lilly's neck.

It was just that spot, while tugging at his collar, that Albert Penny stooped to kiss.

"Little wife," he said.

"Ugh!" she felt.

"Poor little wife, it was ninety-four and a half at six-thirty-eight this morning."

His capacity for accuracy could madden her.

He computed life in the minutiae of fractions, reckoning in terms of the half-penny, the half minute, the half degree.

She sat now, laying pleats in the pink negligee where it flowed over her knees, a half smile forced out on her lips.

"Well, Albert," she said, wanting to keep her voice lifted, "I guess we're in it, aren't we? Up to our necks."

"In what?"

"Marriage."

Leaning to the mirror for the adjustment of his collar button, he paused, regarding her reflection.

"Well now, what an idea! Of course we're in it, and the wonder to me is how we ever stayed out so long."

She reached up to yawn, her long white arms stretched above her head.

"Oh dear! oh dear! oh dear!" she said in what might have been the key of anything.

"Poor little girl!" he said. "I wish I could make it cooler for you."

"It isn't that."

"What then is bothering your little head?"

"I--oh, I don't know. I guess it's just the reaction after the excitement of the wedding."

He came back to kiss the same tendril at the nape of her neck.

"I'm glad it's over, too. Feels mighty good to settle down."

"'Settle down.' Somehow I hate that expression."

"All right, then, Mrs. Penny, we'll settle up. Speaking of settling up, I guess the missus wants her Monday-morning allowance, doesn't she?"

"I--guess--so."

He placed three already counted out five-dollar bills on the dresser, weighting them down with a silver-back mirror.

"See if you can't make it last this week, Lilly. You watch Mother Becker market and you'll come out all right."

"Oh, I can't pick around raw meat the way mamma does. It makes me sick."

"Housekeeping may seem a little strange at first, but I'm not afraid my little wife is going to let any of them get ahead of her."

"Whoever wants it, can have that honor."

"What?"

"Nothing."

"What's the program for to-day, Lilly?"

"Oh, I don't know."

"I'm going to send Joe out from the store to-day with some washers for the kitchen faucets and some poultry netting for a chicken yard. I'll potter around this evening and build one behind the woodshed. Chickens give a place a right homey touch."

"And send out a man from Knatt's to fix the piano. They delivered it with a middle C that sticks."

"Yes, and I'll send a can of Killbug out with the wire. I noticed a cockroach run over the ice box last night. You must watch that a little, even in a new house."

"Ugh!"

"I hope I'm not getting a cold. I feel kind of that way. Mother Becker fixed me up fine with that wet cloth around my neck last time. I'll try it to-night."

"Come," she said, "breakfast is ready."

They descended to the little oak dining room, quite a glitter of new cut glass on the sideboard and the round table white and immaculately spread. There was a little maidservant, Lena Obendorfer, the fifteen-year-old daughter of the Kemble washerwoman, shy and red rims about her eyes from secret tears of homesickness.

"Why, Lena, the breakfast table looks lovely; and don't forget, dearie, Mr. Penny takes three eggs in the morning, and he doesn't like his rolls heated."

The child, her poor flat face pock-marked, fluttered into service.

Lilly regarded her husband through his meal, elbows on table, cheek in her palm. He ate the three two-minute eggs with gusto, alternating with deep draughts of coffee, and crisp little ribbons of bacon made into a sandwich between his rolls.

"This is certainly delicious bacon."

"Mamma sent a whole one over yesterday."

"I like it lean. Always buy it with plenty of dark streaks through it. Don't you like it lean?"

Silence.

"Can't you eat, Lilly? That's a shame."

"Too hot."

"Poor girlie!"

"Lena, bring Mr. Penny some more bacon."

"Certainly delicious. I like it lean."

She watched his temples quiver to the motion of his jaws, her unspeakable depression tightening up her tonsils and the very pit of her scared and empty.

"Albert--"

"Um-hum!"

"I--What if you should find that I--I'm not--not--"

"What?"

"Not right--here. Not the--wife for you."

He leaned over to pinch her cheek, waggling it softly and masticating well before he spoke.

"If my little wife suited me any better they would have to chain me down. Ah, it's great! I tell you, Lilly, a man makes the mistake of his life not to do it earlier. If I had it to do over again I'd marry at twenty. Solid comfort. Something to work for. I feel five years closer to the general managership than I did six months ago. Certainly fine bacon. Best I ever ate."

"Albert--let us not permit our marriage to drag us down into the kind of rut we see all about us. Take Flora and Vincent. Married five months and she never so much as wears corsets when she takes him to the street car, mornings. And he used to be such a clever dresser, and look at him now. All baggy. Let's not get baggy, Albert."

"I agree with you there. A man owes it to himself and his business to appear well pressed. It's a slogan of mine. Clothes may not make the man, but neatness often goes a long way toward making the opportunity. Don't you worry about me becoming baggy, Lilly. I'm going to send one of those folding ironing boards up from the store this day."

"I don't mean only that. You mustn't be so literal about everything. I mean let's not become baggy-minded. Take Flora again. Flora was her class poetess and I don't believe she has a literary thought or a book in her head now except her account book. Let us improve ourselves, Albert. Read evenings and subscribe to the Symphony and the Rubinstein Evening Choral."

"Speaking of Rubinstein, Lilly, I'm going to take out a thousand dollars' burglary insurance with Eckstein. One cannot be too careful."

She pushed back from the table. "We're invited over to the Duncans' to-night for supper. They've one of the new self-playing pianos."

He felt in his waistcoat pocket for the toothpick.

"I'll go if you want it, Lilly, but guess where I'd rather eat my supper."

"Where?"

"Right here. And fry the sirloin the way Mother Becker does it, Lilly, sprinkle a few onions on it. If I were you I wouldn't let Lena tackle it."

"This is the third night for beefsteak."

"Fine. You'll learn this about your hubby, he--"

"Don't use that word, Albert. I hate it."

"What?"

"Hubby."

"All right then, husband. Bless her heart, she likes to hear the real thing. Well then, your husband is a beefsteak fellow. Let the others have all the ruffly dishes they want. Good strong beefsteak is my pace."

She let him lift her face for a kiss.

"I'll be home six-forty-six to the dot. That's what I've figured out it takes me if I leave the office at six-five."

He kissed her again, pressing her head backward against the cove of his arm, pinching her cheeks together so that her mouth puckered.

"Won't kiss my little wife on the lips this morning. I'm getting a head cold. Good-by, Mrs. Penny. Um-m-m! like to say it."

"Good-by."

"Mother Becker coming over to-day?"

"Yes. We had planned to go to the meat market together."

"Fine."

"But I'm not going."

"Why?"

"I--don't know. Too hot, I guess."

He looked at her rather intently.

"That's right, Lilly," he said, his eyes, with something new in them, roving over her figure; "if you don't feel up to the mark, just you take care of yourself. Jove!" he repeated. "Jove!" kissed her again, and went down the front steps, whistling.

CHAPTER XII

At eleven o'clock Mrs. Becker, hatted, crossed the sun-bleached street, carrying outheld something that wetted through the snowy napkin that covered it. At the door she surrendered it to Lena.

"Put this in the ice box for Mr. Albert's supper. It's some of my coldslaw he's so fond of, and a pound of sweet butter, I took from my dairyman. See that Miss Lilly never uses it for cooking, Lena; the salt butter I brought yesterday is for that."

"Yes'm."

"And, Lena," drawing a palm across the banister and showing it up, "look. That isn't nice. In my house I go over every piece of woodwork from top to bottom on my hands and knees. You mustn't wait for Miss Lilly to tell you everything. Where is she?"

"Upstairs, ma'am."

She ascended to a jeremiad of the cardinal laws of housekeeping, palm still suspicious. Her daughter rose out of a low mound beside the window.

"Good morning, mamma."

"Lilly, you should help upstairs wash days with the housework. Eight o'clock and my house is spick span, even my cellar steps wiped down. Take off that pink thing and I'll help you make the bed. It was all right to wear it around the first week for your husband, but now one of your cotton crepes will do. Come, help turn the mattress."

"Oh, mamma, Lena will make the bed."

"Who ever heard of not doing your upstairs work on wash day? Really, Lilly, I was ignorant as a bride, too, but I wasn't lazy. I wouldn't give a row of pins for--"

"Please, mamma--don't begin."

"Well, it's your house. If it suits your husband, it suits me."

"Well, it does suit him."

"Not if I judge him right. Albert likes order. I went over his socks the other day, and he kept them matched up as a bachelor just like a woman would. He's methodical."

"Don't lift that heavy mattress alone, mamma. Here, if you insist upon doing it, I'll help."

They dressed the bed to its snowy perfection, a Honiton counterpane over pink falling almost to the floor.

"Well, that's more like it." Her face quickly moist from exertion, Mrs. Becker regarded her daughter across the completed task.

"Now for the carpet sweeper."

Lilly returned to her chair, lying back to fan her face with a lacy fribble of pocket handkerchief. "You can wear yourself out if you insist, mamma, but I can't see any reason for it. I'm--tired."

Mrs. Becker sat down, hitching her chair toward her daughter's.

"Lilly," she paid, eagerly forward and a highly specialized significance in her voice, "don't you feel well--baby?"

"Of course I feel well, mamma. As well as anyone can feel in this heat. If only you wouldn't harass me about this--old house."

Mrs. Becker withdrew, her entire manner lifting with her shoulders.

"Well, if that's the way you feel about it, you need not be afraid that I'm going to interfere. That's one thing I made up my mind to from the start, never to be a professional mother-in-law in my daughter's home. The idea!"

"Mamma, I didn't mean it that way, and you know it. I realize that you mean well. But I suppose many a family skeleton rattles its bones to the tune of 'they meant well.'"

"Lilly, you're not yourself. I'm sure you don't feel well. Baby, you mustn't be bashful with your own mother."

"Please, please don't ask me that again in--in that voice. You know I always feel well."

"We're both married women now, Lilly. If--if there's anything you want to say--"

"No."

"I always say, a single woman doesn't know she's on earth. Isn't it so, Lilly?"

Suddenly Lilly shot her hand out to her mother's arm, her fingers digging into the flesh.

"You should have told me something--beforehand!"

"I'd have cut out my tongue sooner. What kind of a mother do you think I am? Shame!"

"It's wicked to rear a girl with no conception of life."

"You're no greener than I was. That's what a man wants in the girl he marries. Innocence."

"Ignorance."

"It all comes naturally to a woman after she's married, life does."

"I--I hate life."

"Lilly!"

"I do! I do! I do!"

"You poor child!" said Mrs. Becker, stroking her hand, and her voice pitched to a very private key. "Life is life and what are you going to do about it?"

"Only love--some sort of magic potion which Nature uses to drug us, can make her methods seem anything but gross--horrible."

"What's on your mind, Lilly? We don't need to be bashful together any more. We're married women."

Lilly rose then, moving toward the dresser, drawing the large tortoise-shell pins from the smooth coil of her hair.

"If you want me to go to the meat market with you, mamma, I'd better be dressing before it gets any hotter."

"You're too warm, Lilly. I'll go myself. You can learn the beef cuts later."

"I would rather stay at home and practice awhile. I haven't touched the piano since--"

"Tack up your shelf paper while I'm gone, Lilly--your cupboards look so bare-- and then come over to lunch with me and we'll go to the euchre together. It's your first afternoon at the Junior Matrons and I want you to look your best. Wear your flowered dimity."

"If you don't mind, mamma, I want to unpack my music this afternoon and get my books straightened. I'd rather not go."

"The nerve! And that poor little Mrs. Wempner goes to extra trouble in your honor. I hear she's to have pennies attached to the tally cards. Pretty idea, pennies for Penny. Well, I'm not going to worry my life away! Work it out your own way. I'll send you home a steak and some quinine from the drug store for Albert to take to-night."

Presently Lilly heard the lower door slam. It came down across her nerves like the descent of a cleaver.

For another hour she sat immovable. A light storm had come up with summer caprice, thunder without lightning, and a thin fall of rain that hardly laid the dust. There was a certain whiteness to the gloom, indicating the sun's readiness to pierce it, but a breeze had sprung up, fanning the Swiss curtains in against Lilly's cheek, and across the street she could see her mother's shades fly up and windows open to the refreshment of it.

At twelve o'clock the telephone rang. It was her husband. "Yes, she was well. Pouring downtown? Funny. Only a light shower out there. No, the man had not brought the missing caster for the bedstead. Yes, six-forty-six, and she would put the steak on at six-twenty. Yes, the poultry netting had come. Fine. Bathtub stopper. Yes."

For quite a while after this she sat in the hallway, her hand on the instrument, in the attitude of hanging up the receiver.

She did piddle among her books then, a vagabond little collection of them. Textbooks, in many cases her initials and graduating year printed in lead pencil along the edges. Rolfe's complete edition of Shakespeare. A large illustrated edition of Omar Khayyam. Several gift volumes of English poets. Complete set of small red Poes that had come free with a two-year magazine subscription. Graduation gift of Emerson's essays. *Vision of Sir Launfal. Journeys to the Homes of Great Men. Lucille*, in padded leather. An unaccountably present *Life of Cardinal Newman. The Sweet Girl Graduate. Faust. How to Interpret Dreams.*

They occupied three shelves of the little case; the remaining two she filled in with stacks of sheet music, laying aside ten picked selections marked "Repertoire" and occasionally sitting back on her heels to hum through the pages of a score. Once she carried a composition to the piano, "Who is Sylvia?" to be exact, singing it through to her own accompaniment. Her voice lifted nicely against the little square confines of reception hall, Lena, absolutely wringing wet with suds and perspiration, poking her head up from the laundry stairs.

"Oh, Miss Lilly, that's grand! Please sing it over again."

She did, quickened in spite of herself. Her voice had a pleasant plangency, a quality of more yet to come and as if the wells of her vitality were far from drained.

She could hear from the laundry the resumed thrubbing and even smell the hot suds. The afternoon reeked of Monday. She left off, finally, and rocked for a time on the cool porch, watching the long, silent needles of rain, wisps of thought floating like feathers.

"Who am I? Lilly Becker. How do I happen to be me? What if I were Melba instead? What if Melba were frying the sirloin to-night and five thousand people were coming to hear me sing in the Metropolitan Opera House? Albert--husband. What a queer word! Husband. Love. Hate. Lindsley. Language. How did language ever come to be? We feel, and then we try to make sounds to convey that feeling. What language could ever convey the boiling inside of me? I must be a sea, full of terrible deep-down currents and smooth on top. How does one know whether or not he is crazy--mad? How do I know that I am not really singing to five thousand? Maybe this is the dream. Page Avenue. Lena in the laundry. That sirloin steak being delivered around the side entrance, by a boy with a gunny sack for an apron. Dreams. Freud. Suppressed desires. That's me. Thousands--thousands of them. Am I my conscious or my unconscious self? Can I break through this--this dream into reality? Which part of me is here on this front porch and which part is Marguerite with the pearls in her hair? Bed casters, they're real. And Albert--husband--the rows of days--and nights--nights of my marriage. O God, make it a dream! Make it a dream!"

At six-forty-six Albert Penny came home to supper.

CHAPTER XIII

There was nothing consciously premeditated about the astonishing speech Lilly made to her husband that evening. Yet it was as if the words had been in burning rehearsal, so scuttling hot they came off her lips. There had been a coolly quiet evening on the front porch, a telephone from Flora Bankhead, a little run-in visit from her parents, and now at ten o'clock her husband, shirt-sleeved and before the mirror, tugging to unbutton his collar.

She did not want that collar off. It brought, rawly, a sense of his possession of her. She sat fully dressed, in her chair beside the window, the black irises almost crowding out the gray in her eyes, her hands tightening and tightening against that removal of collar. Finally one half of it flew open, and on that tremendous trifle Lilly spoke.

"Albert."

"Yes?"

"Let me go!"

"Huh?"

"It's wrong. I've made a mistake. I don't want to be married."

For a full second he held that pose at his collar button, his entire being seeming to suspend a beat.

"What say?" not exactly doubting, but wanting to corroborate his senses.

She was amazed at her ability to reply.

"I said I have made a terrible mistake. I can't stand being married to you."

He came toward her with the open side of his collar jerking like an old door on its hinges.

"Now lookahere," he said, rather roughly for him; "it's all right for a woman to have her whims once in a while, but there are limits. I've been as considerate with you as I know how to be. A darn sight more than many a man with his woman."

"I'm not that!" she cried, springing to her feet.

"What?"

"That! Your--that!"

"Call it what you want," he said, "all I know is that you're my wife and I married you to settle down to a decent, self-respecting home life and that a sensible woman leaves her whims behind her."

She stood with her hands to the beat of her throat, looking at him as if he had hunted her into her corner, which he had not.

"Let me go," she said.

He seemed trying to gain control of his large, loose hands, clenching and unclenching them.

"Good God!" he said. "What say?"

"It's no use! I've tried. I'm wrong. Something in me is stronger than you or mamma or papa or--or environment. All my life I've been fighting against just--just--this. And now I've let it trap me."

"Darn funny time to be finding it out."

"That's the terrible part! To think it took this--marriage--to awaken me to a meaning of myself."

"Bah! Your meaning to yourself is no better than any other woman's."

"A month ago it would have been so simple--to have had the courage--then. To have realized then! Why--why can life be like that?"

"Like what?"

"You remember the night coming home from the Highlands? I tried to tell you. Something in me was rebelling. Ask mamma; papa. They knew! That's been my great trouble. My desires for myself were never strong enough to combat their desires for me. They've always placed me under such ghastly obligation for their having brought me into the world. Their obligation is to *me*, for having brought me here, the accident of their desires! But I let the molasses lake of family sentiment--suck--me in. If only I had fought harder! It took this trap--marriage! All of a sudden I'm awake! Don't try to keep me, Albert. I haven't known until this minute that my mind is made up. So made up that it frightens me even more than you. I'd rather be on my own in a garret, Albert! It's kinder to tell you. We mustn't get into this thing deeper. Nothing can change me. Don't try."

She put up her hands as if to ward off some sort of blow, but in her heart not afraid, and she wanted to be afraid of him. He did whirl a chair toward her by the back, but sat down, jerking her into one opposite, facing her so that their knees touched, and she could see the spots on his temples that responded so to beefsteak, throbbing. Her terror rose a little to the volume of his silence. His head was so square. She wanted him to rage and she to hurl herself against his storm. Her whole being wanted a lashing. She could pinch herself to the capacity of her strength without wincing.

But on the contrary, his voice, when it came, was muted.

"Lilly," he said, "you're sick. You're affected with the heat." His look of utter daze irritated her.

"Sick! You mean I was sick before! I'm well now."

"You're either sick or crazy!"

"I'm trapped. I was born trapped, but now I tell you I'm free! Something up here in my brain--down here in my heart--has set me free! You can't keep me. No one can. I want out!"

"In God's name, what are you driving at?"

"You wouldn't understand. Love might have made you--this--possible, but it didn't come. It didn't come, Albert."

He reached for his coat to plunge into it.

"I'm going across for your mother and father. I'm afraid of you. There is something behind all this. One of us is crazy!"

"No, no, Albert. Please, not them. I'll run out of the house if they come. They've defeated me so often. That terrible wall they erect--out of flesh that bleeds every time I try to climb it. They've killed me with the selfishness of their love, those two. They put me body and soul into Chinese shoes the day I was born. I've never ceased paying up for being their child. Suppose they did sacrifice for me--clothe me--feed me--what does parenthood mean but that? Don't you dare to call them over! Don't you dare!"

"In God's name, then, what!"

"Just let me go, Albert--quietly."

"Where?"

She went toward him, her fine white throat palpitating as if her heart were beating up in it, something even wheedling in her voice.

"I've thought it all out, Albert. These unbearable days since--this. I'll go quietly; I'll take the blame. In these cases where a woman leaves it becomes desertion--"

"If you're talking divorce, I'll see you burn like brimstone before I'll sacrifice my respectability in this community before your damn whims."

She quivered, and it was a full second before she was able to continue.

"I know, Albert, to you it sounds--worse, probably, than it is. But think how much worse, how degrading it would be for me to stay here--in your house--hating. I'll make it so easy. It's done every day, only we don't happen to hear of it. That's what makes our kind the marrow of society. We're too immorally respectable to live honestly. We build a shell of conventionality over the surface of things and rot underneath. Nature doesn't care how she uses us. It's the next generation concerns her. She has to drug us or we couldn't endure. We're drugged on respectability. On a few of us the drug won't react. I'm one. Let me go, Albert. To Chicago. I was there once with mamma and papa to the Rope and Hemp Manufacturers' Convention. Or, better still, New York. That's the field for my kind of work. Many a girl with less voice than I has gotten on there. Albert, won't you let me go?"

He was like nothing so much as a cornered bull, trying to bash his bewildered head through the impenetrable wall of things. Little red shreds had come out in the white of his eyes; he was sweating coarsely and feeling the corners of his mouth with his tongue.

"You won't ruin my name--you won't ruin my name."

"I'll take the blame. I'll love taking it. You'll have a clean case of desertion--"

Suddenly he took a step toward her with the threat of a roar in his voice, and again she found relief in the rising velocity of his anger and practically thrust herself in the hope of a blow.

"What are you that I am married to," he cried, "a she-devil? What have I got to do? Treat you like one? Huh? Huh?"

He stopped just short of her, the upper half of his body thrust backward from restraining his impulse to lunge, his face distorted and quivering down at her.

"Be careful," he said. "By God! be careful when I get my blood up. The woman don't live that can touch my respectability. If you go, you go without a divorce.

You're trying to harm me--ruin my life--that's what you are. Ruin my life." And suddenly, before the impulse to strike had traveled down his tightening arm, collapsed weakly, his entire body retched by the dry sobs that men weep. He could so readily arouse her aversion, that even now, with a quick pity for him stinging her eyeballs, she could regard him dispassionately, a certain disgust for him uppermost.

He turned toward her finally with the look of a stricken St. Bernard dog, his lower lids salt-bitten and showing half moons of red flesh.

"What is it, Lilly? What have I failed in? For God's sake tell me and I'll make it right."

"That's the terrible part, Albert. You haven't failed. You're *you*. It's something neither of us can control any more than we can control the color of our eyes. It's as if I were a--a problem in chemistry that had reacted differently than was expected and blew off the top of things."

"Bah! the trouble with you women to-day is that you've got an itch that you don't know how to scratch. Well, it's high time for you to learn a way to scratch yours by settling down like a respectable married woman has to." His voice rising and his wrongs red before him: "I wish to God I'd never laid eyes on you. I thought you were more sensible than most and I find you a crazy woman."

"Then, Albert, you don't want a crazy woman for your wife!"

"Ah no, you don't! No, you don't! I've worked like a dog to get where I am. I'm a respected member of this community and I intend to stay one. No woman gets a divorce out of me unless over my dead body. I'm a leader of a Bible class and an officer in my lodge. I wore a plume and gold braid at the funeral of the mayor of this town. I'm first-assistant buyer and I propose to become general manager. I'm a respectable citizen trying to settle down to a respectable home, and, by God! no woman tomfoolery is going to bamboozle me out of it."

She sat with her eyes closed, tears seeping through them, and her fist beating softly into her palm.

"Oh, Albert--Albert--how can I make you understand? My brain is bursting--"

"Lilly," he interrupted, explosively reaching out and closing over her wrist, and sudden perception lifting his voice, "I know! You--you're not well! You're ailing. Women aren't--aren't always quite themselves--at times. You--Lilly--could it be--"

"No! No! No! I'll go mad if you, too, begin to insinuate--that! I'm myself, I tell you. Never more so in my life."

He regarded her through frank and even tender tears, his voice humoring her.

"Of course, you're high strung, Lilly, and a high-strung woman is like a high-strung horse, has to be handled lightly. Don't exert yourself. If--if I'm embarrassing to you--talk to mother. These are the times a girl needs her mother. You go ahead and pick on me to your heart's content. I--I'm a pretty slow kind of fellow about some things. Never been around women enough. Come, it's ten-thirty-six. You need all the sleep you can get. Come, Lilly. Why--I--I've been thick-headed--that's all."

She suffered him to kiss her on the cheek as she turned her face from him.

"Have it your own way," she said, limp with a sudden sense of futility and as if all the reflex resiliency had oozed out of her.

"We're all right together, Lilly. Just don't you worry your head. We'll get adjusted in no time. You and--and mother talk things over to-morrow. I've been a thick-headed old fool. Pshaw! I--Pshaw!"

She moved to the dresser, removing pins until her hair fell shiningly all over her, brushing through its thick fluff and weaving it into two heavy braids over her shoulders. He laid hesitant and rather clumsy hands to its thickness.

"Fine head of hair."

She jumped back as if a pain had stabbed her.

"Don't forget, Albert, to lock the downstairs windows."

He was full of new comprehensions.

"I understand. Take your time to undress, Lilly. I'll be about fifteen minutes locking up, and I want to attach some new safety locks I brought with me. Everything all right?"

"Yes."

"You don't need to keep the light burning."

"I won't."

He opened his lips to say something, but, instead, turned and went out, the closed half of his collar drenched in perspiration.

When he returned, after a generous fifteen minutes, the room was in darkness except for a thin veil of whiteness from the arc light in the street. Between the sweetly new sheets the long, supple mound of Lilly lay along the bed, her bare arms close to her body.

Her breathing was sufficiently deep to simulate sleep. He undressed in the darkness and the silence.

Half the night through he tossed, keeping carefully to the bed edge, and often she heard him sigh out and was conscious that he mopped continually at the back of his hands. Once he whispered her name.

"Lilly--awake?"

She deepened her breathing.

About four o'clock he dozed off, swooning deeply into sleep, his lips opening and a slight snore coming.

She lay with her eyes open to the darkness, letting it lave over her as if it were water and she had drowned in it with her gaze wide.

She felt bathed in a colorless fluid of unreality. Those Swiss window curtains! To what era of her consciousness did their purchase belong? She and her mother had shopped them at Gentle's. They hung now lightly against the darkness. The blond girl who had sold them to her must be sleeping now, too, in this same curious pool of unreality. She lay sunk in a strange pause. Once she propped herself on an elbow, gazing across the street to the blank front of her parents' house. They were sleeping behind that middle upper window, their clothing folded across chairs, as if waiting. How eagerly they would greet their new day of small duties, small pleasures, and small emotions. What gave them the courage to meet the years of days cut off one identical pattern, like a whole regiment of paper dolls cut from a folded newspaper? She began to count. Uncle Buck, five hundred. Grandma Ploag, one hundred. Mamma and papa, one hundred and fifty. Seven hundred and fifty in the bank in her name! Her own little checking account. The tan-bound check book. The new tan valise, monogrammed, L.B.P. The stack of music marked "Repertoire." New York! She fell to trembling, forcing herself into rigidity when the figure beside her stirred. She was burning with fever and wanted to plunge from the cool sheets. She could have run a mile--two.

Instead, she lay the long night through, her mind a loom weaving a tapestry of her plan of action, and dawn came up pink, hot, and cloudless.

CHAPTER XIV

At seven o'clock her husband awakened with an ejaculation that landed him sitting on the bed edge. She lay with her eyes closed, wanting not to blink. He dressed silently, but she could hear him tiptoeing about, and finally lay with her hands clenched against the gargling noises that came through the closed door of the bathroom. At last she was conscious that, fully dressed, he was standing beside her, looking down. She could tell by the aroma of mouth wash.

"Lilly?" he said, in a coarse whisper.

She continued to simulate sleep.

"Lilly!"

She did not employ the deception of a start, but opened her eyes quietly to meet his.

"Lazy!" he said. "It is twenty-six minutes past seven."

"So late?" she said, twisting into a long, luxurious yawn. He kissed her directly on that yawn between the open lips.

"You stay in bed this morning. Rest up."

"I think I will, Albert, if you don't mind."

"You turn right over and have your nap out. I'll be home at six-forty-six."

"Good-by, Albert," she said into the crotch of her elbow.

He kissed her again on the ear lobe and the nape of her neck.

"Good-by, Lilly, and if I were you I'd have a little talk with mother if I found myself not feeling just right. I'm sending Joe up with a pair of granite scrub buckets and that stopper for the bathtub. All right?"

"Yes."

After a while she could hear him below, the tink of breakfast cutlery and the little passings in and out of Lena through the swinging pantry door. Then the front door closed gently, and on its click she swung herself lightly out of bed, standing barefooted behind the Swiss curtains to watch the square-shouldered figure swing across the street toward the Page Avenue car. Her energy to be up and doing suddenly unstoppered, she turned back to the room, jerking out a dresser drawer until it flew out to the floor.

At nine o'clock she was still in her nightdress, sloughing about in an engagement gift of little blue knitted bedroom slippers. There were the new valise and an old dress-suitcase tightly packed and shoved beneath the bed, and over a chair a tan-linen suit inserted with strips of large-holed embroidery that had been dyed in coffee by Katy Stutz. It had originally been designed as a traveling suit for a honeymoon trip to Excelsior Springs until that project had been decided against in favor of immediate possession of the little house.

"Put that extra money into your furniture," Mrs. Becker had advised, to which Albert had been highly amenable.

There was a large *piece de resistance* of a hat, too, floppy of brim and borne down at one spot by an enormous flat satin rose. Lilly had rebelled against its cartwheel proportions, but in the end her mother's selection prevailed.

She dressed hurriedly, emerging from her bath with her hair wet at the edges, but combing back easily into its smoothness.

Her nervousness conveyed itself to her mostly through her breathing; it was short and very fast, but she was as cool of the flesh as the fresh linen she donned. That was part of the clean young wonder of her. Her vitality flowed and showered back upon itself, like the ornamental waters of a fountain. She awoke like a rose with the dew on. Even Albert Penny, rubbing the grit out of his eyes, had marveled at the matinal bloom of her.

She ran in her movements, closing drawers and doors after her to keep down her rising sense of confusion, pinning where fingers could not wait to fit hook to eye. There were twenty-eight dollars in her little brown-leather purse and a check for seven hundred and fifty dollars, payable to "self," in a little chamois bag around her neck.

The pretty solitaire engagement ring, a little aquamarine breastpin, gift of the groom, a gold band bracelet, and after some hesitation her wedding ring, she placed in an envelope in the now empty top dresser drawer, scribbling across it, "Valuable." She pried it open again after sealing, to drop in a tiny gold chain with a pearl-and-turquoise drop, still another gift, suggested by her mother to the bridegroom. Finally, there were the little trinkets of more remote days which she dropped into her purse. A rolled-gold link bracelet dangling a row of friendship hearts. Her class pin. A tiny reproduction on porcelain, like the one burned into the china plate in the parlor, of her parents, cheek to cheek. Regarding it, her throat tightened and she sat down suddenly.

"O God!" she said, half audibly, "what am I doing?" But on the second she cocked her head to a passer-by and finally leaned out to hail in a neighborhood man of all work, paying him a dollar and car fare to carry her bags down to the new Union Station and check them. Seeing them lugged out of the house was another moment when it seemed to her that she must faint of the crowding around her heart.

Lena she dispatched to the grocer's on the homely errand of beeswax for ironing, and, trembling to take advantage of the interval of her absence, hurried into her jacket and hat, her face deeply within the wide brim. Opposite, her mother was scrubbing an upper window sill, the brush grating against the silence. She waited behind the Swiss curtains for the figure to withdraw.

The wide, peaceful morning filled with order and sunshine! The pleasant greeny light cast by awnings into her bedroom. What devil dance was in her blood? What prickly rash lay under her being? Her mother at that ordered scrubbing of the window sill! Her eyes swung the smaller orbit of the room. The rumpled bed. That discarded collar on the dresser, the two stretched buttonholes like two tiny mouths. That collar...

She caught up her purse and ran downstairs. Her telephone was ringing violently as she hurried toward the Page Avenue car.

On the ride down there occurred one of those incidents that sometimes leap out like a long arm of coincidence pointing the way. A classmate with whom she had once sung in the Girl's High School Glee Club, and whom she had long lost sight of, sat down beside her.

"Why, it's Lilly Becker!"

"Vera Wohlgemuth!"

"Of all people! The same pretty and stylish Lilly."

Remembering Vera's readiness with the platitude, Lilly smiled down upon her.

"And you, too, Vera, you look natural"--but the words almost petered out on her lips. Much of Vera's slender prettiness was gone. She had gone hippy, as the saying is, even her face insidiously wider and coarser pored.

"What are you doing, Vera? Have you kept up your music?"

"Oh no! I'm married!"

There was a little click to the finish of that speech that seemed automatically to lock against the intrusion of old dreams.

"A ten-months-old daughter furnishes me all the music I have time for. Didn't I read where you got married, Lilly?"

"Yes. You had such a pretty touch on the piano, Vera."

"Why, I don't believe I've opened the piano in six months! Marriage knocks it out of you pretty quick, don't it? And, say, wait until the babies begin to come. I said to him last night, 'Ed, why is marriage like quicksands?' He's no good at co-nundrums. 'Because it sucks you down,' I said, and he didn't even see the point. But it's a fact, isn't it? Mine is city salesman for the Mound City Shoe Company. What's yours?"

"With Slocum-Hines."

"Lucille Wright is married. And remember Edna Ponscarme? Twins. Nine months to a day. Maybe she wasn't in a hurry! And Stella Loire, the class beauty? She wheels her past our house on her way to market every morning. More like the class dishrag now. Well, well! it does seem funny. Lilly Becker married and settled down like the rest of us, and we had you down in the class prophecy for a famous opera singer. Well, well!"

At Eighteenth Street Lilly left the car, transferring for Union Station. A sudden exultation was racing through her. She sat well forward on her seat, as if that could quicken transit.

Union Station, one of the first of those dividend-built and dividend-building terminals that were to spring up quickly and palatially the country over, rose with a peculiarly American trick out of one of the most squalid sections of the city. Fifteen railroads threaded into it, a gaseous shed *de luxe*, picking up St. Louis like a gigantic bead upon the necklace of commerce.

The coughing of steam up against a glass roof threw off repetitions of self. The boom of a train announcer's voice rang out, the echoes fitting smaller and smaller into one another like a collapsible drinking cup. A hither and thither! A bustle that caught Lilly up into it. She was immediately drunk with the moment and train smoke. Life was a gigantic drum, beating.

The clerk at the Terminal Hotel, Mrs. Kemble's brother-in-law, in fact, cashed her check for her, without question, but a sort of unspoken askance, sending it across the street, with his additional indorsement, to a bank. There were six one-hundred-dollar bills, two fifties, and five tens. She folded their considerable bulk into the bag around her neck.

True to direction, the checks for her bags had been left at the Information Desk in an addressed envelope. A porter scurried for them.

Backed by the precedent of the trip to Buffalo, Niagara Falls, and Chicago, she bought her ticket, and then, rather more reluctantly and against her sense of thrift, a berth, which already necessitated a foray into the little chamois bag.

Last, she dropped an already stamped and addressed envelope into the station mail box, her heart seeming to swoon to her feet as she did so. It contained a half-hundredth version of a week-old letter finally reduced to:

MY DEAREST PARENTS,--When you receive this I will be on my way. I won't try to explain my action except that now I see plainly my entire life has been directed toward this moment.

Had I found this courage two months ago a great deal of suffering might have been spared one person, at least. I cannot say enough for Albert's patient struggle to make possible the impossible, or for you, my dear parents, for whom my love is as great as my rebellion.

I am not leaving an address. That would be useless. My decision is unalterable. It is futile to come after or try to find me. In a large city I will immediately become a needle in a haystack and that is what I want and need for my work. Do not worry. You know very well I can take excellent care of myself, and in case of unforeseen accident I will always be identified by your name and address on me. So by my very silence you are to know I am well and happy. Some day, when success has justified this seemingly rash step, who knows what happy reunion may be in store for us?

Take Albert into your home. He will be a better son to you than I have been a daughter. God bless you all. LILLY.

At ten-five the B. & O. Limited, for New York, pulled out. In a Pullman, her bags on the seat opposite and her hands locked so that her finger nails bit in, sat Lilly, gazing out over the moving landscape of dirty, uneven fringe of city. Crossing Eads Bridge, the higher and lighter rumble of the train, induced by steel over water, was like thin soprano laughter with ice in it.

She was suddenly terrifyingly conscious of an impulse to join in that laughter--to laugh and to laugh.

CHAPTER XV

There is a sense of detachment from this old planet of ours goes with travel, that is not unlike that instant when the pole vaulter's feet are farthest off ground. It seemed to Lilly, after a while, that both her starting point and her destination had fallen away. She hung in abeyance. She was the unanchored streak of a rocket through space.

Time was dropping away from her with a sense of the same steep declivity that could awaken her out of a doze to a sense of falling. She was rolling through the pleasant monotony of Indiana, against the light slant of a morning suddenly turned rainy. Quick diagonal streaks flecked the pane and she could see the drops spat down into a thick white-plush road, clipping it of nap.

The sleeper was quite empty save for a medley of drummers' talk and the rattle of chips from the smoking room and an old man in a skull cap who dozed incessantly. Even the porter dozed. She sat the day through without responding to calls for meals, the rain falling steadily now like a curtain. At five o'clock the lamps were already burning and a rash of little lights began to break out over the landscape.

"Some day," she mused, "I'll look back upon all this and laugh. I'll tell it in a newspaper interview. Lillian Ploag. No, Luella Ploag. Ploag. No-o, Luella--Luella Parlow! Not bad. Luella Parlow!"

She asked a passing porter the time.

"Six-forty-six!"

* * * * *

She slept fitfully, awakening with little exclamations, and once came so suddenly out of a doze that she awoke sitting bolt upright, bumping her head against the top of the berth. Cup her hands as she would against the window pane, she could not see out, but it seemed to her that dawn must be imminent. She felt for her little watch, leaning to the streak of light the curtains let in. Ten-five! Not yet midnight. She lay back on the gritty bed, trembling.

At six o'clock there were still stars, but a coral tremor was against the sky line and clouds coming up furiously. Suddenly she realized that the clouds were mountains and that the flat territory had flowed through the night into Pennsylvania mountains that were like plunging waves, and with the changed physiognomy, her mood quickened. She would not wait for the sun, dressing in her berth.

At eight o'clock, and for only the third time in her life, she breakfasted in a dining car. It was well crowded, the old man in the skull cap across the aisle from her gouging out an orange. She ordered with a sense of novelty and thrift, passing on from grilled spring chicken, bar-le-duc, and honey-dew melon to eggs and bacon. A drummer with a gold-mounted elk's tooth dangling from his chain ogled her, so she sat very prim of back, gazing out over flying villages that were like white-pine toys cut in the cisalpine Alps and invitingly more clipped and groomed than the straggling Indiana towns of yesterday. She was cruelly conscious of self, and throughout the meal kept the tail of her glance darting at her surroundings, dropping a piece of toast once and apologizing to the waiter, continuing to smile in an agony of strain after the incident. She ate slowly, her little finger at right angle to her movements, masticating with closed lips, her napkin constantly dabbing up at them.

Finally the head waiter, who had been hovering, to Lilly's great discomfiture, directly at her shoulder, steered a young woman, with a great deal of very fuzzy light-brown hair about her face, to the empty seat opposite. She had a certain air of chic, was modishly dressed, wore no rings except a marriage band, and long pink nails with careful half moons. With the ripple of a thrill over her, Lilly registered her as "typical New Yorker." As a matter of fact, she was the wife of a teacher of physics in Brooklyn Manual Training School, returning from a two weeks' visit to her mother-in-law in Indianapolis.

She ordered with somewhat of a manner, asking for an immediate cup of hot water, and to Lilly there was something esoteric even in that. The sturdy, fine machine of her own body had the crass ability to start off the day with bacon and eggs. She blushed for the healthiness of her choice.

A patter of conversation sprang up between them, something like this:

"Would you mind passing me the sugar?"

"Why, certainly not!" from an eager Lilly.

"Going all the way to New York?"

"Yes."

"Live there?"

"No. Do you?"

"Yes, since my marriage."

"Do you like it?"

"New York is not a point of view, my dear. It's a habit. Your system comes to demand it just as an opium fiend comes to require so many pipefuls. You know it's bad for you, but the fumes are delicious."

"What fumes?"

"The fumes of the metropolis, my dear. The perfumes of wealth. The next best to being Mrs. Four Hundred herself is to walk past her Fifth Avenue home and see her step out of her automobile."

"I suppose so, if wealth is what one craves most."

"It isn't a craving in New York; it's a necessity. But to those of us to whom life is pretty much of a compromise anyway, there is something in mere propinquity to wealth that is like smelling into a tumbler with its sides still wet from some rare old chartreuse. It isn't filling, but it's heady."

"That's exactly the way I feel about life; it's worth going after if you only get the aroma. If I can't be Venus, then let me be the star dust that is nearest to her!"

It seemed to Lilly that she was suddenly talking to her own kind. New York spoke her language.

"Fearful coffee. I always say the only place outside of my own percolator I can get a decent cup of coffee is the new Hudson."

"The Hudson? Is that a good hotel?"

"Yes, splendid. Are you alone?"

There occurred to Lilly a swift talent for the moment.

"Certainly," she said, shaping her own voice into a petard against the little clang of surprise in the voice of her *vis-a-vis*. "I always travel alone. I'm a professional."

"Really?" her glance running over the somewhat florid details of the corn-colored linen. "With that fine chest, I'll warrant you're a singer."

"Right."

"I wonder if you know Margaret Mazarin."

"Indeed I do, from hearsay."

"Well, we virtually gave Margaret her start. Madge Evans is her real name. My husband grew up next door to her in Indianapolis. She practically used to make our apartment her home. One day when she was about as close to bed rock as a girl could be, my husband said to her: 'Madge, if the managers won't give you a hearing, why don't you try some of those agencies in the Pittman Building in Longacre Square? I see all sorts of musical and theatrical agencies' signs on the windows.' Bless us, if the very first one to which she applied didn't give her the position that indirectly led her straight to the Metropolitan! Some one connected with one of the biggest patrons of the opera heard her singing down at a little old ten-twenty-and-thirty theater and got her an audience right off."

"Oh," cried Lilly, her face ardent, "if only--I--some day--"

"Yes," continued her companion, dipping into her finger bowl and pushing back, "Madge always says it was that tip from my husband, a mere chance suggestion, gave her a start."

"Wonderful!"

They paid, each her check, leaving small womanish tips beside their saucers.

"Well, I hope some day to have the pleasure of hearing you sing. Are you in concert?"

"Oh yes, concert."

"I must watch for your name," digging down into a reticule for a bit of cardboard. "Mine is Towser--Mrs. Seymour Towser. What is yours?"

"Mine? Lilly Penny," she replied, her whole body flashing to rescind the word no sooner than it was spoken. "Lilly-Penny-Parlow."

They swayed their way through the chain of cars, Lilly's coach running two ahead of her companion's.

"Well, good-by, Miss Parlow, I hope we meet again some day."

"Good-by," said Lilly, making her way relievedly through two more cars of aisle.

Once in her seat, she withdrew hastily from her valise a small red memorandum book, giltly inscribed "Mid-West Insurance Company," plying a quick and small chirography on to its first page:

Pittman Building, Longacre Square. Hudson Hotel.

The day, which for Lilly began with the tickle of aerial champagne, petered out humiliatingly. Quite without the precedent of the previous trip to Buffalo, Niagara Palls, and Chicago, train-sickness set in and the remainder of the day was spent hunched with her face to the prickly hot plush of the seat, her hair and linen suit awry, and not a spot on the pillow mercifully proffered by the porter that would remain cool to her cheek.

It was well past nine o'clock, and two hours behind schedule, when a very limp and rumpled Lilly followed the weary straggle of weary passengers through the pale fog of the New Jersey station to the waiting ferry. She found a place at the very bow, and, standing there beside her bags, hat off to the sudden kiss of fresh air, her prostrated senses seemed to lift.

There was something Trojan, Illiadic, in the way in which they moved out presently, to bay. The first tang of salt air, that rotten, indescribable smell of the sea, tickled her nostrils. It was all she could do to keep from being drunk with it. She felt skittish. She wanted to kick up.

The approach was not spectacular. The great spangled flank of herself which New York turns to her harbor had just about died down, only a lighted tower jutting above the gauze of fog like a chateau perched on a mountain. Fog horns sent up rockets of dissonance. Peer as she would, Lilly could only discern ahead a festoon of lights each smeared a bit into the haze.

She began her trick of dramatizing the moment. She wanted suddenly to claw apart the dimness with her finger nails. She wanted to lean into the beyond, to wind herself in that necklace of lights out there and bend back until she touched the floor of the universe.

They slid into slip. Chains dropped. There was a sudden plunge forward. Night was day, white arc lights grilling into a vast black shed. A few automobiles and a line of horse cabs backed up against a curb--the one-horse variety that directly antedated the general use of the taxicab. A porter shoved her bags into one of these, the driver leaning an ear down off his box.

"Where to, miss?"

"Hudson Hotel," she said, sitting back against the leather tufting.

CHAPTER XVI

They rattled over the cobblestones until her very flesh shivered, and she bit into her tongue and her hands bounced as they lay in her lap, and, trying to peer out of the window, she bumped her head, and finally sat back, forced to be inert as she bumbled over the deep narrow streets of lower Manhattan which at night become deserted runways to slaughter, ghostly with the silent thunder of a million stampeding feet.

It was ten o'clock when they finally drew up at the side entrance of the hotel in a street disappointingly narrow, but which seemed to burst, just a few feet beyond, into a wildly tossed stream of light, pedestrians, and, above all, a momentum of traffic that was like the fast toss of a mountain stream. The cab fare was overwhelmingly large. Her bags disappeared; she followed them, immediately enveloped in an atmosphere of upholstery, mosaic floors that seemed to slide from under her, palms that leaned out of corners, crystal chandeliers, uniforms, rivulets of music. She had dined upon several occasions at the Planters' Hotel in St. Louis, and had once spent a night at the Briggs House, Chicago, and the Hotel Imperial at Niagara Palls, and had objected when her father signed, "B. T. Becker, Wife and Daughter," taking the pen to write out her own name boldly under his, and upon all summer excursions had taken upon herself the ordering of the family meals.

But the Hudson awed her, the very Carrara magnitude of the walls, the remote gold-leaf ceilings, light-studded, the talcy odor *de luxe*. She wanted to back out of that lobby of groups of well-dressed loungers; to turn; to run. Instead, she wrote her name on the register, marveling at her steady chirography:

Luella Parlow, Dallas

A narrow clerk scanned the bulk of her baggage, unhooked some keys, and called, "Front." She was mildly taken for granted and her assurance stiffened.

"Bath?"

"What are your rates?"

"Three-fifty and up."

"Yes--bath."

He shifted among his keys and she noticed that when she returned the pen to him his hand lingered just too long. She had a way of lifting her eyebrows to express her archest scorn. The smile on the clerk's face did not die, but neither did it widen.

She shot upward in an elevator. She padded her way through long hallways deeply carpeted to eat in footfalls. It seemed to her they must have rounded a city square of those hallways, door after door after door as imperturbable as eyeless masks, and yet which somehow seemed to look on.

"Anything else, ma'am?"

"Nothing." She interpreted his wait and felt for a ten-cent piece. He shifted the key to the room inside of the door and went out.

She was alone in a twelfth-story room that enhanced her aerial sense of light-headedness. She looked at the bed. Curly birch with a fine sense of depth to its whiteness. There was a glass top on the dresser, with a lace scarf beneath it which appealed to her sense of novelty. Also an extra light above it which she jerked on, peering at herself in the mirror.

There were soot rims about her eyes, and when she removed her hat her hair was glued to her brow in its outline. But just the same, the pollen that gave to her skin its velvetiness was there. She leaned to the mirror, baring her teeth to scan their whiteness; turned her profile as if to appraise its strong, sure cast; swelled her chest after the manner of inhaling for an octave, letting her hand ride on it. Then she undressed slowly, luxuriating in a deep hot bath that rested her as she lay back in it. She even washed her hair, wrapping it finally in one of the thick turkish towels, and then leaned out of her window for a while, her body well over the sill, and the air, with a cool washed quality to it, flowing through her nightdress. She looked down on what she thought must be the bosom of Broadway. Actually it was Forty-fourth Street. An ocean of roofs billowed under her gaze.

She thought of Tuefelsdroeck alone with his stars. Or rather, wanted to think of herself as thinking of him.

A telephone directory on the desk caught her eye. For an hour she pored over its pages, names that had blazoned themselves incandescently from the pages of musical reviews and magazines mixed in casually with the clayey ones of mere persons. A thrill shot over her with each encounter. The book began to exhale an odor of sanctity.

It was two o'clock when she turned off her lights, just enough glow from the hallway pressing against her transom to reassure her. The sheets were fragrant with cleanliness and she let her body give to the delicious sag of the mattress. The rumble of the train was gone from her ears. She felt washed, light, drowsy; cast aside her pillow; wound her arm up under her head; sighed out of deliciousness; slept.

She awoke with a sense of red. A flame of fear shot through her, and a first thought of fire, but even before she could rise she saw it was static, this crimson gash across the blackness, and shaped like a grin.

She began to tremble, and an unreasoning fear of the depth of the darkness to take hold of her. A sort of paralysis locked her, and, although she wanted to scream, she lay there drenched in terror. Finally, out of contempt for her fear, she sprang, landing both feet on the floor.

A little window in the box of the wall telephone, one of those modern hotel devices *de luxe* and *de trop*, had flashed up redly, spelling out to her dilated gaze, "MAIL IN YOUR BOX." Regarding it, her relief shifted suddenly to terror. Mail! Not even had she herself known what her address might be! Her mother--father--Albert? But how? The drummer with the gold-mounted elk's tooth! The clerk and that almost imperceptible trail of the hand. Detectives! Her window showed a streak of dawn. Five-forty by her watch. She tried to go back to bed, but at six she was up again, dressed fumblingly, finally sliding the linen jacket over an unbuttoned blouse. She had some difficulty locating the elevator, scurrying through the deserted halls only to dash herself against repeated *cul-de-sacs*. It was almost seven when she descended into a lobby that was littered with sawdust in the sweeping up.

She asked for her mail, a strange clerk handing it out to her without askance, and hurried to a chair behind a pillar, holding the envelope between the folds of her skirt without glancing at it, and trying to hide the trembling of her arm. She sat down, forcing her hand around and her gaze to meet it. The envelope was blank; she tore its flap and read: "Valet Service. Suits Cleaned and Pressed in One Hour."

And then she went out into 7 A.M. Broadway, all swept clean and caroling with the song of the car gong and the whistlings of steamboats. A line-up of theaters, early-morning mausoleums of last night's madnesses, first met her eye in the clean light. One of them was violently postered with lithographs of Minnie Maddern Fiske. A three-sheet proclaimed Melba. Broadway became an Olympus, every passer-by a probable immortal. She half expected to pass John Drew there as the Rialto cleaned its cuspidors, polished its brass, and swept its front. She thought she caught a flash of Margaret Mazarin in a cab. An exultant chill raced over her at the vertical sign, "Rector's." A musical comedy full of frothy and naughty allusions to Rector's had once played Forest Park Highlands, St. Louis. It was like strolling the pages of an illustrated magazine. Some one jostled her and smiled around very closely into her face. Suddenly her eyebrows shot up. It seemed to her that the face under the gray derby hat was as coldly and as bonelessly fat as an oyster. Her two hands could have met around the little neck which was tightly incased in a soft blue collar held with a gold bar pin. She quickened her step and, what with the lifted brows, promptly lost him.

She stopped finally at a florid lace-and-glass-fronted restaurant on Forty-third Street, with a mimeographed breakfast menu up against the window. Her food went down through a throat constricted against it. Her tightness would not relax.

At half after eight she was back once more in her room, changing from the tan linen into a pink mull, heavily inserted, too, and throwing up quite an aura of rosiness about her. She had only the tan hat, too wide and too floppy of brim, but it had a picturesque value, which is a greater selling quality than *chic*. In fact, in her own eyes, as she tilted the mirror for a full-length view, the art of Katy Stutz stood unimpeached. Eying her reflection in the mirrored walls of the elevator, she felt as pinkly blown as a rose, and looked it. A head or two turned after her youth. At the desk she inquired for the Pittman Building. Just opposite! A policeman held up traffic to let her cross. She picked a name off a third-story window, "Barnett Bureau-- Musical Service," and rode up to it.

By one of those astonishing flukes of beginner's good fortune, upon the occasion of this very first effort Lilly obtained.

A ground-glass door opened into a room the size and bareness of a packing case and crammed to its capacity with a roller-top desk, a stenographer at a white-pine table, a cuspidor, a pair of shirt sleeves, a black mustache, and a blacker cigar.

Entering, Lilly was surprised at the measured tempo of her voice and the manner in which she permitted her eyebrows to arch ever so superciliously.

"I'm looking for an engagement," she said, speaking through the ticking of the typewriter.

The jaw ate in half an inch more of cigar and swung around in the swivel.

"Voice?"

"Yes. High soprano."

He ran a swift cocked eye over her points and turned to the white-pine table.

"Send her down to Visigoth," he said to the stenographer, who took up where he left off.

She was as blond and as bland as a summer's day. A Pompadour dipped down over one eye and her jaws moved as rhythmically as rigorously to gum with a pull to it. She was herself caricatured. She and Lilly exchanged that quickest of inventories, woman's for woman.

"Sign here."

Lilly signed.

"Ten dollars."

"Why?"

"Our rules. Ten dollars a year bureau membership, and fifty per cent of first two weeks' salary."

"But what if--"

"We always place sooner or later."

"But in case--"

"Take this card down to the Union Family Theater, Union Square, and ask for Robert Visigoth. It's a two-a-day. If you don't do business with him, come back to-morrow morning."

A quick dozen of questions rushed to Lilly's lips, but instead she laid down a new ten-dollar bill, crammed the slip into her palm through the hole in her glove, and went out, the snapping torrent of typewriting already resumed.

The Union Family Theater was the first of a succession of variety houses that was to spread, first to Harlem, then Philadelphia, and later gird the country like a close-link chain. Vaudeville prefaced with stereopticon views, designed to appeal to the strict respectability of the most strictly respectable audiences in the world.

The high-class Rialto houses might pander to low-class comedy and Broadway take its entertainment broad, but Robert Visigoth laid the corner stone of subsequent fortunes when he decided that a ten-twenty-thirty vaudeville audience that smells sour of perspiration and strong foods demands entertainment as pink and as sweet as a baby's heel, and that a gunman in the gallery will catcall his prototype on the stage.

Let the Noras and all the pyschanalyzed Magdas go their problematic and not always prophylactic ways, the Visigoth Family Theaters wanted 'em sweet, high-necked and low-browed.

Robert Visigoth, attorney-at-law, whose practice had suddenly, by one of those arbitrary twists as difficult to account for as the changed course of a river, assumed a theatrical twist, had taken over, on cleverly obtained backing, the Union Family Theater from an insolvent client. Within a year it had made a disappearing island of the law office, flowing over and finally submerging that enterprise in the swifter waters of the new.

At the end of two years, Bruce Visigoth, a younger brother by ten years and snatched from the law the very day he graduated into it, was already in Chicago, launching under the auspices of The Enterprise Amusement Company, the People's Family Theater, Popular Prices, the sixth link of the chain already in the soldering.

When Lilly found out the older of these brothers, he was standing in the black auditorium of the theater, holding an electric bulb made portable by a coil of cord, and directing the reverberating hammering down of an additional brace of three orchestra chairs for which room had been found by shifting the position of the bass drum.

A hairy old watchdog, tilted back against the brick side of the building and smoking a pipe so foul that its tang clung to her hair that night as she brushed it out, inspected her slip of paper and led her through a black labyrinth of wings and properties.

An aroma lay on that blackness that in some indefinable way quickened her, set her nostrils quivering, and ran along her entire being like a line of fire. It smelled of Elizabethans in buckskin. Bottom rollicked through it, thumb to nose. Ophelia leaned out of it. Bernhardt, Coquelin, Melba, intoned into it. Its cold, pink paintiness lay damply to her face. She had never smelled simmering mascara, but her lashes were hot with it. Suddenly to herself she was herself, running ahead of the wind, her aching senses bathed in an odor which somehow intoxicated them. She was on a stage for the first time in her life, a bunch light only half revealing it to her. Through the megaphone of cupped hands and the dimness of the auditorium a voice came at her.

"Come down here, around through the left box."

She groped her way to a steel door, stumbling down two unsuspected steps, and was suddenly in the carpeted silence of an aisle. Robert Visigoth came toward her, the electric bulb held high and dragging the yards of cord behind him.

"I'm from the agency," she said at once, the little beating quality that she was feeling all over her in her voice, and holding out the slip.

"Come out here," he said, "where I can see you."

Some daylight flowed in through a slightly open fire exit and she caught at a last moment of darkness to straighten her hat.

"Sing?"

"Yes."

He shoved open the iron door so that more light flowed over her.

"Why," he said, "you're a big girl, aren't you?"

"I don't know," she said, through a little laugh of embarrassment, and noticing that, regarding her, he wetted his lips.

"That part's all right. What I need is a good refined ballad voice. Understand? The kind that can sing 'The Suwanee River' as if the only thing in the world that mattered is that old plantation down there. Understand?"

"I see."

He spoke through a slight patois, New-Yorkese, but which she misjudged for Virginian. He was in inverse ratio to her stock idea of theatrical manager. Both brothers were to become more and more subject to this soft indictment.

Born in one of those old morose houses in lower Lexington Avenue, each had lived there until he obtained his degree of LL.D. from a state university. It had been a sedate, a mildly prosperous, even an historic home. A Vice President of the United States had once owned it. Then a Major O. Higginbothom, and finally, for fifteen years of tenancy, the Visigoths. One of the kind whose genteel hall light had burned through the fanlight decade after decade, and then suddenly, overnight, as it were, disintegrated into a furnished-room house with a sign over the door bell.

One evening Horace R. Visigoth, of the law firm of Visigoth, Visigoth & Higginbothom, did not answer his wife's soft question to him across the green-shaded reading lamp of their library table. His head was quite sunk forward in a sheaf of proofs. He was dead. One month later his wife failed to awaken to Pauline Visigoth's frenzied attempts or to even a dexterous physician's respiratory methods. The year following Pauline Visigoth married the dexterous physician and moved to Chicago.

The Lexington Avenue house succumbed to a quick sale, and in attempting to divert the law business out of the clayey rut of quiet old conservatism, the Enterprise Amusement Company was ultimately to be born.

Robert Visigoth, twenty-nine at the time, betrayed little of the heritage his name suggested. His Teutonic blood pretty well laid, he was a trifle too short and a trifle too heavy, and with none of his mother's lean patrician quality to which both his younger brother and older sister had fallen heir.

Suggesting future rotundities and a reddishness of complexion that was presently to purple, at this stage his chin was undoubted and as square as a spade, and, as so often happens to chins of this potentiality, punctuated absurdly with a dimple, and he wore a little clipped edge of black mustache which he tried to twirl.

Busy at the mannerism, if not the act, of twirling that hirsute adornment of upper lip, he continued to observe Lilly.

"You understand? What I need is a real heart-to-heart voice."

"I'm quite good at ballads."

"Quite good or darn good?"

"Darn."

"Experience?"

"I'm just in from as far west as--Dallas."

"Now what I want is a turn that hasn't struck the West yet. Understand? It originated right here in this theater. There is a firm of music publishers in this town makes up slides of its songs, and all you have to do is stand beside the screen and sing to the stereopticon illustrations. Understand? You don't have to follow the pictures. The pictures follow you. It is sure fire if it is handled right, only the girl we had on last week must have wrapped her vocal cords in sandpaper. The secret of the whole thing is to make them--out there--live the song. Understand?"

"I see."

"Every woman in the audience has to be the sweetheart and every man the lover you are singing to them about. And to do that the first one to live that song must be you. Believe in yourself before you expect the world to. If you come in here and tell me you sing *quite* good, it won't be easy to convince me of more if you begin to warble like Melba. Now you go up there and let me hear a bar or two. Take care of the last row gallery and the first row orchestra will take care of itself. Shoot!"

"I--haven't my music with me--my repertoire--"

"Nonsense! Just a bar or two--'Suwanee River'--anything with heart in it. Give us some lights up there, Bob."

Through the blackness Lilly moved as if she were sleep-walking in it. Little needles of nervousness were out all over her, and, absurdly enough, there walked across her vision the utterly irrelevant spectacle of old black Willie with her feet bound in gunny sacks and the pencil nubs in her hair, and just as irrelevantly her mind began to pop with a little explosive ejaculative prayer: "O God, make him take me! O God, make him take me!"

The bunch light had been dragged down center stage. She stood beside it, opening her mouth as if to muster voice, then closing it. It was as if water were swirling around and around her, the unseen presence in the back of the house surging at her like a multitude.

"Shoot!"

She looked appealingly in the direction of the hammering down of the seats.

"Never mind that. Sing to the top row of the gallery."

A fearful recurrence of yesterday's train-sickness rushed over her; she could have crumpled to her knees, had even a sense of wanting to faint, but instead she opened her lips again, her eyes fixed on the unseen last two tows of the unseen top gallery, and by miracle finding a pitch that left her plenty of range.

"Way down upon the Suwanee River-"

"Louder!"

"Far, far away,
There's where my heart is turning ever,
There's where the old folks stay.

All the world am sad and dreary,
Everywhere I roam.
Oh, darkies, how my heart grows weary--"

The lay of Page Avenue was before her, swollen through tears. Her mother sewing beside Katy Stutz. The patient back of her father's gray head. Her parents on their knees, far back there somewhere beside her bed of fever. Albert! Their wedding night when the door had closed behind them! "O God, make him take me! Please!

"Far from the o-old folks--at ho--"

"That will do."

She stood with her mouth an O on the unfinished note, hand to the little rise of her bosom.

"Meet me around in my office back stage." His voice was like a call in a fog, retreating and retreating. She followed it. They met in a narrow patch of broad daylight.

"I'm afraid," she began, her voice breaking on a gulp--"I'm afraid I didn't--"

"You did very well," he said, kindly. "Little off key and your voice won't set the world on fire, and it has a tremolo quality that may be rotten-bad singing, but it's the right stuff for the act."

She thought, with a swoop of perception, that in this she discerned the astuteness of a buyer too clever to praise the article he covets. She felt lighter, as if some of her had melted in the ordeal. The machinery of her body began to take up again, the saliva to flow, and her heart to beat without seeming to hit its walls.

"I'll try you out for a week. Twenty dollars?"

"Yes." Trying to seem to pro and con.

"Come to-morrow at ten and I'll have a man down to go over next week's slides with you. That gives you until Monday. Something pink on the order of what you are wearing will do, only fluffier. Rough up your hair a bit, too. No, leave it slick like that, but something fluffy in a hat or a sun-bonnet with a pink bow under the chin. Right there--under that little chin."

Her head flew up from his touch.

"I see."

"Manage it?"

"I think so."

"You what?"

"I know so."

"Good. Never let a think show through your answer. Yes or no!"

"Yes."

He tweaked her chin again.

"Watch out somebody doesn't steal you on your way home, big girl."

"To-morrow at ten," she repeated, going out into the sunshine that smote her with the sting of hot lances. The tweak from his hand lay back somewhere, branded none too pleasantly into her consciousness.

But just the same, when she inquired of a traffic policeman the direction to the Hotel Hudson, even the mundane wording of her asking clicked like happy castanets into her spirit.

CHAPTER XVII

A nd so it came about, through events of surprisingly simple shaping, that her first week in the metropolis found Lilly integral to it.

She liked the consciousness that unless she appeared at the Union Family Theater at two-fifteen and at eight-fifteen she was breaking into the continuity of a sequence of events in which she had her place.

She was already in the rush of assurance that followed her sense of earning capacity, regarding the Union Family Theater merely as a means to an end, and in spare time had registered at two concert bureaus, read off the same building of plate-glass windows, and had purchased the score of "Carmen," humming Michaela's aria, in bed of mornings. There was a letter she had once obtained from Max Rinehardt, addressed:

"*To Whom It May Concern. Miss Lilly Becker has studied with me for a period of three years. I consider her voice a lyric soprano of fine quality.*"

Evidently it concerned no one. The clerk at the concert bureau tossed it aside without comment. Visigoth, when he read it one day in the wings, returned it in just that manner.

She was secretly ashamed of her professional debut in a role that would not have survived the ridicule of even Flora Bankhead's easy standards. Many a time, together at matinees, they had giggled and munched chocolates over acts that hardly rivaled hers for sentimental appeal of about one dimension. Plenty of length and no depth.

To a series of colored views thrown upon the screen, Lilly sang from a dark stage into the warm musk and stale linen-smelling theater, a ballad as slow and sweet as taffy in the pulling.

"Dressed up in her gingham gown,
Just to come with me to town.
How the sun was shining down!
It seemed to bless our lit-tul wedding day."

CHORUS:

"Darling Sue--e dear,
How I miss your laughing!
Seems to me I hear it in the same old way.
Darling Sue dear, don't believe I'm chaffing.
Bless your heart! I love you in the same old way."

Lights! Revealing Lilly in the pink mull and dangling sunbonnet beside the blank white screen. They liked her, invariably demanding encore, this time the words and score of the chorus thrown upon the screen and, to Lilly's importunings and pretty encouragement, the house joining in.

By arrangement with the publishing house, this exploitation of song hits cost the Visigoth brothers nothing. In fact the little novelty soon came to supplement one of the eight acts on the program, thus eliminating a number.

Each week a new song score bordered in hearts and flowers was thrown upon that darkness, the audience eager to find a hum in it.

Lilly's second song, "Mamma, Why Are You So Sad To-night?" went even better than the first, and it so pleased Robert Visigoth, who in those years had his ears to the ground of the daily audience, to hear them filing out, whistling and carrying it on little tra-la-las, that he called Lilly into his office the first day of the second week, to announce a five-dollar raise in salary.

She had been in the habit of oozing past him rather hurriedly in and out the dark passages, conscious that his touch was ever ready to slide down her length of arm, or his knee to find out hers and press it if he sat down beside her as she waited in the wings.

It was before the realty aspect, the buying, leasing, and selling, of theater property had engulfed him, and his presence around the theater, often shirt-sleeved, was hardly a matter of moment.

However favorably he differed in aspect from Lilly's preconception of the managerial genius, her inhibitions concerning him were strong. She always sat on the edge of her chair in his presence. To accept so much as a slip of paper from him meant that his touch would trail to the last long-drawn second. His eyes had a habit of focusing, seeming to move in a bit toward the tip of his nose and grill intimately into her being. And then his wetted lips, as if his mouth were watering.

"You need to be waked up," he said once to her. "You're like a great big sleepy cat."

She jerked away from his touch and his reference, hurrying from the theater, as always, immediately after her act, which came first on the afternoon and evening bill. Secretly she was thoroughly ashamed of what she was doing, putting each performance quickly behind her.

Six hundred and twenty-two dollars still lay in the chamois bag against her bosom, but the additional five dollars a week on to her salary was a saving prop against the not infrequent sag of her spirit.

She was listed at half a dozen agencies, but nothing presented itself. Her first hotel bill, twenty-eight dollars, sent her scurrying, against further and deeper inroads into the chamois bag, to an immediately adjoining side street of brownstone fronts as without identity as a row of soldiers, all of them proclaiming the furnished room to that great sandstorm of New York transients who blow in and out of them in nameless whirl.

Their dreariness flowed over her in cold, soupy odors, that left a feeling of a coating of grease over the surface of her. The poor filbert of gaslight burning into floor after floor of slits of hallway. The climb after a whole processional of spotty landladies whose shortness of breath contributed to the odor-laden air.

The room which she finally obtained at three dollars a week was a third-floor front, shaped like a shoe box, with an aisle of walking space between the cot and washstand, and as dank to her and as shiver-inducing as a damp bathing suit donned at dawn.

But the matting on the floor smelled scrubbed, the bathroom at the head of the stairs contained a porcelain tub instead of the usual horror in painted tin, and except for June bugs that bumbled all night against her ceiling, attracted by the incandescence from the theater sign across the street, was free from those scavengers of bed slats and woodwork which, often as she inspected from room to room, to her agonized flush, had crawled across a landlady's very denial of them.

Robert Visigoth had a habit of appraising this ready blush of hers. It never rushed hotly to her face but what he noted it in persiflage.

"Look at her blush!" he cried, one afternoon as they both stooped to recover her dropped hand bag, their heads bumping so that they sprang apart in laughter.

"The idea, Mr. Visigoth! I'm not blushing!" she cried, stinging with her inability to control the too ready red.

He ran his hand over the smooth glaze of her hair.

"Don't!"

"Let's see if it will muss. I'll wager it's painted on."

"It grows that way," she said, levelly.

"I like it! Clean as a whistle. Interesting. In fact, you're a mighty interesting young woman, if you want to know it, Miss Luella Parlow."

"What is the song for next week, Mr. Visigoth?"

"'My Pretty, My Pretty,'" he said, his intimate eyes watching her wriggle, with a sense of being ridiculous, on the hook of his glance.

"I never know how to take you," she flared, infuriated, and rushed toward the door.

"Take me--with you."

"Really now--this--this is too absurd."

"Where are you going?"

"Home, of course. I have all this time to myself between now and the evening performance. Why waste it sitting around with the dog and trapeze acts?"

"Where do you live?"

"West Forty-fourth Street, near Eighth."

"Where?"

"West Forty-fourth Street."

"Hm-m-m!" he said, with a new easiness of manner that alarmed her.

"Selfish little girl. All this time to yourself."

"You would be surprised how it flies."

"What do you do?"

"Oh, no end of odds and ends. Wash out things. Read. Sew. Practice. Write."

"What do you write? Letters to suitors? Lucky chaps."

"Nonsense!" she said, coloring.

"A girl like you must have a string of them after her."

"No! I write--you see, I've always sort of wanted to write fiction. Magazine stories. I like to scribble in my spare time."

"Story writing? You can't serve two masters in this profession."

"Oh, and then I practice." It was here she had shown him the letter addressed, "To Whom It May Concern." "I haven't a piano, but you would be surprised how helpful it is just to memorize the role from the score."

"What role?"

"I know four. Michaela is my last. I haven't memorized all of her aria yet, but half the time I'm singing her with my mind, if you know what I mean. I once had twelve lessons on Marguerite. With study, Mr. Visigoth, and perhaps some more lessons with one of the big teachers here, do you think I have the slightest chance for opera or--concert? You can be frank with me. Do you?"

He patted her.

"Too much ambition will make that satiny head of yours ache."

"Let it ache."

"What you need more than lessons is some one to wake you up. That will do more for you than all the training money can buy. You need a rousing-good love affair. Love, that's the secret!"

She walked past him now, swinging open the stage door.

"You can be so nice, Mr. Visigoth, and so--horrid."

He followed, laughing.

"I'll walk a ways. Which way you going?"

"Home."

They strolled into the syrupy warmth of a late Indian-summer afternoon. At each crossing he took her arm, closing gently into the flesh.

"Yes, my little lady, that's what you need."

"What?"

"To be waked up."

"Oh, there you go again! Is there no limit to sex self-consciousness? I want to be a person in my work. An individual. Not first and foremost a woman!"

"Why, my dear girl, you talk like a child! Sex is the very soul of art. The greatest songs have been sung and the greatest pictures painted because men and women have loved. Don't tell me a great big handsome creature like you doesn't realize that!"

"Well, just the same," with feminine subjectiveness, "I mean to make my way as an individual first and a woman second. I give nothing to you men and I ask nothing except a fighting chance. I don't believe in all this pay-the-price business. I don't recognize you as the arbiters of my destiny. I'll pay my price with my ability, and if I can't pay up that way then I deserve to fail. Women can fight back at the world with something besides their sex. I intend to prove it."

He closed tighter over her arm.

"I like you when you tilt at windmills, Miss Don Quixote, and I like the way your eyes turn black."

"There you are at it again."

"Certainly; it's the law of life."

"You mean it's the law of men! Why should you set the price of our success? We women are going to batter down the monopoly."

"You're a regular little holy terror for woman's rights. Come in here for a drink and tell me about it."

They were approaching the rapids of Broadway, the quickened torrent of the pleasure zone that leaps high in folly even under sunlight. Sidewalk humanity quickened and had a shove to it. Street cars and cabs plunged in seemingly impassable directions. Frivolity was showing her naked shoulder on lithograph roof garden and matinee stage. The Times Building stood like a colossus, breakwater to the tide. Rector's invited.

"Come in for a drink," he repeated.

She threw him a northwest glance with what for her amounted to quite an adventure in coquetry.

"Aha!" in the key of burlesque. "Either I sully these fair lips with alcohol or tomorrow I awake jobless."

He was visibly annoyed, dropping her arm and hurrying past the mirrored entrance.

"You flatter yourself."

She bit into her lips, again with a sense of her ridiculousness, confessing, in her stress and against the old inhibition, to a state of being unwell.

"It isn't that, and you know it! I'm done up these last few days. Feeling seedy. It must be this Indian-summerish heat."

"Poor pussy!" he said, again good-humored.

It was true that a recurring sense of dizziness would sweep like a sudden wave over her, in street cars, even in bed before she rose mornings, and that very afternoon as she sang into the murky darkness a terrifying sense of it had threatened her.

In the little restaurant in Union Square which she frequented, her healthy young appetite would prompt her to order foods that when they arrived she would suddenly reject. She tried to guard against these nervous recurrences by resolutely permitting no thought of her yesterdays to crop into her to-days. Except, daily, she visited the Public Library, reading over St. Louis newspapers of last week's vintage, and never failing to glance at the death notices. For one week an advertisement under PERSONAL appeared, which every time she encountered it was sure to blur over her vision with quick tears:

Lilly, come home. All is forgiven.

She attributed some of her nervousness to the condition of mind this little paragraph invariably induced. To bear out this conviction she even omitted the visits to the Library for three or four days, but still the flashes of discomfort persisted.

They had stopped at the stoop of her lean-looking rooming house.

"So this is where you live," he said, half a smile out and his lids well down.

"Yes," she said, unconsciously defiant, "and for my purpose it's fine."

"No doubt."

"Clean, quiet, and reasonable."

"I see," he said through the same smile that was somehow hateful to her, and after a moment of apparent indecision raised his hat and walked off.

The following evening, without waiting for the second refrain of chorus or the lights to flash up, and creating some confusion down in the orchestra, Lilly left the stage rather hurriedly, her hand groping ahead of her as if to ward off muzziness, and her very first step into the wings crumpled up quietly in a faint.

She awoke in her little damp dungeon of a dressing room, a trick bicycle rider in sateen knickerbockers fanning her with a spangled jockey cap and immediately rushing off for her act, Robert Visigoth standing and looking down at her.

Embarrassment flooded her. She insisted upon standing immediately, smoothing herself down and brushing at the wet spots where the water had trickled away from her lips.

"Why," she said, through a gasp of apology, "of all things! Why, I have never done such a thing in my life! It was the heat. Oh, how silly of me! How unutterably silly!"

He pressed her down into a chair.

"You had better sit quiet there, my young miss, and get yourself together. One eighth of an inch nearer that bicycle trapeze in the wings and that smooth head of yours might not be so smooth right now."

"I'm so ashamed."

"I'll call a cab and take you home."

"I'd rather you didn't trouble."

"But I'd rather I did."

She smiled through an impulse to dig her nails into her palms and weep her sense of ignominy.

While he procured the cab she hurriedly changed from the pink into the coffee-colored linen, and, frightened at her pallor with the rouge removed, tried to pinch her cheeks back to pinkness.

In the hansom and behind the wooden apron his hand crept over to hers, soothing it.

"Poor little sick girl!" he said.

She tried to withdraw, but the black spots were swimming before her, and to save herself from their engulfing her, as the shields and bracelets must have buried Tarpeia, sat suddenly erect, blinking and shaking her head.

"Oh, I say now!"

"Why, I--I'm all right--"

His one arm was at her waist and with the other he was poking open the little trap door.

"Stop at the corner."

"No--please."

"Yes, please."

She closed her eyes, and almost immediately they drew up at a corner drug store adjoining a long row of brownstone fronts deep in brown studies. He helped her down, reading up at one of them. Dr. Barney Lee. "He leaves his name at the box office once in a while. Suppose you stop in here instead of the drug store. Don't like the idea of soda-fountain cures. You've a little sunstroke, I think."

"No, no, Mr. Visigoth. Why, I've hardly ever had a doctor in my life! The--drug store will--"

"One, two, three--march!"

"Please!"

"March! Got money? Good! I'll have a smoke in the cab. If he's not in, then I'll drive you around to our house doctor."

He was in. But for ten minutes she sat in a leather-and-oak waiting room, beneath a fly-specked Rembrandt's "Night-Watch," a clock ticking spang into the gaslighted silence and the very chairs seeming to meditate as they stood.

Then a pair of black-walnut doors slid back, and on a puff of iodoform Lilly passed between them and they clicked shut again.

When she emerged Robert Visigoth's cigar was smoked two thirds its length and he was slumped down, with one knee hooked comfortably about the other.

He sprang out to help her in.

"Well?"

Her smile was drawn across her face almost like a gash.

"Tired waiting?" she said, holding her lips lifted.

"Fix you up?"

"You were right. A little sunstroke. A good night's rest will fix me up."

"You've been playing 'possum."

"That's it," she said, with the plating of hired gayety over her tones, but her nails printing little half moons into her palms.

"Just for punishment, I'm going to drive you around the Park."

"No, no, no! I don't feel quite up to it. He said rest--a good night's rest."

He regarded her unmistakable pallor.

"Oh, all right," sulkily, "you tantalizing enigma, you! Gad! you--you'd drive a man crazy! There's something over your face. A veil. I'd like to tear it off--"

"You--you're talking like a Third Avenue melodrama."

"I suppose I am," he said, subsiding and regarding the hooked top of his cane the remaining ten minutes of the drive. "I suppose I am."

He dismissed the cab at her curb. To escape his arm she even ran up the steps, and to prove how complete recovery called down over one shoulder:

"You've been kind and I'm grateful. Good night."

"Prove it," he said, up and after her, his arm at her waist.

"What?" she said, his meaning flashing as she spoke. She was crowding away from his nearness against one of the storm doors which folded back against the entrance, sooty light filtering over them through a frosted door panel.

His face twisted out of repose, flooded darker and darker with red.

"You devil," he said, "you knew you'd get me."

"You go!" she cried, her lips pulled with the degradation of the moment.

He grasped her so that the breath jumped out of her.

"Oh," she cried, wrenching herself free, "don't you dare put your foot in this house--"

"Then the Gramatan, Lilly. It's quiet and first class there--we can have a talk. I'll call a cab--the Gramatan. Or my place--I live alone."

"If you do I--I'll bite! I'll bite, you hear?"

"Do it," he said, his face the color that was Iago's, grasping her then in the shadow of the storm door, and kissing her so on the open lips that to evade him she had to wriggle down to her knees and out of his clasp.

The shamefulness of the scene not to be endured, she held her hand with the key in it behind her back; then suddenly let it fly up for her hatpin.

"If you come near me--"

He stood back from her upflung arm, his refinement of feature incongruous under the rush of ox-blood red, his teeth showing whiter as he darkened.

"What the devil do you want, then? You devil! Who are you? There's only one woman in a thousand I'd follow to a joint like this. I'm afraid of them. Now I've had enough of this baby talk from you. It doesn't match this house! What's your game? Let me up."

"House!"

"What do you expect, with an address like this? There's two kinds of women.

You can't be the kind you pretend to be and live here. What is the comedy? I like you, Lilly. Let me up. Come, put that little arm down. God damn it! what do you want?"

With a wrench that threw him backward, a frenzied instant of struggle for the lock, and she was in, slamming the door behind her, and up the two flights with such a sense of pursuit that her breath turned to moans in her throat.

Once within her room, locking her door on its very slam, and her hat sliding down on her unpinned hair, she dropped down on her bed edge so that the springs coughed, seeming to bleed her tears, so roundly and full of agony they came.

The white light from the electric sign opposite created a pallor in the room that enveloped her like a veil. She rocked herself as she sat. She pressed her palms into her eyes until the terrible kind of darkness they induced was sprinkled with red. She clapped her hands to her mouth to keep down the rise of shrieks. She burrowed her head down into her pillow, beating into the surrounding area of bed, chewing at the sheet end, twisting it until it became rigid. She slid to the floor as if for relief of its hardness; sat looking into the white kind of darkness with the rims of her eyes stretched until her gaze seemed to sleep. She fell to rocking herself again and twisting the sheet in an outrageous abandonment of despair that was abashing because it was so naked. Her hands wound each other in a dry wash. She sobbed in long coughs drawn through a resisting throat. Pounded the matting. Dragged her palms down over her face, pulling the hair with it.

Half the night through she paced the narrow aisle of the room, repeating and repeating until the darkness seemed filled with the rushing of a million frantic little wings:

"O God! O God! Help me, God! Make it a lie! Tell me that the doctor lied! God, I need you! Where are you? Save me! Where are you? Help me, God! Help me!"

Thus did Lilly Penny greet the coming of her child.

CHAPTER XVIII

There was no egress for Lilly's state of panic. It hurled itself into this and that *cul-de-sac*, only to dash into a black, a colossal wall of ignorance builded on the sands of false and revolting modesty, and which, as it tottered, threatened to crush her.

Her mind ran hither and thither, panic and anger plunging into storm waves of sobs. Around and around spun her terror in its trap. Each pore of her body might have been a mouth screaming. Distaste for her physical awareness mounted upon her old peculiar aversion. The maternal did not even lift its head. She could have beaten her own head, and did, for the relief of pain. One alternative after another flickered into her consciousness, only to die out again into blackness. Home! But by the merest flash of the incongruous, not to say absurd, vision of Albert Penny's wilted collar on the chiffonier, or his shirt sleeves that were held back with pink rubber garters, bending over the recalcitrant bed caster, knew how impossible that!

Forceps sensitive enough to lay hold of an antenna could not capture the vagariousness of all of this, but none the less it was just that ridiculous and irrelevant flash across her vision that eliminated the almost unbearable tugging of nostalgia at her heart strings.

There were long hours of dizzying and fascinated contemplation down into the cypress-sided vale of self-destruction; that ravine which gets its glance from most and even the best of us. It seemed to her that she could not even think for the rush of its dark waters pressing against her reason; but love of life was strongest of all in Lilly. It was the sweep of her own vitality which she felt pressing.

She tried to desire what had befallen her, to think in terms of beauty; to feel the miracle of her state and the age-old throbs that make maternity sublime. The sense of her aversion debased while it immersed her. She reasoned how valiantly whole eternities of women had gone down to meet motherhood and how proudly those eternities of women had worn the moment. Her mother. Mrs. Kemble. The concept awed her, but then memory came scourging out of that long night of her childhood:

MRS. KEMBLE: "Kill me, God! Put me out of it! Please! I can't suffer any more! Kill me, God!"

She buried her head into her pillow; tried to think in terms of God; to intimidate her rebellion. Finally she did cool to a sort of leaden despair through which slow determination began to percolate.

At nine o'clock the following morning, a Sunday that wrapped the city windily in the first cold gray of autumn, without having undressed the night through, she ventured as far as Times Square for a newspaper, the dark halls of the house and the rows of closed doors suddenly sinister. The wind caught at her flimsy skirts, blowing them forward, and she was forced to clutch the wide brim of her hat. Summer was gone.

But more than that, it seemed to Lilly that a black gauze lay across her eyes, the very complexion of the streets had darkened, the hurried wind-blown clouds stamping the whole aspect of things with turbulence. She could not keep the run out of her steps, and her palms were full of the half moons impressed there by her finger nails. The city, as joyous as Chloe, had suddenly turned a frightening grimace upon her.

She bought a Sunday paper, letting the prankish gale around Times Square scurry the bulk of it through the streets while she stood in the shelter of the news stand, unfolding the Furnished Room section. Wind puffed the sheets up into her face, and finally she crossed to a white-tiled lunch room, ordering coffee and rolls more for the temporary shelter than for appetite. Scanning column after column, occasionally she poked a toothpick through the page, and once tore out a little segment, dropping it into her hand bag. It read:

Neatly Furnished Room near Columbia University and Kroeg School of Music. Three dollars and a half a week and breakfasts if desired. Ideal for refined young lady. Inquire at 9000 Amsterdam Avenue.

She paid her check, inquired direction of the cashier, and, hurrying out, boarded a north-bound Amsterdam Avenue car, riding for half an hour through streets lined in petty shops and presenting the peculiar swept look of Sunday.

She had cooled to apathy, a drowsiness descending that made her reluctant to leave the car; could have ridden on and on in this eased and half-narcotized state, but people had a habit of remembering her. A truckman had followed her only the day before through half a block of snarled traffic to see that she turned properly to the right. New York, mad as a March hare, was eager to direct her. The conductor now walked up the aisle of car to tap her on the shoulder.

"Your corner, miss."

Nine thousand Amsterdam Avenue was a drug store sidled in between a bake-shop that six days a week poured forth sweet hot breath, and an undertaking establishment with a white-satin infant's coffin *de luxe* tilted in the window. The sight of it caught Lilly like a pain. That peculiar power of an obsessed mind to see in everything its own state reflected had set in. Queer that this infant's coffin should tilt at her. A bouncing youngster leaned out of its perambulator to dance its arms.

She hurried into the drug store. Isaac Neugass, Chemist.

It was the older-style pharmacy, with a gilt mortar and pestle for a sign; and as she entered, a bell attached by a pulley rang somewhere in a thin, tattling voice. The soda fountain, fountain pen, the picture postcard, the umbrella, and the face-powder demonstrator had not yet invaded here. Isaac Neugass, Chemist--was just that. His walls were lined in labeled jars of panacea. The pungency of valerianate of ammonia smote the entrant. He pummeled his own pills, percolated his own paregoric, prescribed for neighborhood miseries from an invariable bottle that was slow, sluggish, and malodorous in the pouring, anointed the neighborhood bruises, and extracted, always gratis, neighborhood cinders from neighborhood eyes.

A Madison Avenue physician, erstwhile of Amsterdam Avenue, and more recently of two honorary degrees, his own private hospital, two outer waiting rooms, three assistants, and four-figure operations, still diverted quite a runnel of his clientele to the impeccable pharmaceutics of the little Amsterdam Avenue shop, so that the motor car and the carriage not infrequently sidled up to its curb.

At Lilly's entrance, Isaac Neugass came shuffling around the ground-glass prescription partition, his hands at their perpetual dry washing of each other. There was something of a dressed-up wishbone about him, in the way his clothing scarcely suggested the thin body within them. They had scarcely a point of contact, even with his angles. He was a mere inner tubing to what he wore. A skull cap hid his baldness, a fringe of gray below it suggesting what was not beneath it. His little eyes were like steel, humorously glinting gimlets in the process of boring, the old face wrinkling up around them as pliantly as a dough eraser. In fact, when he laughed his little chin with the tip of beard did curl up like one of those rubber-toy faces where chin kicks brow.

"Well," he said, with a great dip of nose down into his smile, "whad can I do for you?" He reminded Lilly of a great auk, something alcidine in the thin cheeks with the mouth cutting so widely toward the ears.

She had not realized it, but suddenly the terrible, the impersonal detachment of the past weeks smote her. There had been voiceless days and days when the sound of herself asking direction or ordering from a bill of fare had an element of surprise in it, and the toneless voice of public service was the only one directed to her: "Step lively." "Two blocks east." "Don't mention it." "No more rice pudding left, ma'am."

When Isaac Neugass said, "Well, whad can I do for you?" something within her thawed so that she could have cried.

"I'm looking for this furnished room," she said, and held out the slip toward him.

"You wand my wife," he said, waving her the direction. "Go right outside to the next stoop and ring the bell over Neugass."

"Oh, thank you!" she said, suiting her action to his word.

"It's a nize room. I could wish it to an early bird to catch it."

"That's what I want, a nice, quiet room."

"Then you got it," he cried. "It's a room for a needle," his thumb and forefinger indicating an infinitesibly fine point.

"A needle?"

"So it could hear itself fall."

In his own way Mr. Neugass was a jokester, insisting upon the laugh, sitting back upon his figurative haunches, waiting.

"Then it is just what I want," said Lilly, giving him his smile, "only I hope it isn't too--"

He took to waggling his head, his little kindly eyes illuminated with a sunburst of wrinkles and his voice a festooned chant of rising and falling inflections.

"Sa-y, if you can't pay three-fifty, she'll make it three. You doan' need to tell her I told you, but for such a young lady like you, sa-y, the brice in the newspaper doan' always got to be the brice in the hand, ain't it?"

She laughed, the irises that had crowded out the gray in her eyes suddenly smaller and back to normal.

In the little entrance adjoining, with its line-up of door bells, she pressed the button as directed. A clicking answered her ring, and she had to learn from a child who entered with a dangling pail of milk, that she was to speak upward through a tube above the bell.

"About the room?" Yes, she was to come up.

She climbed two flights of dark, clean-smelling stairs, and Mrs. Neugass herself opened the door.

Mary, Rispah, Cornelia, Monica, Martha Washington, Mrs. Whistler, Margaret Ogilvy, and Mrs. Neugass, blessed be their tribe, must all have had about the same look about the eyes. Masha Neugass was sixty, and looked it. A blue-gingham apron held her in at the waist so that she bulged softly and fatly above and below it.

Thirty minutes and one hundred years removed from Millionaires' Row, the apartment was just another of those paradoxes which the city can shake from its spangled sleeve. Built like a coach, each room opening off a strip of hallway, it was a scoured chromo of Victoria's age of horrors. The brilliantly flower-splashed wall paper and carpeting. A front room that smelled and pricked of horsehair. The little patch of dining room brightened by a red tablecloth, two canaries, and a window-sill array of turnips sprouting in bottles. The rush of bead portieres as you walked through them. Hassocks. A freshly washed-and-ironed ribbon bow on a chair back. Pillow shams. Nottingham-lace curtains with sham drapes woven into them. A pair of bisque pugs.

The room to let was the size of a freight elevator and crammed with a fine old walnut bed when there was scarcely room for a cot. Also an overflow of curlicue divan, and a washstand. It was clean to coolness, as if the very air were washed, but, entering it, Mrs. Neugass flecked an imaginary dust particle from the divan with her apron, then wrapping it muff fashion about her hands.

"It ain't big, but it's gumfortable."

"Indeed it is!" said Lilly, sniffing in appreciatively.

"We doan' got to rent this room, miss. It's our first time. My husband, if he had his way, wouldn't. But I say it's a shame for the waste, since our youngest daughter ain't in it no more...."

"It's lovely."

"You see out there between those two chimneys? That's Columbia University. You're from the college? Yes? We brefer it should be a student."

"I--I'm a high-school graduate, but not exactly a college student. I mean--I'm a music student. Voice."

"You doan' tell me! Now ain't that a coinstidance! For why you think I should have this room empty if not my own baby daughter is in Europe with her voice! For three years already, with her gone, miss, and my husband's daughter down to her bookkeeping all day, as I tell him, it's like my heart will burst from the silence."

"There is something I had better explain--"

"I want a young girl in the house again, I tell him."

Standing there, the words pressing for utterance against her very teeth, Lilly swallowed them back again.

"I see," she said, smiling her misery. "Then I'm afraid--I--"

"We're used to a young girl. You read maybe of our daughter only in last Sunday's papers. Millie du Gass, with the Milan Opera?"

Lilly had. "Millie du Gass--your daughter!"

"We got more only last night from her in 'Traviata.' They pulled her carriage after the opera. Felix Auchinloss went special from Vienna to conduct her. That's her picture there and there and there. Say, ain't that a coinstidance you should be a voice!"

Lilly stood regarding one of the framed photographs. A lifted young profile, ever so slightly of the father's aquilinity, a vocal-looking swell to the bosom, and a chin that locked up prettily to the protuberant upper lip.

Regarding her, such a nausea of bitterness flowed over Lilly that her lips were too wry to speak and she could have sobbed out her plight to the simple soul there, with her hands in the muff of her apron, and her gaze soft to tears upon the photograph.

"That ain't so good of her, miss, as some her papa keeps down in the store. In Milan they call her the American Beauty. Auchinloss won't conduct 'Faust' without our Millie's Marguerite. How she used to practice it, miss, righd on that piano you seen in the front room. It's worth all the sacrifices we made for such a success like hers. I doan' know who you study with, but if you come to us here, I wand once you should let her old teacher, Ballman, hear you. He's the man that can find your voice if you got it."

"Oh, I do want to come here, Mrs. Neugass. I--If only--. Will you--will you let me talk to you as I would to my own mother? I--somehow--I--I think you will understand--"

Then Mrs. Neugass came closer, a little whisper of garlic in her breath and her eyes screwed to conniving.

"Sa-y, miss, you doan' need to worry. Doan' tell it to my husband that the reduction came from me, but if three dollars is all you can pay, since it's for some one who will use the piano and liven up things a little, it's worth the difference to me in pleasure."

"Oh, Mrs. Neugass, if you knew what a place like this would mean to me--now! If only you--"

"All righd, then, for a few cents we doan' dicker. Say we make it three dollars, and on rainy mornings coffee and rolls so you doan' get your feet wet."

"But I--"

"We're blain beoble, miss, but we got a respegtable standing in the neighborhood for fifteen years. My husband's daughter by his first marriage is sixteen years bookkeeper down by Aaron Schmoll Paper Box Company in Green Street. We doan' got to rent, miss, unless it should be to the righd person. A nice young lady like you--"

"But what if I were to tell you, Mrs. Neugass, that I'm a mar--"

"You got references? It ain't I don't trust, but business is business, ain't it?"

"I'm afraid I haven't. You see, I'm a stranger. Here from--the West to study. I don't quite like it where I am. In fact, I want to get out to-day."

"Say, doan' I know how things can happen? For two months after she arrived in Munich, where she went first, my Millie used to write home, 'Mamma, I can't get myself settled righd.' In one place bugs and in another they complained of her practicing. I got sympathy for a girl trying to get settled. You can come righd away up into a room of mine, miss. There's no extra cleaning to be done."

"Oh, Mrs. Neugass, if I may! I've only my valise and suitcase."

A complete shrugging of Mrs. Neugass took place, her voice, brow, and manner lifting.

"Valise and suitcase. Is that a baggage?"

"I'm sending West for my trunks later, Mrs. Neugass."

"You'm *Goyem*, not?"

"Beg pardon?"

"You're Gentiles, ain't it? Well, with *Goyem* such things ain't so important. I'll show you sometimes the way my Millie left home, complete even to hand-crocheted washrags. Three of us had to sit on her trunk. You'm *Goyem*, not?"

"I was reared in the Unitarian Church, if that's what you mean, until--well, I guess until I sort of figured out my own religion for myself."

"We're Jews, you know, miss, in case you should have any *richas*."

"*Richas?*"

"Prejudices against us, like some. My husband has one of the finest cantor voices of any temple in the city."

"No, no, Mrs. Neugass. I just love Jewish people. Some of the nicest folks we knew in St. Lo--I ever knew--have been Jews," cried Lilly, with the colossal, the unconscious patronage of race consciousness.

It left no welt, however, across the sensibilities of Mrs. Neugass. The centuries had seen to that. She was craven and she was superb in her heritage.

"I always say, thank God for whad I am, but it doan' matter to me whad anybody else is, just so she is that with the best she has in her."

"Exactly. There--there is something I ought to say to you, Mrs. Neugass. You've made it so difficult, with your kindness, but I--well, I--There are certain conditions I want you to know about. I--Not a--I could only take the room for a few months, Mrs. Neugass, because I--"

"Say, doan' I know how it is with students?"

"No, no--"

"They go home when it comes summer. You doan' got to worry. It ain't like we need it to pay rent with. You got my word it's all righd, Miss--The name, blease--Miss what?"

"Par--Parlow. Lilly Parlow."

"All righd, Miss Parlow; that makes everything fine."

She opened her purse, unfolding a bill.

"I'll pay now," she said, calm with sudden decision.

"Sa-y, I would have trusted you. But you're like me, I always say money speaks louder than words."

"I'll be right back, Mrs. Neugass."

"That's good. I'll have out fresh towels. That's one thing I doan' expect from nobody is to stint on towels."

And so it came about that at the moment Robert Visigoth was confronted with a sudden gap in his program, Lilly Penny, with almost the week's lodging still to her credit, was tiptoeing through the moldy halls of the house in Forty-fourth Street, her luggage hitting against wall and banisters and a palpitating fear fuddling her haste.

At the second flight down she experienced her first and by no means fragrant encounter in these hallways. A door flew open with a rush and, her thin body wrapped in something ornate and flowing that was like a quick sheaf of flame around her, a woman dragged suddenly out to the head of the stairs, by the actual scruff of the neck, the ridiculous figure of a male, his collar--the necktie streaming from it--in his hand.

She spat then a bombardment of screaming profanity that sickened Lilly as she stood unseen and flattened against the wall. A further shove sent him sprawling down the remaining stairs, and from the open doorway a flung waistcoat and coat draped him ludicrously as they struck.

"Cheap skate! Piker! Skinflint!"

Then a slamming, reverberating door, and, while she stood trembling and waiting, the creature on the stairs, a hulk of Swede with short, square teeth and a corner of lip that snarled back to bare them, scrambled into his coat, stumbling out the front door, collar still in his clutch.

Then Lilly wound her weak-kneed way down the flight after him, softly, to save the creak, her luggage held out before her.

The air outside seemed cleansing as water to her. She could not breathe deeply enough of it. For a long and indeterminate period she stood at the corner, Amsterdam Avenue car after car rumbling past, her luggage on the sidewalk and inclosing her in a little island.

Indecision buffeted her. Even Mrs. Neugass and her apartment had suddenly become abhorrent; Broadway as barren as any granite gully and somehow terrifying. She strolled a block toward the station, yet it is doubtful whether in the back of her head Lilly did not know the impulse of home to be a mock one.

The tremendous trifles began their running fire.

Her mother pulling her corsets in so that they bottled her up more and more into the shape of an hourglass. That caster for the brass bed. Those interminable discussions over that caster for the brass bed!

She boarded an Amsterdam Avenue car.

CHAPTER XIX

The following months of her life always seemed to Lilly to have hung suspended without any forward march to them, and entirely surrounded with a colorless fluid which distorted reality, as a hand seen through a fish bowl of water is distorted. There descended upon her whole rows of days that were swollen with inertia. Her little window looked out upon an ocean of roofs, and across her distant horizon was a strident picture in electricity of an old woman in a Dutch cap beating a tub of proclaimed soap flakes into an incandescent froth.

She would sit with her cheek crumpled against her hand, looking out over this, her mind hardly stirring. There still lay three one-hundred-dollar bills, crisply warm, against her bosom, and during the long arid spell that followed her first stroke of good fortune they were to her like a sedative touch, pressing down a more and more frequently recurring rise of fear.

Two or three mornings a week she ventured in among the agencies, occasionally an address handed out to her which she followed up, always vainly.

There was something gone from Lilly, these months, as if a line of resiliency within her had snapped like a rubber band. It showed most in her slowed step and her head not quite so flung up.

One Saturday night she did earn twenty dollars, singing, a red-white-and-blue paper cap on her head, the "Star-spangled Banner" and the "Marsellaise" on the up-and-down-stream excursion of the Annual Convention of Commercial Photographers.

During their clambake and dance at Grody's Grove, just beyond Coney Island, she remained on the boat, lying back in a deck chair, facing a night brilliantly pointed with stars. The machinery of her mind might have ceased with the chugging of the boat. She lay the five hours of her wait, floating in a state of the complete disembodiment of which she was peculiarly capable.

At one o'clock the convention, highly inflamed, came trooping back on board, the boat nosing downstream, brilliant and terrible with orgy.

Twice she was grasped by revelers who were little more than bashing bulls, and before she could fight them off, her face and neck, through the sheerness of her blouse, were covered with hot, wet, and beery kisses. The third time she fought off with her hatpin, inflicting a deep red scratch across a too loose jowl. She took refuge, finally, finding out by desperate instinct the only other woman on board. A cook down in the reeking kitchen of the one-screw steamer, who had grown old so horribly that her only remaining tooth was a tusk that hung deeply beneath her lower lip. But she found out a bench rug for Lilly, so that the trip home she lay there in the stench of strong foods and hot machinery, stupefied with misery.

And yet, withal, a certain exultation had hold of her these strangely unreal weeks, her terror of the life about to be subdued somewhere underneath her consciousness, and each to-morrow reassuringly remote.

The long unfettered days. Her own latchkey to come and go at will. The lay of those three crisp bills against her heart. Her little economies, however, grew against a day which she hardly contemplated and for which she certainly did not plan. Very often she ate in her own room, a sandwich and a bottle of milk from a corner delicatessen. She had already learned those small private economies of the petty and penny wise. The mirror-pasted handkerchief. The gas-jet-brewed egg. The hand-fluted ruching. Once, in her absence, Mrs. Neugass had pressed out her dark-brown-cloth coat suit, wrinkled from weeks in her suitcase, and which she had left hanging before the open window.

The print of these kindly people was like an indelible rubber stamp into the premises. Mr. Neugass had already presented her with a jar of Millie face cream and a preparation for cleaning kid gloves. Sundays she was invariably importuned to dine with the family, and of occasional evenings, Alma Neugass, angular and full of the knobs of protruding neckbones, elbows, and shoulder blades, and with little sacs under her eyes as if she had wept down into them that life could be so tasteless, would knock at her door, and for an hour or two, and sometimes up to midnight, sit on the edge of Lilly's bed, the drone of their conversation surviving repeated rappings from the parental bedroom, adjoining.

There was something about Alma of an old glove just about ready to breathe out and flatten from the print of a recent hand. Fifteen years of debit and credit and days which swung with pendulum fidelity within the arc of routine had creased and dried her of sap.

The whiteness of Lilly and the swift, shining, backward rush of her hair were a source of wistful and vicarious delight to her. "Whoever named you Lilly was right," she said upon one of these midnight confabs so immemoriably dear to women, when hairpins can be removed and the dig of skirt bands unhooked. "You're so snowy, and soft, too; you feel like a kitten's ear. And that shining head of yours!"

"But all my life I've wanted to be blond. Sun people I call them."

"Millie is a blonde," said Miss Neugass, glancing toward one of the photographs that graced even Lilly's wall. "There's a girl was born in the sun!"

"You've been part of her sun, Miss Neugass. Your parents have told me how for eight years half of your earnings went toward her education."

"Life is a beehive, Miss Parlow," said Alma, her rather grandiloquent and apiarian simile highly inaccurate, "some of us are the drones, some the workers, and some the queens. Millie happened to be a queen."

"How can you say that? Happened! What if Napoleon had never left Corsica, or Lincoln the backwoods, or Jeanne d'Arc her village, just because they decided environment had placed them there."

"Quite right, but it is their being queens, drones, or workers determines their action."

"Well, whether or not I was born for it, I aspire to be a queen."

"Fine. Only be sure your arm is long enough to reach what you want."

"But how can I tell if I don't stretch and stretch?"

"You can't. Most of us never know when we've used up the last inch of reach, and keep on straining to touch what God or circumstance, or call it what you will, has placed beyond us."

"Yes, but it is not knowing makes us capable of hoping and striving."

"To me that is one of the tragedies of living. The hearts that pass by the jobs they are fitted for, to eat themselves out struggling to do what they think they're fitted for."

"You're a fatalist."

"Not at all. The way to know the reach of your arm is to sprain it. I sprained mine, and it wasn't until the ligaments began to pull that I had the courage to face the fact that I was made out of bookkeeper instead of concert-pianist stuff."

"You, Miss Neugass, a pianist!"

"Sounds queer to you, doesn't it?"

"What--interfered?"

"My own realization. One night before he moved from the neighborhood Doctor Feldman sent pa a pair of seats for De Pachman. I was seventeen then, and Millie seven. Ma stayed in the store and pa and I went. I remember as if it were yesterday. The concert was at Beethoven Hall and it snowed so that when we arrived I made pa slip off his shoes under the chair, for his socks to dry. I had been studying for eight years then and my teacher was arranging a recital. Strangest thing, but De Pachman played every single thing of Chopin's that I had on my own little repertoire, only under his touch it was real lace played into perfect design. I think pa must have lived through everything with me that night. He's got the finest musical instinct in the family, Millie included. We didn't say a word all the way home, but next day when I told him that I was going to business college on the money we were going to put into the recital, he didn't say a word, either. Just patted my hand. He knew! It wasn't so much a matter of technique, only when I played Nocturne in D flat a hammer inside the piano case hit a wire; when De Pachman touched those same keys a nerve kissed a heartbeat."

"Alma--Neugass! You poor--you splendid girl!"

Curled up there on the narrow bed, her bony profile against the wall and her knees hugged up to her after the manner of the excessively thin, a smile had come out on Miss Neugass's face as if the taste of renunciation were anything but bitter.

"I don't know what kind of a pianist I might have made, but I do know I've made a good bookkeeper and that a little talent took a chance on stepping aside for a bigger."

"You mean your sister?"

"There's a talent for you! Millie has a voice like one of those revolving barber poles, as round at the bottom as it is at the top, and it goes up and up seemingly without end. There never was any doubt about Millie."

"Oh, Miss Neugass, you frighten me! What if my arm is too short? Your sister's teacher, Ballman, to whom your mother sent me, says so little."

"Ballman is a great voice builder, but he doesn't concern himself with the future of his pupils. He's a dear old fogy with a single-track mind."

"What did he used to say of your sister?"

"Nothing much except that he used to call her his wonder-child and shut up like a clam when we tried to discuss her future with him. What you need now, if you're ever really going to get anywhere, is an audition."

"Audition?"

"One of the big opera directors to hear you. It's not easy to arrange at the Metropolitan. Ballman has no pull. It takes a man like Auchinloss or Trieste or one of the big guns."

"If only I could get started, Miss Neugass, on the right track!"

"I'll tell you what I'll do. When Auchinloss comes this winter I'll have him hear you. That may pave the way to something. He's the prince of them all. His judgment never fails. He's only stamped his approval on five or six, but he's never missed. They say he heard Paula Anchutz singing her baby to sleep one night as he happened to pass her cottage, and he rang her door bell."

"Auchinloss discovered Paula Anchutz!"

"He decided her greatness after a few bars. Some day I'll read you Millie's letter home about her audition in Vienna. After about six bars of the 'Jewel Song' he leaped up over the footlights, screamed at her, kissed her, drew up a chair, and began to plan out the entire campaign of her future, so rapidly that the poor child said everything was swinging in circles before her."

Her eyes two flaming orbits, Lilly sat staring, her lips slightly open.

"And that was the beginning."

"Yes, that was the beginning of--everything," said Miss Neugass, with a twist on her lips.

"Oh, I--Even to hear it thrills me so that I--Thrills me so! But what, Miss Neugass--what if he hadn't--"

"That is where you must make up your mind to take your medicine. There's an article about him in this month's **Musical Gazette**. If he thinks you've the stuff great singers are made of, it's a repetition of his scene with Millie every time. But this article goes on to say, if he rubs his hands together and says, 'Very nice,' and walks off, that means he thinks you will probably make a better bookkeeper or baby dandler than you will a prima donna. Millie used to write that around the opera house in Vienna, when Auchinloss started rubbing his hands together after an audition, everybody used to have the smelling salts ready."

"Miss Neugass--you've heard me practice. Tell me the truth! Do you think my ambition is bigger than my voice? Tell me as you would your sister."

The veil of a pause hung between them, Miss Neugass unfolding her legs and letting them hang over the side of the bed, as if she would flee the moment.

"Why, I'm no critic, Miss Parlow. All I inherit is some of my father's natural musical instinct."

"You're evading me, like Ballman does! Tell me! You may save me as you saved yourself. Am I chasing a phantom?"

"I swear to you I don't know. I like your voice. I think it has a beautiful rich quality. I agree with Ballman, it has fine timbre."

"Timbre--I'm tired hearing that--"

"That counts in voice almost as much as range."

"No, no, don't evade. You think it lacks range?"

"I don't know. It lacks something--as if--well, if you'll pardon my saying it, as if it didn't reach as far as your temperament could fling it."

"That's it exactly! I feel that about myself in everything--almost as if--as if it would take another generation of me to complete me--if--if you get what I mean."

"There is something in that."

"I know what you think in your heart. I'm a vaudeville product with a grand-opera aspiration."

"I'm not capable of judging."

"You judged your sister."

"Ah, but Millie's voice there was no mistaking. Her talent needed hardly to be developed. It opened naturally, like a rose. Nine voices out of ten have to be drilled for like precious ore. Just you study on. I'll have Auchinloss hear you when he comes over."

"You're sure, Miss Neugass, they're coming?"

"That's what the papers keep saying. She's to sing three operas in January, with Auchinloss conducting. We're expecting daily to hear from my sister, verifying it."

"You don't know--exactly?"

"No."

"If only--You don't think it will be this side of January? You see, after January my--my plans may be uncertain."

"I understand. He's to conduct his own symphony in December, to be played the first time in this country, somewhere around Christmas in Boston, I think."

"Will you be wanting this room then?"

Miss Neugass swung her face with its considerable dip of nose toward Lilly.

"You don't think this place will hold Millie any more? You don't think, for instance, the great Du Gass could receive the reporters--here!"

"But, after all, it's her home."

A levelness of expression came down over the face of Miss Neugass, as if a shade had been lowered across it, her voice, too, leveled of any inflection.

"Of course," she said, "you know about my sister and--Auchinloss."

"You mean--"

"Oh, I realize everybody knows--that is, everybody except my parents."

"I didn't--"

"That's because you don't belong yet! Wait until you've worked your way in a bit. I've known it long enough. Two years."

"Then she--you--"

"She was a baby when she left, Miss Parlow. Even if there had been the money to send me along with her, we wouldn't have felt the need of it. I could have staked my life on that child. Not that I'm blaming her, only I--God! I could have staked my life."

"He's--"

"Already married. She wrote me the whole story two years ago. It's an old one. So old it's got barnacles. I sometimes wonder it came to me with the terrible shock it did. She was so young--too young to get ahead so quickly even with her gifts. He has a son almost her age. He's forty and she's twenty. The wife in an insane asylum somewhere outside of Paris. Our Millie! I don't think I even realize it yet. Beauty and the Beast they call them in Milan."

"Horrible!"

"That baby. The whole world before her. It was all with her or nothing, she wrote, and she chose all. She sang six leading roles that first year. It made her. I--I don't blame her, somehow--that baby. It's him I hate. Sometimes I wonder how I'm going to hold back, when I lay hands on him, from--killing. But I won't. I'll grin and bear it just as if her beautiful little white self were no more to me than an alabaster vase after it's cracked."

"And your parents?"

"That's all she writes of, now that she thinks she is coming, to keep it from them! I wake up nights in a cold sweat over it. Wringing wet with the fear of my job."

"Your mother and sweet little old father!"

"That's it; they're like two babes in the woods morally. They don't know any gradation except black and white. Virtue and sin. A woman is good or a woman is rotten bad. She falls or she doesn't."

"Oh, I know the relentlessness of that single-track code of right and wrong."

"My stepmother, good soul that she is, would take the last stitch off her back for what she calls honest need, but I've seen her slam the door in the face of one of our neighbor girls in trouble who's come to my father begging for help--medicine. That's what I'm up against, Miss Parlow, keeping from those two old people what their daughter--is."

"Oh, my dear, my dear!"

"I don't know why I'm airing my troubles here. God knows you are bottled up enough about yours, if you have any, but I thought surely you knew. Everyone does. Is it any wonder that my sister's home-coming is a nightmare to me? She doesn't want to come; I can read between the lines of her letter she's fighting it. But you see, Auchinloss is a great man. He's been invited to conduct his own symphony at its American *premiere* and naturally has taken this opportunity to bring about her American debut. You can imagine my parents' pride."

"I can see it. Why, your father can't keep his face straight--he's always sort of smiling, slyly, to himself."

"Their daughter, Millie du Gass, coming home with an opera triumph back of her in every European city, the great Auchinloss himself coming to conduct for her American debut. That is the kind of homecoming they're looking forward to and the kind I must make possible for them. My mother, who screams out every girl in trouble who dares to come into the drug store for help!"

When Lilly bade Alma Neugass good night, they kissed, a dark bony hand lingering on each of Lilly's shoulders.

"You've your decision before you yet, Miss Parlow, and you're young and pretty, too. Much as I love that little sister of mine, and can't find it in my heart to blame her, I know that somewhere there are women big enough not to have to pay the price. You--there's something about you--something so, if you'll permit me to say it, so boyish--so clean--so wholesome. You should be big enough not to have to pay the price."

"If only I felt that your sister--cared. That is so horrible--the beauty-and-the-beast part. To place personal ambition above her body--the body that holds her soul! Ugh!"

"She sent his picture. He's hairy like an ape. My. little white sister--he's--hairy, I tell you, like an ape."

"I think I would have to want something--love something--enough to tear out my very heart for it before I could pay her price. Nothing on earth, Miss Neugass, can be so hideous--as that! I--I imagine it's flying in the face of the first law of nature--nothing so hideous as giving of self to--in--in--payment--"

Tears were racking the worn form of Miss Neugass, Lilly wrapping her in arms that soothed.

"You musn't," she said; "you've your big job ahead of you."

Through the left wall came a sharp trilogy of raps.

"All right, ma. Coming!" cried Miss Neugass, starting up instantly, her voice lifted and absolutely without tremor.

That night Lilly dreamed the whole of her marriage. Her father with his face distorted by lather before his shaving mirror. The Leffingwell Rock Church. Little Evelyn Kemble placing the white-satin cushion. Herself and Albert finally locking the door of their new little home that wedding night.

It was then she awoke with a scream.

CHAPTER XX

About a week later an advertisement in a morning paper caught Lilly's eye.

WANTED:--Refined young woman of good appearance and soprano voice, to sing in music store. Must be able to accompany self. Apply between twelve and six. Broadway Melody Shop, 1432 Broadway.

A recurring and dragging sense of lassitude was over her these mornings, so that it was all she could do to drag herself through two hours of practice in the parlor, scrupulously given over by Mrs. Neugass, who moved constantly and audibly about the kitchen.

Her lessons, one every Tuesday morning, with Leopold Ballman, were tiresome unmusical periods of diaphragm exercises and an entire tearing down and reconstruction process of the previous methods taught her. It was tedious, standing before the long gold-and-black pier glass in the front parlor, watching the tendinous rise and fall of her lower thorax when her forbidden arias were on top of the piano and a cabinet of Millie du Gass's sheet music bulged there at her disposal.

The old disturbing ache would climb up to the back of her neck, and her half-baked power of concentration falter at the arid monotony of, breathe-in; breathe-out.

There were about five months between Lilly and the hour of her supreme travail. They might have been five years, while she paused suspended, as it were, in this state of abeyance that hung between the hot August day of her leave-taking of home and that chimeric hour ahead which depended like a stalactite, stabbing space.

Her most tangible concern was a money one. The breaking of another one-hundred-dollar bill was imminent and it frightened her. She reduced her vocal lessons, at three dollars the hour, to one every other week, finally discontinuing entirely, and took to haunting the agencies daily, leaving her address where no initial charges were required and scanning incessantly the want advertisements under Amusements.

She applied one Monday morning at the Broadway Melody Shop, a mere aisle wedged between a theater and a *rotisserie*, a megaphone inserted through a hole cut in the plate-glass frontage that was violently plastered over with furiously colored copies of what purported to be the latest song hits: "If I Could Be Molasses to Your Griddle Cakes." "Snuggle Up, Snookums." "Honey, Does You Love Me?" "Cakin' the Walk." "It's Twilight on the Tiber." "Tu-Lips for Mine!"

A sort of managerial salesman in a number-thirteen-and-a-half collar and a part that ran through his varnished-looking hair bisecting the back of his head like a poodle's, and a soft, pimply jowl that had never borne beard, stuck up a random sheet of music on the piano, so placed that its tones carried straight through the megaphone to the sidewalk.

She played and sang it off easily, her tones jaunty and staccato and her desire to please quivering through them. He stood beside her, the angle of his body so that the sharp bone of his hip pressed against her.

"Rag up," he said once, insinuating the movement with a slight wriggle that ran through his apparently rigid body. She quickened her speed, leaning forward to read more surely:

"Uh-uh! my ba-a-aaby,
You drive me cra-azy,
Uh-uh! quit shovin',
I'm only lov--in'."

The words running along to a stuttering syncopation that filled her with self-disgust as she sang them. But she finished with quite a flourish, swinging around on the stool to face him.

"You need ragging up, kiddo. You've the speed of a funeral march."

"A little practice is what I need," she said, half hoping to obtain.

"I'll try you at fifteen a week. Eleven to six Tuesday, Thursday, and Friday. The other evenings we close at eleven; fifty cents extra for supper money. You on?"

"Yes."

"Slick, ain't you? Who peeled you to-day, Miss Bermuda Onion? Aw, touchy! No harm meant. You're too big to suit me; I like 'em squab size. Rag up a bit between now and to-morrow, Miss Onion."

For five weeks in the little slit of store that was foul with tired and devitalized air, and concealed behind a screen that shut off the megaphone device, Lilly sang through an eight and sometimes a twelve-hour day, her voice drifting out to the sidewalk with a remote calling quality.

To her relief she quickly learned that Mr. Alphonse Rook--"Phonzie"--spent the greater part of his time at the office of the Manhattan Music Publishing Company, under which auspices the Broadway Melody Shop operated.

He was replaced by a salesgirl of such superlative dress and manner that her long jet earrings were like exclamations at the audacity of her personality. An habitual counter line-up of Broadway mental brevities in the form of young men with bamboo sticks and eyes with perpetual ogles in them, would while away the syncopated hours with her, occasionally Lilly emerging from behind her screen to "come up for air," as Miss Gertrude Kirk put it.

She was "Gert" to the boys, and from the propinquity of that sliver of store and the natural loquacity of Miss Kirk, which would have overflowed a much more generous area, Lilly was to learn much of life as it is lived on that bias which is cut against the warp and woof of society. Miss Kirk had twice been up in night court. Her mother alternated under three aliases and was best known on the night boat that plied between New York and Albany. Occasionally this mother visited upon her daughter, her laughter hitting through the store like cymbals. She had the sagging flesh of an old fowl and cheeks that had not been cleansed of rouge long enough for the pores to breathe in and keep the flesh alive. To Lilly she was as terrible as a plucked hen on a butcher's block, with her head dyed to a vicious cock's-comb red and the wattles of loose skin beneath her chin.

In fact, she was familiarly known around the shop as "old bird," and on one occasion had invited Lilly for a Sunday excursion "up to Albany."

"Lay off, ma," said her daughter. "Fer Gossake, can't you take a tumble?"

Miss Kirk's tongue was as nimble as her fingers. She used them both lightly.

Would tear the flounce off her too lacy petticoat to bind up a messenger boy's cut finger, and no scarf-pin that came within three feet of her was immune from her quick touch. The only hour that ever struck for her was sex o'clock. The unmentionable lay mentioned in her discourse so frequently that to Lilly the Broadway Melody Shop became a slimy-sided vat, horrible with small-necked young men with flexible canes and Gertrude Kirk's slit-eyed stare of calculation.

"I don't know what you're trying to put over, Lilly-of-the-valley; you're one too many for me. But I'd stake my life on one thing."

"What?"

"You got a caul over your face."

"A what?"

"Caul. Sort of veil some get born with. I know a girl carried hers around in a little wooden box for luck. Well, you got that white-veil kind of look that would blacklist you for the Vestal Virgin Sextet. I can pick 'em every time. You look to me like--say, I got a little mud puddle of my own to play in without wetting my feet in yours."

"I'm sure I don't know what you're talking about," said Lilly, crashing out the opening bars of "Oh, Willie, I love you when you're silly."

"No?" said Miss Kirk, the slit-eyed stare of terrible sophistication narrowing down to two blade edges.

That night Lilly eyed herself in all the plate-glass windows as she walked to the car. She was straight as a lance, but before she went to bed she readjusted the gathers of her skirt band, pushing them forward.

One evening, because she saw it in the window of one of the Amsterdam Avenue petty shops, she bought, furtively, a baby dress with a little nursery legend embroidered on the yoke. She stole home with the package up under her coat, like a thief. Once in her room, she laid it out on the bed. It was as tiny as the French apron of the French maid who opens the play, and as sheer. She wanted suddenly to finger it, and did, laying her cheek to it with a rushing sense of sweetness, and then suddenly, on wild lashing tears of her resentment and terror, her hands tightening into and wringing it. Dragging the suitcase out from beneath her bed, she crammed in the little garment, and finally, strapping down the lid again, laid her head against it, silently screaming her despair.

Strangely enough, that very night, long after the street noises had thinned and she had heard Isaac Neugass, creeping up from the drug store, drag the bolt across the apartment door, Lilly sat suddenly up in bed out of a hot tossing period of light doze. She was often crying unconsciously into her sleep these nights, so that her eyes were tear-bitten and dilated into the darkness. The night bell that connected from the drug store was gouging the silence with a long-sustained grilling. Soft-soled feet were already padding down the hallway past her door, a bolt withdrawn, then voices.

The grunty tones of Mr. Neugass and a woman's fast soprano that rose and rent the silence like the tear of silk. More feet down the hallway; sobs that were filled with coughing; Mrs. Neugass, pitched high in the key of termagency; the faint, ex-postulatory voice of Alma Neugass; and finally one throat-torn sob that grated like a buzz saw against the night and the banging, reverberating slam of a door.

Barefooted, trembling in the chill, Lilly peered out into the hallway, the grotesque procession returning down its length. Mr. Neugass bent to his tired angle, nightshirt striking him midships as it were, the two dim white women creeping after.

"What has happened?"

"It's nodding, Miss Parlow. It's a shame for decent beoble they should have to listen. Wash your ears out of it, Alma, and go back to bed."

But instead, to Lilly's importuning arm, Miss Neugass slid into her room, closing the door softly behind her, standing there shivering in the blue kind of darkness.

"It's the old story," she said--"some girl in a fix and trying to get pa to help her. It makes me sick, positively sick."

"A fix?"

"Every once in a while some poor creature comes begging pa to break the law and help her. It gets him wild. Any girl who doesn't want her child is a monster and every girl in trouble a vicious sinner. This poor little thing didn't look seventeen; I couldn't quite understand her. A Pole, I think. Something about the beach at Coney Island. A man she'd never seen before or since. My mother in her righteousness! Her terrible, untempted righteousness. Her easy righteousness. The law in its righteousness. It can be just as wrong and horrible to have children as it can be sublime.

What right has that little underbred girl to bring an illegitimate life into the world? The law doesn't provide for the illegitimate child. Why should it provide for its birth? What right had my father to withhold his help? ... There are worse crimes than taking human life; one of them is to give life under such conditions."

"You mean, Alma, there's a way not to--a way out?"

"Why, you poor baby! Of course there is if you see to it in time. That is, during the first few weeks."

"How--many?"

"Oh, five or six at the outside. Go back to bed, girl; you'll catch your death. O Lordy! such is life!" And went out.

For the third time in her life, Lilly fainted that night, standing shivering in her nightdress for a second after Miss Neugass had left. In a room barely wide enough to contain her length she dropped softly against the bed, and, her fall broken, slid the remaining distance to the floor.

After a while the chill air from the open window revived her and she crept shudderingly into bed.

CHAPTER XXI

Two weeks before Christmas such a gale of house-cleaning swept through the Neugass apartment that the scoured smell of pine-wood floors and the scrubbed taste of damp matting lurked at the very threshold.

Then one Sunday morning Mlle. Millie du Gass and maid, also Felix G. Auchinloss, were registered at the Waldorf.

All that day there wound into Lilly's room the aroma of fowl simmering in their juices, the quick hither and thither of feet down the hallway, and later the whirring of an ice-cream freezer and the quick fork-and-china click of egg whites in the beating. For days she had hardly glimpsed the family, except as they passed her on excited little comings and goings, and always package-laden. A strip of new hall carpet appeared, Miss Neugass nailing it down one night, calling out short, excited orders through a mouthful of tacks. The piano had been tuned.

A sense of delicacy kept Lilly to her room that bright cold Sunday. She did her breathing exercises; washed out some handkerchiefs and stockings; tightened the buttons on a pretty new brown coat with a touch of modish stone-martin fur at the collar which she had purchased, not without qualms, for twenty-seven dollars and a half, at an advertised sale.

Then for two long immobile hours she sat with her cheeks crumpled into her palms, staring out across the sun-washed roofs and roofs.

At noon she took in a bottle of milk from the window sill, thawed it, slid a hatpin along the wrapping of a new tin of biscuit. She alternated between bites and sips, sitting on the bed edge, her gaze into the design of the wall paper.

At home they must be sitting down to dinner, her father adjusting his napkin by the patent fasteners and tilting back his head for the invariable preamble of throwing the contents of his water tumbler down at a gulp. Her mother in the hebdomadal polka-dotted foulard, her bangs frizzed. Albert gnawing close to the drumstick, jaws working.

As a matter of fact, just that scene was at just that moment in its enactment, and in all the fullness of her intuition she now knew it as unerringly as if it had flowed in replica to her through time and space, etching itself in dry point into her consciousness.

How often and with uncanny fidelity to fact her retroactive state of mind had guided her step by step over the site of the domestic disaster.

Her parents' home, reaching around like an amoeba, inclosing Albert in living walls. The slow readjustment, dumfounded rage, and despair simmering gradually to bitterness and hardening finally to despair. The soft, sensitive ground of their sorrow constantly spongy with the wellsprings of grief beneath, but the surface bubbles showing less and less, and ultimately a hard dryness setting in. Her heart would hurt as tangibly as if the surface of her body were red with a wound from it, yet, sitting there at her milk and biscuit, her gaze into the monotonous repetition of wall-paper design, the thought of that Sunday dinner out there, with its invariable roast chicken, bread stuffing, candied sweet potatoes, and lemon-meringue pie; the Sunday-afternoon lethargy; the hypothenuse of her father asleep in his chair, the newspaper over his face; Albert, the celluloid toothpick moving along his lips, puttering around at favorite locks and bells; the mere visualization was such a fillip to her present that she lay back on the bed, stretching her arms and legs like a great, luxurious cat, her lips curved to a smile.

At five o'clock, as she lazed there, Alma Neugass burst in without the usual scrupulously observed preamble of a knock. There were two round spots of color out on her long cheeks, and her white cotton shirt waist, always bearing the imprint of sleeve protectors, was replaced by a dark-blue silk of candy-stripe plaid, with a standing collar of lace that fell in a jabot down the front, held there by an ivory hand of a brooch. There was something of the mausoleum about poor Alma, the grim skeleton of her everyday personality finding but icy warmth beneath the ivory, lace, and the seldom-warn black broadcloth skirt that was pinned over two inches at the waistline to hold it up.

"Did you think I'd forgotten you? I haven't--but it's been such a rush."

She sat down on a chair edge, pressing a bony hand to her brow.

"You poor thing, you're dead tired."

"They're here, you know. Docked this morning, almost twenty-four hours ahead of schedule. They--they would have come up immediately, but customs detained them three hours. They are at the hotel now and won't be up until supper. It's all so confusing. The reporters and photographers on their trail. He won't let anyone at her until she's rested. I talked to him over the telephone. His voice is--hairy."

"I've never seen you look so nice, Miss Neugass."

"If I stop to think, I'll scream."

"Then you mustn't stop, dear."

"You should see my father; he can't sit still. I never realized how little and--old he's getting until I put his black suit on him. He's so full of pride he--Oh, what a mockery--for him to dare to come here--home--with her."

"Miss Neugass--this is not the time. Not now."

A cocaine sort of courage seemed to lock her face back into its rather nondescript immobility.

"You're right," she said. "I'm acting like a fool," and rose. "What I came in to say, get into that little pink dress of yours about nine-thirty and I may be able to manage it for you to-night. Two minutes of his time may mean everything to you and nothing to him."

Lilly flashed to her feet.

"To-night!"

"Keep your head. Sing the 'Jewel Song.' It's always a good, showy standby. Let go--the way I heard you practice the other Sunday morning--and forget that it's Auchinloss or anyone else listening to you."

"No, no, not to-night, Miss Neugass. I--I'm not prepared. It's too sudden."

"It's as good as any other time. Besides, to-night we have him here, and there is no telling when we will again. This isn't what you would call the ideal headquarters for a pair of celebrities. I suppose, if the truth is known, Millie dreads bringing him here at all. Besides, they leave to-morrow for Boston, and with the line-up of entertainments the newspapers say are planned for them, there is no telling when we will get him alone again."

"I'm not in voice these days. It's all roughened up since I'm singing downtown.

I--oh, I'm not ready to-night, Miss Neugass."

"Nonsense! Don't ask Opportunity to wait outside when he knocks. He may move on and not return."

"I--I'm so frightened. I've such--such odds against me--right now. What if he only rubs his hands and says, 'very nice'? What if--"

"That's where you'll have to swallow your medicine. After all, even the great Auchinloss represents only one man's opinion."

"But his judgment has proved itself--time and time again."

"That's why you have the chance to-night that comes once in a lifetime. Take it."

"I will!"

CHAPTER XXII

It was just before midnight, after a four-hour period of waiting in the pink mull dress, when came the summons which brought Lilly into the presence of Felix Auchinloss.

Cramped from the long period of taut waiting, she was so dry of throat that in spite of constantly sipped water she could only gulp her reply to Miss Neugass's knock and eagerly inserted head.

"Quick! He'll hear you now before they leave." She followed her, without a word, down the hallway and into a front parlor brilliant with the full-flare gas jets, a bisque angel in the attitude of swinging dangling from the chandelier, and, swimming in the dance, a circle of faces.

"Miss Parlow, this is my sister, Millie du Gass."

A Greek chorus could have swayed to the epiphany in Millie's voice.

With her short bush of curls, little aquiline profile true to her father's, tilted upward, as if sniffing the aerial scent, her slender figure Parisienne to outlandishness, the stream of Millie's ancestry flowed through the tropics of her very exotic personality. She was the magnolia on the family tree, the bloom on a century plant that was heavy with its first bud. Even at this time, slightly before her internationalism as a song bird was to carry her name to the remote places of the earth, a little patina of sophistication had set in, glazing her over and her speech, which carried the whir of three acquired languages.

"And this is Doctor Auchinloss. I've told him about you and your eagerness for a foothold. He's going to give you a little home-made audition. Will you hear Miss Parlow now, Doctor Auchinloss?"

The face of Felix Auchinloss, also to become familiar through subsequent years of American dictatorship, seemed by the hirsute vagary of a black beard joining up *via* sideburns with a Pompadour of sooty black, to peer through a porthole. It did just that. A face in window looking out with very quick perceptions which ruffled it not at all, upon a world that came to him chiefly through two channels, his supernaturally attuned hearing and his palate.

He could detect a slurred note of the sixteenth violin in the crash of a ninety-piece ensemble of orchestration, and one-eighth-of-a-second miscalculation of his two-minute egg could embroil a breakfast table. A creature of elbows and knees, such as a chimpanzee is, the backs of his hands were hairy, but the eye seldom strayed from his face. It knew its Huxley, that face, its Hegel and its Kant. It loved the smoothness of young girls' bodies. It was attuned to the music of the spheres. It could hold in leash the outrageous temperaments that responded to his baton and look with impassivity, even cruelty, upon torture. Mostly the torture of women. Also it could brighten out of its imperturbability at the steaming sight of a dish of *sauerbraten.*

There had been no *sauerbraten* on Mrs. Neugass's festive board, rather fowl, in a white glue of gravy and great creamy dumplings, and under three helpings and the steady pour of an extra lager the great Auchinloss had expanded and expounded.

His glance, still warmed, took in Lilly at a sweep finding resting place at the swell of her bosom.

There was something about Lilly as she stood thereof the winglike smoothness of a little wild duck, wet from a skim across water. A slick and pale kind of beauty which ordinarily held little appeal for him except that her bosom was very white. Very, very white, he thought.

"Zoprano?" he asked, his gaze still beneath her chin.

"Lyric soprano."

"Om-m-m-m!" After the manner of having his doubts.

"You accompany her, Felix," said Miss du Gass, not unkindly and actually with an intensive kind of eagerness, as if for the diverting of his interest.

He seated himself at the piano, his great knees at a wide stride, hands riding down the keyboard in an avalanche of improvised octaves.

In black silk that stood away from her, Mrs. Neugass sat by, not releasing hold of Millie's hand, her eyes as if they could never finish their feast of her. Her timidity forbade her much that she would say, and so she sat smilingly silent and held the little ring-littered hand, stroked it and lay it to her cheek. To Lilly, who had never seen her out of the cotton-stuff uniform of housewife, it seemed to her that something of her Old Testament beauty had died beneath the bunchy jetted taffeta that brought out in her the look of peasant--her husband in camphoric broadcloth suffering the same demotion.

"Now doan' get egcited," said Mr. Neugass, himself shaken of voice. "Remember it is home folks."

"She's all right, pa, if you don't make her nervous," said Miss Neugass, seating herself stiffly on a stiff chair, her face, as the evening wore on, cold of its flush, and tired rings coming out beneath her eyes.

"What do you prefer to sing?" asked Millie du Gass, again, kindly.

"The 'Jewel Song.'"

On her words the opening bars crashed out, and, to Lilly's consternation, far too rapidly, so that she ran with her breath, as it were, for the opening notes, lifting to it nicely, however, and, by miracle, quite at her truest.

The state of her invariable vocal exultation began to mount, her consciousness of scene to recede, and, anticipating her coloratura climax, she started to climb, building for warble. Her blood was pounding and her voice in flight. Up went her chin. It was then Felix Auchinloss swung on the stool, snipping off the song like a thread, his face in its window, full of a new impassivity, and this time his eyes off somewhere behind Lilly's left ear.

"That is verra nize," he said, moving restlessly about the room as if to throw off an irksome moment, and then winding his hands and winding them, "a pretty voice as far as it goes, and verra, verra nize."

There was a silence that seemed to wait, and Millie du Gass, her laugh like glass beads falling from a snapped chain:

"You must come down to the hotel, dear, some day, where I've a concert grand. This darling old tin pan! You should have seen, Felix, the way pops used to make me practice on it, rapping me over the knuckles. You old darling pops!"

"Papa's baby-la," he said, pinching her cheek.

"If you will excuse me now, please, I--won't, intrude any longer."

"Good night, dear; it was just lovely. Good night," joined in everybody, too kindly.

Walking out of that room, Lilly was conscious suddenly of passing through a prolonged stare, especially from Mrs. Neugass, who leaned forward slightly in her chair--a stare that prompted her somehow to quicken her departure almost to a run.

*　　　*　　　*　　　*　　　*

Out of a night that had flowed around her in a bitter sort of blackness that fairly threatened to drown her, she floated up toward morning to an exhausted doze, her face tear-lashed and her breathing sucked in sobbily as she slept.

It was out of this that she awoke suddenly to a bombardment of knocks at her door.

"Come!" she cried, sitting up rather alarmedly in bed, and holding the blanket over her chest. She was lovely and disheveled with sleep, her whiteness whiter because of the most delicately darkened oyster shells beneath her eyes.

It was Mrs. Neugass. She was pleasantly shapeless again in cotton stuff, her bosom bulging down and over the jerked-in apron strings.

"Wait, I'll get up and close the window, Mrs. Neugass!"

"You doan' need to," she said, slamming down the window herself, opening the floor register, and seating herself rigidly on the chair that faced the bed. "I want a little talk with you, blease."

"Why, yes, Mrs. Neugass!" A wave of memory and a sense of physical misery swept over Lilly so that it was difficult for her to force the smile. But she did, sitting up in bed and hugging her knees with bare shining arms.

With nervousness patent in every move, Mrs. Neugass sat forward, pleating and unpleating a little section of her apron.

"I guess you know it, Miss Lilly, that with all the honors we got by our daughter, we're still blain, respegtable beoble."

"Of course--"

"For fifteen years in one business in one neighborhood we've such a standing that from three blocks around they come to my husband he should keep their savings. My girls--I can say it on a bible--more than anything around them was always respegtability."

"But why--"

"If I'm mistaken, Miss Luella, and blease God I should be, then excuse me for a foolish old woman, but is--is everything all right with you, Miss Luella?"

"Mrs. Neugass, I--What do you mean?"

"I took you in for a student, a girl alone from her home town, but not once since you're with us--I can't help it I got eyes--so much as a postal card. All right, I said time and time again to my husband, she don't have friends to come and call on her, because she's a stranger in New York. Neither did my Millie have so many friends, I guess, the first few weeks in Munich. But no letters--not a line! I know *goys* ain't so strong on family ties, but once in a while a letter--"

"I don't quite see where the matter of my correspondence can be of interest to you, Mrs. Neugass."

"No, but it is of interest to me if everything is all right with you. If everything is over and above-board, as the saying is, Miss Luella!"

There was a throb to the silence, as she sat upright there in bed, that seemed to shape itself about her, like a trap. She buried her face suddenly into her hands.

Then Mrs. Neugass rose, edging around the back of her chair as if to get clear of even propinquity.

"I'm right?" she cried, hoarsely and rather coarsely. "I'm right, then? I took into my home a bad girl?"

"No!--No!--No!--"

Out of bed, her feet hastily into slippers and fumbling into her kimono so that the flow of her hair went down inside it, Lilly approached Mrs. Neugass, her gesture toward her and entreating.

"Mrs. Neugass, you're horribly wrong in what you suspect. You must listen to me--"

"You can exblain nothing to me except to get your clothes packed. How it goes to show you never can tell beoble from looks. Even my husband, who never gets deceived in human nature, 'She's a refined, intelligent girl to have around,' he says. My stepdaughter! A girl I am as careful with as if she was still eighteen, should go out of her way to get you before Auchinloss! No wonder he says it you are limited and that you fall just short of fine talent. You don't deserve it no better. Ain't you ashamed? You bad girl, you! I'm only sorry for the mother you say you got--your poor mother!"

"Mrs. Neugass, this is outrageous! You haven't the right to speak to me like this! It was wrong, I admit, to--to deceive you. But I had my reasons--you wouldn't have taken me in. I'm not what--what you think I am!"

"I don't care what you are and what you ain't. I only want you to pack your bags and go."

"I won't go until you've heard me out!"

"We're respegtable beoble!"

"Oh, I know, Mrs. Neugass, your kind of respectability. I was reared on it. It's the cruelest respectability in the world. It has no outlook except through the narrow little bars of the small decencies you have erected about yourselves."

"That fine talk don't save a girl's skin when she's in such a fix like you!"

"I've more claims to your precious kind of respectability than you--than you think!"

"I don't *think* no more. I know! I don't say it's the nicest thing I should have looked once through your things. Even then I must have felt it in my bones. That little dress with the nursery rhyme on the yoke--how it was I didn't get suspicious then? All of a sudden last night, though--even while you was singing, it come over me, all these weeks I must have been blind."

"I tell you I'm a married woman. I was married last July in the Leffingwell Rock Church in St.--in a city I don't care to name. I suppose that constitutes me a moral woman in your world of cautious morality. But in my eyes I'm a moral leper. Not because I did not marry, but because I did. Married for every reason in the world except love. No marriage ceremony in the world can condone the immorality of that! Society may, but God doesn't. From your point of view, then, I'm a respectable woman. From mine, I'm rotten."

"I don't know what it is you're talking aboud. If you are what you say you are, what does it mean living around in decent beoble's houses in a condition like yours? It's an insult to my daughters you should be here. The right kind of a married woman don't live around New York in such a way like you. There is something very crooked in the woodpile."

"If that is what bothers you, won't you please, dear Mrs. Neugass, sit down and let me tell you the whole story? I need you--"

"The whole story, Miss--Mrs. Parlow--or whatever it is you call yourself--ain't what bothers me. All I want is you should go while my husband is down in his store and my daughter in her position. I am ashamed they should know. I'm lucky yet I saved myself from having a disgrace in the house a few weeks from now."

"Oh, Mrs. Neugass, be careful! You may have cause some day to--"

"A singer she wants to be! Is it any wonder, miss, you got no luck? A girl like you don't deserve it. I'm sorry enough for your poor mother. Married or no married, I want you should leave here. Quick, you bad girl, you! I'll wait outside till you go."

So Lilly was subjected to the bitter, the unspeakably vulgar humiliation of gathering her belongings like any culprit servant girl, cramming them, blind with tears and frenzy, into the suitcase and valise, tears scalding down and rolling over her hands as she dressed.

As she staggered finally down the hallway, the two bags grating the walls and her hat awry from haste, Mrs. Neugass stood at the door, holding it open.

"Here," she said, "is your rent back for four days--"

"Don't you dare, Mrs. Neugass, to offer me that! Only let me out, please, from this outrageous predicament."

"You got righd. It is a outrageous predicament. Ach! shame on you! Such a fine, clean-looking girl like you. Indeed, you don't got to ask to be let out twice."

Thirty minutes later, and because her wildly beating brain could figure out no alternative, Lilly sat on a bench in the waiting room of the Grand Central Station, bags at her feet, trying to subdue her state of trembling.

Eleven o'clock moved around largely on the station clock. She was due at the Broadway Melody Shop. Still she sat on, the palpitating surface of her gradually slowing its throb. The reverberating terminal, then at the excavating state of its gigantic reconstruction, rang to the crash of steel with the fantastic echo of tunnel and of blasting. Its constant conglomerate of footfalls reduced to the common denominator of a gigantic shuffle, it swelled toward the noonday schedule, with more and more rapid comings and goings. A light snow was announcing itself in little white powderings across overcoat shoulders and in the crevices of derbys.

The new brown coat enveloped her warmly enough, but she shivered as she sat, at the same time committing the paradox of unbuttoning and flinging its double-breastedness away from the beating of her very being. After a while she gave over her bags to the obliging eye of a shawled Polish girl on the bench beside her and crossed to the Information Bureau. A clerk gave her precedence over two men.

Yes, there was a St. Louis train out at two-five. Another at six.

She returned and sat in the midst of a third bustling hour. A young woman with an infant, and a whole archipelago of luggage surrounding her, finally replaced the Polish girl. She was as fadely and straggily pretty as a doll that has been left lying on the lawn throughout a night of heavy dews. Every so often the tiny head would spring back from the soft fount of her breasts, a cry rising thin and spiral as smoke.

"Sh-h-h, baby! He won't eat," she said, plaintively. "It's just terrible; we've tried everything and he won't eat."

Lilly put out her hand toward the small ball of head, but withdrew it.

"Poor little baby!"

"My sister's gone to the matron to get him some barley water before he gets on the train. There is a grand matron here at the station. I left him with her all morning while we shopped, and he never whimpered. The barley water was her idea. He won't eat. It's terrible. He 'ain't gained in six weeks. The doctor says we've just got to keep trying until we hit a formula that agrees with him."

"Formula? How funny! Sounds like chemistry."

The young mother cast a commiserating eye.

"I'd hate to tell you what it sounds like about two P.X. I've been on a visit to my mother in Brooklyn, but he yelled so of nights the whole flat was kicking. You ain't, by any chance, taking the two-five St. Louis Limited, are you? Brazil, Indiana, is mine."

"I--don't know--yet."

"Ever been there?"

"Where?"

"Brazil."

"I've passed through."

"Some dump, believe me. I keep saying to him, 'Keep me out here much longer, Fred, and you'll have to ship me home in a wooden kimono.'"

"Wooden kimono?"

"Coffin. Get me?"

"Then Brazil isn't your home?"

"By transplanting, yes. I never married out there, believe me. We was both born and raised right here on the little long and narrow island, till he got a better job out there with the telephone company. Believe me, I'll take my little old fifteen a week in New York to thirty a week out there, bungalow setting thrown in. Bunk-a-low, I call it."

"But isn't it better for the baby?"

"That's right, too. I always say to my twin, I say, 'Myrt, if you don't think I got harder hours than when I worked next to you in the Five and Ten, and no pay day, neither, just trade with me one day and take care of the kid and the bunk-a-low.' I always say to Fred, I say, 'If you think you're dog tired, fasten a speedometer on my ankle and read it when you come home nights and see who's taken the most steps.' It's hell, anyways, when they won't eat and you can't hit the right formula."

"Poor baby!"

"You wouldn't give 'em up after you got 'em, but believe me it's a wise girl will think twice before she has 'em. A girl gains a lot by marrying--maybe. But believe me, she gives up a lot--sure."

"But you married the right man."

"Yeh; but Nature is a trickster. How you going to know where her intentions leave off her and your own begin? Fred and me ran off. Regular love affair. I suppose I am one of them that picked right; right as a girl with my disposition could ever pick. If I hadn't, believe me, eight hours for me behind the counter in preference to eating the rest of my breakfasts across from the wrong face. Sh-h-h, Freddie baby! Can't you see my back is breaking? Sh-h-h! Auntie Myrt's gone to nice matron for barley water. For the love of Mike, sh-h-h! or mamma'll spank."

The twin fluttered up then, a vivid italicized prototype, on slim tall heels that clicked and a very small red hat set just at the angle of sauciness. They moved off together after a bickering over luggage, the slim silhouette with the chin sharply flung up and the accentuated sway-back figure of the little mother, her skirt sagging over run-down heels, and, for want of a free hand, blowing up the loose strands of hair from out her eyes.

For a time Lilly sat quite intently, her gaze on a small sign that hung at right angles from an open doorway, "MATRON." After a while she gathered up her luggage and walked over, entering a little room fitted up with the efficient and institutional unprivacy of public service. On a couch, her face to the wall, a woman in a traveling duster lay stretched, hat and all, in an attitude of exhaustion, a young girl with a wayward fling of posture, sitting sullen in a corner, her very pointed and heeled shoes toeing in. A three-year-old child with a large tag pinned across his little dress played with railroad-owned blocks; the matron, a sort of stout Lachesis, with a string of keys at her belt, gray with years and the rather sweet tiredness of service, sorted towels at a rack. It was to her that Lilly spun out a ready tale, reddening as she talked, but stanch to it.

"I'm from Indianapolis. I want a quiet place for the next few months. Two, to be exact."

Sweeping her with a look. "Are you in any kind of difficulty?"

"No--not that! I've left my husband. We agreed to separate. I want a few weeks of quiet until--afterward, and then I can arrange to start out on my own."

"You're too nice a girl to--"

"I'm not asking anything. I am not the kind you are evidently accustomed to deal with here. It is simply that I'm strange."

"Have you no friends?"

"None with whom I desire to communicate."

"Well," doubtfully, "there is the Nonsectarian Home for Indigent Girls and the Hanna Larchmont Lying-in Hospital--"

"Oh," cried Lilly, with a sting of color to her cheeks, "you don't understand! I have funds. I tell you it is just that I am strange. I want a medium-priced place to live for the next few weeks, where it won't be embarrassing."

The matron unlocked a drawer.

"I have a few addresses here of private rooming houses in the Hanna Larchmont Lying-in Hospital and Bellevue districts, if that is what you want. Personally inspected places that can be recommended for their cleanliness and respectability."

"That is exactly what I need."

"You will find no questions asked so long as you conduct yourself quietly, and of course you are expected to make your plans for leaving well in advance of any emergency. There are several private sanitariums in the neighborhood."

"Of course."

"Here are three addresses. The first is in East Seventeenth Street, just in back of the Hanna Larchmont. It's a very nice place run by an old Irishwoman who has a lace-curtain establishment in the basement. Here are two others on the same block, in case she has rented her room."

"I'll go there at once," said Lilly, taking the memorandum.

"If I were you I should go back home to friends. It is too bad that a girl like you should find herself in this position. Won't you let me help you?"

"Thank you"--lifting her bags again--"you have helped me a great deal."

That night Lilly slept in a small back room, two flights up, over a lace-curtain-cleaning establishment. It was cruder and rougher than anything she had yet encountered; a white-pine table with a washbowl and a toothbrush mug, and a black iron bed that at first glance had sent darting through her a sinking sense of institution. But it was clean, and a sparse Irish landlady with a moist pink presence that steamed hot suds had left her without question and one week's advance payment tucked into her bosom.

Before going to bed, after she had looked under it and turned out the gas jet, she went over to her single window, opening it wide to the bite of a winter's night and shooting up the shade. Her view was again of roofs and roofs and chimney pots, dirtier, this time, and dingier, and marching against the sky line, like a dark herd of buffalo, a long range of buildings, blackened of bricks.

It was the Hanna Larchmont Lying-in Hospital seen from the rear.

CHAPTER XXIII

When Lilly returned to the Broadway Melody Shop that morning following, there was already a voice driving with such nasal power into the sidewalk din that she hardly needed to enter to learn of her successful replacement.

There was an entirely new hauteur incasing Miss Kirk, who upon her entrance wound into an attitude.

"Well!"

"I was ill."

"I--see."

"I guess the place is filled. Oh, it's all right!"

"Better go over to the office and see Phonzie about it. All I know is they sent over a pair of lungs that can stop traffic when they let out. Forty copies of 'Cinderella Ella' just like hot cakes the first time she telephones it out to 'em! Hauls in a netful every time she opens her mouth, and, some mouth! 'Phonzie,' I telephones over to him this morning, 'thank God she's screened from the public or somebody would buy her for codfish balls.'"

"Do you think there might be something over at the office for me? I've had some training for desk work, too."

"Don't know. I always told you to put some nose into your voice. Let out, that's what they want in this business. You never came out enough from behind your tonsils. The refined stuff through a megaphone has about as much chance as a violet in the six-o'clock rush. In other words, dearie," finished Miss Kirk, her rather close-set eyes focusing upon the tip of Lilly's nose, "I think you're fired. Canned, so to speak. Replaced, as it were."

Lilly laughed, forcing her head high to deny disconcertment.

"Well, anyway, that saves me the trouble of resigning."

"Yes," said Miss Kirk, her gaze suddenly long and full of portent, "I wouldn't be surprised."

To Lilly's heated consciousness the grilling quality in that gaze was so unmistakable that it plunged into her like an arrow. She walked out, stinging with it.

Hurrying toward the music-publishing office, she caught suddenly her reflection in the plate-glass window of a shop devoted to Broadway's intense interpretation of the prevalent in modes. She stood, in the very act of motion, regarding this snapshot of herself. Then she entered, emerging presently in a full-length dark-blue cape with gilt buttons and little pipings of red along the edge. It was neither so warm nor so durable as the brown coat, and cost her the rather sickening sensation of breaking into a hundred-dollar bill for twelve dollars and ninety-eight cents.

But it was immensely becoming, this flowing wrap, enveloping her like a wimple, her face rising out of it as clear as a nun's. Nevertheless, it was her realization of need for it that quite suddenly ended her quest. She turned for home, stopping at the Public Library for one of her frequent perusals of the St. Louis newspapers. She read quickly, her eye skimming the obituary, personal, and social columns. For a week there had daily appeared a little insertion which invariably caused her a twist of heart:

To Sublet: Furnished. Seven rooms and bath. Brand new from top to bottom. Every convenience. Will sell furnishings if desired. Spacious front lawn. Poultry yard. 5199 Page Avenue. Apply 5198 Page Avenue.

Then one day it disappeared and something lifted from Lilly's heart. This time, as she opened the St. Louis paper of just one week previous, a small oval photograph leaped at her from a row of them, choking her as if it had clutched at her throat.

In a full-page advertisement, Slocum-Hines Hardware Company announced to its many friends a twenty-fifth anniversary, the entire sheet bordered in small oval photographs of the personnel of valued employees.

"Albert Penny, first-assistant buyer." Regarding it, her consciousness of his promotion was secondary to a feeling that straight lines joining the four corners of Albert's face would have produced almost a perfect rectangle. A little farther on was Vincent Bankhead, buyer, and on a lower row, Ralph Sluder, with whom she had graduated from grade school.

Strangely enough, in this very edition the name of Horace Lindsley sprang out at her from the tiniest of type in the marriage-license column. Horace Lindsley, 3345 Bell Avenue. Carol Ingomar Devine, 3899 Westminster Place. The name of the bride was associated in Lilly's mind with the society columns of the Sunday *Post-Dispatch*. A hundred little pointed darts shot through her, and even now the old sinking but delicious sensation of too sudden descent in an elevator.

That night she went to bed with a toothache, a biting little spark of pain that toward morning became a raging flame rushing against the entire inside of her cheek. She could not trace its source, every tooth seeming to stampede.

All of the day following she lay with her face buried into her pillow, abandoning herself utterly to creature discomfort. Toward evening she ventured down as far as Fourteenth Street for a bowl of milk and toast, but the pain raged on, tightening her throat against food, and she crept back to the haven of her cheek to Mrs. McMurtrie's scorched pillow slip.

After another two nights of local application and the rather futile business of holding warm water in the sag of her cheek, she found out, at the direction of Mrs. McMurtrie, a neighborhood dentist who occupied a suite of rooms over a corner drug store, the large grinning picture of a boy, with a delighted hiatus of missing front tooth, painted on each window and giltly inscribed, "It Didn't Hurt a Bit."

It is inconceivable, except that under duress of great pain Lilly could have engaged services so obviously quasi professional, but she was past that perception by now, her nerves from brow to shoulder crackling like a bonfire.

Examination by a dentist with gray pointed side whiskers that flared and brushed her cheek unpleasantly, revealed a pair of abscesses gathering within the gum, and for weeks of mornings she lay back to the agony of steel incisions, for the remainder of the day stretching out on her iron bedstead, face to wall.

Then for a few days a premature spring came out teasingly. The East Seventeenth Street block, with its rows of houses, going down none too debonairly, from gentility to senility, showing a bud here and there. There even remained one private residence with a polished door bell and name plate and a little cluster of crocuses in an iron jardiniere set out in a front yard about the dimension of an army blanket.

Crocuses, whose cold, moist smell, with all the pungency of associations an odor can arouse, somehow suggested, to Lilly, Taylor Avenue and little Harry Calvert. She did not remember it, but Harry had once stolen two satiny red ones for her from a Taylor Avenue flower bed and been soundly cuffed by a housewife.

A block away, Gramercy Park, a rectangle of the Knickerbocker New York of the woodcut, red-brick sidewalk, salon parlor, and crystal chandelier, was already lacy with the first leafwork of spring. Several times, when the sun lay warmest, Lilly ventured into its Old World sobriety, strolling around the tall grill fence that inclosed the park. It was locked against the public, nursemaids from surrounding homes and a few old ladies stiff with gentility holding keys. Children from the raggedy fringe of Third Avenue played without awareness, against the outside of the iron palings, too young, and, anyway, too imprisoned in class, to resent one more monopoly even of God's sunshine and the brown, warm earth already swollen with life about to be.

It seemed to Lilly that almost any of these mild days Washington Irving, in pot hat and lace in his sleeves, might come strolling this pompous Square. She bought a manhandled copy of Volume I of Knickerbocker's *History of New York* off a secondhand bookstall one day, and read it sitting on the sun-drenched stoop of one of the old houses whose eyeless stare and boarded windows bespoke one absent family. Off this same stall she also purchased a volume of Wordsworth's poems, feeling a vague, a procreative, and who shall say mistaken need for beauty. Over and over she read, milking each phrase dry:

Our birth is but a sleep and a forgetting.
The soul that rises with us, our life's star,
Hath elsewhere had its setting and cometh from afar.
Not in entire forgetfulness and not in utter nakedness
But trailing clouds of glory, do we come from God who is our home.

She read of daffodils as if she would steep her soul in the sun of their yellowness, bought some one morning and propped them in the toothbrush mug.

She practiced her shorthand, too, these days, in a blank book bought for the purpose, sometimes an hour--even two or three--until the sun receded off the stoop.

Then for a week it rained, and from the patch of back yard, two stories beneath her window, began to mount the moist smell of living earth. Beside this open window, after the harrowing mornings of dentistry, with a soft rain falling from a sky swift and low with clouds, she wrote, her pencil dabbing constantly at the well of her tongue, a short story of some six thousand words composed out of the fabric of an idea that suddenly presented itself. She copied it in her most painstaking handwriting, on one side of foolscap, and sent it, with return postage, to a popular magazine. She was venturing out less and less, preparing over a portable oil stove her own breakfast, and very often her own lunch and dinner. She tried to sew, too, cutting up one of the sheerest and prettiest of her nightgowns into a litter of small garments, but almost immediately her hands would fall idle and the great waves of terror begin to surge.

Certain inevitable decisions crept closer. She decided against the Hanna Larchmont Hospital, its very foyer awakening in her such a sickening sense of public institution that she ventured no farther, but engaged a tiny room in a private sanitarium in Nineteenth Street, at twenty dollars a week, and the privilege of boarding on two or three weeks after her discharge.

Her bag of three new one-hundred-dollar bills still hung in all its reassuring entirety from the little pink ribbon about her neck, but the confronting dentist's bill of twenty-five dollars, and the slow but acid process of daily expenditure eating into the thirty or forty dollars left in her purse, lay uncomfortably against her consciousness.

By a series of constantly repeated calculations, particularly if the short story should bring in even a check large enough to cover the dentistry, Lilly planned to span the weeks of her narrowing interval with the three bills intact, but pretty shortly the first piece of mail she had received in New York arrived in a long, bulky envelope:

MY DEAR MISS PARLOW,--Thank you for submitting the accompanying manuscript. It does not quite get across in this office, but it is near enough to our standard for us' to want to see anything more you may care to submit.--THE EDITOR.

That night Lilly cried again all through her sleep, presenting herself next morning at the dentist's with heavy, rimmed eyes. It was her final visit, and before mounting the chair she laid down her carefully counted-out payment, five five-dollar bills, in a little pile on the revolving stand.

Doctor Hotchkiss, with the offshoot of white whiskers from each jowl, and who was fond of pinching her cheek as she lay under his touch, moistened his fingers and counted.

"The charges are fifty dollars," he said.

She was immediately startled.

"Why, Doctor Hotchkiss, you said twenty-five!"

"Fifty, with the bridgework, my dear young woman," he said, the words swimming in the oil of his suavity.

"You said twenty-five."

"You misunderstood, my dear young woman. Twenty-five would not pay for the amount of gold I used. Fifty is what I said. Fifty dollars," his voice rising.

She looked her despair.

"I--It's not honorable. I asked you distinctly. What if I haven't it to spare--"

"That is not my business," he replied, his entire manner roughening up. "You have forty dollars' worth of my gold in your mouth and the law provides for receiving goods you can't pay for. You've got it, all right, and if you haven't, from the look of you, there is some one behind you who has."

She colored so furiously that her eyes smarted to tears as she reached down into her blouse for the little chamois bag.

"Give me fifty dollars," she said, cramming the five five-dollar bills back into her purse, holding a crisp new hundred-dollar bill out to him, her voice as fluttering as a broken wing; "but nothing--nothing will ever convince me that you have not taken advantage of me."

He counted her fifty dollars off his own roll, all the more suave.

"You will find you have made a mistake, my dear young woman. This is a strictly one-price office. Now I will take out that temporary filling and finish you up."

She was loath to mount the chair, except that the nerve was jumping again. For half an hour she lay under his touch; finally, as he fumbled to untie the bib-like towel about her neck, his lips descended so close to her cheek that she could feel their cold, liver-colored caress touch her finally in a kiss. She sprang to her feet, jerking the towel away from her neck and rubbing it across the defiled spot.

"How dare you! You cheat! You miserable creature! How dare you! You come near me and I'll call the police. Let me out of here! Out!"

She ran from the place with her hat in her hand, across the street, and up two flights to her room. Panting and drenched with perspiration, all day she lay on the little iron bed, her face to the wall, shuddering.

"O God, where are you driving me? What are you driving me on for? Where? Why? What does it mean?"

At dusk, with a sense of weakness entirely new to her, she rose to undress, resting after each discarded piece of clothing.

She could hear Mrs. McMurtrie passing through the outer hall, a tin bucket, on one of its frequent errands to Joe's place across the street, grating against the wall. The room took on a deeper and soupy color of twilight, the great pachyderm of the Hanna Larchmont Hospital casting its shadow.

Suddenly, one of those boltlike perceptions that can spring out apparently from space, Lilly clapped her hands to her throat, her breast, the back of her neck. Her bag, the little chamois bag, and the pink ribbon at her neck were gone! She shook through her clothing in a frenzy of haste; she tore each piece inside out; slapped her hands over the washstand; flung back her mattress, plunging her fingers into every imaginable crevice. Dragged out the bed; jerked up the tacks from the carpet, turning back the corners; felt along the dark, narrow halls and down two flights on her hands and knees; shook out her clothing again. The hair came down over her shoulders and her reasoning seemed to go. That hand fumbling to untie that bib-towel. Those pointed whiskers approaching her cheek. The little pink bow at her neck. Those liverlike lips. That soft, boneless hand at the back of her neck had jerked out the bag! O God! that soft, slimy kiss and the little jerk of the bow at the back of her neck! and fell down with a screaming that brought Mrs. McMurtrie.

At noon of the next day Lilly Penny lay in the public ward of the Hanna Larchmont Lying-in Hospital, a premature mother by some weeks.

Lilly Penny, whose trousseau had included twelve of the sheerest batiste ones, in a coarse, unbleached nightdress not her own and the least gentle to her flesh she had ever known.

There was a row of her of which she was the whitest; wan women, big-eyed with pain, who had gone down into the canons of death that there might be life.

She had a slow, vagarious notion that all of the cots were tilted, so that they appeared each on a cross, these mothers. It was sad to lie there in that etheric world, yet somehow pleasant. The frieze on the auditorium of the St. Louis Center High School was unaccountably before her. It was still sown with lilies, but with babies' heads for calyxes. Her mother, her teeth set with effort, was scrubbing something. A window sill? Who was calling? Mamma--Flora. You wouldn't give 'em up after you got 'em, but: it's a wise girl that'll think twice. She felt so white. Never, in fact, had she enjoyed such a sense of her whiteness. She held up her arm to regard the column of it, and wanted to laugh, but it was easier to cry.

They brought her child. Hers, Lilly Becker Penny's. A huge tray of them, like a vender's street-corner offering of spring flowers. Tiny human blooms with a tag at each wrist. Incredible!

"Three guesses," said the nurse, through a smile, and held out the human bouquet toward her. She could scarcely breathe. She wanted to scream, to draw up the sheet over her head. To suffocate. Herself, external to herself, was breathing out there--off somewhere in that tray. She tried to pull up the covers over her head. A hand would draw them away. There was a black one in that row of little pink nubs of humanity! Heads like hard-boiled eggs not quite cooked through. No! No! No!

Suddenly Lilly raised to her elbow. The second from the end! The big head. The full-blown spring-tight curls! The color of honey. The blue eyes that were almost ready to turn gray. The tag on the wrist. Number two. The tag of her own unbleached gown? Number two!

"Give me!" cried Lilly, on a sudden mounting note that left a little resonance like a plucked violin string.

"Right the first time," cried the nurse, lifting the second from the end, "and a little beauty she is."

That little living ball of head in the crotch of her arm! She leaned forward to the flameless heat of it, her lips moving and wanting to speak.

"What is it, dear?" asked the nurse.

She moved them again, but still silently.

The nurse bent lower, her ear to the pillow.

"Now what is it, dear? Say it again."

This time through the veil of a whisper she could hear quite clearly:

"Zoe."

Book Two
THE GRAPE

CHAPTER I

There were vagrant little streams of water, released by thaw, hurrying along against the curbs of Second Avenue, the absolutely impeccable spring day that Lilly Penny walked out of the Hanna Larchmont Hospital into the warm scented bath of its sunshine, a blanketed bundle in the crook of her arm that mysteriously seemed to animate the nap of the wool, lifting it and suggesting the little life it enfolded.

She felt strangely light and giddy that life could have gone clattering on outside those dim weeks of hers inside the walls.

She had gone down in a dark, a fantastic hiatus in her scheme of things, and it was incredible that out here were street cars still clanging for right of way, pedestrians weaving in and out the great tapestry of a city day, factory whistles splitting asunder with terrific cleavage the fore--from the afternoon. There was a hurdy-gurdy rattling tinnily through the morning that must have played on uninterruptedly through this strange demise of hers.

School children, the air raucous with them, sped home for luncheon through streets that already smelled of sun on asphalt. She had never really noticed them before. That little fat girl with the braids. How pretty to loop them up that way behind each ear with bright red bows. She pressed against the little warm life at her bosom. She felt throaty with laughter, and the tears of a delicious weakness that made her ache to lie down somewhere in this sun, close to the soft bearing earth whose secret she knew now, and open this bundle. Hers! It was the first moment of her actual ownership. Reality was reclaiming her from that unreal realm of doctors and nurses and the dozy detached period of her convalescence.

She wanted to run with her living loot to some quiet corner and open it up. There was a little square of park with a municipal-laid-out bed of tulips across the street, but its benches were crowded with humanity, like sparrows sunning themselves on a wire, and the winding of its asphalt paths swift with the hurry of all the strangely uninterrupted world outside.

She hurried toward Seventeenth Street--could have run, in fact, such a resurgence of the old vitality was upon her. Before one of the private houses a rheumatic-looking oleander was in the supremest moment of its full bloom. It lit up the old street as if a bride had donned her veil there. Outside the cleaning establishment were two stretchers of lace curtains sunning themselves against the wall.

Lilly hurried up the stoop and pulled out the bell that rang dimly in one of those subterranean retreats peculiar to landladies.

Mrs. McMurtrie herself opened the door, as usual her great hands steaming and swollen with suds.

"Well?" she said, her arm immediately flung up to the virago's akimbo and her foot sliding in between the door.

In an agony of anxiety over possible exclusion, Lilly's words came so fast they hardly allowed for the coherence of spacing.

"How do you do, Mrs. McMurtrie? I've returned and I'm fine. I'm so sorry about that--that night and the trouble I must have caused you. Thank you for sending my bag after me. It's a girl. She's the best little thing, Mrs. McMurtrie. Doesn't cry at all. I'll only be wanting her with me for a few days until I can get her placed somewhere near me, so I can spend evenings and Sundays with her. I've such plans! I'm ready to take a position again and forge right ahead. If I might have the old room, Mrs. McMurtrie, I promise you that you won't know she's in the house these few days. It won't mean one thing in the way of extras for you, but I'm willing to pay more. Nothing except a little alcohol stove, and if your little girl could watch her for an hour or two once in a while, when I'm out, I'll pay her, too. Gladly. My bag is at the hospital. I'll send for it--"

"Be saving your breath," cried Mrs. McMurtrie, flinging her gesture upward with a cluck of the fingers. "I wouldn't give that for your yarn! You're a hussy, from the looks of the whole business, and I've a mind to be suing the railroad station for the sending of you to me. You mentioned the husband of your own free will. Your husband! Faith, and not so much as a relation turning up to be with you in your trouble. Husband! You'd better be going and telling that to the Home for Indigent Girls. Your husband! Bah!"

To a door slammed full in her face Lilly stood there for a stunned instant, hugging at her bundle. She would have liked to crumple up, to have felt the earth open and drag her down to a merciful oblivion, but after a while she turned and walked down those steps, fumbling with her free hand for an address she had applied for at the hospital information desk, against possible emergency.

The slip of paper read Nineteenth Street, almost in a straight line from where she stood. It was a morose, lean building, only two windows wide and five stories high, with a porcelain sign above the bell, "ROOMS." A wrinkled pod of a woman opened the door.

"I'm looking for a room for myself alone except for a few days until I get my baby placed--"

"Nothing," answered on the click of a closed door.

With her lips almost ludicrously lifted to stimulate the crescent of a smile, Lilly descended. There were passers-by and one or two of them turned for another glance, and more than ever she kept the smile looped up.

Then she instituted a campaign down one side and up the other of two blocks of Nineteenth Street. Finally there came a whimper from the depths of the blanket, and a light and coughy little cry against and into her heart.

She stood on the corner, arguing with herself for a clear brain, the easy fatigue of weakness beginning to descend and a queer unsteadiness of limb setting in.

"Don't lose your head, Lilly," she admonished of self. "There is a way, only you haven't yet struck it. Don't let your brain feel trapped. Keep cool. Quiet. Dove. Peace. Cathedral. Sweet and low. Sweet and low. Neugass. No. Gertrude Kirk. No, no! If only Mrs. McMurtrie--Indigent Girls--No--no--no!"

However, after a while she did turn back through toward Second Avenue, her feet quickened with a destination she could not bring herself to admit, and so she loitered, inquiring at three more front doors which had now come to have an angry scowl for her as she mounted their front steps.

Between a Home for Lithuanian Aged and a Swedish bakery and lunch room that she had more than once frequented, a black-and-gold sign spanned what at one time had been the noncommittal front of a stately residence--"Nonsectarian Home for Indigent Girls."

Ascending these steps, she could feel the glance of every passer-by boring into the very back of her head, awls crawling through and through her. She tried to drag her hat down over her eyes. Her black velvet sailor, modish enough when new, had suffered somewhat in the hurried packing off of her things after her. The buckram rim, misshapen from too close quarters, flared rather outlandishly off her face, so that after she had pulled the bell she stood with her back to the sidewalk, while the sign above seared into her.

Induced by the warmth of the day and the bundle of blanket she carried, a pox of perspiration had burst out on her face, but the little whimperings against her heart had died down so that she dared not risk the jolt of reaching for her handkerchief.

She was admitted finally into one of the large salon parlors that had lost its beauty as a woman can lose hers. Stripped of the jewels of crystal chandeliers, long mirrors, and glittering floors, it remained now a gaunt strip of room, divided by a low fence and swinging gate into office and waiting room.

There were long windows that looked out upon the polyglot of Second Avenue, which even then, over a not quite abandoned elegance, was donning its Joseph's coat of seventeen nationalities and dining, bartering, and gesticulating in as many languages.

On a strip of bench between the windows Lilly sat and waited.

The movement of the room coagulated about the figure of a woman seated at a desk on the office side of the partition. Girls, to Lilly it seemed a whole phantasmagoria of identical ones with short hair and eyes none too young, passed in and out of the little swinging gate. Suddenly it struck her, with such a wrench that she almost cried out, that here was no illusion. They were uniformed, these girls. In dark-blue cotton stuff, with three rows of white tape running around the skirt hem and white bone buttons up the back. Through the doorway one of them was washing down a flight of stairs, raising a cold, soap-and-lye smell. Another, with a splay smile that was terrible as a wound, wiped in and out among the spokes of the banisters, her face as without muscle as a squeezed orange, and smiling without knowing that it smiled.

Sitting there with her bundle closer and closer to her heart, Lilly closed her eyes to that smile.

Above all, she knew that she needed to keep clear, and yet across the swept horizon she tried to create, silhouettes of thought such as these would move, fantastic as cloud shapes.

"Who am I?" And then, with her old untrained probing after reality: "How do I know I am not dreaming? Where am I going? What is it I want? How terrible! Me, Lilly Becker. This place is like the poorhouse at home, that time the High School sociology class visited it. Zoe, are you real? Mine alone! Not his. Mine. You must be the miracle and show me the way, Zoe. You shall be me plus everything that I am not. To have missed the ecstasy of you is not to have lived. If Auchinloss could hear me now. Who knows? I may, yet. What if I am like Joan of Arc, heeding a vision, only I don't know which way the vision is pointing. Funny. Oh, but I'm going to clear the way for you, Zoe. No Chinese shoes for your little feet or your little brain. Free--to choose--to be! That's the way I'll rear my daughter. My daughter! Queer I never think of him, her father. Zoe--what if you don't want to be saved from what I'm saving you. The fatness--the sedentary spirit of--out there. But you are me plus everything that I am not. You will want to be saved. You will."

It was out of this limbo that Lilly was finally summoned, through the little swing door to an empty chair beside the desk.

She thought she had never beheld such eyes as were turned upon her through polished eyeglasses with the complement of a wide black-ribbon guard. They were the color of slate and cleaned for impression. The eight cases that had preceded Lilly were gone from them just as the eight cases to follow would erase one by one.

"Sit down," she said. Then, "Girl or boy?"

"Girl."

"Name?"

"Zoe. Oh, you mean my name? Let me explain. You must understand that I am not--indigent. I am looking for a room. I've just come out of the hospital with my little one, and you have no idea how difficult it is to find lodging where there is a child."

"What is your name?"

"I--I must beg of you not to--to take an attitude toward--"

"If you want me to help you, my dear, you must trust me. What is your name?"

"Lilly. Your files won't help you. I'm not on record--that way. Lilly Parlow for professional reasons, but I want her christened by her full family name--"

"What is your family name?"

"Why, Lilly--Becker--Penny."

"Your last address?"

"You mean?"

"Where did you sleep last night?"

"I told you. Hanna Larchmont Hospital. I received my discharge to-day."

"Is the father of your child your lawful husband?"

"Indeed, yes!"

"Where is he?"

"Out West--where I came from."

"Exactly where?"

"D-d-denver, I think."

"Why are you here and he there?"

"Oh, you mustn't question me like this! I left him of my own free will, after I found I had made a mistake. I am not asking anything of you. I can pay. I want a room for me and my baby, for a few days until I get her placed. I can make certain arrangements for her and take up my work again."

"What is your work?"

"I am a singer."

"Where are your friends?"

"I have none."

"You are quite sure that this man whom you call your husband--"

"I won't be talked to in that tone."

"Of course, you realize that you are a highly specialized case."

"Do these institutions merely function as machines? Is no provision made for the exception? Rent me a room for me and my baby. I will pay you in advance. See, I have five five-dollar bills in my purse. I must have a place to sleep and I won't leave here unless you forcibly eject me. I must have my luggage; it is still at the hospital."

"How is it they did not help you there to make further provision for--"

"I didn't explain. It seemed inconceivable that I could not find immediately lodgings."

"I see," said Lilly's interrogator, with the air of seeing not at all. "Your case does not come under our kind of jurisdiction. Our girls are unfortunate mothers who are cared for here until such time as arrangements can be made to place the child. But no girl is entitled to our nursery and infirmary service for more than four consecutive weeks, and then, as I said, only in the event of unfortunate motherhood."

"Can only the unmarried mother be unfortunate?"

"I hardly care to discuss with you the wisdom of our policies."

"But you must," cried Lilly, now thoroughly beside herself. "What about the girl who would rather fight out her own destiny than live through the miserable and immoral--yes, immoral--process of a marriage that she realizes has been a mistake? Is there no provision for the woman who hasn't a man-made grievance against society? Who simply wants her one-hundred-per-cent-right to live? Women are coming to demand it more and more, that right! I venture to say that ten years from now they will be voting themselves that right. Now we're like a lot of half-hatched chickens pecking through the shell. I've pecked through! My daughter may live to see them all pecked through."

"Really, I can't see--"

"To-day a woman on her own with a child has only one meaning. I've been treated like a leper. Suppose, for argument, my child hadn't had a legitimate father. All the more reason a hand should have been held out to us. But I'm not asking anything. A night's lodging, madam, for which I can pay. Here it is in advance. I'm not going to leave!"

The child was whimpering now lustily and wanting to lift its little body from the long confinement of wrappings. There were tears and anger and a brilliant sort of challenge in Lilly's voice and in her glance that seemed to dart and glance off the starchy shirt waist of the figure behind the desk. She sat clicking her pencil against her teeth, eyes averted, as if to galvanize herself against a personality that dared to intrude itself through a "case."

She openly regarded her work, this Miss Letitia Scullen, who was one day to lay down her life valiantly enough at the altar of typhus in war-stricken Rumania, as an exact science. Indigency, like typhus, was a pandemic which must ultimately respond to an antitoxin. It was as if her forty-seven charges were sick, and she reading the blood test of indigency, prescribing in toto.

"If you are what you say you are, then you are not entitled to the benefits of this home. Our girls here receive absolutely collective treatment along lines worked out for their general needs. Your case is an isolated one. You are not in need."

"But please, please, please, is there no need except that covered by vice? Can you not conceive of a plight being all the worse because there is no provision for it?"

"It is unthinkable that a woman like you, of evident refinement and education, should find herself in the predicament you describe."

"Then thank God for being a rebel, if it will make you ponder on what is new, untried, and not according to formula. There are only two kinds of women you social workers recognize. The sheltered ones and the unfortunates. What about the woman who is neither, but merely out on her own? I try to meet life as an individual and not as a woman. What happens? Doors slam in my face. I can't buy a night's lodging for the child in my arms. It sounds like a thirty-cent melodrama. And now you, whose life study is life--I tell you I won't be turned off. You must take me in."

"It's very irregular."

"I'll pay."

"We don't accept paying inmates. You may make the institution a present if you so desire. I'll put you up in the infirmary--it happens to be empty; and you may have the use of the nursery equipment adjoining, and there is a practical nurse in the house. Understand that this is entirely outside the regulations of the institution and I must ask you to make different arrangements as soon as possible."

"Thank you," said Lilly, ashamed to be grateful and the tears pressing against her eyeballs. "Oh, my dear, thank you! Thank you!"

And so it came about that in a room of five white cots and three barred windows, with the aid of a practical nurse and a tiny gas stove on a tin mat, Lilly prepared her daughter for the night.

In her bag, lugged over from the hospital by one of the uniformed girls, was the little layout, parting gift of the institution, including a machine-stitched flannelet nightdress that Lilly could have wept over as she fastened the thick button at the throat.

Still, with the chapped-faced nurse moving about the bare, ugly room on her everlasting mission of efficiency, diluting the formula to just the proportion required, rubbing the little bud of a body with coarse cornstarch, the sense of ownership did not descend upon Lilly.

She wanted to feel this new estate of hers. In all the three and a half weeks there had never been a moment of privacy, to give reality to this pink-and-blue-and-yellow bloom that had somehow flowered from the tree of her being.

She wanted the quiet to reconcile this new, this terrible, this throat-throbbing sweetness with the Medean fury which had flung her, a shuddering, choking mass upon that rooming-house floor. She wanted to feel again and again the quick, ecstatic brash that could race in a wave over her when she held this warm rose of life to her breast.

At just before nine there was a wordless round of inspection from the white starched shirt waist surmounted with the spectacles and the black-ribbon guard, a final look-in from the nurse whose face was Swedishly blond and pink from chapping, a bottle of milk placed in the small refrigerator, and the little bundle on the pillow covered with an extra thickness of murky blanket.

At nine o'clock the lights went out just as Lilly had slid into her own gown. She tiptoed to the door, barefooted, locking it and thereby violating a rule of the institution. There must have been a moon somewhere behind housetops, because through the three shadeless windows a sort of gleam whitely powdered the silence.

She was suddenly full of fear there in the darkness and the aloneness, and ran over to the cot for the miracle of that soft body to her flesh. She lifted it from the nest of coarse pillow, even in sleep the tendril of a little finger closing about hers.

There were crisscross shadows on the floor, cast there by the iron bars at the windows. Her child lay asleep in an institutional garb of charity. The father of that child, ignorant of its very existence, was at that moment, and at a distance of one thousand miles, adjusting a new rubber stopper to the bathtub in the home he shared with his parents-in-law.

On one of the empty cots the rather silly silhouette of Lilly's hat, its buckram rim sadly broken, persisted through the gloom. Her shoes, in a little attitude of waiting beside a chair, lopped slightly of a tipsiness induced by run-over heels. In the jumble of changing hands the black valise of her underwear, handkerchiefs, and baby garments had disappeared, so her little washed-out chemise, quite dainty, hung drying over a table edge.

Outside the Home for Indigent Girls a city that took absolutely no reckoning of Lilly wove its pattern toward another to-morrow.

She was alone with the first realization of her child, in a moment that might have shaped itself to crush her. She felt a throbbing that seemed to make a rush for her throat. She sat down on the bed, leaning over until her body formed a sort of cave about the child. She had a sense of the power to strangle both their lives out there in that strange darkness. An old fear leaned out at her.

"Am I mad?"

More and more the sense of wanting to strangle flowed over her.

"Here--to-night--now!"

A cry leaped up under her pressure, startled, and with a stab of pain in it.

She swooped the little squirming burden up under her chin; she buried her head into the warm froth of curls, the light wind of her laughter suddenly sweeping the room.

"Mother's darling! Twiddle-de-darling. Moonlit flake! Beautifulest. Zoeist flower in the world. Mine alone! Alone mine! Oodle-de-dums. To-morrow! To-morrow!"

*   *   *   *   *

There followed for Lilly a week of scars, each exactly as deep as the day was long.

First, the heartbreaking business of giving over her child to the chappy-faced nurse and a rear room of nursery hung in the odors of formaldehyde and lined up into a ward of white iron cribs, each screened in with a clothes horse of little flannel garments of a thickness that wrung Lilly's heart.

There were now two additional occupants--a poor, top-heavy infant with a fourteen-year-old mother, father unknown, and the teething baby of one of the blue-uniformed inmates whose routine allowed her periods of the day to nurstle her child.

That was the wrench that began each day. To abandon the pink-and-white bloom that slept all night without crying in the cove of her arm, to the grayness of a nursery that should have been pink and white and sweetly fragrant with powders and puffs and the rosy kind of tufted coverlets with scent between them that her mother had once sewn over with bowknots for the Kemble baby.

She was guilty of extravagances that ate menacingly into the four remaining five-dollar bills. Against the protests of the practical nurse she promptly discarded the long muslin swaddling dress, whose superfluous length wound around the little feet, purchasing three short and sheer ones, also a doll-size toilet set painted in little clumps of forget-me-nots. The hair brush had a thick, soft nap which would spin out her child's curls into a cloud of gold. They really were the color, these curls, of a jar of strained honey seen through sunlight. It was as if she could never tire of feeling them wind to her finger.

The nurse she kept placated with tips in outlandish proportion to her funds, and often a memory of that dip of lip curving terrifyingly across her consciousness would scurry homeward to this gray-and-black abode of theirs, which only contained them on a tolerance that day after day seared deeply into her being.

Slowly but surely her none too immaculately shod feet ceased their pilgrimages to the agencies. She did apply one sultry morning in answer to an advertisement for a "refined indoor entertainer, city work," only to find the usual fee exhortation thinly backed by promises. For the most part she marked off at her breakfast table in the adjoining Swedish lunch room, under the newspaper heading, "Help Wanted, Female," the demands for stenographers, companions, hat models, and, on one occasion, for a cashier's vacancy in a Madison Avenue florist's.

A persistent streak of circumstances seemed to prohibit her success. Upon three occasions it happened that she waited all morning in a line, only to see the applicant directly in front of her chosen for the position. At the florist's shop, bond was required. A lawyer in the Flatiron Building asked her to type a specimen letter for him, and laid heavy lips on the curl at the nape of her neck as she bent to his dictation. R.L. Ginsburg, of the Ginsburg-Flatow Millinery Company, engaged her services, and kissed her squarely on the lips to seal the bargain.

The straight line of those lips had undeniably softened. She walked about with them usually moist and slightly open, and the arch of her brows very high. She had softened ineffably, like a ripened fruit; was more liable to the backward glance of the passer-by.

During these days that were lifting now, each its frankly lashing tail of terror, there were smiles all along the way for Lilly--old faces smiling at and young faces with her, often to the assuagement of the tightening knot of terror at her heart.

With her trick of mind that could close itself against any concern beyond her immediate future, her one burning desire was for a competency, to be earned preferably at stenography, since that would leave her evenings free, and which would tide her over these first weeks of difficult readjustment. To find and afford for this amazing liability of hers the kind of temporary asylum that would set her free for the scheming out of her new cosmos.

She found out, at the instance of the practical nurse, a sort of semi-private institution on Columbus Avenue, but a trip through the wards and nurseries sickened her. There was a score of little blue gingham dresses, dingy fabrics that seemed to darken childhood, flapping on a rear clothes line, and one two-year-old child lay asleep on a step, his little white frock, with black anchors printed into it, furiously smeared, and one hand clutching a sticky gingersnap.

She did not even inquire further, but got out quickly, trembling.

The proprietor of the Swedish bakery gave her an address of a Mrs. Landman, a practical nurse who might consent to board the infant of an employed parent. So on the very day of the lawyer's encounter there was another sickening journey to what proved to be a tenement in West Fifty-third Street. The newel post to the entrance was defaced with obscene handwriting, the hallways were like cellars, and there was a sign in the window, "Madam Landman, Midwife."

She did not linger to ring the bell, but worked her way downtown again, toward the lawyer's office *via* the florist's establishment, always with an eye to minimum car fare.

That night she lay awake the night through. Another bed in the infirmary was occupied. One of the girls had spilled scalding tea along her arm, and all night to her groanings Lilly lay staring into the darkness, her child so in the cove of her arm that its slight breathing fanned her flesh.

It was one of those long, calculating nights full of alternatives no sooner contrived than rejected. Only one state of surety came crystalline out of it.

There was no going back.

Twice she rose and, with much of her old revulsion curiously gone, greased the scalded arm by the puny aid of a night light that flowed in from the hall when the door was opened.

At five o'clock her child began a lusty paean to the dawn. She heated the milk and held the warm bottle tilted until it was emptied with the strong, deep draughts that delighted her. There was distinctly more gold out day by day in the ringlets, and the eyes were turning gray and could fill blackly with pupil.

After that Lilly sat in her nightdress beside the window, her eagerness for the day allayed to an extent by her rising sense of panic. She tried to lay her despair. Unthinkable that this new day, dawning so pinkly over chimney pots, would not prove itself a friend in her great need. By eight-thirty, at the instance of a newspaper advertisement, she was the first applicant at the Acme Publishing Company, East Twenty-third Street, a narrow five-story building with ground-floor offices and a tremor through it from the champ of presses.

She obtained this time from a woman who accepted her lack of reference rather negligibly.

She, too, asked her to compose a specimen letter acknowledging receipt of a translator's manuscript. She accomplished it with a glibness that brought a flush to her cheek and a smile to the face of her employer.

Lilly thought she had never beheld such spick-and-span efficiency as this woman's. The smooth white hair arranged with a conservative eye to the prevailing mode. The clean, untired skin and rather large, able hands. She made mental note of the crisp organdie collar and cuffs, and was suddenly conscious that her shoes were too short of vamp, and her heels run down because they were too high. A revulsion of taste flowed over Lilly; she hated suddenly the rather tawdry cape piped in red, and mentally retailored herself with a new feeling for simplicity.

Her sinkage of heart at the proffered eight dollars a week was followed by a quick resurgence of vitality at the prospect of the advancement held out.

Her predecessor was being promoted to first reader!

The Paradise Trail, a best seller of the moment, had been written in those same offices during spare moments of one of the proof readers.

The Acme Publishing Company printed paperback editions of translations from the more highly papriked of current French novels. The instinct to write rose in Lilly, the quick flame of her faddism easily aroused. Here was nothing more than a stroke of fate. A long-laid plan for a novel lifted, an entire panorama of resolutions dramatizing themselves.

The easy hours from nine to four. Long evenings at work beside the crib. A ***nom de plume***, of course--Ann something. Ann Netherland. But eight dollars! Her heart tightened.

She had obtained, the day previous, at a Lexington Avenue Children's Hospital she chanced to pass, the address of an institution at Spuyten Duyvil said to be conducted for the children of professional parents, and conducted by Minnie Dupree, an old stock actress remembered by the generation preceding Lilly's for the heavier Shakespearean roles. Her mind leaped to this. Yes, she would return at two o'clock, ready to begin work, and went out into a day warm with sunshine.

A quick resolve formed itself. She inquired at some length in a corner drug store, finally taking a train for Spuyten Duyvil, and fifteen minutes later descended to a little station upon the edge of a park that was brilliant with new green.

More inquiry, the disdaining of a cab, and a twenty minutes' walk along curving asphalt walks with houses far enough back to lose their identities among trees. A sense of summer and hope swept her.

The Dupree place was an old homestead of painted gray brick and ugly with the millwork and gable bulging wall and tower of American architecture in most horrific mood, but a smooth green lawn fell plushily away from it on four sides and it was all Lilly could do to keep from running up the walk. Her child in the sweet air of this fine old spot! Out of her eight dollars a week she could manage four, even five if need be! Her embarrassment was only temporary. Any arrears incurred she could make up later if only it could be arranged.

There were long, cool halls, a sun-flooded kindergarten, an open-air playroom on the roof, and a white-enameled nursery with a row of ducklings waddling across the walls, and Mrs. Dupree herself, who stopped at each stair landing for ready and copious explanation.

She was very corseted, very mannered, and quick to attitudinize. A flight of framed photographs of her followed the staircase upward step by step, in which she registered at a considerably younger period such staple states as Anger, Meditation, Humiliation, Vengeance, Love.

She was still a commanding figure with copper-colored hair that for ten years had wanted to turn gray, a face of furiously combated wrinkles, and eyes deep with black or blackened lashes.

She was the declamatory kind of Lady Macbeth who had stepped into the role flatly on a No. 7 last, rather than from a Juliette who had fattened into the part; that congenial stateliness now thrown completely out of plumb by a violent limp, which, resulting from a railway accident, threw out her entire left leg as she walked.

All the velvet was unconsciously out in Lilly's voice coping with the Dupree extravagance of manner.

"Do you accept them as young as four weeks, Mrs. Dupree?"

"Bless you, dearie, the three weeks' duckie darling of Cissie de Veaux is our youngest at present."

"The comic-opera Cissie de Veaux?"

"Why, honey child, Cissie tells it on herself, she never would have had those ducky twins of hers five years ago if she hadn't known there was a Minnie Dupree Infantary. That is our aim, here, you know. To give the child of superior professional parents the most superior environment that money can buy."

"How much--"

"Elaine Bringhouse, daughter of Harold Bringhouse. Ever seen him in 'Hamlet'? Before your time, I guess! Poor Harold in his day was the best all-around Hamlet in the country. Cry! I wish you could have seen that child's father cry on Elaine's fifth birthday. We don't keep them over five years of age here, you know. Bless her! she's in a road company of 'Little Miss Muffet' now. Yes, indeedy, dearie, that's a book of testimonials there on that table from my children's parents. I take it you're a professional, dearie?"

"Oh yes--yes. Concert and--vaudeville."

"I'm a retired member of the profession myself. A little before your time, bless you, but ask anyone who remembers the Manhattan Stock Company about Minnie Dupree. Why, I played Lady Macbeth opposite Claude Melrose when he was making thirty dollars a week in Fredericksburg Stock. Did he use my cutting of the banquet scene all those years after he struck Broadway? He did. Did he give credit where credit was due? He did not. Oh, my dear, I could tell you tales! The dirt I've had spun me in my day. Maybe Minnie Dupree never saw Broadway, but dirt! If there is so much as a speck on my name, God strike me dead. You voice, dearie?"

"Yes."

"Ah, voice! Ask anyone who knew me in the Manhattan Stock if they remember Minnie Dupree in 'The Silver Lute.' Donald Deland as fine a Macbeth as ever strode the boards! That's his picture there as Iago. I'll show you his little grandchild up in the nursery. 'Min,' he used to say, 'if you'll throw over Edward Dupree, I'll give you a year's voice training at the academy and put you up against Melba.' Ah, my dear, I hope yours is a happy one."

"How much--"

"I threw away a career for the caprice of a man who cast me off like an old glove. Be careful, dearie. Here in the Infantary we never ask questions of parents, believing it the right of everyone to work it out her own way, but look twice before you leap in this life, dearie. I could tell you tales! The dirt I've been spun!"

"Oh, Mrs. Dupree, what a sunny, lovely nursery! How happy I would be if my little girl could come to you here."

"My people want the best, dearie, and I give it to them. I've put the last ten years of my life, since the accident, dearie, to making this home one the profession can be proud of. My nurses and doctors are the best. We only accept them from two weeks of age to five years, but look over that album of testimonials--"

"Oh, this bright, lovely nursery is sufficient--"

"Look, at that one! Ever see such a flower? God love it, that's Esther Deland. Her mother's playing Canada. And this is little Sidonia Vavasour--mother out in one of the highest-priced sketches in vaudeville. Know it? 'The Snake.' Every morning that God sends comes her good-morning telegram to this little mite, just as regular as clockwork."

"I hope, Mrs. Dupree, it isn't going to be too expensive."

"Our service divides itself into three classifications, Mrs. ----?"

"Penny."

"Not Alonzo Penny of the old Trenton Stock?"

"No. You were saying, Mrs. Dupree, three classifications?"

"Yes, I'll give you a booklet, dearie. The rates vary according to age. Up to one, then one to three, and three to five. We've our own cows, sterilizing machines--"

"How much did you say, Mrs. Dupree, up to one year?"

"Six hundred dollars a year, in quarterly advance payments."

They were down again in the wide, cool hallway, little kindergarten voices of children shrilling through from one of the playrooms.

A white nurse passed them, tilting a white perambulator down a flight of white stone stairs.

"Six hundred dollars a year. That--that would make one hundred and fifty dollars--in advance," said Lilly, trying to keep the muscles of her face from quivering.

"Right, dearie."

"I--why--I--I'm afraid--"

"No hurry, dearie. Think it over. It just happens we have a bed on the infant floor right now, so I'd make up my mind right quickly if I were you. Think it over. You know best."

Out on the sun-swept lawn, the white perambulator and the white nurse just ahead, Lilly broke into a run. Tears were beating up against her throat and there was a knot of sobs behind her breathing. She wanted to throw herself on the warm slope of terrace and kick into it. That vision of that large bone button at the throat of that little muslin nightgown somehow became the symbol of all her misery!

After a while she dropped down on a little grassy knoll just off the curving sidewalk, and leaned her head against a tree, large tears, since there was no one to see them, rolling unheeded down her cheeks toward an inverted crescent of bitterly disappointed mouth.

The sun at her back must have acted as a sedative, because, after a while of crying there tiredly, she started up out of a light doze, all her perceptions startled, and began immediately to run back toward the station. Within view of it she met a pedestrian, inquiring of him the time. Ten minutes before two! This set her to running again, so that she fairly flopped with a little collapse on a station bench. A train was just pulling out. There was another at two-twenty.

It was ten minutes past three when she burst into the outer offices of the Acme Publishing Company, her lips trembling with a prepared apology she had hardly the breath for.

An office boy brought her out an immediate message. Her place had been filled at five minutes past three.

All the way down Second Avenue she was inclined somehow to laugh. She found herself finally in the Swedish bakery and lunch room, ordering, without appetite, but with a growing sense of need of food, a dish of rice pudding and a cup of coffee. She broke into the only remaining bill in her pocket, leaving a five-cent tip beside her saucer, and pouring, with quite a little jangling, one dollar and eighty-five cents back into her purse.

In the hallway of the Home she encountered Miss Scullen, hurrying with a sheaf of papers in her hand.

"Oh yes, Lilly, I want to speak to you."

"Yes?"

"Have you made different arrangements? You know it is highly irregular your remaining on."

"I am expecting to take a position and get baby placed any day now, Miss Scullen. I've just returned from Spuyten Duyvil, where I have something very good in view. If you could see your way clear to let things run on a few days longer, Miss Scullen?"

"Not beyond next Tuesday evening. It is very irregular and I've a board of directors' meeting Wednesday."

"Yes, Miss Scullen, not beyond Tuesday evening."

When Lilly entered the infirmary the smell of iodine smote her queerly and with an unnamable terror. Her child lay sleeping on a pillow hedged in with a chair, and, bending over, the aroma struck her squarely and with a close pungency. There was a great yellow stain on the little forehead, a welt rising and purpling through it. Even the honey-colored curls were stained with a great blotch of the vicious greeny yellow, one little eyelid swelling.

With a cry somewhere from the primordial depths of her, Lilly snatched up the pillow, rushing with it and its burden to the door, kicking it open in a gale of terror, her voice tearing down the hallway.

"Help! For God's sake--quick--help!"

The nurse came rushing with a stack of sheets in her arms, and in an instant the corridor was a runway of blue-clad girls, ready, even eager for stampede, and finally Miss Scullen herself pushing through.

"My baby! What has happened to her! Quick--my child!"

With immediate realization of the situation, the nurse pushed her red-elbowed way through the tightening congestion, her voice strident above the dreaded hum of panic.

"Get back to your room. It is nothing. The child fell off the bed and bumped its head. Get back, every one of you. I painted the bruise with iodine. It's nothing but a bumped head. Back, I say!"

There was a blur before Lilly's eyes that waved like a red flag, and her voice shot up to a shriek.

"You've hurt her terribly! You! Devil! Pig! How dared you! You've pinched her! too. I know now what those little blue marks are from. Her head! Her little eye! I could kill you! Devil! Pig! You let her fall! I could kill you!"

Through the snarl of the corridor Miss Scullen emerged, her lips very thin and her voice a steady sedative to the rising murmur.

"You get your things and get out! Leave the child, if you want, until you find a place, but you get your things. You thankless, ungrateful girl. You were taken in here on sufferance and against my better judgment. This is the reward which comes from placing myself liable to censure from my board of directors. Girls, go back to your rooms at once and forget this wayward girl's disgraceful scene. Now you go!"

"Indeed I'll go! But leave my baby here? Not likely! Why, what's one baby's brain more or less to you? One case more or less for your filing cabinet, that's all. If I were one of these poor girls and found myself stuck in one of these places that screams out their indigence above the very doorway, dresses them in the blue calico of indigence, and then seals and stamps indigence all over them, I'd show you what real indigence is, once you insisted upon stamping me with it. But you're not going to make an indigent out of my baby. No, you're not! No! No! No!"

She was presently marching down the street with her head high, her eyes black with iris, a bag in one hand and the bundle of her child clutched under her chin.

She did not heed where she was going, but as she tramped she was saying audibly over and over again:

"My baby. My baby. My baby."

CHAPTER II

She was not afraid. The blood was rocking in her veins like a sea, and she was raging with an anxiety that mounted as the heliotrope dusk, turping out sky lines, began to blow in like fog through the narrowness of the cross streets.

But neither was she alone. That was the miracle of her state. That peculiar living magnetism was through the blanket she carried and in a current along her arm. A lusty little storm of crying rose once, quite suddenly, and she kissed down into the pink little mouth that was full of the breath of life--her life.

There were three bottles of still warm milk in her bag. She fumbled for one, kneeling right there on the sidewalk, jerking out the stopper with her teeth and fitting on the rubber nipple. The little lips closed over it with the pull and strong insuck of breath which never failed to thrill her.

She was sobering, though, slowly and surely into a state of panic. At Broadway the swirl of the dinner-bound was already tightening. Lights began to pop out in the tall, narrow office and loft buildings of the vertical city.

She boarded an uptown car, counting, and truly enough, upon the chivalry of the mob toward her burden, for obtaining an immediate seat. At West Fifty-third Street she alighted into a day gone two shades darker. A stiffening breeze blew in from the river, whipping up the odor of garbage from curbs. A group of dirty children were building a bonfire of some of these slops and bits of flying paper, lending a certain vicious redness to the scene.

She thought suddenly of Page Avenue at this hour of pinkish mist. The little patch of front porch with the green chairs and tan-linen covers.

"O God, what have I done!"

The window with the midwife's sign was dark and there was a little coagulation of bareheaded women on the steps. They parted to give her passage, their babel immediately resuming after her.

The hot, sour smells of the hallway smothered her, but she fumbled for the bell, plunging her hand into the damp, clinging gauze of a cobweb that sent her back shuddering. What proved to be Mrs. Landman herself opened the door upon a rushing smell of hops and a cookery and a glimpse of violently disordered interior. It was not so much the furiously stained figure that sent Lilly a step backward, but a black flap tied over one eye and knotted at the back of her head struck her as so unutterably sinister that without a word she turned and, with her head charging the way for her, ran out through the hallway, through the group on the stoop, and the entire length of the block, catching a downtown surface car that stopped for her after it had started.

She was palpitating with the kind of fear that gave her a sense of fleeing through a dark corridor with some one at her heels, and so rode on until her breath caught up and she could relax into a grateful sort of inertia.

At Forty-second Street, on a sudden impulse, she left the car, hurrying into Grand Central Station. In its undress of semicompletion, the swirl of home-going commuters caught her, so that she was swept down a temporary runway and shunted finally into the waiting room. At its far end the "Matron" sign still hung at right angles. She hurried to it, and to her relief was met by a new face above the gray-and-white uniform, rather little and old and framed kindly in white. There was a small boy asleep on the couch this time, and the usual frowsily tired traveling public relaxed against various of the chairs.

"I want to leave my baby here until I get in touch with friends who have failed to meet me."

A quick suspicion of foundling crossed the old face.

"We don't take the responsibility of infants."

"But this is urgent. I must locate my friends in Brooklyn. I cannot find them in the telephone book and evidently they have not received my telegram."

"We don't do it."

Then Lilly went gallantly down to her last handful of change, all but a ten-cent piece.

"She's the best little thing. Sleeps the night through. I've two bottles of prepared food here in my bag. Her next feeding time is at ten and her next at six--"

"We don't keep infants for nothing like that long, madam. I go off duty at seven and--"

"I haven't any intention of leaving her that long, just until I get in touch with my friends."

With the mound of change ingratiated into the old palm and the little bundle transferred to arms more or less reluctantly held out for it, Lilly lifted back a corner of the blanket.

"Wait until nice lady sees mother's beautiful, then she'll be glad to watch over her."

Mysteriously, it seemed to Lilly, there was nothing of the button nose so peculiar to infants about her child. Its was tipped with character; so, too, the little mouth in the firm way it had of closing.

"Say, but ain't she a beauty!" capitulated the matron.

"Isn't she! Isn't she!"

"Look at them curls. You ought to enter her in a show, ma'am."

"You will see to her carefully until I return, won't you? She sleeps that way always, sweetly and deeply."

"Why, I'll sit and rock her myself this very minute."

When Lilly went out into the darkness there were the ten cents in her bag and the blurry outline of things she finally laid to hunger. She walked downward for some blocks, finally entering a Third Avenue lunch room and ordering a ten-cent bowl of beef stew. She took it from a tablespoon like a thick soup, its warmth flowing through her and dissipating a chilly discomfort. But her face still felt rather drawn, and, regarding herself in the pink net-draped mirror, she took to rubbing her cheeks, an old, schoolgirl device against pallor. She was quite becomingly large-eyed from the deadly aching tiredness that lay over her, but otherwise the old whiteness of her skin flowed unmarred and intact, also that unadorned look of nun to her face where the hair left it so cleanly.

Beside her at one of the marble-topped tables a great, hefty motorman in uniform kept finding out her knee and pressing it.

"Stop it," she said, "or I'll call the proprietor."

He drew surlily back, draining his thick cup of coffee and shambling out, chewing a toothpick. At the door he looked back with his lips pulled down, mouthing a filthy epithet at her.

After a while she followed, almost slunk, with a sense of no tip left beneath the saucer, her pace swinging into the indefinable tempo of destination, but more and more indeterminate as she approached Madison Square.

She kept close to Third Avenue, something reassuring in the sidewalk gabble, the air of cheap carnival, the white arc lights over open fruit stands, and the percussive roar of Elevated trains. Presently even Third Avenue would withdraw to over its shops, the sidewalks fall quiet and darken, pedestrians become sinister. She shivered against that lateness; stood for a period outside a bird store, watching a pair of Japanese mice chase their little eternities in a wheel cage. At Twenty-third Street a youth with a prison complexion, a cap pulled down and a sweater pulled up, sauntered out of a pool room, matching his pace with hers, and at once easily colloquial.

"Hello, sweetness!"

Her eyebrows shot up. She could smell, feel, and taste the cheap beer on his breath, and anger rather than fear possessed her.

"Cat got your tongue, sweetness? Where you goin'? Lonesome?"

After a while he fell back, flecked off as it were like a burr clutching for a metal surface.

It was her conviction, many times put to test, that such situations lay within her shaping, and that man took his cue from the yea or nay of her attitude.

At the sight of a crowd tightening about a street corner she edged her way in. The iron plug to a corner sewer had been removed, a policeman and the shirt-sleeved figure of a man prone on the ground, red-faced and arms inserted their length.

"What is it?" asked Lilly, tiptoeing.

"A feller's gold watch rolled down."

"Who'll go down on a rope?" called out the owner.

"I will," cried Lilly.

The crowd turned its face to her.

"I will, for a hundred and fifty dollars--now--here!"

In the derision and boo that went up she escaped, hurrying this time and without uncertainty.

The Union Square Family Theater showed the lighted but quiet front of a performance in progress.

At the stage entrance the old doorman with his look of sea dog recognized her, admitting her with a nod. The titter of music came back through the wings and quick, loud thumps of a tumbling act in progress. The smell of grease paint, like the flop of a cold, wet hand to her face, smote her with a familiarity out of all proportion to her limited experience in the theater.

She wound, unchallenged, up the short spiral staircase.

Through an open doorway of an office that had been refurnished in large mahogany desk, filing case, and a stack of sectional bookcases, Robert Visigoth sat tilted on a swivel chair, his hands locked at the back of his head, gaze and cigar toward the ceiling.

She stood in the doorway a second, watching his perceptions dawn.

"Hel-lo!" he said, finally, uncrossing a knee grown slightly corpulent and his rather small eyes crinkling to slits. "Hel-lo!"

She was arch and laughed back.

"A bad penny, you see."

He swung a chair toward her without rising.

"Turned up, didn't you? Good."

She seated herself, with that coquetry of hers which she could force on occasion, feeling his glance as it ran over her dawning shabbiness as searingly as a flame. It darted on downward to her feet, and because that very day the leather in her right shoe had cracked, showing a grin of white lining, she wound that foot up around the chair rung.

"I took sick--that time," she explained, fatuously.

He lifted her hand, bending back each finger to match his words.

"You are a naughty girl. Why did you run away?"

She sat swallowing through obvious gulps, but increasingly determined to be arch.

"Please--don't," trying to withdraw her hand.

"Come now," he said through a half smile and watching her redden almost to purple, "you don't hate me that badly or you wouldn't be back here."

"I know I don't."

"What?"

"Hate you."

"Good! Now we're getting on."

"I need something, Mr. Visigoth--terribly."

"We're not using that song specialty any more," he said, kindly.

"I've given up that sort of thing, too, Mr. Visigoth. I'm a stenographer now."

"Smartest thing you ever did."

"I--I'm in a little difficulty right now--a money one. That's why I thought if you--Could you use me in the office? I know stenography and typewriting. I--It would be a godsend, Mr. Visigoth. I dislike having to put it so strongly--but my present difficulty is serious--very."

"What's troubling you?"

"I must have an office position. I want my evenings free and I cannot be situated so that I might have to go on the road at any time."

"Married?"

"Why, I--I thought--assumed that you knew I was married from the beginning. I--We aren't together, though; haven't been--"

"Umph!"

"It's just that I'm temporarily embarrassed."

"That was a pretty rough way you left me in the lurch. Those actions don't get a girl very far in this business."

"It was sickness."

He leaned forward to pat her hand, his lids somehow seeming to thicken.

"You're a queer little duck," he said, "but I like you. Always have."

"Then you will, Mr. Visigoth?"

"Well, let's not bother about that now."

"But--"

"There is quite a change taking place in these offices. My brother is coming from Chicago to take charge of the booking end and I am going out there after he comes on, and I'll see if he can use you. Let us talk about you now."

"No. No. I haven't made you understand. That isn't all. I'm in immediate need. So immediate! I need as much as--as a hundred and fifty--two hundred--here, now, to-night!"

"Whew!"

"It is so difficult to explain, but if you would. If you could! I will work it out for you, beginning tomorrow morning. To the last penny. Two hundred dollars advance on any salary you may see fit to pay me, if you would! I'm not afraid to start small. Within a week I'll prove my value to you--that's how I'll slave for advancement. Just two hundred dollars advance on my salary--one hundred and fifty if--"

"Well, well, well," he said, stropping up and down the back of her hand, "that does put a different face on things, doesn't it? I just don't know what to say."

"Say yes. It is only my predicament gives me the courage to ask. But I need money, Mr. Visigoth. Need it. Need it. Now--to-night! I'll pay it back in service. I--"

"Come now," he said, his eyes crinkling again. "You don't mean that, Lilly. I'm a man and you're a woman. I don't want your money."

"I'll go any length for yours."

"What length?"

"Any--you say."

He leaned forward at that and kissed down into her lips so deeply that her neck was strained backward to hurting. She sprang to her feet, wiping her hand across her mouth until her lips dragged, but trying to laugh.

"You hurt."

"That's what I want to do--hurt, hurt," kissing down into and crushing her lips again and again.

"Oh! oh! oh!" she moaned rather than cried, pummeling at his chest.

"Devil," he said, jerking her back to him until the breath jumped from her.

"I--I hate you!"

"Good!"

"I'm not what you think I am. I hate you. I hate--sex. I--"

"I don't care what I think you are. I only know that I want to be the one to wake you up to the knowledge that sex is life and life is sex. Ice maid. I don't care what you are. I know that I like you. I know that I like your lips. Give me."

"Quick, then," she said, trying not to shudder.

*   *   *   *   *

She squirmed from him finally, pushing against him with all her strength.

"Ugh. How I--I--hate--"

"Gad! how I like your lips!"

"Let me go now."

He looked down at her through slits of eyes.

"To the last cent, you said."

"Yes."

"Come, then," he said. "I live alone."

"Please," she said, her palm pat against her mouth and looking at him with streaming eyes. "Please--not that--"

For answer he kissed her again so brutally that she sat down, moaning her shame.

"You're a woman of the world, Lilly. You don't want anything for nothing. Life wouldn't balance up that way."

"But I'll--"

"Yes, yes, I'm going to give you a position, too. Fifteen a week to start with, to show you I mean well by you. You beautiful sleepy-eyed thing!"

"I'm not what you think--"

"All right, I know. Never again after to-night, so help me God! This isn't my kind of thing any more than it is yours. Any position you want in this office to-morrow morning and me off to Chicago for permanent headquarters next month. I'm good pay. Are you? Now? To-night?"

"My hundred and fifty--"

"Two hundred!"

"Yes--I'm good pay--now--to-night!"

CHAPTER III

With a flaying intensity that kept her teeth unconsciously ground together so that when she relaxed their pressure the gums fairly sang, Lilly took up her work in the office of the newly incorporated Universal Amusement Enterprises.

The clerical department occupied a large unfinished room, obviously makeshift, that had previously been used for the storage of stage properties. There were two flat-topped desks, placed so that their swivel chairs faced across a considerable expanse of surface, two bookkeepers' perches also rigged up to meet the exigencies of run-away affairs, and her own little table with its brand-new typewriting machine.

Yet Lilly never entered the rather cold breath of this atmosphere without a sense of haven. It was as if she had turned the key on those areas that lay outside of the immediate present. She could take the dictation of a letter to the printers, or a manufacturer of slot machines for opera glasses, or to a ventriloquist guilty of disorderly conduct behind the scenes, with the whole of her concentration brought to bear upon her pencil point until very often it snapped under the nervousness of her pressure.

Then Robert Visigoth, who dictated with his ten fingertips together to form a little chapel, would invariably wedge a pleasantry into her tightly maintained attitude, but there was a freshly sharpened pencil always at hand in the little patch of shirt-waist pocket, so that even this slight schism was seldom accomplished.

Her work consisted of some correspondence, mimeographing of programs for distribution to orchestra leaders, scene shifters, printers, bookkeeping and publicity department. Quite a bit of communication by wire, letter, and telephone with the Chicago office, and upon one very recent occasion she had been summoned down to the auditorium together with a Mrs. Ida Blair, one of the bookkeepers, for the try-out performance of a sketch, with the request for a written opinion on its box-office value.

Lilly alone had sent in a negative report--"Too sophisticated and not sufficient emotional appeal for vaudeville." On the strength of several opposing yeas, the play-let was booked, and removed after the second performance--a little secret feather which Lilly wore jauntily on a little secret cap.

In these eight weeks a quiescence that was like a hand to the reverberating parchment of a drum had come over her. It was, in fact, as if the whole throbbing orchestration of her universe had stopped as it sometimes can seem to upon the motion-picture screen, leaving the action to click on quietly without the excitation of music.

She had taken, at the instance of Mrs. Blair, a room in an Eleventh Street house. The odor of Bohemia, which is the odor of poverty through cigarette smoke, lay on the hallways. There were frequent all-night revelries reverberated down from the skylight room on the top floor, and one evening a passing group had beat a can-can of invitation on her doorway; but she could lock and bolt herself into her room, a box, it is true, at two dollars and a half a week, but it boasted half curtains of yellow scrim, a couch-bed with a moth-eaten but gay wool cover, and a small square of table with a reading lamp attached by a tube to the gas jet.

She found herself during the routine of her business day looking forward to these long, quiet evenings beside the tiny table. There had been eight unbroken weeks of them, and each Sunday a fresh little mound of sheer garments to be carried out to Spuyten Duyvil. Her old inaptitude with the needle, by no means overcome, hampered her so that her stitches were often wandering gypsy trails to be ripped over and over, and then her fingers leaving little prick stains to be washed out.

She had grown thinner, so much so that a slight jaw line had come out, but the shells were gone from beneath her eyes and it pleased her, when she brushed out her hair before going to bed, to see that its electricity, which had departed for a while, was out in it again, so that it would snap and stand out horizontally from her head. The little spark of a smile was constantly over her face like a mirage before her lips and her eyes and seeming to hover on the very peak of her brows when she arched them.

She liked to stand before her wavy mirror, folding the completed garments and looking back at herself. Newly freed, probably by the great Auchinloss and her daughter between them, from the bondage of an idea, she felt corporeally lighter, and was. The toothache of her being had ceased its neuralgic stabbings.

It was not unusual for her to stand before this mirror before climbing into bed, her mouth bunched to mimetics.

"Zoe, come to mother. *Mother!* Daughter, they're shouting for you! Let me hold your flowers, darling; they'll smother you!... You mean the one with the yellow curls, madam? The valedictorian? That's my daughter!"

All the spots would come out in her eyes, like little "niggers" in a pair of diamonds, and more often than not she would fall asleep then with a crescent moon of a smile lying deeply into her face.

One day, after these weeks of minute fidelity to routine, she was startled somewhat by a request from Robert Visigoth, in the form of a note sent over to her desk, to remain after six to take some dictation. The big temporary-looking office with its absence of partitions and staring lack of privacy had become a paradoxical source of security to her. In all the eight weeks, three of which, it is true, he had spent in Chicago, she had not once encountered Robert Visigoth alone. She had subconsciously developed the habit of peering down the dark stairs that led to the stage door before descending them, and on one or two occasions, when they chanced to pass, had flattened herself rather unduly against the wall. Her comings and goings, whether by maneuver or not, were seldom alone. She and this Mrs. Blair, a sparse, umbrella of a woman with a very bitter kind of widowhood, had formed the noonday habit of taking a dairy lunch of milk and cereal at a near-by White Kitchen and of departing evenings for there, too, since it spelled strong, hot, simple foods and a very superior kind of cleanliness.

It was with a distinct sinkage, well laid over with office imperturbability, that she showed Mrs. Blair the note, saw her stab into her greenish-black bird's nest of a hat and depart alone. Then the office boy; the publicity man, whistling; a clerk or two, and finally a sixteen-year-old girl who pasted clippings into scrap books.

The pleasantly cool summer day had thickened up rather suddenly into the beginnings of dusk, the electric sign down over the theater throwing up a sudden glow through the windows. She sat before her machine, shorthand book in lap, her attitude quiet enough except that her hands, as they clasped each other, showed whitish at the nails, and she would not swerve her gaze by the fraction of an inch, even with the consciousness of a presence behind her.

It was Visigoth at her shoulder, the male aroma of him, a mixture of cigar smoke, bay rum, and freshly washed hands, and the feel of his rough-serge suit very close.

She rose, withholding herself stiffly from his nearness, marveling, as always, at this power of hers to endure him so casually.

"Letters?" she asked.

He placed a knee on the chair rung, tilting it toward him, and leaning across the back at her.

"You funny, funny girl," he said, regarding her intently through the crinkling eyes.

She met his stare in a challenging sort of silence.

"My, what big eyes you have!"

"Please," she said, retreating from the look in his, her weight against the table until it slid.

"Please what?" he rather mimicked, advancing the exact distance of her withdrawal, the smile out on his never quite dry lips.

"Please--don't."

The corpulency which was one day to envelop him like suet was already giving him the appearance of ten years his senior. He had upon occasion been mistaken for the father of his younger brother, and some of Lilly's acute distaste for him, across the slight enough chasm of the seven or eight years between them, was already that of youth for lascivious age.

"Shall I take those letters now--Mr. Visigoth?"

"I would rather take you--to dinner."

"I might have known," she said, rather tiredly.

"What?"

"That you would not keep your word."

"I have though, for eight weeks."

"I thought your promise meant--"

"Ah no. I never broke a promise in my life, but even I cannot be expected to keep one indefinitely with a girl like you within eyeshot."

"That can be easily corrected."

"Come now, I'm giving you your chance here to make good."

"Well then, let me take it."

"My dear girl, never expect the best of us to be more than human."

"I suppose, then, this is to be the regulation, theatrical-manager-dangers-of-a-big-city kind of scene."

"Come now," he said, his voice plushy with the right to intimacy. "We understand each other--Lilly."

She stood silent, flaming her humiliation.

"And I like you for it. If there is one thing to my mind less interesting than another, it is the untempted kind of woman who--"

"I never pretended to you, Mr. Visigoth, that I was what you are pleased to term--tempted!"

"No? But how much more redeeming if you had been."

"Nothing can ever redeem that--night--except--"

"Except?"

"Oh, I don't know--maybe--except--God."

"You funny, funny girl!" he repeated. "I like you."

"I know your kind of liking. You like me for the kind of thing you would protect your wife or your daughter from with all the fury of your little elemental soul."

"I haven't a wife, I haven't a daughter, and I like you."

"No, but you will have presently. Your kind always does and you'll be the ideal family man who telephones home from the office three times a day to see if the baby has taken her cough medicine regularly, and you'll knock the man down that brushes your wife too closely in a crowd, and because of your attitude toward all but your own women you'll suspect every man who even approaches your daughter. In the eyes of the world you're entitled to your wild oats. That's what I am, a wild oat to be sown at your pleasure. If you haven't any letters, Mr. Visigoth, I'm going. I--"

"No," he said, closing his hand over hers. "Don't."

"You force me."

"Nonsense! Haven't I promised to let you be, Lilly? I've respected that promise to the letter, as I always respect a promise. The past is dead, it died with that night. I swear it over again."

"Dead, with your reminding me with every word you utter--every look."

"Nonsense, I tell you! I've treated you like everyone else in this office. Made things easy for you. Helped you."

"And I've tried to justify my position in your office. To hold it by sheer merit so that this--this wouldn't--couldn't happen. And now you--your daring to keep me here like this shows me I've failed."

"You haven't. You've raised the efficiency of the office forty per cent. I'm turning you over to my brother as a prize. I've got you in mind for the booking end of the business. That's what I think of you."

"Oh, Mr. Visigoth, if you knew--if you knew what that would mean to me. I'll give you my best! Let me go on proving to you that I want to stay here to make good on my merits--as man to man!"

"I wish to God I could figure you out."

"I made it clear--that night--"

"But I flattered myself at least that--"

"You hadn't that right. Ours was a cold business deal. So much for so much! I never for a moment pretended otherwise. I was in need. Terrible need. I didn't think when I came to you that you would do business on any other terms than you did."

"I envy the fellow that awakens you."

"Oh, I've been awakened! Awakened to the fact that a woman out in the world has to fight through a barrier of yourselves that you men erect. But I'm not afraid of your barrier. In the last analysis I know, that I have the situation in hand. Every woman has. It is a matter of whether she will or she won't! I had an alternative-- that night. Could have taken it, but wouldn't. Would do the same over again. A man invariably takes his cue. You took yours. Even a street masher takes his cue from the look in her eyes whether he will or won't follow up."

"Right, but public sentiment is all on the woman's side."

"It's worth more to me to know that the situation was in my own hands than it is to play the sensational role of more sinned against than usual."

"You're immense."

Dryly, "Doubtless, from your point of view."

"From any--"

"Now look here. I need this position here more desperately than I ever needed anything in my life. It means the success or failure of something that I've staked every card on, of a fight that nobody in the world would understand--possibly not even myself. But that doesn't change the fact that the situation again is mine. I am in a position now to demand fairer terms than I was--then. I return to work to-morrow only on those terms, Mr. Visigoth."

The veil of light from the sign fell upon her in the rigidity of her pose and pallor. For some reason she was hugging one of the book-shaped letter files, all the black out in her eyes.

He sat down, straddling the chair, his arms across the back and his chin down upon them.

"Who are you?" he said, regarding her with the intense squint of one in need of glasses.

She felt her power over the moment, and with her old slant for it began to dramatize.

"I'm the grist being ground between yesterday and to-day. Sometimes I think I must be some sort of an unfinished symphony which it will take another generation to complete. I am a river and I long to be a sea. I must be the grape between the vine of my family and the wine of my progeny. That's it, I'm the grape fermenting!"

Then she felt absurd and looked absurd and stood there with the quick fizzing spurt of exultation died down into a state of bathos.

"Let me stay on here on my terms, Mr. Visigoth," she finished with a sort of broken-wing lameness of voice.

"What terms?"

"The terms you have been generous enough not to violate up to now. I've the most glorious reason for wanting to make good that a girl--a woman could have. I don't think the career stuff, as you once called it, is rankling any more. I'm suddenly glad and quiet about my job. Let me stay on. Let me make myself indispensable to this growing, interesting enterprise of yours. Why, even watching the letters grow in numbers and importance, and using the little individuality in handling them that you are beginning to allow me, is a game worth playing! I'm like a bad girl who has been spanked by life and is all chastened and ready to be good. If you are the clever business man I think you are, you'll let me stay, Mr. Visigoth, on my terms."

There was a shine to her there in the half light, probably because her eyes were wide and the muscles of her face lifted so that her teeth showed, but not in a smile.

"I played the game on your terms, Mr. Visigoth; now meet me on mine."

"Put your cards on the table, then; no fine flights of speech either. Who are you?"

"I told you from the first I am a married woman, with nothing to be said against my husband except that he was part of a condition that was intolerable to me."

"Where is he?"

"West."

"Stage ambition, eh?"

"Yes or--I don't know. Too many ambitions of all kinds crawling over me like a terrible itch, for God knows what. Fermenting. The grape fermenting! But I'm quiet now. So quiet that sometimes I think I wouldn't change it for even the--the singing wine of fulfillment. I don't think I can make you understand. I seem to have been stretching all these years for--for something my arm isn't quite long enough to touch, and now my child--my little girl--"

"You have a child?"

"A little girl."

"How old?"

"Eleven weeks."

He looked at her across a long silence.

"Good God!" he said, and then again, "Good God."

"Yes," she said, watching belated comprehensions flood up into his face, "that was it."

"You mean you had on your hands that night a--"

"Yes, a three-and-a-half-weeks-old one."

"You were broke?"

"Stony."

"Good God! You--poor--"

"I'm not pleading for your sympathy, Mr. Visigoth. Only a square deal. Will you give it?"

He walked over to his desk, turning on a green-shaded bulb, the clip back in his voice and manner.

"That will be all for this evening, Mrs. Parlow--"

"Penny."

"Mrs. Penny," he said, picking up a random sheaf of papers and not meeting her eyes. "I want you to go over to Newark Monday afternoon and bring back a report on an act over there; and, by the way, you are to begin your new week in the booking department at twenty dollars."

She wanted to speak and her lips did move, but the tears anticipated her, and, blink as she would, they sprang, magnifying her glance, and besides, there were footsteps coming up the flight of stairs that led from the stage entrance, and a young, a lean, a honed silhouette rather suddenly in the doorway, the right side borne down by the pull of a dress-suit case.

"R.J?" Peering into the gloom.

"Good Lord!" from the figure at the desk, leaning forward on the palm of his hand. "That you, Bruce?"

They met center, gripping hands.

"When did you get in, youngster? Didn't expect you for another couple of days."

"Just now. Took a chance on finding you here."

"Another five minutes and you wouldn't have."

"So these are the new diggings?"

"There is your desk."

He deposited his hat on the flat top indicated, his silhouette cutting vigorously into the dimness, particularly the rather heavy double wave to his hair causing Lilly to grope with a vague sense of having seen him before. It was merely a rather remote resemblance to the remote Horace Lindsley, but not for days did she stumble across this realization.

She knew, instinctively, even while she marveled at his youth and the merest and most lightninglike resemblance to his brother, that here was Bruce Visigoth, and what she did not know was that a certain throaty resonance to his voice had a tendency to gooseflesh her and that quite suddenly her eyes were very hot and her hands very cold.

"Well, R.J.," he was saying, and she noticed that his head came up with a fine kind of young defiance, as if a pair of invisible Mercury wings flowed with the sleek nap of his hair, "I'm for taking a chance on the Buffalo lease. I stopped over yesterday and the little theater looks good to me."

It was then Lilly began noiselessly to move toward the door.

"Oh--here--Mrs. Penny. My brother, Mrs. Penny. Sort of secretary on the booking department, and a darn good one."

"How do you do, Mrs. Penny? Mighty pleased," he said, through the resonance that had a little aftermath of a ting to it.

Her five fingers rather trailed along the palm of his hand as he slowly released her.

"Thank you, Mr. Visigoth," she said, smiling up at him with her eyebrows, pressing down her sailor hat, and hurrying toward the staircase.

Outside, the darkness had the quality of cool water to her face. The palm of her right hand and the tips of her fingers were tingling as if they had been kissed.

She could have run before the wind.

CHAPTER IV

From now on for many a month to come, the curve of Lilly's life would have shown a running festoon; six days whose uneventful continuity was bearable because they were looped up by the rosette of the Sundays at Spuyten Duyvil.

When Zoe was two years old this hebdomadal consciousness was already borne upon her. Into her earliest vocabulary, as haphazard as if the words had been dished up out of the alphabet of a vermicelli soup, crept the word "Sunday," mysteriously boiled down to "Nunk," the first time her mother heard it, the pride seeming to crowd around her heart, fairly suffocating her.

As if the luster of this girl child could be any brighter, yet here was the new shine of the mental beginning to radiate through. Nunk!

Was there any limit to this ecstasy of possession? It ran through her days like a song.

It meant that while the home-going six-o'clock rush at Union Square, which of face is the composite immobility of a dead Chinaman, would presently cram into street cars and then deploy out into the inhospitable cubbyholes of the most hospitable city in the world, Lilly, even in her weariness, could be deterred by the lure of a curb vender and a jumping toy dog. There was never a time or a weather that she could pass, without pause, Westheim's Art Needlework Shop on Broadway and its array of linen-lawn dainties, and, remarkably enough, the purchase of the toy dog or a five-cent peppermint cane could send her home with an actual physical refreshment as if she had slept off, rather than cast off, fatigue.

She would line up during the week, Monday's toy dog, Tuesday's peppermint cane, Wednesday's cap rosettes (fashioned out of five yards of baby ribbon at one cent the yard), and so on to Saturday's climax of bootines, and on one occasion a large circular wooden arrangement, a sort of first aid to the first step, which she carried out herself, standing with it on the train platform.

With her three months' running start, paid in advance and duly receipted by Mrs. Dupree, Lilly's weekly expenditures, by the nicest calculation, reduced themselves thus:

```
Room rent. . . . . . . . . . . . . . . . . . . . . . . . . . . . . . . . . $2.50
Car fare (one round trip to Spuyten Duyvil). . . . . . . . . .60
Breakfast (gas-jet boiled egg, an apple, three biscuits from
    a tin, and coffee) . . . . . . . . . . . . . . . . . . . . . . . . . . . .50
Lunch (milk, cereal, sandwich) . . . . . . . . . . . . . . . . . 1.50
Dinner (lamb or beef stew, green vegetable, pie, coffee.
    Tip) . . . . . . . . . . . . . . . . . . . . . . . . . . . . . . . . . . . . 3.50
Laundry. . . . . . . . . . . . . . . . . . . . . . . . . . . . . . . . . . . .75
                                                        -----
                                                        $9.35
```

There were already forty-two dollars and sixty-eight cents hoarded in a little biscuit tin in the depths of her valise, and out of it had come a gift for Mrs. Dupree, a rather interesting relic of an old silver thimble wrought in cunning filigree which she had bought in two payments of seventy-five cents each, and largely by eliminating the pie for a month, from a rapidly diminishing keep-chest of Ida Blair's.

A friendship had sprung up here, which, born out of the merest propinquity, had sent down strong roots into the common ground between them.

One or two nights they had attended the theater together, on orchestra passes given out to them by one or the other of the Visigoths.

One Wednesday evening they saw the "School for Scandal" presented at the Academy of Music, and once, just before the permanent departure of R.J. for Chicago, he had tossed negligently across the desk a single balcony ticket for Eames in "Faust."

"Here is something ought to keep one of you busy this rainy evening."

Ensued a highly feminine parley.

"Mrs. Blair, you take the ticket. Really, I'm too tired and I've some sewing to do."

"Nonsense! You're musical and I'm not. Besides, it will do you a world of good."

"I don't know," said Lilly, her lips giving a sensitive quiver. "I've put it so out of my mind that it might only tantalize."

But in the end she did attend, seating herself, for the first time in her life, in the F-minor, the perfumed twilight of the Metropolitan Opera House, just as the velvet curtains swished sibilantly apart.

Day was breaking, and in all the passion and churchiness of Gounod, the student calls for death, the echoes of human happiness rustling through the background like the scything sound of harvesting.

Lilly could scarcely breathe for the poignancy of sensation. She was all throat. Faust's opening greeting to the dawn, his challenge to happiness, pierced her. She sat forward on her chair, anticipating the lyrical vision of Marguerite, her hands clasped over the handle of her wet umbrella, and her knees crowded up unconsciously about its dampness.

She bought the libretto, humming down into it between acts and leaping ahead to verify her memory of the score.

Poor Lilly, it is doubtful if she was by endowment more than a lovely melomaniac doomed never to emerge from her musical primaries. A mere tonal accord could assail her nostrils like a perfume set to music. And yet her quick ear, though, was not exact. Her capacity for fine vocal distinctions in her own singing had been distinctly limited, and a note landing just this side of itself could drop down into her state of ecstatic coma with hardly a plop. She had neither capacity for exactitude nor tireless fidelity to tone. It made her neck ache. She had never graduated from musical sensation to cerebration; a theme washed her over with all the voluptuous abandon of a Henner sea siren letting the water tickling up the beach to roll over her lightly.

There was unrest in the balcony because Faust was singing through laryngitis and a cloud of fog in his throat. A critic who wrote in terms of elliptical rhythms and tonal arabesques tiptoed out for a smoke. One of those sympathetic fits of coughing swept the house. But Lilly sat hunched in her habitual beatific attitude against the chair back, the old opera flowing back to her in association that caught her at the tonsils.

"Lilly, play that over, the left hand alone."

"Oh, mamma, mamma!"

That blue challis wrapper shotted with pink rosebuds.

"Lilly, play that over."

Eames down there flinging up the "Jewel Song" like a curve of gold. Her place!
She half rose to her feet.

Down in front!

She sat again, but a sudden, an inexplicable sense of wanting to plunge from
the height of the balcony seized her. It had been so long since the old neuralgic
stabbings of spirit. She wanted to jump and had a ludicrous vision of herself landing
down in the cream of white shoulders and crashing through the U of one of those
immaculate shirt fronts. She could have torn and scratched the indestructibility
of her failure and wanted suddenly and terribly to wrap those pearl-twined taffy
braids around the rising throat of Marguerite as she sprayed the auditorium with
the "Jewel Song," a great fire hose of liquid music finding out every cranny.

In the deep-napped velvet of this melodious darkness Lilly rose suddenly, pushing her way out through knee-impeded aisles and a string of protestations.

An usher helped her to find a door. She ran down several flights and into a side
street. A slant of rain met her and she charged into it with bent head and umbrella.
Bubbles with a tap of sleet in them exploded like little torpedoes on the sidewalks,
curbs were rushing water, and Broadway was as black and oily-looking as a found-
ry. She tried to visualize it as she had seen it that first morning from her window at
the Hudson Hotel, pink with sun.

The picture would not conjure, and finally, because her shoes were full of bubbles and her damp skirt clung and hindered walking, she boarded a street car and
sat looking out of the water-lashed windows, her throat full of little moans like the
song of a kettle just about to boil.

When she reached home there was an envelope beneath her door. It contained
a snapshot picture of herself and Zoe taken by Mrs. Dupree one Sunday afternoon.
Still wet, she sat down with it on the bed edge. Against a background of shrub and
stone steps Lilly was little more than a blur, but Zoe, with five little fingers dug into
her cheek, leaped from the picture, all her dimples out.

The mood induced by the opera fell off like a cloak, a warm, easy tear splashing right down on the adorable little face. She wiped it off ever so painstakingly, holding the little print up to the gas to dry.

Then she stood it up on the table so she could gaze down and smile while she undressed, and even placed it on the floor as she leaned down to unlace her shoes. She climbed into bed with it under her pillow, but rose in the darkness to transfer it, against crumpling, beneath the mattress.

She went to sleep right off with a little smile on her lips, as if the picture had kissed it there, but it was many a day, sixteen years, in fact, before she could be induced to enter the Metropolitan Opera House again, and then only in the most crowded hour of her life.

CHAPTER V

Quite a friendship was thriving between Lilly and Mrs. Blair. The older woman had opened the door to her upon that family skeleton, one of which, by the way, lurks in the cupboards of most of us--the unproduced play! This one, a sketch called "The Web," read by Lilly and even placed by her with a written word of appreciation on Robert Visigoth's desk.

He carried it with him to Chicago, mailing it back one day without comment.

"Just the same, there is a corking idea there. You ought to develop it into a long play, Mrs. Blair."

"I will some day," she replied, with a cryptic something in her voice that Lilly was only to understand a year later.

One spring evening, that year later, as she and Mrs. Blair sat in her small room beside the open window that looked out over the twilighted rear of housetops, Lilly was induced to sing, quietly, almost under her breath, sitting there on the floor with her hands clasped about her knees, her invariable shirt waist and dark-blue skirt discarded for a pleasant sense of negligee in a pink cotton-crepe kimono, her hair flowing with the swift sort of rush peculiar to it.

They had just completed, as a relief from the nightly round of lunch rooms, a wood-alcohol meal of canned baked beans, cheese, crackers, and tinned sweet cakes. Even Mrs. Blair, at an age when the years are at the throat of a woman, shriveling it, had opened her blouse at the neck, revealing an unsuspected survival of its whiteness.

Lilly sang "Jocelyn," a lullaby dimmed in her memory by the mist of years and full of inaccuracies. She had last sung it at Flora Kemble's.

It lay on the twilight after she had finished.

"How pretty! Why don't you let one of the Visigoths hear you? It might lead to something."

"Robert V. has heard me."

"Well, I don't pretend to be a judge of music, but considering your youth and looks and when I see the kind of thing that does get across--"

"I know. I used to feel that way about it, too--hot, rebellious--but, somehow, not any more. Strange that it should have taken my child to show me. I realized it last winter when I heard Eames. I simply hadn't it to give, except in desire. Why, her voice--it seemed to climb up around an invisible spiral staircase to the stars; and that wasn't all! There was something so richly colored through it--like the candy stripe through a crystal. I know now--and I'm glad I know--that my ambition was bigger than my talent."

"I suppose that is what you thought about me, too, when you read my sketch."

"No, no. I admit I did think it amateurish, but there is an idea in 'The Web.' Almost as if you had lived it yourself and had written it in blood. Besides, you know the secret of concentration; it shows in your work at the office. I couldn't stick night after night over one of those trial balances of yours. I'd throw it over. I've never in my life really worked for anything. Even as a child I used to cheat myself--move the clock; hadn't that sublime capacity for grind. That was part of the lack. How clear it all seems now!"

"The cruelest clarity in the world is wisdom after the event."

"Oh, but I wouldn't have one thing different! It simply wasn't in me to want badly enough, and therefore I didn't attain. But I know--I know, Mrs. Blair, that there is a logic running somewhere through it all. Nothing has been in vain. I'm out on a highroad now with open running ahead. I'm going to rear her into a super-woman. She is my song, Zoe! There is logic, I tell you, Mrs. Blair--straight through the apparent mix-up. Off somewhere in Corsica a vine is putting down roots that there may be wine in somebody's glass some day. The vine. The grape. The wine."

"The vine. The grape. The wine."

"Don't you understand now a little better, Mrs. Blair, why this poor little fermenting grape couldn't stay on the vine?"

"You've told me so little, dear."

"More than I've ever told a living soul. There's one thought I love to carry about with me about Zoe. She was born out of captivity. No Chinese shoes for her little mind or her little soul or body. I'm vague about it now, just as I'm half crystallized about everything. But this time my will to do is unlimited and unfaltering! Her whole life is going to be a growth toward fulfillment of self. I want life to dawn upon her in great truths, not in ugly shocks and realizations. She is a plant and I am her trellis toward the light. Do you see? Do you? I may be as wrong as you think I am, Mrs. Blair--terribly, irrevocably wrong--but I wouldn't take her back there into that--that--sedentary fatness--I wouldn't--"

A musing sort of silence had fallen into a gloom that was thickening into darkness.

"The more I see of your case, Lilly, the less I understand it. To think of anyone in this world of suffering deliberately bringing it upon herself. Why, my dear, it isn't any of my business, but when I think of those parents of yours out there, comprehending nothing, and that poor bewildered husband of yours, I could cry for them."

"Do you think I don't, Mrs. Blair, whole nightfuls of tears? Why, yesterday at the Library in my home paper I saw a little local notice of my mother's euchre club meeting at our house--it was a knife, somehow--the pain of it--"

"I'm not saying so much about the husband, only, God knows why a woman should throw away a life-time of protection just because a man chews with his temples and--"

"Surely you haven't taken that literally! I only tried to symbolize for you that the unimportant mannerisms that may even delight in one person can become monstrosities in another. Oh, I haven't made you understand--"

"Yes, dear child, you have made me understand this much. What a fine sense of satire the power behind the throne of the world must have. Take me--that first little two-by-four home of mine over in a back street of Newark. Talk to me of freedom! I married to get away from it. Somebody who cared whether I came or went. Somebody who cared enough to want to restrict me."

"Ah yes, but--"

"We had a little house on Dayton Street; must have been a hundred years old, with funny little leaded panes and a staircase rising out of the parlor to a queer old box of a bedroom with slant walls. We painted the floors ourselves and Lon did the doors in burntwood. He had a feeling for the artistic, Lon had. That was the way we met--that was--the way--we--met."

"How?"

"He was a police sergeant then, and I was bookkeeping for the time for Metz Producing Company. Lon used to drop in once in a while for passes. Then he got to waiting for me evenings with little pencil drawings of all the funny things that had happened to him during the day. I was strong for him to get off the force and take up art, but even then, now that I look back on it, I can see that Lon was fed up on propositions that it was driving him half mad to resist. That in itself should have put me on my guard, but it didn't. I don't know why I'm telling you all this--"

"Go on."

"Oh, I must have known in a way that Lon was drinking in his effort to keep his eyes shut to the bribe money that could have come his way. He never came home to me under the influence, but toward--the end--his eyes began to glassen up. I was all for getting his beat changed. You see, it took him down into the gang and red-light districts. More than that, I had my heart set on seeing him off the force altogether. I wanted to keep my position for a year or two after we were married and send him to Paris to study art. I've some cartoons in my trunk. That boy would have made good as--Well, it didn't happen. I blame myself. Marriage made a great baby of me, Lilly. You see, I'd never been coddled in my life--all those years of struggle on my own. Well I just turned soft and he loved to baby me. Why, when I went back to book-keeping I had to learn it all over like a beginner--that's how wrapped up I became in that little home of ours!"

"How long, Mrs. Blair, did you live in it?"

"Fourteen months and five days. It was a tiny place and we didn't have much to spend at first, but what I had I managed to good advantage. Lon hated makeshift. He couldn't get the fun out of simplicity that I could. He wanted to dress me up. He wanted a big house. Big. Everything big. That was his undoing. That's what they called him in the Ring, I learned later, 'Gentleman Lon.' And I never knew there was a Ring! Never knew the filthy inside workings of the graft game existed. That's the way he protected me from everything ugly--from poverty. Me, that had never been protected from either. O God! if he'd only been truthful with me those last few months. I--I can't talk about it--I--"

"Then don't, dear Mrs. Blair, I didn't mean to--"

"He began bringing home more money than was natural, but he always explained it--a tip from a bucket shop on his beat--extra duty. If I had been right strong those days I might have suspected. Once he walked the floor all night, said it was a toothache, my poor boy! and let me fix a hot-water bottle for him. Then two men came one evening and there was some loud talk down in the parlor and I heard words like 'squeal' and 'gangsters.' He told me when he came upstairs that one of them was Eckstein. But how was I to know who Eckstein was? Didn't, until I heard it was he who had been--shot. I--You see, the captain had closed in on Eckstein's place because of a personal grudge, and Eckstein came running to Lon to save him. Threatened to squeal on Lon--on the whole business--if he didn't. Lon was hot-headed--got frightened--lost his head. O God! I don't know what--never will know--"

"Know--what?"

"That evening he stayed home and helped me fix up the nursery. Yes, I was expecting in the spring. That's why he was so for keeping things from me. We painted the woodwork white and gave a couple of coats to a little brown crib I had picked up second hand. He was for buying an enameled one on casters--he loved the best. Next night--next night--he--didn't come home--and at eight o'clock the following morning the extras were on the street--about the killing. Even then I didn't tie up--Lon and Eckstein. O God! God! how could I--"

"Tie up what? Who?"

"He was a cat's-paw, Lilly. Never believe otherwise. My boy was caught and trapped in the filthy cesspool of politics. There are men in this city--men whom I named at the trial, all the good it did me, living and prospering for doing worse than my boy died for. You wouldn't know of my boy, Lilly; you were too young then. The whole country knew him, eleven years ago. Lon Elaine. It's easier Blair; no questions asked. It was the beginning of a cleanup that my boy blazed the way for. He went to the gallows, Lilly--my boy--"

"No! No!"

"He died a gunman. Thank God his child was born dead. But he lies in my heart, Lilly like a saint washed clean. He sinned for love, and because stronger forces than he wanted him for a tool. May every man on his jury live to carry that truth to his grave. He killed in self-defense and he sinned for love. I'll exonerate him in a play, yet! I will! I'll tell them! I'll tell them!"

Told without hysteria, her tale had almost a droning quality on the twilight. She was grim in her tragedy, and her lips were as twisted and dried as paint tubes, yet Lilly crept closer, laying her cheek rather timidly against the corduroyed one.

"Ida Blair," she said. "I see now. 'The Web'! Oh--Ida Blair."

They fell silent, the two of them, dry-eyed, cheek to cheek, drowning back into a long twilight that finally blackened.

"I don't know why I've told you all this. It's been ten years since I've talked it. But your telling me that you threw it all over--that little home out there, and a man that was driving down deeply the stakes of his home--threw it over because the black spot from his collar button made you feel hysterical--Oh, I tell you there is a grin through the scheme of things. A laugh. What old man Metz used to call a belly laugh."

Chin cupped in hand, Lilly stared out into a back yard that was filled with the tulle of winding mist, the lighted rear windows of the houses opposite blurry, as if seen through tears.

"Just the same," she said, her lips in the straight line peculiar to this not infrequent reiteration, "I'd do the same if I had it to do over again."

"How do you know that some day your child is not going to turn upon you with the bitterest reproaches?"

"She won't; she's too much like me. That is why it is going to be something sublime to have the rearing of her. It is going to be like living my life over again the way I once dreamed it. I know even now what she wants, before she puckers up her little lips for it. Of course, you are right--he--they have the right to know. But take the shine off that creature? Clip the wings of her spirit? Fatten her little soul back there in that sluggish environment? She'd hate it as I hated! Oh you must have seen for yourself that Sunday I took you out there. The little live stars in her eyes. The plunge and rear to her little body. Never! She's mine! We two! Out on the open road!"

"I shouldn't want the responsibility of rearing my child in a paid institution if I had better to offer."

"I haven't better! I've proved to myself, Mrs. Blair, to what limit I would go to--to save her from back there. Proved it--horribly! No--no, she's mine. No, not even mine. She belongs to herself. As soon as her little brain is ready to take it in, she shall decide; but until then--she's mine."

"Lilly--Lilly--a father ignorant of his child!"

"They'd suck us back, I tell you! Self-preservation even against family is a first law of life! Owls eat their young! So can human beings feed on the thing they love. It's not these first years would matter. But ten, fifteen, twenty years from now. They would hitch her vision, not to a star, but to a--a tin dipper. You don't understand. You know it seems to me, Mrs. Blair, that most people, women, anyhow, are like great big houses with only half the rooms in use. The mentality closed up and musty from disuse because they have never found or made the keys. I want my child to live roundly--in all her mental rooms. What is the use closing off any part of a house that was meant for light and sunshine? I want her to know the world she lives in from attic to cellar. The good from the bad, so that, knowing the bad, she can love more the good. The right to live!"

"You're for woman's rights. You're one of those suffragists."

"I guess I am if woman's rights mean more breadth, more beauty, more realization of our latent selves. Oh, I don't know what I mean. That's been my curse."

In the darkness Mrs. Blair put up a hand to the sheen of Lilly's flowing hair.

"You poor child! You funny girl. You need--"

"What?"

"The right man to sweep you off your feet."

"I knew you were going to say that. No, you're wrong. I'm not essentially a man's woman, Mrs. Blair. Sex isn't even as big a part of my life as it is of most women's. I can't flirt. I haven't an ounce of coquetry in me. I think I almost hate--"

"You mean you hate what your experience has been. The right man for you, dear, a man with enough of the materialist to hold you in check and enough of youth and vision and ideals to soar with you. No, no, you don't hate him, Lilly."

"Why--why--who?"

"Oh, I've seen it flash between the two of you. I've watched it being silently born. Lilly child, look at me!"

"Why, Mrs. Blair! Why--Mrs. Blair! I've never seen him outside of office hours in my life. I never laid eyes on him until he walked in that night from Chicago. Why, I--I'm a married woman! He's younger--than I--a year! He knows there is

Zoe. He sent her up a little hobbyhorse from the property room. Why, Mrs. Blair--of course if you look at me like--that--"

She was suddenly in the older woman's arms, a passionate, a peony red flooding her face and waving down her words. She was all for further resistance, but her denial had taken on an archness for which she somehow blushed.

Besides, it was suddenly delicious to huddle there, tingling in the darkness.

CHAPTER VI

There were a quality of voice, of eye, and a fine, upstanding rush of sooty black hair which he tried to japan down with a pair of swift military brushes, in the way of woman's safest judgment of Bruce Visigoth.

By the quieter kinetics of his own sex, he was a man's man. He commingled easily in his clubs, a university, a Mask and Wig, a Long Island Canoe, and the Gramercy. Preceding his brother in this last and later proposing him.

The resemblance between the two was neither of form nor of feature. Rather, it was fleeting as a wing; in fact, was just that. There was something in the batting of the eye, a slant of lid, that showed the mysterious corpuscles of the same blood asserting themselves. Yet it was more the likeness of father and son; the older man shorter, wider of thigh, and with none of that fleet, rather sensitive lift of head, partly because his neck was shorter and not upflung as if so sensitive to the very rush of air that the flanges of the nostrils quivered.

There was a more nervous organization to Bruce that gave him something of the startled look of wild horse, particularly with the laid-back Mercury wing effect to his hair.

In anger Robert had a repertoire of oaths that stained the air like the trail of a wounded shark, his pupils receding to points and his mouth pulling to an oblique.

Bruce, if anything, whitened and quieted. He had once, with hardly more than a lightning lunge, broken a truck driver's wrist in an office altercation over some manhandled scenery, and gone home rather sick because the fellow's opened cheek had bled down over his desk.

His office manner was clipped, brisk, and highly impersonal. He cultivated a little mustache to enhance that manner, yet the two sixteen-year-old girls who pasted clippings into scrap books spitted their curls for him, and, since his advent, even Ida Blair had discarded her eye shade.

In moments of high pressure he stuttered slightly, grinding and whirring over a sibilant like a stalled tire. Upon one occasion that was to be memorable Lilly sat between the brothers, notebook in lap, her head bent to dodge the fusillade of high words passing over it.

It was her third year in a firm that had not slipped a cog. She had likened its growth to her child's--fine--sturdy--normal. There were seven theaters now, lying at points between New York and Denver, a quickening nervous system of them with New York its ganglia. An eighth had just been acquired, through which transaction she had endured with a vicarious anxiety that amazed her. There had been arduous after office hours of deed, mortgage, and bill of sale, and to growing demands had invested herself with power of notary public, proclaiming the same in a neat sign above her desk.

It was the day of the consummation of this last deal, a Bronx Family Theater, in fact, that occurred between the brothers one of those bloodless chasms no wider than a sword blade, but hilt-deep.

After a morning series of conferences with two representatives of Philadelphia capital and the vice president of a Surety Guarantee Company, Lilly in her new capacity thumping down on document after document that slid beneath her punch, the transfer was completed, and, bursting out into the corridor, rather hoyendish with elation, she drew up shortly to avoid collision with Robert Visigoth, himself still warm with the occasion.

"Well," he said, slapping the side pockets of his waistcoat, "we pulled it off, didn't we?" The possibility of an evening train back to Chicago and of a big deal creditably accomplished quickening his well-being.

"Indeed we did!" she replied, heartily.

More and more, on these intermittent visits of his, the icy edge of her self-consciousness was beginning to thaw. Probably because the years had done their sebaceous worst with him. Somehow he had receded behind the dumpling of himself.

"Have you seen this one of Rufus II, Mrs. Penny? I want to show you a picture of a youngster with some kick to him. Look at those legs, will you!"

He had married, three years previous, a Miss Hindle Higginbothom, the only child of a Chicago leaf-lard magnate of household-word kind of fame, and brother-in-law to his father's one-time law partner, O.J. Higginbothom.

For three years now, as if caught in a suet destiny, he had lived in the Lake Shore mansion of his father-in-law, making the Western city his official headquarters for as long as seven and eight-month periods. Ten, the year his first child was born.

Often his wife accompanied him on his trips to New York. She was an enormous girl, looking ten years her senior, but with that fat kind of prettiness which asserts itself so often in clear skin and apple cheeks.

Her capitulation to matrimony, rather than to Robert Visigoth, was complete. She was one of those inevitable mothers with little broody household ways that no immense wealth could dissipate. The first year there were twins. One of them died, but annually thereafter, until there were six, she presented a chuckling grandfather with a literal heir. Literal, because on each such nativity old Rufus Higginbothom, who had found it easier to make millions than to learn to write, signed his famous "X" to a five-hundred-thousand-dollar check of greeting to the new arrival.

Robert Visigoth carried photographs of his babies and wife in a leather pocket portfolio, referring to it constantly and with a great show of casualness, "Oh, by the way, have I ever shown you--"

Lilly returned this to him now, with a rush of amused pleasure at the bouncing rotundities of his newest born.

"He's a darling!"

"He was a little croupy before I left and I'm taking that six-three for Chicago, Mrs. Penny, and I wonder if you would do something for me. I'm caught empty-handed. Would you take a cab down to Ryan and Steger's (the wife says they are the best for stouts) and select me a couple of right nobby waists for her? Get the best, and you know pretty much about size. The largest--you know. A few pairs of black silk stockings, extra quality and extra size, would be nice, too. It would save me considerable rush."

"I'll do my best."

"Well, that will be a darn sight better than the wife's when it comes to clothes. She gets them tubby. Pick out something slick--on the order of what you've got on."

"Why, this is only a two-dollar blouse!"

He flipped her a one-hundred-dollar bill.

"Don't come back with any change."

Late in the afternoon of this day which had transmitted its tremor of large transaction throughout the offices, long since partitioned off into ground-glass cells and softened with sound-eating rugs, Lilly was summoned to the office of R.J., carrying with her the box containing her purchases. Bruce was there, too, pacing between windows.

He met her up with an immediate inquiry.

"Mrs. Penny, did you go up to see that 'June Blossom' sketch last night?"

"Yes. I'm writing my report on it."

Constantly now requests like this were tossed in the form of a pair of tickets on her desk.

"Well?"

"Sweet, clean, and obvious."

He nodded in a short corroborative manner he had, drawing up alongside the desk.

"Take a telegram, please. 'Mr. Sam Sadler, People's Theater, Cleveland, Ohio. Book *June Blossom* for week of nineteenth.' And now if you'll sign and stamp this mortgage after my brother and I sign."

The box proved cumbersome, so before she took up pen she held it out to R.J.

"The blouses," she said. "There is a blue and a maroon. I hope Mrs. Visigoth is going to like them. And here is the change."

"That's mighty fine," he said, smiling until a second chin appeared. "A trinket or two up his sleeve gives a fellow a right to ring his own door bell."

He reached then, fumbling at the hasps of his alligator bag which stood by, opening it out and stooping to insert the package.

Simultaneously, as the mouth of that valise yawned, the two men leaped forward so that their heads came together resoundingly and absurdly, but not before the bag had exposed its surface articles: a pair of tortoise-shell military brushes, a packet of documents, and a precious silver and lapis-lazuli box about the dimensions of a playing card, the kind usually dedicated to such elusive addenda as stamps, collar buttons, or sewing box in a lady's overnight bag.

From where she sat, shorthand book open, pencil poised, Lilly had observed it quite casually, although it was some time before she could co-ordinate it with what ensued.

Suddenly there was the flash of the two men to their feet, R.J., an ox-blood surging into his face, kicking shut the valise, his brother whitening and quivering.

"Why did you lie about that box!"

"What do you mean?" said Robert, through his teeth, his color so livid that teeth and eyeballs seemed to whiten.

His voice like the splitting of silk, Bruce plunged down a pointing forefinger toward the bag.

"Open that up," he said.

"The hell I will."

With one swift stroke from the lighter and lither of them, the bag was on its side, spilling its contents of tortoise-shell hair brushes and the silver box, Bruce standing above it, tightening of jaw and knuckles.

"Liar!" he cried. "Liar!"

To Lilly it seemed that out of these years of apparently placid relationship, with something avuncular, even of father and son in it, here were suddenly and terribly Cain and Abel, elemental with an itch for each other's throat.

"Say that again, by God! and you'll regret it."

"Liar! Liar!" he reiterated over and over, standing and towering over the spilling bag. "Why did you lie to me about that box? Three years ago I asked you for it. The spring after her death. Just before the auction. Wasn't it sufficient that I let you and Pauline settle her personal effects between you? Only that little box--somehow I wanted it. Father gave it to her the first Christmas of their marriage. She always kept it on her table. You were welcome to all the rest between you. All I asked for was that little box of mother's. And to think that yesterday, the anniversary of her death, I mentioned it again. Liar! Liar! Lost! Never been found among her effects! Bah! Liar! It's a little thing, a trinket that she loved, but I wanted it. You hear, I wanted that trinket. She used to keep jelly beans in it for me when I came in from school. It's little--the littlest thing that ever happened between us, but it's the meanest, and God knows in my dealings with you all my life there have been enough of the little meannesses to contend with. But you have won your last mean little advantage outside this office. You and I can play the cards in business, particularly when we play them six hundred miles apart and where it is a case of man to man out on the mat. But outside this office we play quits! There aren't going to be any more nasty little personal issues with you, because there aren't going to be any at all. You're a liar and a hundred per cent bigger one over that little trinket of a box than if the stakes had been bigger. You hate to give, unless it's so much for so much. Your sense of fairness is vile! It's penny mean! Liar!"

With a lowering of head Robert lunged then, his lips dragged to an oblique, threads of red cut in his eyeballs.

"Eat those words or, by God! I'll ram them down your throat."

"The hell I will."

"Gentlemen!"

They were crowded against the door, their breathing flowing against each other's face, gestures uplifted.

Her eyes black and her notebook crushed up to her, Lilly's voice rang out like the crack of a whip, springing them apart. There were a whiteness and a sense of emptiness upon her and she wanted to crumple up rather sickly and cry, as if the blows had been diverted to her.

They were suddenly and quiveringly themselves again, the panther laid.

"You'll rue this," said Robert, walking back with some uncertainty of step to his desk, his eyes still slits.

Bruce lifted the box rather tenderly, even with the greeny pallor of his rage still out and his features straining for composure.

"I'll have it valued and send you a check--"

"Damn you!" With snarl-shaped lips the older brother lunged again, this time their bodies meeting and swaying for clutch.

"Bruce!"

The use of his given name, the curdled quality to her voice, had their way. There was a moment of blank staring between the two men, of Bruce placing the box gently on the desk and walking out without slamming the door, and Robert sinking down into the swivel chair, trying to bring the oblique pull of his lips back to straight.

"Get out," he said, without looking at her.

She did, tiptoeing and fighting down the sense of sickness.

And thus, out of a bauble of silver and lapis lazuli, was reared a tower of silence between these brothers as high as fifteen years is long. Large affairs for their joint unraveling lay ahead, dramatic in their magnitude. The Union Square Family Theater was very presently to become first a tawdry, then a discarded link in the glittering chain of playhouses that was to gird the country.

Toward this end R.J. and Bruce Visigoth steered, with an impeccable oneness of purpose, the destinies of an enterprise audacious in its concept and ultimately to be spectacular in its fulfillment.

But outside the sharply defined inclosures of their business lives, the brothers went down into a wordless vale of fifteen years of estrangement, not in enmity, but rather as a hatpin, plunged through the heart, can kill, bloodlessly.

CHAPTER VII

When Lilly put on her hat outside in the now darkening and deserted offices, it seemed to her that the roar of men's passions was a gale through the silence. Quite irrelevantly she was clutched with a terror of catastrophe. The possibility of fire! Only last week there had been a devastating one in a children's hospital out in Columbus, Ohio. She beat down these flames of fear. Yet what strange and horrible passions lay just a scratch beneath the surface of the day-by-days. A little girl aged four had once been found battered and dead beside a farm hand's dinner pail in St. Louis County! Suddenly all the faces she could conjure began to form staring circles around her--the Visigoths. Minnie Dupree. Ida Blair. Auchinloss. Phonzie. Phonzie!

She decided to walk fast and long and ran downstairs out into the little areaway that ran like an alley from stage entrance to sidewalk. A newly installed nickelodeon, adjoining, was already lighted, throwing out a hard white shine and tinned music at the instance of five cents in the slot. In the glaring pallor Bruce Visigoth was suddenly at her side, his felt hat bunched up in his hand and his hair wet-looking, as if drenched with perspiration.

"I couldn't let you go without apologizing, Mrs. Penny."

She smiled with lips that would pull to the nervous impulse to cry.

"The idea!" she said, feeling the words tawdry and provincial as they came.

"It was my fault for permitting it to happen in the presence of a third party--you especially."

"Those things cannot always be avoided," again biting down into her tongue for its banality.

"Will you forget it as if it had never occurred?"

She turned her gaze, that could be so singularly clear, full upon him.

"It is already forgotten."

Strangely enough and with unspoken accord they took to walking then at a clip that was almost a rush and created quite a wind in their faces. It was their first meeting out of office and here they were half running through a cool and winey half darkness and utterly without destination.

She stopped abruptly at West Fourteenth Street, beyond the thunder of the Sixth Avenue Elevated and where the sky line began to dip down toward the piers.

"Good night," she said, throwing back her head to look up at him from under the low brim of sailor.

He whipped off his resiliently soft hat, hugging it under one arm.

"Of course," he said, "of course," mopping at his forehead and so unstrung that she could have laughed. "I'm sorry. I beg your pardon. Is this where you live?"

They were before a greasily lighted taxidermist's window of mounted raccoon, fox terrier with legs curled for running, and an owl on a branch.

"No," she said, eying the owl, "I don't live here," and were both off into a gale of laughter that swept down the barriers of self-restraint.

"We've both been walking it off," she said, easily. "Here is where I turn for home."

He caught her hand.

"D-don't go. I'd be so grateful--so grateful if you'd have dinner with me to-night."

"Nonsense!" she said, amazed at her fluency of manner. "You're a bit unstrung, that's all. Look in at your club or a show."

"Please."

"All right," she said, suddenly, on a little click of teeth. "I'll come--this once."

"You're a brick," he cried, releasing her hand with a grateful pressure.

She was excited out of all proportions to the event, flushing up with a sense of adventure and crowded moment.

He began to scan for a cab.

"Let's walk."

"Not a bit of it," bringing one down with a cane. "We're out on a party."

"But--"

"No buts," helping her in and climbing in after. "Waldorf."

"I'm too shirtwaisted."

"Nothing of the kind. You're as trim as a dime. I like those waists you wear. They make you look smooth--shining. That's it, you've a shine to you."

The odor of another drive in an open cab through this same snarl of traffic was winding about her like mist. That doctor's outer office with its row of thoughtful chairs. Rembrandt's "Night-Watch." That frenzied moment of finding the lock! The run up two flights. She sat forward on the slippery leather seat.

"I--I shouldn't have come."

"If you're serious, of course I'll take you home. But I can't tell you how much I want you not to feel that way."

She sat back again.

"I'm behaving like a shop girl."

They both laughed again and complete thaw set in.

He selected one of the lesser dining rooms where the formality of evening clothes was still the rule, but here and there a couple like themselves, in street attire. It was her first New York meal that was not read off a badly thumbed menu and eaten off thick-lipped china. A stringed orchestra played the Duo of Parsifal and Kundry, which was enough to set the blood rocking in her veins and some of its bombastic maternal passion to dye her face.

He ordered a man's dinner: Clear soup with croutons. Long oysters on the half shell. A thick steak with potatoes deliciously concocted beneath a crust of cheese. Light wine. Ices in long glasses as slender as the neck of a crane. Turkish coffee brewed at the table over alcohol.

She sighed out finally, warm with well-being: "I didn't realize how deadly tired I was of just--grub. You see, it's the first time I've dined at a first-class place since I'm in New York."

"You don't mean that."

She nodded, smiling.

"I think I'm as surprised as you are. It's just one of the things that never occurred to me."

He regarded her for a long moment and without smile.

"You queer, queer girl."

"If anyone tells me that again, I'll begin to believe it is my inevitable epitaph."

"No epitaph is inevitable. It is what you write it."

She leaned her chin into the cup of her palm.

"Do you think that?"

"Yes, and therefore yours should embody courage and dauntless idealism and love of truth."

She looked off through the atmosphere that was talcy with soft odors and the warm perfume of bare shoulders.

"Love of truth," she said, her eyes lit, "would be enough."

"Love of you, would be an epitaph to my liking."

She was afraid he could see the little beating at her throat and wanted to be facetious. Poor Lilly, to whom persiflage came none too readily.

"Now, you're making sport of me."

"Probably it is a case of laugh that I may not weep."

"Even tears can be idle."

"Or idolizing."

"I suppose I am to surmise over the quality of yours?"

"Well, you have had me guessing for three years. Mrs. Penny. Lilly! I can't say the other, it--won't s-say itself."

She asked her question with a cessation of her entire being, as if her heart had missed a beat.

"Hasn't--your--brother--told--you--anything?"

"Oh yes. I know how you threw over the professional end of it for what you decided you could do better. I thought that pretty plucky; so many of us mistake inflated judgment for genius and stubbornness for perseverance, when that same perseverance applied to the job within one's capacity may lead to fine fulfillment."

"It's good to hear you say that."

"But that is about all I do know--Lilly--except, of course, that there is a youngster and somewhere in the background a husband whom I would like to meet out some dark night when I happen to be wearing my favorite pair of brass knuckles."

Something nameless and shapeless had lifted; there was a gavotte to her heartbeat.

"My husband was--is a good man."

"But not a wise one if he couldn't hold a creature like you."

"And my child! You talk about shine! Of course I know it is only her hair and eyes and now her little teeth, but sometimes it seems to me there is an actual iridescence to her. Just as real as the gold circlets the Italians loved to paint about heads they adored."

"Your head is--"

"You see, the fuzz of her curls gives that effect. Those new stereopticon views that move, that we used on the bills last week, show it--that aura off the hair. Even the nurses and Mrs. Dupree have remarked Zoe's. She's really the show child of the place, you know."

"By inheritance?"

"No. She's only like me about the eyes, and like--him--in the honey color of her hair. Hers is as brilliant and curly as mine is dull and smooth. And she's so big. So golden and burstingly big. I can't look at her without fairly gasping, 'can this be mine'!"

"And to think a man let you go, once he had you captured."

"He didn't let go. I went. I can never hear him referred to slightingly without feeling myself a rotter not to explain. My husband was so terribly all he should have been, Mr. Visigoth. As decent and God-fearing a man as ever--chewed his beefsteak with his temples."

He threw back his head for one of his sustained laughs.

"It's horrid of me to belittle him. Let me explain further."

"Lord! you don't need to. I know everything about him there is to know. A fine, hefty truck horse trying to do teamwork with a red-nostriled filly."

"I--I think that's it--I've never been able to get it across to anyone before, but--"

"He was just cast wrong. That's all there is to be said against the chap. Right?"

"Exactly."

"I understand. In a way I'm in a similar position with my own brother. Only, I've stuck it out because it was my mother's great wish to see us get on together. After what you have observed these years, particularly to-day, none of this can be particularly new to you."

"I've noticed, of course, you--you're different."

"It is the little things about Robert I cannot swallow. Never could. He is the better business man and keeps my head out of the clouds, but many a time I've wanted to duck these years of apprenticeship and produce the things I believe in. I will some day, but that is another story. Robert has vision. His sense of land and theater values is unfailing. He--"

"Well, so is your vision just as unfailing in your work. The chain didn't even begin to form before you took over the booking end."

"He has fine traits, too. Big ones. His word is his bond. He has business foresight and integrity, but somehow it is his little meannesses. I remember once in my father's house he took a thrashing for something outrageous he was not guilty of, because he had promised some youngster across the way he would shield him, come what might, and somehow I thought it pretty fine of him. But another time he let me take a thrashing for something he had done and stood by without opening his mouth. It is those indescribable smallnesses in his make-up. Once when I was in favor of branching out and producing a legitimate three-act play which I happened to run across--a rare thing from the French--he--well, I won't go into it--but this thing--to-night--that bauble of my mother's--it--it's the climax of a lifetime of such flea bites--a trifle hardly worth the mentioning, and yet--it's the most utter--the most damnable--"

There was a half crash of his clenched hand among the silver and a rise of suffusing red up out of the white of his soft collar.

"I beg your pardon. I didn't mean to let you in for any more of it. I'm sorry. And after you were gracious enough to come alone, too. Come, here is to making this little party a gay one."

He held up his glass. "Here's to the shining child."

"Oh!" she cried, and drank quickly.

"Like it?"

"Not much. It burns."

"You should see your eyes."

"You should see hers."

"Whose?"

"My child's."

"Do you know what I should have done in your husband's place?"

"What?"

"Harnessed you, too, but to a moonbeam."

"I once knew a man to whom I never spoke ten words in all my life, and yet I always imagined he might have talked to me like that--not literally--not in terms of tin dippers."

"Of what, you queer, queer girl?"

"Now I know of whom you remind me! An old school-teacher I once had. Odd."

"I would never have let you slip my harness through."

"And have deprived the Amusement Enterprise Company of my austere services!"

"You've been invaluable. Ninety per cent of your judgments have been ninety-nine per cent there!"

"Luck."

"Luck nonsense! Judgment isn't horseshoe-shaped."

"I love it! Feeling the public pulse for what it wants. The psychology of your vaudeville audience is as elementary as a primer and as intricate as life. It is a blood-hound when it comes to detecting the false from the true. Take that little sketch, 'Trapped,' you sent me out to see last week. A more sophisticated audience might have mistaken its brittle epigrammatic quality for brilliancy and its flippancy for cleverness. But not your ten-twenty-thirty's. In real life a husband doesn't psych-analyze his wife's lover. He horsewhips him. And that lovely blank-verse fantasy that you attempted on your own. That is the sort of thing you are going to stand for some day in the theater. I loved your wanting it. But right now, while you are on your way up to the goal, is where I come in. Sort of mediator between your ide-als and the box office. Of course you loved the fantasy. So did I, and I loved your wanting to do it. But it took vaudeville just one performance to decide that it wasn't ready for that kind of mysticism."

"And you forty minutes."

"You would never have backed it even over my O.K."

"Then you don't realize how far your O.K. goes with me."

"What is this," she smiled, "a mutual-admiration fete?"

"I don't know," suddenly leaning toward her, reddening. "I can only speak for myself. Lilly--you're wonderful--"

She chose to be casual, most effectively, too.

"Indeed it is mutual. I need hardly to tell you what association with your office has meant to me. The romance of an organization like yours. The thrill of seeing it triple proportions in these few years. The fine stimulating something that comes with the acquisition of each new Amusement Enterprise Theater. The chats we have had over plays, play writing, producing. Your own fine aim. Oh, it has made bearable even the monotony of the secretarial end of it!"

"I am afraid your secretarial services are about to be dispensed with."

She placed a quick hand to her heart.

"What do you mean?"

He flecked his cigar, laughing over at her.

"You're delicious. What could I mean except that you have outgrown your job?"

"You--mean--"

"I mean that I am going to officially place you in charge of the booking department at--well, your own idea of salary."

"I--I don't know what to say."

"Don't say anything."

"You can't know--"

"I do know."

"You see, she is almost four now, and beautifully cared for, but, now that her little mind is beginning to unfold--I--Oh, to be able to afford a place of my own--next year--when she has outgrown Mrs. Dupree's. You see, I've never really had her. I've such plans for the day when I can have her rearing all to myself. I want life to unfold so naturally to her. Like a flower. That's why I am so terribly jealous of every day we spend apart. That's why you--you cannot know what it means to have you tell me that I've made good. It means that the time is nearing for me to have her with me, to--to--Well, you cannot--cannot know!"

She sat back, feeling foolish because her eyes were filling and trying to smile back the tears.

He reached over to place his palms over her hand.

"How rightly named you are! 'Lilly.' One of those big, milky-spathed, calla lilies. Calla Lilly."

"We'll be going now," she said, feeling for her jacket.

They rode down to Eleventh Street in a cab, almost silently, and as she sat looking out, unsmiling, she could feel his gaze burn her profile.

He left her at the stoop, standing bareheaded.

"You've saved me from an evening of horrors."

"I'm glad."

"You're not angry--Calla Lilly?"

"Of course not."

"How soon again?"

"No."

"Yes, yes!"

"No."

And somehow the word was like a plummet deep into the years ahead.

CHAPTER VIII

One hot Saturday afternoon, at least a twelvemonth later, as Lilly was rushing down from the children's department of one of Broadway's gigantic cut-rate department stores, she stopped so abruptly that she created a little throwback in the sidewalk jam.

Her miracle was broken. Her first impulse even now was to dart back, but the tow of the crowd was strong, and, besides, she was suddenly eye to eye with an exceedingly thin youth with a very long neck rising far above a high collar, a pasty and slightly pimpled face evidently slow to beard, and a soft hat pulled down over meek light-blue eyes, himself even more inclined to push on than she.

It was her first encounter since her clean cleavage from a strangely remote dream phase of her existence. For the first three years she had carried about a fear of some such meeting, a passer-by brushing her shoulders or a sense of presence at her back sending a shock through her. Once she had hurriedly left a Subway train because of a fancied likeness to Roy Kemble in a young fellow across the aisle. Even now there were days when fancied resemblances seem to people the crowds.

"Why, Harry Calvert!"

"Hello," he said in the tempo of no great surprise, but purpling up into his lightish hair. "I know you. You're Lilly Becker."

"Harry, I cannot believe my eyes! I haven't seen you since you were in knickers. And to think we remembered each other! Come here a minute out of the crowd. I want to talk to you."

He followed her with some reluctance and a great sheepishness out of Broadway into quieter Thirty-fourth Street, twirling his hat, his nervousness growing.

"You look fine, Lilly."

"What are you doing here, Harry? How is your grandma? St. Louis?"

She could have embraced, cried over him, the loneliness of years seeming to rush to a head.

"Gramaw and I live here."

"Harry, not really!"

"Nearly two years, now."

"Where?"

"'Way out near Tremont Avenue."

"And you, Harry, what do you do?"

"I was window dresser for a gents' furnishing store up to a few weeks ago, but it--it changed hands. I'm out of a job right now."

"Harry, do you ever hear from--home?"

"No, Miss Lilly, we never see anyone from there. You're the first."

"I'll tell you what. I'm going home with you. Take me out with you to visit your grandma. I haven't seen her in years--it's been so long ago--everything."

He was wringing his hat now and shifting.

"It's a long way out, Lilly. It's hardly built up out there at all."

"I don't care. I'll buy some pastries on the way and we will make a party of it. Does she still keep boarders?"

"Roomers."

"Poor, dear Mrs. Schum, fancy her living here!"

They rode out on a surface car, changing twice and jammed face to face on a rear platform, a brilliant pink out in her face.

"Harry, I just cannot realize it. You a full-fledged man!"

"I'm twenty-four."

"What is that yellow on your fingers? Not from smoking?"

"I used to a lot, but not now."

"Is your grandmother just as wrapped up in you as ever, Harry? Poor dear!"

"Yes, she is. You sure look fine, Lilly. You're pretty!"

"And what in the world brought you to New York and what ever became of Mr. Hazzard and--"

"Oh, gramaw read in the paper once that he died of that sore on his face."

"And old Willie and Mr. Keebil and Snow Horton--ever see any of them, Harry?"

"No; you see it is nearly two years since--"

"I have a little daughter--almost five years old!"

"Gramaw followed up in the papers when you were married. Flora Kemble and Roy, they're both married, too."

"Harry, didn't you ever hear anything about--well, about my marriage?"

"Yes, there was something about it. I forget. You live in New York?"

"Yes, and, Harry, don't say anything when we get to your home. Just let me walk in and surprise her."

"Yes."

More and more she noticed his indoor whiteness and the eyelids which would twitch nervously.

"Do you keep well, Harry?"

"Fairly."

There was quite a walk from the car, across a viaduct, down a flight of steps, and into a steep new street of flimsy-looking apartment houses of the dawning era of vertical homes. But the Harlem River, neat as a canal, flowed within easy view and there was something very scoured about the expression of the just graded street of occasional vacant lots, showing the first break in the continuity of city brick that Lilly's tired eyes had encountered.

"Why, Harry, I've never been away out here before! How nice and clean!"

"Here we are."

They entered one of the tan-brick buildings, "El Dorado" writ in elegant gilt script across the transom. Then up three flights of clean, new, fireproof stairs, Harry inserting his key into one of the two doors that faced the landing.

"Sh-h-h, Harry! Tell her it is just a friend."

Old odors laden with memory rushed to meet her; that pungency which, un-accountably enough, reeks of the cold boiled potato, and which old upholsteries, windowless hallways, and frequent meat stews can generate.

There was a blob of low-pressure gaslight in the hallway, a weak and watery eye burning from a side bracket into the odor so poignant with association. Tony Eli drowned at eighteen. Her father peering behind the dresser. "Where's Lilly?" "Here I am!" Herself hugging up her knees in their stout ribbed stockings, her round gaze on the red-glass globe with the warts blown into it.

There it was, that same glass globe around the puny light; and the hatrack--the one with the seat that opened for rubbers and school bags.

"Gramaw, come out. Here is some one."

A long cooking fork in her hand, and a puff of steam hissing out after her, Mrs. Schum peered into the hallway. She was strangely smaller, Lilly thought, as if the flesh were beginning to wither off the rack of her bones.

"Mrs. Schum! Dear Mrs. Schum!"

"Who's that?"

"Come out, gramaw. It's no one to be afraid of."

"Harry!" Her voice came cracking out like a shot. "Harry, are you in trouble?"

"No--no--"

"Who is hounding you? If you are here about my grandson, madam, they are all the time trying to get the best of my boy. He hasn't broken parole since old Judge Delahanty down in the Twenty-third Street Court--"

"Mrs. Schum! Dear Mrs. Schum! Don't you know me? Please! Think, dearie, the little girl out in St. Louis who used to plague you for bread and butter--"

The old face loosened, the eyes peering through spectacles held across the nose with a bit of twine.

"It isn't--Lilly--Becker?"

"Right the first time, gramaw!"

"Bless my heart! Bless my soul! Let me sit down. I'm right weak. Little Lilly--Becker!"

They embraced there in a hallway hardly wide enough to contain them. These two, who ordinarily might have met again, after such a span of years, in the mildest of reunions, here in each other's arms, hungrily, heartbeat to heartbeat.

"Lilly, Lilly, come in here and let me look at you. Light up the front room, Harry. Well, I declare! Let me sit down. I'm right weak-kneed. Law! pretty is no name! Well, I declare!"

In the little front room of chromos, folding bed with desk attachment, a bisque knickknack or two, they were finally knee to knee, Lilly's hat tossed aside, her hands clasping the old veiny ones.

"Begin at the beginning, Mrs. Schum. Everything. First, tell me, dear, how long since you have heard of my folks?"

"Harry, you go out in the kitchen and keep the things warm until gramaw comes out to dish up. Set the table with a cloth on, and run over to the delicatessen for a bit of cold cuts. He's a right smart help to me, Lilly. Not like some boys, too proud to help. And now--now--let me see--why, it's two years since I met your mother downtown in St. Louis before I had any idea of coming here."

"How did she look?"

"Splendid. She was with one of her euchre friends, so I didn't have the chance for an old-time chat, but she made me promise to come and see her, and 'pon my word, just as young and pretty as you please, with a fine face veil and a purple feather boa and shopping out of the Busy Bee bins just the way she used to do."

"She looked--happy?"

"Indeed she did! Buying some menfolk stuff. Wool socks, I think she said, for your father, was it, who is subject to colds in the head--"

"No, those weren't for papa. Oh, Mrs. Schum, it's so good to hear of her first hand like this! What--what did she say about me?"

"Told me about you off here studying opera, and your husband was making his home with them. I--I took it from what she said you were none too happy with him, but I had no idea of your being here still! Aren't things well with you, Lilly? I always said you reminded me of my Annie, and she would have turned out something big if she had lived. I expect it of you, too, Lilly."

"What else?"

"She put up a bold front with me, I will say that, never letting on that there had been trouble. And then just before I left--we came away mighty unexpectedly--Katy Stutz--"

"Katy Stutz--"

"Yes, came to sew for a family I had boarding with me, and she said she heard you had left him for good and that your parents took sides with your husband and had him in their home, occupying your very room, and that your mother was as fussy over him as she ever was over you, babying him to death. Lilly, Lilly, what is wrong with you?"

"And my father, Mrs. Schum?"

"Fine. Mary says he's a bit whiter, but not a whit changed. He's done well in the rope business, hasn't he? Although I always say it was your mother's practical ways got him on his feet, and from what I understand that young man you married has given him many a lift. They've gone in business together, haven't they? They tell me, Lilly, there is not a steadier or more advancing young man than yours. Ah me, the ways of young ones are strange I guess you haven't heard about Harry, either?"

"No."

"He's a good boy, Harry is, Lilly, but I've been through trouble with him. That's the reason for our being here. You see, Lilly, him being a poor orphan all his life, they're all against him. The little fellow never had the right raising, knocking around with all those nigger servants, and me with never the time to do for him."

"Oh, Mrs. Schum, how can you! Why, there wasn't any of the youngsters in the boarding house had a sweeter influence over him than Harry."

"No, no. It was all my fault. I was too pressed trying to make ends meet. I should have given up that big house years ago for a few roomers like now. He got in bad ways, Lilly. Not noisy and with gangs like some rough boys would. But quiet--solitary-like. I never knew him to hang around with that gang of boys that used to loaf over at Pirney's drug store or anything like that, but after the Kembles and you folks left, Harry got to stealing, Lilly. Little things. The child never took anything more than a bit of lead pipe from Quinn's empty house across the street, and once a little silver trinket from a milliner I had up in the third floor front--"

"He used to do little things like that when he was a child, don't you remember, dear?"

"It's his father in him, Lilly. Maybe you don't know it, but that's what killed my Annie, that same streak which was the ruination of a fine, educated man like his father. But Harry's got too much of his mother in him to be all bad; he--"

"Of course he has, dear."

"To get back to our coming East, Lilly. One night he--Harry brought me home a brooch, Lilly. A right pretty gold one with a garnet in. It used to hurt him that I never had any finery. He wouldn't take anything to buy drink and bad times for himself like other boys, but he'd steal something to bring home to his old grandmother. All that night, Lilly, down there in the basement kitchen, I was nearly crazy trying to get out of him where he got that brooch. The next day they was after him, for it and some--nickel-plated facets from out of the washroom where he was working. They hushed it up. Old Judge Mayer, you remember his sister used to board with me. But the next time there was a little trouble--this time a--a little finger ring--not even all gold. I--we--we had to sell out and come here--where we could be swallowed up."

"Oh, Harry, Harry, how could he!"

"Wasn't his fault. It wasn't the place for him out there any more with everybody against a poor orphan. I've cut him off, Lilly, from his bad ways out there. You're the first I've seen or heard of since we left, and I don't want you to even write it to your folks that we're here. There's the little matter of that ring--not even all gold--and--some lead pipe--forgotten, now--please God, but they might want him back for it--that's how down on him they are. He's a good boy, Harry is, Lilly, with respect for his grandmother. He's had a slip up or two, but the best of us have that, haven't we?"

"Yes."

"It's to be expected. A boy can't shake off his inheritance overnight, can he? Can he?"

"No, I suppose not, dear."

"Don't let on, Lilly. He's sensitive. We'll win yet, Harry and me will. The world hasn't taken much stock of a poor little basement orphan, but with the kind of mother he had, his grandmother will live yet to see the day that it does take account of him. Harry's right smart with draping and decorating around the house, and if I do say it, when he dresses a window the traffic stops. He's a great one for reading and following up the magazines, too. Smart. I'd stake my all on a boy that has got it in him to treat his grandmother with the gentleness he does. And children! There is not one on the street he can pass for love of them. A boy like that cannot be all bad, can he, Lilly?"

Her eyes magnified with the glaze of tears so that one blink would have overflowed them, Lilly laid her lips to the veiny old hand, her voice down into the lap of blue-checkered apron.

"We mothers--Mrs. Schum--God, how we love to suffer to them!"

"We!"

Her face in the tired old lap, the little room seeming to crowd up with voice, Lilly talked on then, until the little clock inset into a china plate ticked out an hour, and in the kitchen, Harry, with all his old capacity for meekness, lay asleep with his head in his arms and the little dinner cloying on the stove.

"I'm afraid my old brain don't take it all in, Lilly. You mean your mother-- father--none of them--know?"

"It isn't for you to understand, dear. The mere telling of it has somehow eased things. We are bits of seaweed, dear Mrs. Schum, tossed up on the same shores. You and your fugitive from environment. Me and mine. If your secret is to be mine, mine must be yours."

"God have mercy on you, Lilly, wherever it is your ways are leading you."

"He has had, Mrs. Schum."

"I don't know. I don't know. You know best, I guess, what is in your heart."

"I do. It's this. Why can't you take--us?"

"Who?"

"I want her with me. She is getting big enough for the kind of training I have all mapped out for her. And now you--it's nothing short of destiny led me to you. I could put her in day school. Can take her myself in the mornings, say, and you, dear Mrs. Schum, are to call for her? I can pay, I can help you and you can help me. Later we may take a larger place with extra room. Mrs. Schum, don't you see, we've been thrown together!"

"Why, Lilly--I believe--I do."

It was after ten o'clock when, over a belated little meal, they ceased their planning. Eleven, when Harry finally walked with her across the viaduct to the street car. Stars were out. Thick white ones. She skipped a little, ran a little, and stood a moment at the parapet, looking down at the lights which followed the narrow course of the river. She felt suddenly wild for bauble. Her flesh, which never particularly craved the lay of fine fabric, felt cheated. She wanted to wind her body to its utmost flexuosity, bare her throat to the wind, and fling out a gesture the width of Vegas to Capella.

At the corner she took Harry's face between her hands, kissing him soundly on the lips.

"Good night, Harry, and God bless you for letting me find you."

Long after that kiss, ever so lightly bestowed, lay burning against his lips and she had boarded the street car, he stood looking after, with his very light-blue eyes.

Book Three
THE WINE

CHAPTER I

When Zoe Penny was still in knee frocks she graduated, first in her class, from the public grade school. It was a period of great stress for Lilly, of happy shopping and the sweet anxieties of ribbon and frock, and there were always two high circles of color out on her cheeks, and from time to time she would force herself to sit down, uncurl her fingers of their tensity, as Ida Blair had taught her, and thus, starting in at the hands, try to relax.

After two or three moves from the makeshift of the Tremont Avenue apartment, they were finally installed in an old brownstone walk-up house in West Ninety-third Street, a stone's throw removed from an avenue of Elevated structure and petty shops, but with a quiet enough, if gloomy, dignity. One of those tunnel dwellings, the light from the front room and kitchen gradually petering out into a middle room of almost absolute darkness.

Lilly and her daughter occupied what corresponded to the parlor, a room of white woodwork, flimsy white mantelpiece, and gilded radiator; one of the vertical layers and layers of just such city parlors. Two narrow front windows looked down into Ninety-third Street and there were closed white folding doors with again a rented piano against them. A pretty screen of Japanese paper with a sprig of wistaria across it shut off a bureau with a layout of much juvenile claptrap of hair ribbons, side combs, and the worthless treasures of childhood. Between the windows a "lady's" desk with hinged writing slab, really Lilly's, but mostly the dangling place for a pair of Zoe's roller skates and its pigeonholes bulging with her daughter's somewhat extraneous matter. But there were a two-tone brown rug, and yellow silk curtains saved the room from the iniquitous Nottingham and Axminster school of interior defamation. The walls, too, were tempered of their whiteness by brown prints of the "Coliseum by Night," "The Age of Innocence," and Watt's "Hope," blindfolded, atop the world.

These pictures had been shopped one Saturday afternoon at the cut-rate department store and were largely Zoe's choice, happily corroborated by Lilly.

"Remarkable selections for a miss," said the clerk.

"Do you really think so?" cried Lilly, herself turning away from an inclination toward the more chromatic and immediately exhilarated out of a state of fatigue.

"Zoe, you're wonderful!"

"You're wonderful, too, Lilly."

There had been scarcely any baby talk.

At three, it was "Zoe, are you happy to see mother this week-end?"

"Ees, ummie."

And then one day out of the pellucid sky of babyhood, in answer to this invariable query, it was:

"Yes, Lilly," so suddenly that something seemed to catch at her heartbeat, but after a pang she let it stand.

Let Lilly's Zoe dawn upon you through this rather typical conversation between them, the night before the graduation from grade school:

"Lilly, am I beautiful?"

"Why, yes, Zoe, so long as you remain fine and unspoiled by it. That is the rarest kind of loveliness--inner beauty."

"I don't mean that kind. Am I pretty--for boys to look at?"

"You are pretty enough as little girls go, if that is what you mean."

"Is it wrong to have beaus?"

"That all depends. Why?"

"Oh, I just wanted to know."

Silence.

"A boy in my class, Gerald Prang, says he is my beau."

"Silly fellow."

"Ethel Watts has one. They kiss."

"That's horrid."

"Is it horrid for me and Ethel to kiss?"

"No, Zoe, you know it isn't."

"Would it be horrid for me and Gerald--Gerald and I--to kiss?"

"Yes."

"Why?"

"Listen, Zoe, a new word. The most beautiful and the most horrible thing in the world can be sex."

"Sex?"

"Yes, dear. We haven't used the term in our talks--yet."

"Isn't it nice?"

"That lies with you."

"Then what is sex?"

"Zoe, the world of human beings is divided into two great classes, isn't it? Boys and girls."

"Oh, I know! It's me and Gerald."

"In a way, yes, but--"

"If me and Ethel kiss, it isn't sex, but if me and Gerald kiss, it is."

"If only you wouldn't keep your mind running ahead. I want to be so sure you are going to understand. That's what our botany and physiology study has been for. To prepare you to understand. Now take the kingdom of flowers, a rose, for instance--"

"Begin with us, Lilly. I don't want to hear any botany."

"But, Zoe--"

"Storks cannot bring babies, can they?"

"No. No. Who put such silly nonsense into your head? Don't let that stupid fable hide from you the beautiful truth of birth. That is an absurd story, Zoe, invented by those to whom the most sublime fact in the world seems nasty. Babies are born, dear--out of lo--out of the union of the sexes."

"Lilly, you are all trembling."

She took her daughter's face between her hands, her eyes probing and yearning down into the brilliantly blue ones.

"It is because I want to keep life clean and beautiful for you. Nothing that is natural is ugly, Zoe. It's only when we make something dark and shameful of nature's methods that we are apt to misunderstand and to err."

"Did you err, Lilly?"

"How?"

"With him?"

"Who?"

"Penny."

"Zoe! Zoe! why will you refer to him that way? Yes, I erred out of ignorance, the kind I want to save you from. In my case your father had to pay for the ignorance of a girl who married him without knowing what marriage meant. Ignorance!"

"How funny to hear that--word."

"What word?"

"Father."

"Zoe! Zoe! Have I made it clear to you about him? How good--how kind--how wronged by me?"

"You are always so afraid I won't understand that. Why shouldn't I?"

"Because it is hard, dear, for you to grasp it all--especially its effect upon you. Some day you will understand how gradually I have tried to prepare your mind to judge me. Even this little graduation to-morrow is a milestone and makes me want to talk to you just a wee bit plainer. Zoe, I--Zoe, does--does--"

"What?"

"Does it ever make you unhappy among the other children to be questioned about your--father?"

"No."

"Do you ever feel that you would like to see him?".

"No."

"Why?"

"Because he is dull. He would spoil things for us."

"But doesn't it ever seem terrible to you, Zoe, that I haven't given you the opportunity to judge him for yourself? If the day ever comes--to-day, tomorrow, next year--that you want your father, you understand, dear, don't you, that I will be the first to--"

"I tell you No! No! Why do you always keep telling me that? No! No! It's better his not knowing there is a me! He makes me feel all suffocated up the way he did you. I couldn't stand it. I want to be what I want to be!"

"Oh, want it badly enough then, Zoe; want it badly enough!"

"The greatest singer in the world! That's what I want to be, and stand on a stage with all the music there is around me as if I was in the middle of an ocean of it. Lilly, will you take me to another matinee to see Bernhardt? She makes me feel what I want to be. Just--just her being what she--is makes me--want to be what I--am."

"You funny muddled youngster! Why, you didn't understand either what she said or what the play was about."

"I didn't need to. It was her voice. Something she says with her voice that I feel inside of me, only I can't say it. I wanted to cry. Isn't it queer, Lilly, to feel so happy you want to cry? Oh, I've learned a new one--only my voice won't say it the way I feel it. It's in our school Wordsworth. Something inside of me cries all the time I'm saying it:

"Our birth is but a sleep and a forgetting;   The Soul that rises with us, our life's Star,   Hath elsewhere had its setting,   And cometh from afar;
Not in entire forgetfulness,   And not in utter nakedness, But   trailing   clouds   of glory do we come   From God, Who is our home.

"Oh, Lilly--Lilly--I love that!--trailing clouds of glory--"

"You recited it beautifully, darling. See, you've made me cry."

"And I--I love you, Lilly. Hold me tight. I love you."

"My baby."

"Lilly, will you be--angry if I ask you something?"

"What?"

"Why--do you cry in the night sometimes?"

"Why, Zoe! Do I?"

"You know you do. I can feel you crying, and sometimes when I touch your face--"

"Why, child--that's just my way. At night--things can be so real--so terribly real. It is something you cannot understand yet."

"Do I make you sad?"

"No! No! No! My light, my life."

"Is it--Bruce?"

"Why, child--you talk nonsense! Don't speak of him as Bruce."

"I hate calling him Mr. Visigoth. It sounds--meek. I won't be meek! Are you sure, Lilly, it isn't him--he?"

"Why, child, in Heaven's name should it be?"

"He looks at you so, Lilly. Maybe he makes you cry the way Bernhardt makes me cry. By what he doesn't say. Saturday afternoons when I call for you--he looks at you so when you're not looking."

"Why shouldn't he? We've worked together for all these years."

"You and he, when you stand up together you look so--so--*right*."

"Zoe, you are talking nonsense."

"But you're all red, aren't you?"

"No."

"Was it sex to say that?"

"No."

"Are you glad he is coming to-night?"

"Mr. Visigoth and I have business together, Zoe. We cannot sit around in public places and discuss matters. I'm reading Mrs. Blair's play to him. Go to bed now, dear."

"Mayn't I stay up?"

"No."

Her child looked up at her, chin cupped in her small hand and crystals of light out in her eyes.

"Please, Lilly--why do you cry?"

"Why, darling, I don't cry because of anything you are quite ready to understand. You know that, don't you, dear? There is nothing mother won't talk over with you as soon as you are ready to take it all in. That is part of her scheme for keeping life beautiful and free of rude shocks for you."

"But I do understand--Lilly."

Long after her child slept that night Lilly sat beside her. She loved the willful way the curls flung across the pillow. She leaned to the full deep-chested breathing; leaned to kiss the lips which, slightly parted, were perfect with the pollen of vitality.

CHAPTER II

She drew the screen finally about the little davenport, fussing at the room, straightening it into a sort of formality with a woman's intuition for this chair one-half inch closer to the hearth and that picture ever so slightly straighter. The sheer frock she hung up in a closet, covering it with a shroud of tissue paper, wadding her daughter's none-too-carefully flung stockings into her shoes and tiptoeing to place them beside the davenport. They were strong, ribbed stockings, still warm and full of curves. She stroked over each. Once she paused at the mantelpiece mirror, drawing back her lip from the even whiteness of her teeth, perusing her points rather absent-mindedly.

Time had handled Lilly with a caress. At past thirty she was herself at twenty, with even more youth, because at twenty she had looked herself almost ten years hence. She had rounded out a bit, but not fatly. If stouter at all, it was only in the slightly deeper look to the cream-colored skin. There were two lines across her forehead, but they had been there at eighteen and were quite obviously the result of tilting her eyebrows so that the flesh folded; and besides, they relieved her clearness, these horizontal traceries, of utter limpidity.

She had drifted, not all unconsciously, into a certain picturesque uniformity of dress and could smile now over the large, cart-wheel hats, coarse embroideries, and short-vamp shoes; neither was she often above mentally contrasting herself in her annual seventy-five dollar suit of dark-blue serge, natty sailor hat, and impeccable blouse, with a certain coffee-colored linen with its slashings of coffee-dipped embroidery, and the blouse that twirled with yards and yards of cotton Valenciennes.

There was still something of the look of the nun to Lilly, but a bit too pinkly, as if she had dressed the part for Act One, but wore the ballet skirts for Act Two underneath.

Her reaction asserted itself in her child. At thirteen Zoe wore straight frocks of navy-blue alpaca with wide patent-leather belts and deep Eton collars. They were mistaken sometimes, and, strangely enough, to Lilly's invariable chagrin, for sisters, and Lilly, in her refutation, could be smitingly swift.

At nine o'clock, to the staccato of three rings, she admitted Bruce Visigoth, leading him down the tube of hallway. It annoyed her unspeakably that Harry Calvert, collarless, poked out his head from a doorway as they passed, and she was suddenly conscious of the smell of stew. She had meant to burn an incense stick.

But she walked with that free, Hellenic stride of hers, without apology and ahead of him.

"This is our room. Zoe is asleep there behind that screen. Won't you sit down?"

He placed his hat and a light bamboo stick across the center table, obviously oppressed with a sense of close quarters.

"Tell you what! Suppose we taxi over to Claremont. It's mild enough to sit out on the terrace."

She met him with her levelest gaze.

"Aren't you going to be comfortable here?"

"Of course I am. There you go, getting sensitive right off. Only it is a warmish evening, and why keep the sun-child awake?"

"Zoe can sleep," she said, with the barely perceptible arch to her brows, "even through the fire of your presence."

"Good!" he said, seating himself in great good nature and trying not to be quizzical. "So this is where you live."

He was frankly curious, his gaze humorous, but traveling over details, his head upflung and the scenting movement to his nostrils. He had not changed in weight, but in compactness and as if the house of his being had settled with a fine kind of firmness. He was a bit squarer of jaw and shoulder and ever so prematurely, and to the enormous fancy of women, inclined to a hoar frost of gray at the temples.

She seated herself across the little square of table.

"You don't seem to care for us here."

"Certainly I do, only--only--"

"Only what?"

"Only--well, hanged if I make you out, lady. This place--it just isn't you--that's all."

"Nonsense! I don't count. I'm just a sort of a means to an end, anyway."

"What end?"

"The wine!"

"The what?"

"Oh, nothing," she said, and laughed.

"Laugh again."

"Why?"

"I like it."

She looked her most serio-comic disapproval and held up a forefinger with a warning little waggle to it.

"Please," she said, with an inlay of something deeper in her voice, "don't begin by spoiling things."

"Rather not," he said. "I'm going to live up to your letter of the law."

Except for the frequent conferences now in the new Forty-second Street offices that commanded a view of two rivers and a vast battledoor and shuttlecock of the city, it was the first time in all those years that stretched from the night at the Waldorf that they had sat thus tete-a-tete. The day of the move she had ridden up from the old Union Square offices with him, a stack of files in her lap. Once, too, on a Saturday, the day of Zoe's invariable luncheon downtown and subsequent opera matinee, he had strolled by what seemed mischievous chance into the tea room where they were dining, but the occasion had hardly been a success. There had been a great deal of badinage between him and Zoe, but Lilly had finished her meal almost in silence. The day following, a toy piano of complete range and really excellent workmanship had arrived. She returned it without showing it to Zoe. These incidents lay between them now.

"So this is where you live," he repeated, as if his long curiosity could not find satiety in fact.

"That I have an abode seems to amaze you."

"It does. You're such a detached sort. You rise so above the mundane things that clutter up life, that it is pretty much of a shock to realize that you use tooth powder and carry a latchkey. It's hard to reconcile Chopin and George Sand probably to those famous raw-meat sandwiches they loved to eat at midnight. Well, that's about the way I feel about you--hemmed in by--dull reality such as this."

"I like raw-meat sandwiches," she said.

"Me too."

They laughed.

She took up a sheaf of manuscript.

"If it doesn't bore you too much, I'm going to read it straight through."

"Oh, I forgot; the play, of course."

She looked up at him as if over spectacles.

"What else?"

"You say it has been the rounds?"

"Yes. Peddled in every office in New York. Kline and Alshuler kept it two years. Forensi paid her two hundred and fifty dollars advance on it and then let his option lapse. For another year there was some talk of Comstock and Comstock doing it, and then finally Hy Wolff got hold of it and the very month he died paid her a second two hundred and fifty to renew his option on it. I've always felt that if Ida had kept after Hy Wolff he would have produced it. He had faith in it, but somehow just didn't seem to get to it. You see, Ida hasn't any gumption--not the kind of aggressiveness the game demands. That is why in fifteen years you scarcely know she is in your office. That is why I plunged in and tried to rewrite 'The Web' with her. It's a big story, sweated out of her own agony. She may never write another. Probably won't. My little part in it has merely been to help her co-ordinate--round up the jumble of her ideas, so to speak. There is a big play somewhere in this story. I know you didn't like it as a sketch--I didn't, either. A short play cannot contain this drama. But out of a clear sky it occurred to me that you might see it as a three-act play. Oh, I know it isn't the kind of thing you've your mind's eye on, but why not take that step over into the legitimate *via* a big popular success? It may pave the way to bigger, finer things. Who knows--Ida Blair--'The Web'--may mean the beginning of your dream come true."

His mouth had straightened and thinned.

"You're right there. Ultimately I'll get into the other. If my brother knew as much about the booking end as he does the realty, I'd have gone over long ago. That is the most the success of the Amusement Enterprise can mean to me--to afford some day the legitimate as a plaything. It costs money to educate the public to better things. It's been profitable playing down to its taste--some day it is going to enable me to afford to be sufficiently altruistic to foot the bills for serving up the best. It costs to educate.",

"Fine! And it is only a question of time until you are ready for that inspiring fray. Meanwhile, why not help foot those bills with a little side flier in 'The Web'?"

"You are a little opportunist, aren't you?".

"I know 'The Web' isn't art. But it is a cross section of reality with the veins exposed and the sap of life running through them. Mrs. Blair, poor dear, can't write. God knows I can't. That is why the play has been through years of lying around in every office in New York. But the idea is there. You see, it is everything she has lived through. You know her story?"

"Yes."

"There is a scene when he comes screaming out of the room after having been through the third degree, half blind from the terrible lights and the terrible circle of terrible eyes, that isn't writing at all. It's life--a raw, palpitating picture of a social abuse that can touch the public as a reform measure can never hope to. Then the character of the boy--a delinquent. We've one right here in this apartment. One of those sweet, shy, half-frightened boys as gentle as a girl. The kind that tells the neighborhood children Peter Pan and reads his grandmother to sleep. I would trust him anywhere with Zoe, and yet there's the streak! The criminal, congenital streak through him that is as pathological as measles. Only we handle it under the heading of criminology. It's like taking an earache to the chiropodist. The boy is a thief. It's through him like a rotten spot, but instead of curing him the law wants to punish him. It's like spanking a child for having the measles. But to get back--Mrs. Blair has him in this play--just as if she had lifted him out of this apartment. She wrote him from the life, too. A young fellow who used to be on her husband's beat. It may not be fine writing, but 'The Web' has the throb of reality through it, and it is my opinion that one pulsebeat of life is worth all your chastity of form."

"Right."

"We're one on that? Good! Well, here is your opportunity to solder the first link into the legitimate. Keep it in mind while I am reading Ida Blair's play and remember I am not talking Ida Blair or Lilly Penny to you. I'm talking this play just as I would talk an act to you. Because I believe in it."

He seemed to look at her through her words, a smile out in his eyes.

"You're not listening."

"I am," he said, "but your hair looks like it is painted on, the way it comes down to that smooth little peak in front. Jove! it's pretty."

She looked off, wanting not to color.

"Come," he said, "I apologize. Read. I'm as predisposed as I can be toward anything conceived by that little dormouse of a person in the office."

"That's the trouble. You men are too often satisfied with a surface inventory. The vault of heart sometimes yields up rare treasures."

"How like you to say that."

"Ready?"

"Go!"

And so, with her head bent so that the light burnished its smoothness, she read him "The Web" through two uninterrupted hours, her voice throbbing into the quiet. In the third act, when a half-crazed victim of the third degree is led out in shuddering and horrible invocation, she sprang to her feet for an instant, her gesture decrying its fullest arc.

She was like Iphigenia praying for death, he thought.

Later, when the shades of the prison house begin to dawn upon the stunned consciousness of the woman, there were tears in her voice and on her lashes, and one fell to the back of her hand, which she wiped off against her skirt, like a child.

At eleven o'clock she finished, regarding him brilliantly through her flush.

He had wanted to smoke, but thrust the case back into his pocket, sitting tilted, his hands locked at the back of his head and gazing at the line of the picture molding. Her lips parted as the paused held.

"Well?"

He uncrossed his knees, straightening.

"Well?"

"Strong."

"Then it did grip you?"

"Yes, but I can see why it gathered dust as it went the rounds. From the average commercial manager's point of view there is a question about that seamy kind of thing getting over with the playgoer. He wants to be entertained, not harrowed.

That's pretty raw stuff. Except for the little woman and the poor delinquent young-ster, it is an out-and-out--what shall I say?--an out-and-out crook play, to coin a phrase."

"Exactly. It is a section of life about which your average playgoer knows little or nothing and yet one for which he nourishes a tremendous curiosity."

"It's crude--"

"I know, but the idea is bigger than the writing is crude. If I had the money I would take a chance on producing it to-morrow. It has social and sociological value, and at the same time is corking-good entertainment. I read the police-inspector scene to my little girl just to see what she would get out of it. 'Why,' she cried, 'a man would confess to anything with that white light on him and those big police-men's eyes on him. That's not fair! That shouldn't be allowed. Isn't there a way to stop it?' That from a thirteen-year-old! It's one of those man-made abuses that if we women ever get the vote we'll go after! Don't answer me on this play now, Mr. Visigoth. Take it to your hotel. Read it over again. Talk it over with your brother when he comes next week. How's that? No snap judgment."

"Good. The play is on the docket for the evening. Now let us get the taste of the underworld out of our mouths. How would the Claremont appeal now?"

"I'd rather not."

"Well, I suppose that amounts to my *conge?*"

She smiled with her brows arched.

"It is after eleven."

He was incessantly feeling for his cigarette case and then with a certain unease refraining.

"You may," she said, "one, before you go."

He held the case to her. She took one gingerly, accepting the light more gin-gerly.

"I don't like them," she said, exhaling with the violence of the unaccustomed.

"Then whyfore?"

"Because it is a stupid convention which says that a man may and a woman may not. Why should it be a matter of course for you and, in most cases, a matter of comment and even vulgarity for me?"

"Usage."

"Usage isn't a reason. It's Time's trick for applying the brake to progress."

He lit up gratefully, waving out the match and hesitating for a spot to dispose of it. She reached across the table, palm up. "Give me."

He caught her hand.

"Lilly!"

She jerked back with a little clicky catch of breath.

"Don't."

"Lilly, you're maddening! Lilly, can't you see what I haven't the words to tell you? For years--since that night at the Waldorf--I--I have been living for this moment. I realized it to-night as you read that play. Lilly, is what is between us insurmountable?"

She jerked back her head, her irises at their trick of growing.

"You don't know what you are saying!"

"I do know what I am saying. I know that you are the most delectable woman in the world--and for me."

She held out his hat and cane.

"My little girl is asleep. Hadn't you better go?"

"That's not fair," he said, taking the hat and cane, but flushing up furiously.

"I know it isn't. But what is there I can say to you?"

"You can talk it out. Man to man."

"Sit down," she said, clasping her hands and regarding him through swimming and revealing eyes.

"Now--what is there to say--Bruce--between you and me?"

"Where is he?"

"You know."

"Are matters unchanged?"

She nodded.

"I love you, Lilly."

"And I have a husband and a thirteen-year-old child, making of the triangle a rectangle."

"You have held me off on that dagger point now for ten years. Good God! women don't martyrize themselves to a past these days. What are you doing with your life? Sacrificing it on the altar of the old burned-out husk of a marriage? Canonizing a mistake!"

"It is the one thing I am able to do for him in some little reparation!"

"Mock heroics."

"No, it is more than mock heroic to save him that precious shred of his respectability. That is about all I have left him to cherish. There are some human beings you simply cannot conceive of in certain situations. Albert Penny and divorce are irreconcilable. Tear his heart out if you will, but hands off his respectability. It may sound absurd in the face of the enormity of what I have done to him, but it is a great solace to me to be able to sacrifice that much to him and to drag him through my life like a ball and chain. Somehow it seems that I ought to suffer that."

"Stuff and nonsense! You made your mistake and you had the courage to tear away from it by the roots. Unless those roots have a drag?"

"No. No drag! And yet I sometimes think my revolt has been a half madness. You cannot know the sheer folly, the crazy kind of tenacity that has driven me on through all these years! And for what? This mediocrity? Or is it that I am an instrument clearing the way for her? Zoe! Is there a divinity shapes our end, rough hew them how we will? Listen to something incredible. Do you know that Zoe's father doesn't know that he is a father?"

"Good God!"

"Yes, jealous truth going fiction one better."

"You mean to say you have fought this out alone?"

"He doesn't know. Neither do my parents. They would suck her down. Dwarf her with their terrible kind of love. She belongs to herself. She's a beautiful thing God has loaned me to rear into a rose, but the world is her garden in which to bloom and expand."

"In all these years they don't know your whereabouts?"

"Oh yes! I write home every Christmas. Just a line that I am well and happy. Occasionally I pick up notes of them in the St. Louis newspapers. I keep them pretty well under glass. It's all so dreamlike--I've always been obsessed with that consciousness. How faint can be the line between the dream and reality."

He drew her toward him by the hands, their faces lit, quivering, close.

"Lilly, Lilly, let us not stop just short of happiness."

"All my life I have done that."

"I cannot put you out of my heart now that I have put you in."

"No. No. No." But his embrace had already shaped itself, and, springing back from it and her own singing of the flesh, she crowded up against the wistaria-painted screen, shielding it.

"How dared you--here--in this--room! With her!"

"Lilly!"

"Go, please! Go, please!"

"You mean that?"

"You know I do."

He bent low in the attitude of kissing her hand, but without touching it.

"Forget everything I've said, Lilly, and forgive. We'll go back to the old. Good night, Lilly! Mrs. Penny."

He must have departed on the balls of his feet, because presently through the roaring of the silence she heard the door slam without having been conscious of his passage down the hallway; and then, after a second, Harry Calvert tiptoeing to her open door to look in with his light-blue eyes.

She sprang forward, throwing herself against the door as she locked it.

"Don't," she cried through it--"don't you ever dare do that again, Harry! Walk on your heels. You frighten me when you sneak like that--you--you--frighten--me."

Then she undressed, crying, tears rolling down to her high white chest and finally on to the crispiness of her plain nightgown. Crept to bed finally, into a darkness as sleek as a black cat's flank, silently, to save the sag of mattress, her body curving to the curve of her child's.

Once from the inky pool of that long night Zoe's hand crept up, finding out her mother's cheek.

"Lilly," floating up for a drowsy second to the surface of consciousness--"Lilly--you're crying. Are--you sad--again?"

"Yes, Zoe--terribly--terribly--"

CHAPTER III

The year that Zoe entered High School, 1914, out of an international sky of fairly pellucid blue, the thunderclap of world war burst in fury.

It was strange, though, even after the subsequent plunge of her country to the Allied flank, and the menacing and shifting tides of affairs creeping closer and closer to the edge of everyday life, how little the complexion of Lilly's routine was changed.

True, her national consciousness flared suddenly from lethargy to blaze. The evening after the sinking of the *Lusitania*, she attended a mass meeting in Astor Place with Zoe and Mrs. Blair, beating out an umbrella-and-floor tom-tom for redress, love of country suddenly a lump in her throat.

The day the Rainbow Division swept up Fifth Avenue in farewell, she could see the rank and file from the roof of the Forty-second Street office building, as if the avenue were running a clayey stream, and she was torn between the ache and the thanksgiving of having no one to give.

But, for the most part, war kept its talons off Lilly. Twice, and as if his exemption from the draft lay heavily, Harry Calvert had tried to enlist, his grandmother, with a zeal that was hardly accountable, exerting every effort toward that end.

It was almost as if war had revived her somewhat fainting faith in Harry's ultimate justification.

But he was underweight and still in a weakened condition from an operation for an adenoidal complaint. This last he had undergone before the war and at Lilly's urgent instance. She had read, in the mass of books on child hygiene, psychology, and physiology she was constantly accumulating, the debilitative effects that adenoidal breathing might exercise upon an entire constitution and mentality.

Poor Harry, and his cancerous predilection for the kind of thievery that almost invariably stacked up to not even petty larceny! He could withstand a jewel chest, but not a tool chest. Would steal the robe from an automobile, provided it was not a luxurious one. Once, when his grandmother at great difficulty had procured for him a clerkship, he confiscated the nickel-plated faucets out of the wash room, barely escaping prosecution. Only the utter triviality of his thievery and the fight in Mrs. Schum saved him from the law. She was as indomitable in her protection of him as the granite flesh of rocks.

Quiet, sensitive, with rather a girlish face, slow to beard and quick to quiver, Harry was invariably liked during the period he held a position, but month to month saw him from a clerkship in a real-estate office to window decorator for a retail paper-flower concern, salesman in the novelty and stationery department of a bookstore, and once in the children's book section of a department store.

He was rarely apprehended, usually abandoning his position, with his absurd loot already under cover, and the loss leaking out later, if at all.

Invariably, as if by way of confession, he brought home to his grandmother the proceeds from these petty sales, effected by who knows what device, dropping down into her lap, almost sadly and with a shrinkage from what was sure to follow, either the few dollars or the bauble of a bit of jewelry.

She would cry up at him and wring her poor hands, and then he would go off into his little room adjoining the kitchen, originally intended as maid's room, and sit with his head down in his hands, back rounded, and all his throat-constricting capacity for meekness out in his attitude.

And, presently, her sobs subsided, Mrs. Schum would creep in after him, and behind that closed door there was no telling what long hours of pleading and abjuration took place. But, next morning, in her little black bonnet, the rust out in her black dress and the "want ad." sheet cockily enough beneath her arm, Mrs. Schum would set out with him to combat, by the decency of her presence, some of the difficulties of seeking a new position with only one or two time-and thumb-worn references.

His grandmother's and Lilly's possessions were sacred to him, but every morning, after the two roomers had departed, Mrs. Schum would tiptoe after, locking their doors and inserting the keys in her petticoat pocket.

"I like to keep things locked," she explained to Lilly one day, upon being intercepted. "You can never tell when a sneak thief will break into these apartment houses that haven't hall service. I've even heard of them entering through the fire escape."

"Of course, dear," said Lilly, through heartache for her.

There was an indescribable sweetness in Harry's attitude toward Zoe. There had been countless long evenings of her little girlhood when no waiting beside her bedside was too tedious--sometimes during three and four evenings a week of Lilly's enforced absence in the pursuit of vaudeville novelties. He was tireless and faithful as a watchdog, keeping awake by whittling at something no more fantastic than a clothespin. There were hundreds of them scattered about the house. It was the sole form his idleness took. He painted heads and eyes on them--cleverly, too-- for Zoe, but as she grew older she began to disdain them, bullying him in much the fashion her mother had before her.

"I can hop up four steps on one foot," Lilly, with a little catch at her heart, chanced to overhear on one occasion.

"No, you can't," said Harry, smilingly and a little teasingly.

Catching at her ankle and flinging her curls, she made an unstaggering and easy ascent of not four, but eight.

"There!" she cried, slapping Harry boldly and resoundingly on the cheek. "Don't you ever dare say I cannot do what I know I can do."

It left the red print of her little hand, and it was literally as if, as he looked away from her, he had turned the other cheek.

Almost immediately she caught his hand, placing her warm face to its back.

"Harry, I'm a devil! I'm sorry. You know I don't mean to be a devil. Harry! Are you angry? You're not! Please! Be nice, Harry--tell me a story--Har-ry."

"Once upon a time--" he began, his light-blue eyes almost with the patient look of the blind.

A little later, there occurred an infinitesimal but telling incident which served to dissipate whatever growing qualms may have disturbed Lilly over the rearing of her child in this atmosphere of petty crime.

One evening, while Harry was performing his willing chore of carrying out for his grandmother the little dinner prepared by Mrs. Schum and partaken of by Lilly and Zoe at a small card table opened up beside the window of their room, Zoe announced, with a certain high-handedness with which Lilly was more and more hard pressed to cope:

"I want my dresses longer. That big red-headed boy in the white jacket said to me when I went into the drug store over on Columbus Avenue to-day for some licorice drops: 'That's right. Wear 'em short; you've got the stems.'"

"What a vulgar, horrid remark!"

"Well, I want my dresses longer."

Lilly regarded her daughter with concern troubling up her eyes.

"Don't ever go into that store again, Zoe. I've a mind to stop in there myself and talk to the proprietor."

Later that same evening, Harry, with a purpling eye and an opened lip which he tried vainly to smuggle past his grandmother, crept into his room. But she was too quick for him, and at her high cry of shock Lilly rushed into the hallway. There was an utterly alien and vibrating note of anger in Harry's voice.

"For God's sake, gramaw, be quiet! It's nothing. Had a row with that red-headed clerk down at the drug store. Took the freshness out of him for a while."

Lilly tiptoed back to her room. All through a fitful night she woke in little starts, kissing into the bare white arm of her child as if she could not have done with the assurance of her safe proximity.

It was less than a month later, and over a year after the adenoidal operation, that Harry returned home one evening from the real-estate office with nine dollars and forty cents in his pocket from the proceeds of the nickel-plated wash-room faucets and several liquid-soap attachments.

*   *   *   *   *

About eight months after Ida Blair's play had lain gathering mold in the lower drawer of Bruce Visigoth's desk, he sent for Lilly.

Their office relationship since the stuffy June evening over the reading of the manuscript had been resumed, with invisible joindure. Together they continued in biweekly conferences to compile the endless cycle of programs that moved like a chain along the cogs of city to city. There were nine Enterprise Amusement Theaters now, the newest red-headed pin on the circuit map as far west as Tulsa, their

booking route as yet independent of any of the larger and recent vaudeville merg-
ers.

It was an office boast and pleasantry that Lilly could recite offhand through the
current program of any of the nine theaters, leaping glibly from motion picture, to
acrobat, and sister acts.

This was hardly true, but her touch at the steering wheel of her department
was sensitive and sure. She could substitute for a quarantined team of jumping Ar-
abs in Springfield, Illinois, with hardly more than a sleight of hand through her
card index and a telegram or two. She knew that Memphis would not stand for a
pickaninny act, and that the same was sure fire in Trenton, and was familiar with
every house manager by long-distance-telephone voice. The department was more
and more the well-oiled engine under a light steering hand that Lilly wielded well
and wisely.

Her judgment of the incoming reports of the various house managers, or a try-
out act, although technically subject to Bruce Visigoth's signature, went usually
unchallenged. She virtually was her department, particularly as the realty aspect
of the enterprise came more and more to assume the proportions of big business.
Within her little office of mahogany appointments she worked with an allotment
of stenographers and clerks. She had an assistant, too; at least, she confiscated him
from the press department--one Leon Greenberg, a young night student from New
York University, with an enormous profile rendered positively carnivorous of thrust
by his struggle up from First Street and Avenue A, which is mire with a pull to it.

Her own capacity was unnamed. She was probably still down on the books as
stenographer, although at fifty dollars a week now, and it was six years since she
had taken a letter.

It was a gray day in cold and tardy spring when Bruce Visigoth sent for her-
-one of those heavy afternoons that darken up at four o'clock and press thick as
gravy against the windows. He was seated at his desk, hands laced at the back of
his head and one foot propped on an open drawer, his male stenographer typing at
the remote corner of a wide and rather luxuriously appointed office. Except for the
green cone of light over him, the room was plushy with dusk.

"About that play--" he began.

"What play?" she said, seating herself in the entirely easy business manner she had with him.

"'The Web.'"

Her strong white hand out from its immaculate linen cuff lay unnervously on the glass top of his desk, but the fingers now began to lift in rotation.

"Yes?"

"I talked it over with my brother before he returned to Chicago yesterday. Thought the firm might be interested."

"Yes?"

"He doesn't see it."

"He--wouldn't."

He bent a sliver of ivory paper knife almost double.

"I should have taken this matter up some time ago, but the sudden death of my sister Pauline's husband, Doctor Enlow--"

"Mrs. Blair understands that."

"And you?"

"Well," she said, looking off and resolutely keeping her smile, "I guess it means 'The Web' must resume its journey again."

"No, it doesn't."

"Why?"

"It means that I am going to produce it on my own."

She slid to the edge of the chair, her hand closing over the desk edge.

"Oh! Oh!"

"Isn't that what you want?"

"Yes."

"Well, that is my reason."

"You mean you don't see it, either?"

"But you do."

"But--"

"No 'buts.' She goes into rehearsal for a spring try-out in Baltimore, Stamford, or any of the dog towns. I'm giving the manuscript to Forbes to read this week. He's the man to direct that type of thing. I'm going to throw in ten or twenty thousand on your judgment."

"You're serious?" He held out his lean hand. "Ill send for Ida Blair."

"No--please!"

"Why?"

"Sit down."

She did, biting back excitement.

"I don't know how to talk to that little woman. She depresses me. This is your venture and mine."

"But her play! Its production will mean her resurrection. Her monument to a memory. Her protest. A chance to get her on her feet. An opportunity for a home, a background, a reason for living to a woman who has lost every reason. It's her play and her chance."

"And it is our venture."

"I'm not afraid."

"Are we partners, then?"

"If I had the money, yes, to my limit."

"I don't mean that."

"I do."

"All right; go your limit."

"My limit? How far would six one-hundred-dollar municipal bonds and--"

"Good. I'll sell you six per cent of a twenty-thousand-dollar venture for the six hundred."

"Six--percent--twenty--thousand--Why, that's not a man-to-man proposition! You're treating me like a child."

"All right, then; three per cent for the six hundred."

"Done! But no nonsense. If I lose, I lose. Man to man."

"'Man to man,'" he said, clasping her hand and drinking down deep into her gaze. And so, when she hurried out to the high ledge to which Ida Blair's figure had somehow shaped itself as the years went on, she stood for a moment to steady the hand she placed on that shoulder.

"Ida!" The older woman raised her eyes of the peculiarly washed quality of gray that has faded from repeated scaldings in hot water. "Mr. Visigoth wants you in his office, dear--now."

She kept her voice out of quaver, but it had a singing quality like a plucked violin string.

CHAPTER IV

As Lilly's months went, the one that followed was abloom with events. In her vague, untutored way she was already reaching out, through her daughter, toward a subject about which she knew nothing, but, in an inchoate way, felt a great deal.

The New York State fight for woman's suffrage had not yet reached its victorious culmination, and, reading announcement of a great parade up Fifth Avenue for a Saturday afternoon, she took Zoe.

The smell of spring was dancingly out. Shop windows bloomed with the millinery of May. Open street cars, open skies, and openwork shirt waists had arrived.

They climbed the flank of an omnibus and rode down to the Washington Arch in a midair snapping with bunting.

It was on one of those irresistible afternoons--radiant with the sun-washed geometry of three architectural renaissances, a monastic-fronted fur emporium, a Parthenon of a library, a Doric-columned bank--that Lilly and Zoe lumbered their omnibus way through the daily carnival of the most rococo avenue in the world.

There was the flare of a sea gull to Zoe--no containing her. Little snatches of song bubbled. She was a freshet of delight.

"Look at that tray of violets, Lilly! I must have a bunch."

"Zoe, don't lean over so far!"

"See the yellow satin in that shop window, Lilly! I'd love to wind it round me. It's like sun!"

"See those jams of women in white, Zoe, waiting to form into line!"

"I'd love to march!"

"Why?"

"Oh, I don't know, there--there's something sort of onward about it."

"Exactly! Onward! Forward! March!"

With a precocity that never ceased to amuse and delight Lilly, Zoe, while only half understanding the content of an occasion, could somehow imbibe its essence. She leaned now over the rail of the omnibus, the cross-town streets, as they jogged past, already colloid masses of women waiting to fall into line.

"Isn't it queer, Lilly, that after all these centuries and centuries women are just beginning to--what did that woman on the program call it down at Cooper Union hall the other night--function in the government? Why has it taken them so long to ask for their half in the say-so of things?"

"Any great movement, Zoe, must have very slow beginnings. Think for what ages man lived without Christianity!"

"Yes; but look how long it has been here."

"Reckoning in geology, Zoe, and compared with the age of mountains and oceans, two thousand years isn't long."

"I think it is."

"You darling!"

They alighted at the Washington Arch, jamming their way into the tight battalion of spectators already lining both sides of lower Fifth Avenue. The head of the parade was already forming, a slim young leader holding in her white mount with difficulty.

"Lilly, she looks like our picture of Jeanne d'Arc when she sees the vision!"

"She is heeding a vision, Zoe--of to-morrow."

"I feel so--so thrilled, Lilly. Do you?"

"Yes," said Lilly, for some reason breathing hard. "Oh, I do!"

There was a break of music, and all about them women darting into line, sudden banners floating out, and the white horse prancing in the archway, for all the world as if spun at a tangent off the narrative frieze of the arch.

At the Eighth Street curb, where they stood, five hundred women, with standards lifted, stiffened suddenly into formation, a deputy from their ranks, a buyer, by the way, for the largest cloak-and-suit house in the world, calling short, quick orders and distributing American flags.

The air was rent with silk and brass; a simoom of rapture raced over Zoe. She danced on the balls of her feet. It was then that a deputy, with a face that recalled newspaper reproductions of it, spied her.

"Here, little girl! You! Oh, lovely! Could you manage this banner, dear, and lead this section? Miss, is this lovely child your sister? Do let her lead!"

"She's my daughter."

"Come; you may fall in line right behind her. Do you mind if I unpin your sister's curls? Oh, she's lovely--"

"I said she's my *daughter!*"

"Here, right in front, dear--my--oh, what a find!"

And so, with her somewhat bewildered parent in the ranks behind her, her little black frock wrapped in a purple-and-yellow banner, head up, eyes stars, Zoe Penny led the largest district of Greater New York up Fifth Avenue, a constant and running line of applause following her lead.

She was youth sonnetized. Cameras clicked after her, and, with the martial music tickling her blood, her head went higher still, like a stag's. To her mother, following after, it seemed that the loudest of all must be music within her own heart, and so she marched on, sprayed, as it were, by the wave of constant applause as it broke over Zoe and died down at the rank and file.

It was dusk when they reached Fifty-ninth Street, and in the jam of disbanding and quite a little demonstration over Zoe by the section she had distinguished, they worked their way out finally toward the cross-town street car, hand in hand, like two ecstatic, rather bewildered babes in the wood.

At a touch upon her shoulder Lilly turned, spun, rather, under high tension, to encounter the well-bred hesitancy of an exceedingly slender woman, a very small head set on the stem of a long, gracile neck, something hauntingly familiar in the somewhat heart-shaped face and the far-apart eyes that were considerably younger than the white hair which framed them.

"I beg your pardon"--in a voice perfectly rounded of edges--"but my husband is so enchanted with the little girl that we are taking the liberty of asking to meet her. Won't you permit me to present my husband, Gedney Daab? You have heard of him, I presume."

Lilly had. The "Dolorosa" above her desk was a print from a Gedney Daab.

He stepped forward then, lanky and rugged, with a great shock of upstanding gray hair, with the path of his fingers through it and his features with no scheme at all. Just very delightfully irregular, he jutted out of any crowd.

"Zoe, Mr. and Mrs. Daab want to meet you."

She lifted her clean gaze, dropped a courtesy, and held out her hand with the short, curved gesture of childhood.

"Hello!" he said, the timbre of real youth in his voice, which childhood is so quick to detect from the silly enameling of tone coated on by grown-ups for the occasion. "I want to paint you, youngster."

"Oh, Lilly, what fun!"

"Then she is your sister?"

"Oh no, Mrs. Daab; she is my daughter."

"But the name--"

"It's our way together."

"How droll!"

"Do you think I'm pretty?"

Gedney Daab looked down at her ardent artlessness without a burst of laughter.

"Oh, as little girls go."

"Zoe knows God has merely given her a fair urn of a body, Mr. Daab, which she, in turn, must fill with beauty of mind and spirit."

"You are the Dolorosa, aren't you?" continued Zoe, turning to Mrs. Daab. "The sad one with the tears that don't show, from crying on the inside of you."

It was not until then that this dawned upon Lilly. Those eyes of the Dolorosa, bleeding tears, were Mrs. Daab's.

"You'll have to paint me as glad--won't you?--glad all over clear from the inside."

"Yes, Sunlight; I rather think I will."

"Will you permit my husband and me to take you home, Mrs.--"

"Penny."

"Oh, please, Lilly!"

"We live rather far up from here--Ninety-first Street, West."

"And we live at Park Hill; so you see we hardly regard that as far."

They were presently riding through the Park, Zoe facing the three of them in the soft gray interior of the Daab limousine. She was absolutely artless.

"I've been in a taxi three times and a hansom once. But I prefer this. I shall have my own some day--only, purple upholstery instead of gray--sort of wine color--"

"An early eye to effect, I see, young miss."

"I'm the class beauty," she explained. "I didn't care to be that at first--Lilly says it is just a lovely accident and might happen to anyone else. She wanted me to be class president; so I decided to be both."

"You will observe that my daughter is not chiefly notable for her reticence."

"You come to my studio, little lady, and I am going to paint you just as golden and radiantly innocent as you are."

"What is 'radiantly innocent'?"

"Good Lord! I don't know any definition of it except--you."

"Zoe has no innocence in one sense, Mr. Daab. Her real innocence lies in the fact that life has no ugly secrets from her. She knows the beautiful from the ugly, and why it is so. I think that is what Mr. Daab means by 'radiant innocence,' Zoe.' Fearless knowledge of truth."

He whistled softly in the gloom.

"Extraordinary!" said Mrs. Daab. "And you are one of us--aren't you, dear?"

"For suffrage? Oh yes; and I am going to be a real one when I grow up."

"What else are you going to be?"

"A singer."

"You said that as if you meant it."

"I do. I've already heard nine operas. I am allowed to be anything I want so long as I get to the biggest--the very biggest!"

"Are you studying?"

"I've had piano lessons for five years."

"I'm looking about now for a vocal teacher for her. She may be too young, but at least I want her voice tried. I--we think she has quite an amazing range."

"Have you tried Trieste?"

"Oh, I haven't dared contemplate anyone so inaccessible as he."

Mrs. Daab turned her head.

"Gedney," she said, "couldn't you give her a note to Trieste?"

"Good!" he said, feeling for a card and scrawling across its face. "This will pass you directly to his nibs."

"You couldn't have granted us a bigger favor," said Lilly, feeling her face glow.

"Then you grant me one. Bring your little girl to my Fifty-ninth Street studio. I want to paint her."

"Indeed I will!"

"When?"

"Saturday afternoon is our only time."

"Fine. To-day two weeks?"

"Yes."

They Were at Ninety-first Street now, and he saw them up to their door.

"Good-by," he said. "You're a great youngster, and you've picked a great little mother for yourself. Mrs. Daab and I want you both at the studio often."

Up in their room, they embraced, Zoe's arms tight about her mother's neck.

"It's begun, Lilly, to be wonderful!"

"What?"

"Life!"

                  *   *   *   *   *

The Saturday afternoon following, in a brownstone house in West Forty-sixth Street that was more like a museum of the storied loot of many lands, Trieste himself opened the pair of Florentine doors, originally unhinged from a campanile outside of Rome, of his very private studio, without appointment, to the magic of Gedney Daab's scrawled card.

He had a head, Lilly decided, like the one of Praxiteles in the St. Louis Museum of Fine Arts--only, the bust implied young hair, and Trieste's curls were full of gray and the lines of his face were slashed deeply. He listened, while Lilly talked her brief preamble, as he invariably did, with his eyes closed and finger tips touching. Finally, he opened them, regarding Lilly from under swollen, rather diabetic lids.

"You should sing," he said, his acquired language grating slightly against the native one.

"No! No!"

"You are young," he said, running his eyes down her body, "and fine and big and strong."

She rose as if to throw off the crowding stress of the moment.

"Once," she said; "but that is all over now. My little girl--"

"You have temperament--let me hear," he said, reaching out to the piano and striking out a bold C. "Sing the scale."

"Please!" she cried, the situation an agony to her. "Not me. My little--"

"Why, Lilly!" said Zoe, regarding her mother with wide, unaffected eyes. "Sing the scale, dear."

"Do-re-mi-fa-sol-la-si-do"--through a crimson flush.

He seemed to lose interest then, turning to Zoe.

"Let me hear you," he said.

"Shall I sing 'Jocelyn' or 'How Like a Bird'?"

"Anything--something simpler."

"Schubert, then, Zoe."

In her straight frock, with its wide patent-leather belt and flat white collar, the cascade of her hair down over it, Zoe held the center of the vast studio, singing straight into her mother's eyes.

It seemed to Lilly, at the sound of that voice, not yet cleared of childish treble, but as ready to rise as a lark, that every ounce of her blood must be gushing against her throat; so, after it was finished, she sat on quite dumbly, staring at the manner in which Trieste remained sitting with his eyes closed.

"Lyric soprano," he said, finally. "Fine! Big! God-given!"

"*Maestro*--you mean that?"

"Heigh-ho!" he said on a sigh, walking over and placing his hand on Zoe's curls. "I make up my mind I am seeck of this business. I wait only for this war to live my day quietly in Capri, where I have my *casa*, and now a new nightingale flies in at my window. Twice now. Ten years ago comes Carrienta out of just such a clear sky, and once more, when I am again sure that one voice is only more unmusical than the rest, comes this--"

Standing there, Lilly was fighting an impulse to faint. She remembered, with terror, previous sensations, and fought off the vertigo, biting down into her lips. She wanted to smile, but her mouth felt numb, as if it dragged instead of lifted.

"You--you make us very happy--*maestro*."

"Some day," cried Zoe, still thrilling from her effort, "I will sing until my high C hits the sky!"

'I think you will, **bella mia**, if you have in you the power to work for it."

"I have."

"Art is the most cruel paymaster in the world. It exacts full recompense, toil, and heartache before it deals out a first payment in success."

"I'll pay! I'll pay for what I want, and most of all I want to sing!"

She trilled up a brace of scales for him then, and there were minute questions of health and habits, and, finally, in a waiting pause, Lilly found word to ask the question against which her lips stiffened.

"What--are--your terms--**maestro**?"

Something strange happened then, his well-known acumen immediately asserting itself. It was as if he had slipped into another personality.

"Fifteen dollars a lesson. She must have three a week and her school work and other studies should be reduced."

"Lilly--we're too poor for that!"

"I--I'm afraid my little girl is right, **maestro**. I--I couldn't even pay that for all three. I'm employed myself, you see."

"Oh," he said, and walked off to the window, dilly-dallying on his heels and looking out.

Finally he turned, with a gesture of dismissal.

"I have never before, except Carrienta, done such a thing. It must be a secret between us. My belief is that art should be as well paid as any life work, whether it is dentistry or lawmaking or storekeeping. But your child here--they do not come so every day. In ten years, with hundreds of pupils each year, she is the greatest since Carrienta. But I must have first right to her. You hear, first right! I will teach her free of charge. Leave your name and address with my secretary as you go out. Send her Monday at four. Loose clothing. Not even corset waists. Good afternoon. Good-by--Zoe"--placing his hands on her curls as if for their warmth.

In the room adjoining, under whisper of a very soft pedal, some one, probably a waiting pupil, was playing the indomitable pianoforte composition, "Melody in F." Staring at her daughter, an old conceit of Lilly's girlhood came flowing back. It seemed to her that a proscenium arch of music was forming over Zoe and that her voice, a high-flung scarf of melody, was winding itself reverently round a star.

*   *   *   *   *

That afternoon, Bruce Visigoth again asked Lilly to marry him.

Taking advantage of the quiet of a Saturday afternoon half holiday, she had returned to the office to clear her desk of an accumulation of loose ends.

In spite of herself, an extraordinary depression, low as storm clouds, was gathering over the excitation whipped up by Trieste's acceptance of Zoe.

The tight squeeze of a lump was gathering in her throat. Finally she laid her cheek to the desk and cried a little pool of her unaccountable melancholy on to the glassed surface.

Bruce Visigoth found her so, although, at his entrance, she sprang from the mound of her misery, violently simulating affairs at a lower drawer.

"Hello!" he cried, then, eying her crumpled cheek and the lane of tears: "Ah, I say now! Come, come; this won't do. What's up?"

She rubbed her bare hand furiously across the ravages of her sharp depression.

"Nothing. I--I guess I'm blue," she said, in a half laugh. "Something wonderful has happened to Zoe, and I--it's made me so happy, I'm blue. That's it--so--happy--I'm blue."

"What is the wonderful thing?"

She told him.

It was then he caught her hands.

"Lilly, marry me! Make it possible! Don't let the years lead you into a blind alley. You are bound inevitably to lose a child like Zoe--to life. That's why you are so unaccountably blue, Lilly; the writing is on the wall."

"No!" she cried, plunging past him, her hat in hand and her throat now a cave of the winds for her unreleased sobs. "The years have brought me, Zoe. She is my fulfillment. You can't frighten me--life cannot take her from me. I'm not afraid--only, I can't bear anything to-night, least of all from you--"

"Lilly, you're not--"

"Let me go! I'm all right--only tired--that's all. Terribly--terribly--tired."

She was presently on her homeward way, walking swiftly, almost, it would seem, a little madly, through a May evening that hung as thinly as one thickness of a veil.

At Seventy-second Street she veered suddenly and rather unaccountably to Riverside Drive and down into a ledge of park that dips like a terrace to the Hudson

River.

An asphalt walk led in festoons from high parky nooks that sheltered couples, down to the water-slapped edge of docks, where the tidey surf had a thick, inarticulate lisp, as if what it had to say might only be comprehended from the under side.

At one of the lowermost curves of the walk, the width of a brace of railroad tracks between, a coal dock jutted out into the river. Across these forbidden tracks, indeed, as if they did not exist, Lilly wandered.

At the last inch of dock, so that the water licked up at her shoes, Lilly stood poised. Not, it is true, with the diver's blade thrust of arms, but rather the unskilled, the indeterminate movement of one vaguely prompted from the unfathomable places of the heart.

It was upon that move that something, a terrifying restraint, laid hold of Lilly's jangling nerve ends.

"Hey there! None o' that to-night!"

A dockman's hand, hairy as an Airedale, had her by the arm, and somewhere at her brow, cooling it, the fine hand of Bruce Visigoth, pressing her against him, and at that touch Lilly's hysteria shot up like a geyser.

"Don't!" she screamed, and would have struggled for the edge except for the two firm hands now pressing her arms to her sides.

"Lilly, for God's sake, get hold of yourself!"

"Let me go! Let me go!"

"Aw no; we don't leggo. It's a good stroke we both happened to spy you at the same minute. There's nothin' gives strength like a spell of the craziness. You'd 'a' jumped me alone, sure!"

"No! No! It wasn't that--God, not that! Tell me, Bruce, it wasn't--that."

"Of course it wasn't, Lilly."

"That's what they all say once they git their senses jerked back. Come in here and pull yourself together, girl, or I'll call an ambulance or a patrol, suiting your pleasure."

"Let me go, you! I won't stand it. I must have been mad! Bruce, you tell him, please--it wasn't--that!"

"You're wrong, old man. Here--take this for your trouble, but this young woman is my sister. We walked out here together."

Quieted suddenly to the merest timbre of insolence, the old man shambled off.

"Sure!" he said, far too knowingly. "Sure!" And faded shaggily, impudently into darkness.

Bruce Visigoth took Lilly home in a taxicab. At her door she broke her shamed silence.

"You understand, Bruce, it wasn't anything--like that. It must have been nerves--tiredness--but nothing, Bruce, that you think it was. That old man was wrong. You must understand--for her sake--it wasn't that."

"Of course it wasn't, Lilly." His voice drained off, as if from exhaustion.

But for years, like a wound whose jagged lips were slow to close, the memory of this night lay palpitating between them.

CHAPTER V

The Web" was tried out in Baltimore the following April, Zoe, Ida Blair, and Bruce Visigoth traveling down on the same train with the company. It cost Lilly a pang for Zoe to miss the two days of school and a vocal, a French, and a piano lesson, but the theater attracted Zoe like the blithesome little moth she was. The duties of her High School combined with the unrelenting tutelage of Treiste molded her young days pretty rigidly to form, but more than once, during the rehearsals of "The Web," Lilly, seated in the black maw of the auditorium, would turn suddenly to the feel of her daughter's gaze burning like sun through glass into the darkness. The company adopted her as a pet. The director babied her. Once, as the afternoon rehearsal was disbanding, she crept up through a box to the stage. The footlights were dark, but she came down quite freely toward them, seeming to feel their mock blaze, and sang a snatch or two from the tenderest *Lieder* ever written, bits of Schubert and Hugo Wolf, the company gathering in the wings to listen and applaud.

The incident, slight as it was, brought the scratch of tears to Lilly's eyes and the pull of half hysteria to her lips. What if, after all, an incredible fulfillment was gathering about her like a vast dawn? "O God! please!"

And so, to the unending delight and amusement of Bruce, Zoe went along to Baltimore, Lilly pinching a little over the expense and pressing out ribbons and girlish accessories up to the last minute.

With Ida Blair, who had sunk back against years the colorlessness of cold dish water, herself more colorless, it was as if she had fired her one and only shot and run retreating behind the explosion.

Already her name had been linked with a co-author on programs and three-sheets, because a collaborator, a professional mender of plays, had been called in at the last moment to riddle the drama's somber story with a few "laughs." A character policeman, a comedy jury foreman, and a subplot of love story between the character policeman and an Irish cook had been "written in." The last act entirely revised, a happy ending substituted, and the theme of the story extricated like a jumping nerve.

It was the heroic treatment administered by experts to save what looked like unmistakable demise after the first Baltimore performance, and all the while Ida Blair sat mutely by, trying to probe through the actuality of her play or what was left of it, actually in the acting.

"The Steel Trap," as it was renamed, played to indifferent reviews and receipts the remainder of the Baltimore engagement, and lost money in Washington, but to the director, Bruce Visigoth, and certainly to Lilly, looked a potential property.

So after two weeks the play was removed, revamped, recast, still another play diagnostician called in, and under his surgery the third and fourth acts combined, and the original role of love story made to predominate what sociological note the play still contained. After an October tryout in Stamford and a New York opening of still doubtful reception, when the production hung between life and death and all the well-known exigencies of oxygen were applied in the form of "papering" the house with two weeks of free tickets, press-agenting, *et al.*, the public decided to like it.

"Who Did It?" as it was re-renamed, settled down to a run of forty-three New York weeks, and along the Rialto the source of its authorship leaked out and became curbstone, and finally newspaper, patter.

At the end of six months Ida Blair had resigned her bookkeepership, erected a small but perfect plinth of blue granite in a certain hillside cemetery, purchased a story-and-a-half bungalow in the heart of two Long Island acres, and was raising leghorns and educating a niece by marriage.

For the forty-three metropolitan weeks, not to mention stock, foreign, motion pictures, and road incomes that were to accrue later, Lilly was receiving her share, never less than one hundred and twenty-five dollars a week and often considerably more.

It was a windfall pure and simple. The years of petty pickering suddenly seemed more horrid to her in retrospect than she had ever realized they were in the living.

It was hateful to have reckoned in car fares and to so often have appeared to do the niggardly thing before the unspoken reproach of her child.

That same winter a cashier's note with her weekly check announced a thirty-three and a third per cent advance in salary. Life had suddenly quickened its tempo. She was passing through one of those eras when events, long crouched, seem to spring simultaneously.

*   *   *   *   *

In April, 1917, the United States declared war against Germany. Daily life, even to the indirectly touched, took on a new throb. Fourteen men employees of the Amusement Enterprise Company enlisted the first week. A service flag went up. Bruce Visigoth, outside the draft limit, immediately enrolled on a service committee, spending two days out of every week in Washington. Vaudeville ranks sagged suddenly and for a brief moment the gray-haired actor came back into his own. Office tension tightened. A nervousness set in. A telephone ringing could set Lilly's nerves to quivering and the telephone not ringing fill her with a nameless sort of anxiety.

More and more, too, it seemed to her, with the emotions always just a scratch beneath the surface those war times, that the agony of pretense between her and Bruce Visigoth could not endure. That he had applied for a commission in active service Lilly knew, but merely from correspondence. There had been no talk about it. She awoke nights, heavy with a dread she could not name.

Only the violent conjuring of her child and a vision of Albert Penny carried her rebellion past these bad places. Their frequent enforced conferences; the chance touching of their fingers, only to fly too instantly apart; the impeccable masks of indifference and elaborate casualness of manner; the forbidden singing through her entire being as he walked into the office and the imperturbability of the manner she must present to him. To contemplate a future futile with such dreary repetition became almost more than she could bear, and bitter with that salt were the lonely tears she cried at night.

Even the occasional appearance of Robert Visigoth came more and more to be a sort of biting irritant to a gangrenous spot she thought long since had hardened.

He had grown enormously fat and Rufus G. Higginbothom, dying, had enhanced that glutted look by bequeathing to his only daughter, Hindle, without stipulation, a leaf-lard fortune of some seventeen million dollars.

When his daughter, Pauline, was thirteen, he brought her to New York on one of his frequent fliers, parading the fat, freckled, and frightened youngster from one department to another.

"How much do you think she weighs?" he was fond of interrogating, with his small parental eyes full of pride. "Hundred and thirty-six for thirteen years. Not bad, eh?"

With about the sickest sensation she was ever to know, Lilly saw him this day lead his daughter past her open door, his face averted and the roll of fat at the back of his neck redly conscious.

It was after this incident that a half plan, long dormant, lifted its head. Every day in her comings and goings through the wide fireproof corridors of the Forty-second Street building a sign on a ground-glass door waved at her like a flag:

MISS NELLIE TERRY

Playbroker

Authors'
Manuscripts
Placed

She had little doubt of her ability to launch out into a scheme of this sort for herself and liked to incubate the idea in the back of her head, going so far as to inspect a tiny office on the fifteenth floor, mentally furnishing it up, and visualizing her name in neat black letters on her own ground-glass door.

She did broach the subject to Zoe one evening, who, with her head wrapped in a brilliant fez improvised out of an old cushion top, stood before the mirror, attitudinizing her part in school entertainment.

"No! Don't go into anything tin horn like that! I hate for you to keep playing *second fiddle*."

In the pause that followed, hardly perceptible enough to hold the drop of a pin, Zoe flashed toward her mother, the colossal ego of her youth somehow penetrated for the moment.

"Why, Lilly--I--I mean--You know what I mean--"

"Of course I know what you mean, dear. Second fiddle!"

And so what with Zoe's growing demands and Lilly's rooted fear of any jeopardy to them, time marched on rather imperceptibly, except that Lilly thinned and whitened a bit, slendering down, as it were, to more and more sisterly proportions as her daughter shot up to meet her. They were shoulder to shoulder now, if the truth were known, Zoe a little in the preponderance.

Meanwhile, Zoe was growing restive of the somewhat irksome limitations of the Ninety-first Street apartment. She complained that the room was oppressive for her long hours of study and practice. Visits to the Daab studio, faithful in effect to a Doge's palace and where she was more and more a favorite, and also to the pretentious homes of one or two school companions, had an upsetting effect upon her. The long, gloomy neck of hallway depressed her and she voiced bitterly a secret aversion of Lilly's for the single bathroom with the ugly wooden floor and shallow bathtub. "Dump" she called the little flat, her brilliant blue gaze blackening up.

"I can't have the girls and boys visit me in this little two-by-four, dear. It's a dump!"

And so early in the run of "Who Did It?" the little group moved again. This time to a strictly modern, pretentious apartment in West End Avenue, whose upper apartments boasted a river view and three baths and rented as high as four and five thousand dollars a year.

For twelve hundred Lilly obtained the ground-floor rear, no view, but five fairly large rooms and two capacious baths. And since such a house takes its tone from its highest-priced tenants, they enjoyed with them the uniformed hall service, the ornate entrance *de luxe* and foyer *de trop*.

In lieu of maid, Harry again occupied those quarters, his grandmother sleeping on a davenport in the sitting-dining-room. There were no roomers, Lilly carrying the resultant deficit.

She and Zoe again shared what corresponded to the parlor, this time a fairly large room, with alcove curtained off for sleeping quarters. They furnished it themselves, quite charmingly, too, and with a consensus of taste except where Lilly gave way to Zoe's really superior intuition.

There were plain ecru walls, not papered, but, at Zoe's instance, painted and roughened up with a process called "stippling." The two-tone brown rug. An over-stuffed couch of generous proportions and upholstered in a nicely woven imitation of Flemish tapestry. Along the back of this piece, which occupied virtually the center of the room, was a long, narrow table the exact length of the couch, with a pair of Italian polychrome candlesticks, gift of Gedney Daab, at either end.

A piece of old red brocade hung over the fireplace, covering the ugly mirror, and facing it a brown-rep fireside chair, coarse tan fishnet curtains, a pair of huge black-velvet floor cushions with orange-colored balls in each center, bespeaking a new art era which was dawning as colorfully and as formlessly as a pricked egg yolk.

An upright piano was stacked with music, and, in spite of Lilly's argument for them, no pictures on the walls, only a brilliant panel portrait of Zoe, signed Gedney Daab, her young form in faint profile against a background of cloth of gold, the face up-flung to a flow of sunlight that crossed the picture in a churchy ray.

"If we cannot have originals or etchings, we won't have any. I hate middle-classness."

"But, Zoe, dear--a few good prints. 'The Age of Innocence'--"

She kissed her mother on the mouth with all the outrageous patronage of youth.

"You're a darling, Lilly, but they just aren't doing it that way any more, dear."

So there were no pictures.

At the time of this move, Harry had been holding the position of clerk at the cigar, magazine, and book concession of one of the newest and noisiest of Broadway's terrific commercial hotels.

The hours were difficult, from noon to midnight, but within the seventeen months he had advanced from fifteen to twenty-five dollars a week. A new, a surprising spruceness had laid hold of him. He took to exceedingly tall small collars and vivid neckwear, his suit very narrow and making him look less than ever his years.

Mrs. Schum, too, had taken on some of that well-being, and, though she complained constantly of a sciatic twist in her side, something had lifted from off her. Her patter about the house, in the slippers with the rubber insets, was lighter; she discarded the old jet-edged dolman with the humps on the shoulders and the slits for the arms, for a decent full-length black coat with a stitched braid border and self-covered buttons, gift of her grandson. There had been a present for Lilly, too, a light-blue, drugstore-purchased celluloid toilet set.

He no longer sat idle in his room, his light eyes futile with staring at space or his head down tiredly in his hands. Something had indeed come over Harry.

"After all," said Lilly, always readily buoyed, "the operation did accomplish!"

Sometimes, since his mornings were free, he rode down to the office with Lilly, eagerly insistent to pay her car fare and cram a return Subway ticket into the warm pink aperture of flesh where her glove clasped.

Once he bought her a little spray of heather off a vender's tray.

"Harry, you mustn't spend on me this way. You must begin to save your money for that right girl when she comes along."

Never quick with retort, he stood watching her dart into the foyer of the Forty-second Street building, a sudden silence shaping around him that had in it the little noises of birds singing. "Right girl," he kept repeating after her, or something like that, and remained there loitering for twenty minutes after her presence had fluttered through the revolving doors and into the elevator.

And then suddenly a quick succession of events set in.

One night Lilly and Zoe, returning from a Boston Symphony concert for which they held first-balcony season seats, found Harry trying to pour brandy between the clenched lips of Mrs. Schum, who lay rigid on the hall floor where she had fallen, her head bleeding from a sharp contact with the door.

Her poor face with the shriveled bags of flesh seemed suddenly shrunk, and, holding the flask against her teeth, Harry's hands were trembling so that the liquid poured in a thin stream off the edge of her mouth.

After half an hour of desperate and unavailing use of home remedies, Lilly sent for a doctor, one in the building, who came down in dinner clothes.

At twelve o'clock that night Mrs. Schum, without regaining consciousness, was rushed to the Saint Genevieve Hospital in East Seventy-eighth Street, for an emergency operation that had to do with a growth in her side.

It was Lilly's first contact with the casualty of sudden illness. In the little anteroom of the hospital, her hand in Harry's, she sat the remainder of the night through. He was constantly wiping away the tears from his light eyes and looking away to gulp. She reassured him where she could, tightening her hold of his hand.

"Don't--let them hurt her."

"They aren't hurting her, Harry dear. She can't feel at all under the anaesthetic."

"But they won't know. Gramaw won't let them know. Tell them, Lilly, she's that way--not to hurt her--please."

"Harry--dear!"

At dawn milk wagons began to clatter through streets no grayer than Harry's face. But at six o'clock Mrs. Schum was reported "as well as could be expected" and the operation apparently a success.

They rode home through the early morning, Lilly insisting upon a taxicab and Harry lying back, quite frankly spent, against her arm. Her vitality was unquenchable, mounted, in fact, under stress. Untired, she brewed him hot coffee, forced him to drink it and lie down; tidied up the little flat there at six-thirty o'clock in the morning, with a hit-and-a-miss it is true, but allaying all signs of confusion; fluted an Eton collar for Zoe and packed her off to school; and at half after eight, just out of a cold and invigorating shower, was combing out the fine electric rush of her hair, a pink Turkish bathrobe, the color of her firm, cool skin, wrapped tightly about her and caught in by a cord at her waist line.

Suddenly through the mirror she saw the door open, and before she could call out, Harry stood in the center of the room, his eyes running quite unmistakably over the contour of her sheathed body.

It was the first time he had ever violated the slightest nicety, and, outraged even in her pity for him, her hand flew up, drawing the robe closer at her breast.

"Don't come in!" she cried, retreating up against the dresser and turning her shoulder with the hair flowing over it toward him. "How dared you come in here without knocking! Go!"

He was crying, not seeming to know it, because he continued, even as she stood blazing at him, to stand staring through the rain of tears.

"Harry, you're forgetting yourself. You mustn't give way. Your grandmother is over the worst now--"

Suddenly he was on his knees, his back round and shaken with sobs.

"Lilly--Lilly--can't you see?"

"See what? Is anything wrong? Harry," she cried, stooping to shake him by the shoulder, "has anything happened again? Are you in trouble?"

He would not rise, following her, to her horror, by walking on his knees, pressing and pressing the hem of her garments, and before she realized it burning his kisses down into it. She fought him off, tearing from his grasp and staggering back against the wall.

"Harry--you're in trouble again."

He caught her bare arm, pressing his lips into the yielding flesh.

"Lilly, I can't hold back any longer. I love you. I'm all alone. With gramaw here I could hold back--somehow--but now--Lilly--Lilly--I love you."

She could only stare, her mouth fallen open and the rim of her eyes their widest.

"It's been so long to--hold back--so long. Since that first day at the street car--you kissed me--and now with gramaw gone--Lilly--"

She jerked him up from his knees this time, holding him firmly, even absurdly, by the coat lapels, shaking him.

"Harry, you've gone mad!"

"I love you, Lilly. All these years. I'm all alone now and--"

Her glance shot to the egress of the door, but, seeing that he anticipated her, she did not dart, but held herself back from him, her hands in an X across her breast.

"Harry," she said, trying to keep out of her voice a rising sense of fear, "you're not well You don't know what you are saying or doing."

"You treat me like a child, but I'm a man. Your age! You hear--a man with a man's feelings for a woman--for you--Lilly. You're my--be my--"

"You get out," she cried, her terror bursting out like a flame. "Get out or I'll call Mr. Alquist."

She referred to the superintendent of the apartment building, although she knew him to be well out of hearing. It is probable that Harry knew, too, because he had her by the elbows, pressing them in against her body and her hair flowing across his face.

"Lilly, Lilly, Lilly!" he kept repeating, breathing so heavily it sickened her to hear and feel it, and all the time fumbling with his free hand down into his waistcoat pocket, bringing up a bit of tissue paper which he tore at with his teeth, revealing the icy flash of a great oval diamond ring set up high in platinum. "It's yours, Lilly. I want to cover you with them. I want you to blaze with them--"

He pressed it on her finger, pushing it down the entire length, danced her hand before her, catching her to him finally and crushing her and the flow of her hair to him, kissing so fiercely down that red marks came out against her whiteness, and when her cry finally rose to a shriek let go of her, staggering back, his face, never quite clean of pimples, suddenly fat-looking and with a lionlike thickening up of the features.

"Ah--yah--yah--yah--yah!"

His incoherence was horrible and she began to sob at him through hysteria.

"You go! You get out! You stole that ring! You're a thief! You stole that ring!" she cried, thrusting it with a sudden quick hand down the V of his waistcoat. "Get out! Get out! Your grandmother--your--" Then, because words failed and her knees threatened to give way, she snatched up a book from the table, standing quivering and in the attitude of hurling.

He did go then, as if the book had actually struck, making a detour of her and his knees quite bent as he walked.

She finished her dressing in quick, fuddled movements, voice out in her breathing, buttoning up wrong and tearing open again in the grip of a nervous frenzy.

A panicky need to gain the outdoors seized her; air to sweep and somehow to cleanse her.

Before she was quite dressed, her belt not yet adjusted, in fact, the bell rang in three titters and a prolonged grill. She stood arrested, for some reason beginning all over her trembling. When Harry did not answer she went out herself, opening the door to a mere slit. A foot was pushed immediately in, crowding her back against the wall. Two men walked in, without removing derby hats, and at sight of them the nameless terror pinned her there in silence.

"Harry Calvert live here?"

She stood with her answer locked in her throat, conscious, on the moment, of Harry appearing in the kitchen doorway behind her. She wanted, for the same nameless reason, to motion him back, to shriek out a warning, to throw herself against his presence. To herself in quick repetitions:

"O God, make him go back!"

"Harry Calvert?"

"Yes," replied Harry from where he stood.

"Warrant for your arrest. Charged with entering the apartment of Mrs. J. King at Hotel Admiral and stealing one four-carat diamond ring valued at five thousand dollars. More evidence than we know what to do with. You better come quietly."

"Harry, deny it! They've made a mistake! You haven't the right to come here at a time like this. There is sickness. His grandmother is dying at a hospital. You've made a mistake. Take me. I'll appear for him. I'll give his bail. All you want. Deny it, Harry. Harry!"

For answer a sharp explosion rang suddenly into the narrow hallway, banging and reverberating against the walls, crowding faces out behind an immediate purplish smoke.

"Harry! Harry! My God! Harry!"

He crumpled up quietly, one shoulder in the lead and his left leg bending under him, straightening out then, with half a writhe to his back.

"No! No! Help him! God! No! No! No!"

But yes. Harry had shot himself, very truly, too, through the heart.

CHAPTER VI

There followed black weeks, with Mrs. Schum lying there on the edge of death, yet reluctant to go, Lilly's days an intricate pattern of hospital, office, and home.

She was more tired than she knew and for days after the tragedy went about with a springy little sob just behind her throat, which was perpetually taut from holding back tears.

The effect upon Zoe was telling. She whose solicitude for her mother had never been any too noteworthy and who with all the unthinking blitheness of an unthinking childhood had taken much for granted, developed, suddenly, a new consciousness.

She would literally drag Lilly away from the pressing board.

"Don't, Lilly. I'm old enough to iron out my own ribbons." Or: "Don't polish my shoes, Lilly. It's outrageous!"

"But, Zoe, I would rather you put the time on practicing or reading."

"I can do both."

One Saturday morning she was even awakened to an aroma of coffee, her daughter standing attendant at the bedside with a tray of steaming breakfast.

"Stay in bed this morning, Lilly. You look fagged. Let me take a message down to Visi for you. Oh, Lilly, do! I'll wear my new red tam."

"Nonsense! I'm going down as usual."

"But, Lilly, I want him to see me in it."

Probably Lilly regarded her daughter a second longer than the occasion warranted, because Zoe broke away from the gaze somewhat redly.

"Faugh! I hate him. He reminds me of a wild horse. But I'll show him some day that I'm on earth. I'm as full of my own ideals as he is of his."

"Of course you are, dear; but why so angry?"

"I'm not."

Then Lilly rose, smiling as she dressed.

The household was not easy of readjustment until finally were procured the services of one of the charwomen from the Bronx Theater, who prepared the meals and could flute Zoe's collars to the utmost delicacy.

At this time Zoe was an advanced junior in High School, president of her class, although the hawklike tutelage of Cleofant Trieste had delayed graduation for a year, slowing down her curriculum to meet his demands of harmony, languages, rhythmic dancing, and sports. She had a long, sure swimming stroke that could carry her again her length, rode with the fine fluid movement of a young body at one with her mount, and because of her five hours a week at gymnasium excelled in the rather uncommon sport of handball.

She no longer wore her hair in its great avalanche of curls down her back; they were caught in now with an amber barrette. Nights Lilly loved to brush them out until they flared to a dust of gold about her head. There was no light too dull for this hair to catch. It sprang out in radiance against any background.

"When you sing Marguerite, Zoe, you won't need a wig."

"Ah, but when I sing Electra--Thais--the real me--no namby-pamby Marguerite--no pearls--that's how I feel about Thais--as if she were a great opal full of fire. Hair," flopping her head backward with a bounce of curls, "is hot--it restricts. These curls--they are all hot and crawly around my neck, holding me."

"Poor Harry! You remember how he used to love to take you out walking to show off your curls?"

"Lilly, is Mrs. Schum going to get well?"

"I don't know. It frightens me. I cannot bear to look ahead for her, poor dear."

"If she gets well she'll have to know, won't she, that Harry didn't go to war?"

"Yes, and somehow--I couldn't stand her knowing that."

"She'll know it some day, anyhow."

"Yes, but then maybe where it will be easier for her to understand."

On her own responsibility Lilly had employed this subterfuge with Mrs. Schum. Slowly as she came clutching back at consciousness, the name of her grandson more and more on her twisted lips, Lilly whispered it down to her, closing her hand over the tired old bony one.

"Listen, dear Mrs. Schum, I've--news for you."

"They're all against him--"

"No, no, dear. While you've been so ill, what we had hoped for has happened. Harry's been accepted, dear--he's enlisted."

She crinkled her brow, trying to understand.

"They wouldn't take him. He wanted to fight for his country. They were all against him--"

"No, no, dear. It's all different now. Since our country is at war Harry has been accepted. The boys were rushed overnight to training camp. Thousands of them. He came weeks ago to tell you good-by, but you were too ill to know. He's on a transport now, dear, sailing to fight for his country. Aren't you proud? Aren't we all proud?"

The poor hands began to tremble, feeling their way up along Lilly's arm.

"Harry's gone--to war?"

"Y-yes--dear."

She seemed to speak then, through a pale transparent sleep, into which a new contentment pressed lightly.

"Harry's gone. Annie, he's a soldier. He's so gentle with me, Annie, a meek child, like you were. Never any back talk or a harsh word. Whatever wrong he did was forced on him by those working against him. They were all against him. His Mamma-Annie knows. She bore him and I raised him. Fight, Harry! The streak from your father can't keep you down. Show them, Harry, show them. Whatever wrong my boy did was forced on him by those working against him--"

"That's all past now, dear."

"He liked you, Lilly. He'd have gone through fire for you. You were always good to my soldier boy. I was forever finding old bits of things that you had thrown away among his belongings. Don't tell him I told you. Old pencils and old gloves. He was a great one for gathering up things for keepsakes after you had thrown them away. Gloves--found some old ones of yours under his pillow one morning. Not taking things, you understand, but just pulled out of the rubbish heap for remembrance."

"I do understand, dear."

And so the weeks of her illness and of Lilly's deception dragged on.

There were holes in the fabric of the story, obvious to any but Mrs. Schum's tired consciousness, and a too sudden inquiry could throw Lilly off her guard, but there was a flag with one shining service star glowing above the narrow bed, and evenings straight from the office Lilly would hasten to the hospital with fruits that could only be looked at, and newspapers to be unfurled and read.

"Is his name in the papers yet?"

"Not yet."

"Why?"

"I--You see, dear, the transport has just reached the other side."

"My boy will show them--"

The kindly spirit of the deception had fallen over the entire corridor. A maternity case in the room adjoining sent in a silk flag with hand-embroidered stars. The head nurse, herself on the eve of sailing for service, had shopped the flag with the one bright star. The doctor, fathering the lie, called her "captain" and saluted her upon entering the room with a flash of palm and a click of heels.

She could smile at this, but with lips as blue and shriveled as drowned flesh.

One night after she had dozed off and wandered into some phantasmagoria where she seemed to fancy herself seated in the bow of a boat with her daughter, she opened her eyes suddenly, reaching out for Lilly's hand.

"Lilly, your poor mother. Do you ever think of her?"

"Yes, yes, I do, dear."

"You remember, Lilly, how she used to rush down right from the breakfast table to the bargain bins for those pink and blue mill-ends she used to dress you so pretty in. My! wasn't she one for Valenciennes lace, though! Wouldn't she just dress Zoe up, though--"

"Wouldn't she!"

"She was a good woman in her way, Lilly, even with all her fussing and nagging. My! how she did used to nag! I understood her. The ketchup. She was a great one for condiments and would have them all over the other boarders. Ketchup and the best cut of the meat for you and your father. There was just no pleasing her. But I understood her--she's a good woman, Lilly."

"Indeed, mamma is good!"

"It's not that I don't glory in you, Lilly, and your having a wonder child. You know I've always gloried in you. You've a head on you I always say that's going to carry you beyond us all, but don't you ever feel, Lilly, that maybe your doings have been wayward?"

"I do. I do."

"Your mother. Your father, as patient and as fine a man as breathed. Your husband, I don't know him, but life is so short. So terribly short. So full of pain and regrets for what can't be undone. That's why I cannot go and leave my boy behind--to suffer alone. I want him to go first. He's not strong. What is life, except doing for those we love? Don't you ever feel that about them out there, Lilly? Life is so short--such a struggle--alone--"

"Dear Mrs. Schum, you--you--you're right."

"Ah, I know---the young man in the box with you at 'The Web' that night it opened. Your boss. I know! He likes you, that young man does, Lilly. It's easy to see it in his eyes for you. That's why it's dangerous. Harry likes you, too--but not that way, I think. He saves your old gloves. That's always struck me as funny. They're all against him. The fire escapes; that's why I lock the doors. You hear--the fire escapes. Poor Lilly! just a little too much ambition and not quite enough talent to reach. I used to predict for you all the things that are cropping out in your child. Zoe is to be the one, Lilly. Not you--or Harry--or Mamma-Annie--Zoe! Funny his saving your gloves--"

These were the times that Lilly would sit there crying, old musty memories rising around her like kicked-up dust. There were whole evenings when her mother's name was constantly on the not always coherent lips, and to Lilly the old sense of the unreality of her universe, or was it herself, laid somewhat, by the busy years, would come surging again. Where were the visions for which she had climbed, spike-shod, up that loving wall of living flesh back there? How long since her last dream of self had vanished? Zoe was her answer.

One evening when Lilly arrived home from the hospital she found Zoe squatting in bed, her face naughtily screwed into a little grimalkin knot, elbows pressed into her sides, palms up, and all attitudinized to emulate a Chinese god. Holding this pose for a full minute after Lilly had entered the room, she began to bounce in hilarity up and down on the mattress, probably to allay her own sense of inner unease.

For the full round of the minute Lilly stared, her glance widening and darkening. Something had happened to Zoe. Something horrid.

"Don't you love it, Lilly? Don't stand there like you're frozen. Everybody loves it. All the models down at Daab's are wearing it this way. Thais does. Jeanne d'Arc does. Don't look at me that way."

Zoe had bobbed her hair. It hung quite straight, and in an outstanding shock, because of its thickness, just below her ears. Franz Hals would have loved the rectilinear contour of her. She was saucy. She was abbreviated. She was naughty; and liked to flop her head about for the soft throw of her hair.

Her mother dropped rather than sat on a chair edge, trying to keep down the storm of anger that had her by the throat and eyeballs.

"Your curls! All gone! Your beautiful hair! What have you done? You wicked girl! You--wicked--girl--you!"

It was the first time in all the largesse of her youth that such a tone had assailed Zoe. The very seventeenness of her revolted; she dropped her attitude.

"Why, Lilly--you--you're talking like other--mothers."

But the spank in Lilly's hand was suddenly singing against her palm and there was a rush of her not so forbearing forefathers to the very front.

"You horrid girl! How dared you? Don't come near me! Your beautiful hair that I've never been too tired to brush for hours! To have realized those gorgeous curls in you and for--for this! You horrid, selfish girl--selfish--selfish!"

All during this, her naughtiness fallen from her like a cloak, Zoe sat regarding her parent, her lower lip less and less steady. She might have been stunned, trying to keep her equilibrium by a series of rapid little blinks, Lilly meanwhile sunk into a heap and crying down into her hands.

"Lilly--dearest--darling--est--"

"Don't talk to me."

"But, Lilly--you--you've always wanted me to be true to myself."

"You're not true to yourself. You're true to a pose, a silly fad that you've picked up around the Daab studio."

"You always said if I wanted to be a circus rider I could, just so I was better than all the other circus riders. Well, I wanted to have my hair bobbed and I bobbed it bobbiest."

"Your comparison is stupid. You know it is. You've never taken a step before without talking it over with me. You know perfectly well I should not have interfered. I should have tried to make you see the folly of cutting off your beautiful curls, but if you had still insisted, off they might have come just the same. I think it is that as much as the loss of the curls. Your privilege has become a license. You've made everything seem ridiculous--me--you."

"Then you've made me so. If you want me to be like other girls you should have reared me like other girls. Have other girls' fathers who don't know they are on earth? Have other girls' mothers who--"

"Zoe!"

As if the words had been live coals scuttling off her lips before she knew, Zoe sat back, staring at her mother's stare, scalding tears already welling.

"Lilly, forgive me. I--I wish I could cut my tongue out. I didn't mean it that way; you know I didn't. If you don't forgive me I can't stand it," the stabbing consciousness of that impulsively flung reproach already through her like a hurting wound.

"You are right, Zoe, I--"

"I didn't mean one word, Lilly darling, not one eeny word. It's just that all of a sudden it seemed to me to be the freest, gladdest thing in the world to cut off my hair. That's it, free! Haven't you ever had that feeling, darling? Free! I wouldn't have done it, Lilly, if I had known how it would hurt. Lilly--darling--mother. If I've hurt you I want to just die. My own dear--Lilly--"

Her voice caught on the crest of a sob and she was at her mother's feet, seeking out her lap, tears rushing down over her incoherence.

"I'll grow it back again for you, Lilly. I'll make it up to you, sweetheart. I didn't mean that--what I said about fathers or--or other girls--you know I didn't. I'm bad. Terrible."

In some alarm, Lilly placed her hand on the shorn head, shuddering in spite of herself as if the ends were bleeding.

"Sh-h-h, Zoe! It upset me, dear, that's all--the shock of seeing you sitting up in bed there--with it off."

"I'll make it up to you, Lilly. In so many ways. Soon. It's settled, dear, that Auchinloss is coming to America in the fall to conduct. Trieste is going to arrange my audition for September. He promised to-day I'd be ready. Think, Lilly, my audition so soon. I'll have the wig made out of my own hair, dear, for Marguerite. Don't feel badly, Lilly; the wig will look--"

"I don't any more, Zoe. It was just the shock--"

"I know it was silly, dear, but it will grow quickly and I just had that feeling to be free--you see, dear--"

"I do see, dear, I do. Zoe, look at me. Doesn't it ever come over you, on the eve of so much, dear--that perhaps you do need his--your father's guardianship--"

"Now just because I said *that*. I tell you I'm a devil. I didn't mean it--not one word--"

"I know you didn't. It cropped out unconsciously. You're not to blame. He's a good man, Zoe, your father, and his steady hand might do much where I--may have failed."

"If you talk that way I can't stand it. You tell me so often he's a good man, I wonder if he really is--"

"You're getting beyond me, Zoe. I wonder if the day isn't inevitable when you are going to break out more and more into unconscious reproach."

"Lilly--no--no--"

"Oh, I don't only mean what you said just now. But it's on my mind more and more, now that you are old enough to decide for yourself. You cannot be sucked back any more into a life you would not tolerate. You can choose. That is what I have been waiting for. Doesn't the ache ever come over you, Zoe, to see your father? Just a natural instinctive ache, if nothing else--your grandparents--"

"No! No! No! I hate it all as you hated it. If you want to punish me terribly--for saying something I didn't mean--just talk them to me. I want wideness, must have it! Room! I--I could say it in music better than in words. Some day I shall compose a song that says it for me--the--the way I feel it. Don't stop now saving me from them. Wait. Wait, Lilly, until I sing. Trieste understands even better than you. I'm the surprise he keeps hinting about to everyone. I'm going to bowl them over at my audition. Lilly--have I ever failed you? Have I ever come in second for you? No, and I never will. You won't ever be sorry, Lilly--on my account. You won't even care that I've cut off my hair. Lilly dear, do you believe me? I'm always going to come in first for you. First!"

"I do, dear, I do."

And of course in the end they sobbed together, and lay far into the dawn, cheek to cheek, until finally Zoe dropped off to sleep and Lilly lay wide-eyed beside her, the perfume of her child's soft breathing against her cheek.

The next morning in the reading room of the Public Library a notice catapulted itself at Lilly from the second page of the St. Louis Globe-Democrat:

L.H. Hines, president, and Albert Penny, vice president of Slocum-Hines Hardware Company, leave shortly for Washington, where they have been called to give expert advice upon installing American Canteen Service.

CHAPTER VII

The day that followed seemed to Lilly vague with a sort of fog. A disturbing something lay against her consciousness and one of her unquiet nights was filled with the unaccountable crying. But morning invariably brought back reality and her workaday could envelop her busily, even happily.

Meanwhile, war, like a spreading wing, had blackened against the international sky. Somme, Vimy Ridge, Aisne had been bled, and more than ever the streets that led toward the embarkation points were the color of khaki, women frequently running alongside, crying and laughing bewildered farewells.

Some of this war hysteria, of which she was really no integral part, had, however, hold of Lilly. Her throat ached with it. Her state cropped out in her work. One afternoon she traveled to Newark for the purpose of seeing a Japanese sleight-of-hand act, and came away without sufficient impression of any kind to pass judgment.

Bruce Visigoth eyed her closely.

"You're tired," he said, commenting upon her failure to turn in the report. "You need a rest."

"No," she said, "it's just--a little of everything--I guess--then Harry Calvert--that was a shock, you see, and now his grandmother. I'm with her at the hospital every evening--and then this war--this futile bleeding--horror."

He could never, with her, keep his tone as level as his manner.

"Lilly," he burst out, "drop it all for a couple of weeks. You and the youngster come out to the place in Tarrytown. There are some things I want to talk over with you. I'm working now to obtain the rights to that little beauty from the Spanish you gave me to read. I'm going to produce after this war mess slows down. It is the exquisite kind of thing I'd expect you to find."

"I didn't. Zoe read it to me one evening. She was the one to see its possibilities."

"It's spring, Lilly, and I want you to see the place. My sister Pauline moved in last week. I want you to be our first guest. It's spring, Lilly--"

It was his first mention to her of the recent purchase of a one-hundred-acre estate at Tarrytown, although in her capacity of notary public she had officiated at the drawing up of certain papers and deed. Blue prints of plans had passed through her hands. That he had furnished it she knew, too, from the magnitude of breath-taking bills from decorators and dealers exclusive antique. It had piqued her more than she would admit, his failure to solicit even her advice or opinion. There was a framed photograph of plans on his desk in the office which her eyes studiously avoided. Furtively and with the edge of her gaze, she knew the house to be a low-length with Tudor peaks to it that gave her a nostalgia for pools of green quiet and the leafy whisperings of English countrysides she had never seen.

"I want you out at the place, Lilly, more than I can say. Please come. The way things are clouding up, there is no telling how soon they'll let me over for active service. Lilly?"

She shook her head.

"I can't. Zoe graduates next month, and--"

"Good Lord! the youngster!"

"Seventeen."

He whistled.

"Well, I'll be hanged. The sun-kid. Bring her out too, Lilly."

"Trieste is very strict with her. She is preparing for her audition in September, and even if it could be managed, there is poor Mrs. Schum, you know."

His eagerness would not endure obstacle.

"Bring her out, too. How's that, Lilly? I'll send a limousine full of pillows for her. It will take Pauline's mind off her loneliness, having some one to mother. We'll put her up in a sun room with a view of pine woods and Hudson River that cannot be surpassed. It's spring--Lilly--"

"Poor Mrs. Schum!" she replied, her smile tired and twisted. "I'm afraid her next journey will be a longer one than that."

"Poor soul! Does she still think that boy of hers is fighting?"

"Surely there is no wrong in saving her from the horror of the truth."

"You dear girl, of course, no. It's only that--somehow don't you think that before she passed on she ought to know that he's gone on before--even if you have to tell her that he died--gloriously?"

"I've thought of that," she said, looking away, "thought and thought of it."

"Lilly," he cried, reaching for her two hands She drew them back quickly and walked out.

That evening when she presented herself at the hospital the nurse met her outside the door with her finger to her lips.

"She is sinking, but conscious."

Confronted with her emergency, Lilly stood before that closed door, beating all over with her silent little prayer:

"O God, help me! Help me, help her!"

Mrs. Schum was quite conscious.

"Lilly," she said, reaching out a thin old hand that was covered with veins as round as cables, "I've been waiting."

"Here I am, dear."

"I think I'm done, Lilly. I--dream so much--of God."

"Why, you're better, dear!"

"No. I'm going. I wanted so to wait for my boy. The doctor, can't he help me to wait, Lilly? Ask him to help me to wait. I keep thinking he's over there somewhere--Harry--funny isn't it? Over there waiting. You've heard no news, Lilly?"

In this moment more propitious than she dared hope Lilly leaned over.

"Yes, dear, there is news."

"Harry?" she said quickly and sharply, lifting her head.

"Yes, dear--Harry--is--over there--waiting."

"His Mamma-Annie's boy--they were all against him. He can't stay back here alone--he needs me, doctor--help me to wait for him--"

"Listen, dear--Harry's gone."

"Where?"

"Why--over there--just as your intuition told you."

She pulled at the sheet with fingers as fleshless as the feet of a bird, moving her lips, vainly at first, and suddenly jerked herself up with a strength no doctor would have conceded her.

"He's dead, Lilly. My boy's dead. Please--please--it is so--isn't it? My boy's dead?"

"Yes."

"I knew it. Oh, Annie, you're the mother of a soldier. God wouldn't let me leave him back here--alone. I wouldn't have left him. There wasn't any good ahead for him. That's why I wanted him to die like a soldier. Before he should come to the bad places ahead. I can go so easy now. I'm done. God fixed it for me--Lilly."

She held the racked old form to her, kissed away tears that the washed old eyes could hardly yield, made a couch of her arms, and held her close so that their heartbeats met.

"Lilly, I feel so easy. I never felt so easy."

"Lie quietly, dear."

"Life can be hard, Lilly. And now--war. Make it easier for yourself. Don't let him out there--go over there--anywhere--reproaching. Your parents--your child--it's his as much as yours, Lilly. If I had gone first, my boy would have reproached. There is nothing so terrible, Lilly--as eyes that reproach--eyes--Lilly--don't."

"I--won't."

She drifted off then in the placidity of a sleep from which she was not to emerge.

*   *   *   *   *

Lilly walked home that early morning following. Her direction lay in a straight line through Central Park. Spring was out in firstlings of every kind. The baby nap of new grass. Trees ready to quiver into leaf. The sun came up from behind a sky line of skyscrapers, and as she was crossing the Mall a fountain rained up a first joyous geyser, some sparrows immediately plunging for a bath.

She sat down on a bench there in the lovely quiet, quite lax, and, because of its pressure, her natty little blue sailor in her lap. The air was like cool water and she closed her tired eyes to it.

Finally children began to trot past on their way to school. She heard their shouts and watched them. A father passed with his little girl by the hand and carrying her sheaf of books. A boy in knickerbockers lunged furiously on roller skates. Another drove his ball under her bench and she smiled as she drew aside to let him drive. A private in khaki threw her a flirtatious glance. The sun found her finally.

Then Lilly followed one of her curious and absolutely irrepressible impulses, one that must have been smoldering who knows how long.

She completed her walk through the Park. At Seventy-second Street, where she emerged, a family hotel, one of those *de luxe* mausoleums to family life, reared showily. Without pause she turned in there, finding out the telegraph desk; wrote her message largely and flowingly, leaning over while the operator read out the words to her:

Mr. Albert Penny, 5198 Page Avenue, St. Louis, Missouri. Won't you include New York in your visit to Washington and if possible bring parents. Try to. Lilly Penny, 2348 West End Avenue.

Hearing that telegram repeated, the pencil marking time word by word, it seemed to Lilly that each one of them was released with the spring of an arrow from its bow, and that the operator recoiled, stunned, from the impact of the message.

"Well," she said, leaning farther over the desk, and for some reason shaping the word to a breathless question.

"Fifty-one cents," said the girl, through the inimitable laconism of gum chewing.

CHAPTER VIII

Six hours later there was a reply folded in Lilly's purse:

We leave to-day for Washington. Arrive New York next Sunday 2.03 *via* Pennsylvania. Albert Penny.

An incredible state of calm set in. She had the sensation of each intervening day a shelf of terrace down which she was walking into a deepening sea. Dreams ill-flavored as Orestes' filled her nights, and how tired she was must have sopped into her pillow, but her capacity for the present lessened her dread and made more bearable the fluent and fateful passing of the time.

There were the details of the poor little funeral to be arranged. Lilly, who had never known death, was suddenly face to face with it again, at a time, too, when the incipient beginnings of pandemic that was later to scourge the country was reaping its first harvest; a strange malady carried on the stinking winds of war, shooting up in spouty little flames, that, no sooner laid, found new dry rot to feed upon. Spanish influenza, it was called, for no more visible reason than that it probably had its beginnings in Germany or India.

On the Wednesday of Mrs. Schum's funeral five of the Amusement Enterprise office force were home with it, one little telephone operator, who occasionally laid the surreptitious offering of an orange or a carnation on Lilly's desk, succumbing.

It was amazing how light the imprint of Harry and his grandmother. Of effects there were practically none. A few tired-looking old dresses of Mrs. Schum's. Eleven dollars and some odd change in a tin box behind a clock. Harry's pinch-back suit with the slanting pockets. A daguerreotype or two. The inevitable stack of modest enough but unpaid bills. Odds. Ends. And in a wooden soap box shoved beneath Harry's cot, old door bells, faucets, bits of pipe, glass door knobs, and, laid reverently apart, a stack of Lilly's discarded gloves, placed to simulate the print of the hand.

For days, Zoe, who had taken the tired willingness of Mrs. Schum so for grant-ed, cried herself bitterly into a state that threatened to take the form of a fever, and then to the strophe and antistrophe of her young grief, becoming self-conscious, burst, with not particularly precocious rhyme, reason, or meter, into the following, which was printed in her school paper:

"Teach me to live, O God,
If sorrow be to live,
Then let me know
All pain that it can give."

"Teach me to live, O God,
To know the gold from dross,
To live, dear God, to live.
I care not what it cost."

And Lilly, the dear mother dust in her eyes, had the page framed beneath a faded photograph of Mrs. Schum, taken when her lips and breast were young.

To attune Zoe to the coming of her family was no small matter. She was outra-geously rebellious, flagrantly irreverent, and for every outburst Lilly bled her sense of blame.

"You've made a farce of everything, Lilly. You've fought for a principle and, with it won, turned maudlin. What is the idea? To drag me back there to join the sewing circle and the local society for the prevention of spinsterhood to maidens?"

"You are not funny at all. You know you are clear of that kind of thing. You're like an arrow on its way to its goal. Straight and sure. Nothing can deflect you. That's why I dared."

"Well, then?"

"Realizations can come, Zoe, even to a selfishness as great as mine has been."

"Sacrifice is not always beautiful. It can be silly and futile."

"Zoe!"

"Yes, and bring rewards to neither side. Half the people who are sacrificed for become tearful tyrants, and those who do the sacrificing sour and meek, or holy with righteousness."

"You are reciting the kind of thing you hear down at Daab's."

"I'm reciting you."

"You darling boomerang!"

"I suppose now you are sorry you didn't stay at home in your canary cage to no one's particular advantage and your own terrific disadvantage. Now that you have reared me into the kind of human being you set out to be, you renig. Do you want to throw me back into that bowl with the greased sides that you managed to climb out of? Not much."

This from Zoe, mixed metaphor and all, who at seventeen kept **Doll's House**, Freud, **Anna Karenina**, and Ellen Key on the table beside her bed.

"Theories go down, Zoe, before life--and death."

She sat haughtily young, and without tolerance, her profile averted and trying to keep the quiver off her lips.

"Just when I'm ready to graduate and preparing for my audition--to have this---"

"Zoe--Zoe--don't make it harder--"

"I'm a dog, Lilly--forgive me."

"The entire abominable condition is my fault--"

"Then thank God for the abominable condition. I love you and everything you've done."

"Then be sweet to them for my sake. Your grandmother, she's going to be un-like anyone you have ever known. She's a great one to pick up the bread crumbs of life with a great ado. That's been her existence, dear--little things. And your grandfather, Zoe, he's so gentle. Somehow I imagine he is even gentler now. You remember I used to tell you how we'd play at hide and seek long after I was grown. Oh, Zoe, be sweet!"

"I will, dear."

"And--your father. Whatever his attitude may be, remember the fault lies in me--not him."

"Trust me, Lilly, if only he doesn't drop dead when he sees me!"

"Zoe!"

Between them the little drama was carefully rehearsed.

"Visi would pay big money for this act."

"You'll be your own natural sweet self, Zoe? No posing?"

"Don't worry. I suppose if the truth is known I'll have an aggravated case of stage fright."

"They'll know--everything, Zoe, before I let them see you. Just be simple, dear--and please--no dramatics!"

"It's all too dramatic for dramatics," she replied, cryptically.

It was finally decided that Lilly was to meet the train alone, settle the trio at the Hotel Astor, and arrive at the apartment in time for a dinner prepared by a cook and waitress especially brought in for the day.

"Break the news in a public place, Lilly--the hotel lobby or a taxi---and avoid family fireworks."

"My news can't be broken."

"Why?"

"Smashed, rather."

At four o'clock the morning of the arrival, Lilly was up, moving with the aimlessness of great nervousness about the apartment. At that same hour Mrs. Becker was emerging backward from her sleeper, kimono-clad, and bulging through the curtains into the dark aisle.

"Carrie," her husband whispered after her, jutting his head out with a turtle's dart, "it's only three o'clock, Eastern time. Why are you getting up?"

"Because I want to," she said, plowing on.

Once in the dressing room, she fell to crying as she staggered and dressed, apparently because each object, as she took it up, fell from her fingers.

And yet the meeting occurred, as dreaded and anticipated moments often do, damply, and as a heavily loaded bomb, for one reason or another, can go off with a cat cough.

To the observer, what happened that early afternoon was simply a very trim and very tailored young woman, her boyishness of attire somewhat accentuated because her swift clean-cutness was so obviously its inspiration, greeting, in the marble vastness of Grand Central Terminal, a trio of what was plainly a pair of travel-stained parents and perhaps an uncle.

Standing there peering between the grillwork as the train slid in through the greasy gloom, watching the run of "red caps" and the slow disgorging of passengers, Lilly saw it all in waves of movement, waves of heat, waves of gaseous unreality.

Then she spied them. Her mother in the old, familiar vanguard, her father with that bulge to his back from which the gray coat hung loosely, Albert struggling to save his luggage from the fiery piracy of a "red cap."

Her first sense was of fatness, their incredible, caravaning, lumbaginous fatness! There was a new chin to her mother. Gone was the old pulled-in waistline, but the old love of finery was out on her hat in ostrich plumes, a boa of marabou lending further elegance. And her father! He was somehow behind himself, slanting out from neck to quite a bulge of abdomen, then receding again to legs that caught her throat with a sense of their being too thin to sustain him. The fringe of hair that showed beneath his slouch hat was quite white, too, and with that same clutch at her throat she saw that it was thin as a baby's can be thin.

It is doubtful if she would have known Penny. He was himself in sebaceous italics. The old stolidity of stature was there, but hardly the solidity. Like Mrs. Becker, he had chubbied up, so to speak, until he looked shorter. And Albert was bald. It showed out under the rear of his derby, like a well-scrubbed visage awaiting some deft hand to sketch in the features, as poor Harry had done it to the clothespins. His Scandinavian blondness was quite gone; there was just a fringe of tan hair left and his jowls hung a bit, of skin not quite filled with flesh.

All this in a telegraphic flash as she stood there waiting, and at the sight of her father, on his too thin legs, dragging his cane slightly so that it scraped, and in the other hand a sagging old black valise that she remembered, all the tightness at her throat relaxed suddenly, the tears coming so easily that she could smile through them.

The dragging of that cane, it hurt her poignantly, as little vagrant memories can.

They spied her out even as she spied them, and, bodybeat to bodybeat, she and her mother met, shaking to silent sobs and twisting hearts. Then her father, pressing the coldly smelling mustache to her lips and lifting her in the old way by the armpits, so that the instant closed over her like a swoon.

With Albert it was strangely easier; there was a pause as wide as a hair while he stood there blinking, and weighted with his unsurrendered luggage.

"Albert," she said, finding the word at last.

At that moment, a "red cap," wild for fee, made for one of the brand-new leather cases.

"Let go," he cried, in small anger. "That is a six-dollar-and-ninety-eight-cent bag you are jerking."

Then he brought his gaze back to Lilly, his Adam's apple above the gray necktie throbbing so that it seemed to her his entire body must reverberate to the pistonlike process.

"Well," he said. "Well, well," the words dropping down into the dry well of a gulp.

But somehow after the episode of the luggage, everything was easier, for Lilly at least. She could smile now.

Very presently they were actually in a taxicab together, the talk of the moment echoing against the silence of unspoken words taking shape between them.

"Papa!" she said, finally, from the little folding seat opposite him, stroking his hands and steadying herself with them against the throw of the cab. "Oh, papa, papa!"

He smiled back through crinkles that were new to her, patting her in turn and looking off.

Mrs. Becker fell to crying, pressing her handkerchief up against her eyes and trying to lift her veil above the tears.

"After all these years," she kept repeating. "Years. Years."

"Now, now, Carrie--you promised."

"What hotel?" asked Penny, one of the bags across his knees and one weather eye for the other on the driver's seat.

"The Astor; that is one of the best. I've your rooms all arranged for. My--my place is too small."

"A less expensive would do, wouldn't it, mother?" addressing himself, without once meeting Lilly's eye, to his mother-in-law.

"You're my guests," she said, trying to smile down old aversions. "This is my party."

"Years--" sobbed Mrs. Becker. "She looks the same, but I'm a stranger to my own child. Ben, we're strangers."

They were all suddenly in tears, Mr. Becker laying a clumsy hand to his wife's arm.

"Carrie, you promised--"

"Can't help it--can't help it," her lips bubbling. "I'm bursting with it. All these years. I can't hold in. What mother could?"

Only their arrival at the hotel stemmed the rising tide, but, once up in their aerial suite of rooms, the last bell hop tipped out, then broke the storm wave, flaying them all.

"Lilly--Lilly let me look at you. Baby--are you my baby--are you mine? Years--O God--years--"

"Mamma--mamma--"

"Feel my heart. Ben--tell her--what I've suffered--"

"Carrie--now--now--what is past is past; we must look to the present now."

"Papa dear--you look so changed and yet so--natural--"

There was an air of indescribable prosperity that rose off Mr. Becker, in the nondescript but excellent quality of the gray suiting, the polished, square-toed, custom-made shoes, the little linen string of necktie, one for each day, the kind, despite family suasion, he had always worn. But it was difficult for him to speak now because he was always blinking and looking off.

"You've given us a great sorrow to bear, Lilly," he said, in a tone of rehearsed reproach. "We tried to be thankful for our health and--bear our--"

"There he goes on health again at a time like this. I'm a broken woman. Years! Years of explaining lies to the community. Years of holding up our heads over an opera singer that nobody ever hears about and that never came home to her folks. Years of feeling them laugh behind our backs--your father and husband trying to hold up their heads in business under the lie. What have I ever done, I've asked myself all these years--to deserve it? I've never harmed anyone. I've--"

"Carrie--please."

"Where do you live? How do you live? A stranger to my own child. Worse than a stranger!"

"I've a well-paid position with a producing firm, mamma, and I live nicely. You shall see, dear."

"Producing? Producing what? Trouble? A position! For that she threw away her life. Her big talk of prima donna, and we find her in a position. The girl that was going to set the world on fire. That's why we looked our eyes out all these years for her name in the paper, only to find her in a position! Ben, what have we ever done to deserve it? Albert, I'm her mother, but my heart bleeds for you--"

He was tugging at his bag straps, industriously keeping his head averted, but the red up in his ears.

"Mother," he said, "did you pack my throat atomizer?"

She licked up at the taste of her tears.

"It's wrapped in between your socks. You're standing in a draught, Albert; close that window. You heard that man in the train about the epidemic of colds that is starting all over the country. O my God! I'm just so upset. And now that it has happened everything is so different. I could tear out my tongue for what I want to say and I can't say anything--not so much your father and I--at least we had Albert to help make it up to us. We know what a son he has been, don't we, Ben, but to think of him, the upstandingest boy that ever wore shoe leather--him having to suffer for it--"

"Carrie, Carrie, it's time to go over all that later. Let's get our bearings. Lilly, you've not changed except for the bones kind of setting and--"

"I don't like you in those shirt waists. Too mannish. The lace I used to dress that child in! The way I used to love to poke in the bins--sacrificed for her. These years--years. Lilly--tell me you've been a good girl--that your sinning has only been against us--child that I raised--Lilly--"

They were locked in embrace again, Mrs. Becker blown hot and cold by the ever-shifting clouds of her emotions, the two men standing by in a state of helplessness that was always in inverse proportion to the lavalike eruptions from the crater of her nerves.

"Mother, father and I will leave you alone for a while and you have your talk together first--"

"No! She's your wife. You have yours first! It's about time you were coming into some of your rights!"

Such a fiery redness was out in Albert's ears that against the lights they were of the translucency of red-hot iron, and even through her pity for his *malaise*, her old poignant distaste of him would not be laid. She wanted him to lunge somehow with that bull-like head of his with the bashedin squareness to its top, but since nothing like that happened, she sprang up instead, grasping her mother's hand.

"Not now," she cried. "I want to tell you all something first, and then I want to take you--to my place--to see where--the way I live--"

"Yes," said Mrs. Becker, rising with a crinkling of nose and drawing her mar-about boa about her, "I want to see the way you live--first. Guests of hers at a hotel like this. A position, she tells me. Lilly--Lilly--for God's sake tell me you've been a good girl--"

"Carrie!" At the sound of rare thunder in her husband's voice she did subside then. Later she began.

"Nice rooms. Nicer than in Chicago that time. Albert, let me give you a clean handkerchief out of the valise.... No, you don't know where they are. Don't like that shirt waist. Too mannish. Don't worry about those pillows, Albert. I brought your little one along. Glass tops. That's nice, isn't it? How would you like one for your chiffonier at home, Albert? Quit whittling toothpicks on the floor, Ben--Oh dear! if somebody don't say something, I'll scream--"

"Come, mamma--papa--Albert. I want to take you--home, and while we drive up there I want to talk to you."

But once within the cab and with her mother's constant runnel of talk and its threat of hysteria, courage failed Lilly, so she sat back, holding herself against rising panic and her mind refusing to hook tentacles into the situation toward which they were speeding.

"You look mighty well, Lilly," her father would repeat, gently; "not much changed, but a little more settled--in the bones--"

"Who does your darning and mending?"

"I do, mamma. See, this is Broadway, papa. We're just rounding the famous Columbus Circle."

"I don't see much difference between this and St. Louis. Do you, Ben? Just stores and stores like there are on Olive Street. Oh, look! There is one of the Ryan Cut Price Drug Stores, just like we have at home. Look at the crowds around that thing--what's that? 'Subway,' it says--"

"Lilly, Lilly, it makes me tremble when I think of you in this great city alone."

"Why, papa, I never was so safe."

"It's not decent, that's what it's not."

"Now, Carrie--"

"Stop cutting me off every time I open my mouth."

"How far is it?" asked Albert, speaking for the first time.

"Why, I guess it ought to take about ten minutes from here," replied Lilly, grateful for the question and trying to meet his averted glance.

He withdrew quite a disk of silver watch, reading it carefully.

"We're already on the way seven and a quarter minutes," he said.

"Albert," she began, "there is something I want to--ought to--tell you--first--"

"Albert, close that window next to you."

"I--don't quite know--how to begin--"

"Close it all the way, Albert, you're still in a draught."

Suddenly Lilly sat back, silent holding her father's hand the rest of the way.

But no sooner were the three of them safely into the little front room than, without even seating them, she rushed out to forestall Zoe.

But too late. That young lady herself had already appeared between the curtains of the alcove. She had done the outlandish, the outrageous, the irrelevant thing. An old red rep portiere wound tightly around her body to below the armpits, and held there by skillfully adjusted bands of black velvet, a fillet of the same so low that it touched her eyebrows secured about her boxed and brilliantly blond hair, she held the half-profile pose of a Carmencita, a pair of ten-cent-store black earrings dangling and her upflung gesture one of defiance, mischief with an unmistakable dash of irrepressible dramatics.

In a silence that shaped itself to a grin, Lilly, caught midstep as it were, stood regarding her daughter. She wanted to scream, to throw back her head and shout her hysteria, to spank her daughter bodily there across her knees, and more than that she wanted to laugh! Enormous laughter, to allay her sense of madness.

Instead she found voice, which, when it came, was not her own, for thinness.

"Albert," she said, "this is your daughter--Zoe."

"Ben," whispered Mrs. Becker, out of a fantastic cave of silence and rising suddenly from her chair to plant herself on the overstuffed divan, where there was more horizontal room--"Ben, I think I'm going to faint." And she did.

CHAPTER IX

Yet within a week Mrs. Becker, through all the fog of her bewilderment, was embroidering seed pearls on her granddaughter's white graduation slippers.

Forty years of dogged loyalty to the white string ties, fresh every day, had gone down before seventeen's mandate; and to Ben Becker's unspeakable sheepishness, he had appeared one evening in an impeccable dark-blue knitted cravat, his collar, of cut heretofore easily inclusive of chin, snugger to his neck, and flowing out to slight points.

"So you let her bamboozle you into something I couldn't accomplish in thirty-eight years," was Mrs. Becker's sole comment through a mouthful of seed pearls.

"Nonsense! The child has ideas. These collars don't dig in."

"Humph! She's had you around her little finger from the start."

"Now, Carrie, why do you say that?"

"Because it's true," trying not to smile.

It was.

An immediate *entente cordiale* had shaped itself around Zoe and her grandfather. She named him with her usual fantastic aptitude.

"Dapple-dear," she would have it, and could not explain the choice. It must have been some such remote analogy as his likeness to an old dapple-gray family horse, patient flanked and thoroughly imperturbable to the fleck of the whip.

Her grandmother she promptly christened "Tippy," also for a reason she could not or would not divulge. But one evening, to her secret amusement, Lilly found a sheet of paper in the litter of the desk, jotted all over with Zoe's joyous scrawl, "Zantippe," in every case the first syllable crossed out.

All but Albert. She addressed him quite studiedly, "Father," her teeth coming down in a little bite over her lower lip, her use of the term never failing to elicit the rush of red to his ears.

He seemed tranced, falling into all plans, just so they included the presence of his mother-in-law, without comment. To her proverbial apron strings he kept firm hold, literally not permitting her out of his sight. Even when he addressed Lilly or his daughter his gaze was straight for Mrs. Becker, and the flags of her moral support that he must have had the eyes to see waving for him in her glance.

The impending interview began to take on the proportions of a delayed tooth-pulling. Repeatedly Lilly had cleared the way for it; just as repeatedly he had fled to cover. A week passed.

Meanwhile something disquieting happened. It developed in further correspondence from Washington on the matter of canteen equipment, that there was some thought of sending Albert to France. An increased stolidity was his sole reaction, but there was no doubt that the prospect of an impending ocean trip weighed heavily.

The submarine situation, at a time when the seas were sown with the menace of sudden death, was of greatest and worrying concern to him.

No new device was overlooked. His room at the hotel was littered with rubber suits, guaranteed to keep the body floating upright for thirteen hours. Adjustable cork life savers. Patent propellers. Wings.

There was talk, in the face of the impending contingency, of applying for a commission. Albert in olive drab! To Lilly he would not conjure.

But meanwhile, to the slow champings of a huge governmental machine in travail, there was little to do but wait, and in the interim not a day that he and Mrs. Becker failed to follow up this or that newest device against bone-cracking seas.

"Albert, there must be a way out! Don't tell me there are not plenty of men who could help install canteen service. Let them send Vincent Bankhead. He's younger. You leave it to me if they decide to send you. I'll find you a way out. It's done every day."

"Wait until I'm called, mother; then there's time to act."

But his eyes were worried.

One day when the strain of holding together the precarious threads of the situation was becoming almost more than she could bear, and the end of the ten-day vacation period she was allowing herself from the office was at hand, Lilly spread three matinee tickets out on the table of a tea room where the five of them were lunching.

"Zoe, you and your grandparents are going to the Hippodrome this afternoon. Albert and I will take a walk or a drive and meet you at the hotel afterward."

"Mother, you come, too."

"No, Albert, Lilly's right. I want this thing settled. I want something decided or I'll go mad. My husband has got me muzzled; I'm afraid to open my mouth; but if I don't know something soon, I'll go crazy. Why are we here? When are we all going back? I don't like it here. I can't stand the noise. My servant girl is out there eating me out of house and home. I didn't even lock the grocery closet; that is the state of excitement I left home in. Something has got to be settled. The minute I open my mouth to talk about what is in the back of all our heads, everybody shushes me up. Now you two go and talk it out. I want to go home. I want us all to go home. I'm a wreck. I--"

"Carrie--"

"Oh, I'll shut up! Next time you travel with me, get me a muzzle. All I'm good for is to bear the brunt of everything. You've dribbled my head full of enough these last seventeen years to drive any woman but me crazy. But with her, it's a soft mouth. I'll shut up, but for God's sake settle things. I'm going crazy. I can't stand it."

The look of one trapped settled over Albert,

"I think I'd rather walk," he said; "those cabs are reckless and the meters run up so."

"Don't curl up your lips so, Lilly, over a little economy. Albert's right. What good does it do you to earn, the way you spend? Your husband has forty thousand dollars to show, and what have you to show? Taxicab rides don't draw any interest. Don't be so ready to curl up your lips."

"Why, mamma, you imagine things!" And to Albert, "Of course, let's walk."

For two hours, then, oftentimes stopping to face each other, they paced the wind-swept rectangle of the reservoir in Central Park, spring out in the air, but quite a tear of breeze across their high place.

He was sullen, casuistic, and impenetrable as a sea wall under a dashing, and the thought came to her that had he presented any other surface it would have been easier.

"Well, Albert," she began, facing him there in the wide afternoon light, "what is there that we two can say to each other?"

"Words," he said, stodgy in his bitterness, "mean nothing against seventeen years."

"You're right. And yet--I want you to know, Albert--before you go across--"

"Don't be too sure you'll be rid of me that way."

"Or before you go back home--that she is yours as much as mine and--"

"Generous," he said, dryly.

She could have beaten her head with a sense of futility.

"You've been a bad woman with a streak of devil in you. Tried to ruin my life, but I didn't let you. No, siree! I've worked things out. I've gotten on. I'm big in my way--in my business--in my home."

"Albert, I love to hear you say that!"

"You! You don't love anything or anybody outside yourself."

"Why? Because I took my chance to save myself from everything I--I hated! Not you--not they--but everything it stands for out there. Does self-preservation imply only selfishness?"

"Whatever it implies," he answered, stung to dark red by his effort for quick retort, "you're selfish--rotten selfish. But you haven't kept me down. I've gotten up these eighteen years--and you--you--Bah!"

"You've been happy, Albert? Tell me you have."

"Happy! I'm not a hog for happiness. You to inquire about my happiness! Lots you care! I've had my share of contentment. Contented as a man can be in a community where he has kept up a farce for seventeen years that his wife is off with his consent studying opera. But I've kept my name--kept it in spite of you. I don't know what's been what with you. Guess if the truth is known, I'm afraid to think what's what!"

"Albert--"

"Oh, I don't put anything past you. I don't even know if that girl is mine. For all I know you're a--"

"Albert!"

"Bah! I don't put anything past you!"

She faced his words as if they were blows, letting them rain.

"You're lying, Albert," she said, evenly. "She's yours and you know it."

"I've kept *my* name! Kept it and tried to make it up to your parents, who deserved better than you!"

She quivered and the red that sprang out in her face was almost purple, and yet by her silence bared her chest for more, as if grateful for the sting of the lash.

"Bah! Don't be afraid. I don't want to know anything, but I'm not the booby I may seem to you. When a woman has lived around this way for all these years, in with a gang of show folks--Bah! I don't want to know." And spat.

"She's yours, Albert, and you know it. You know it!"

"Yes, I guess she is, from the look of her, not that I put anything past you. But that's your business. You're nothing to me. I'm cured of you. You couldn't make me suffer the way they do in books. I've kept my name, so if it's divorce you have on your brain, you might as well get it out, because--"

"No, Albert--"

"I've kept my name, whatever you've done to yours. Your life is your business. But the girl. That's where I have a right or two coming to me."

She was prepared for just this, but somehow when it came it was a full moment before she could answer, for the rush of fear that choked her.

"That's for--for Zoe to decide."

"That's for *me* to decide. She goes to a decent, respectable home where she belongs. You're not fit to raise her. Look at what you made of her. A fine specimen. A short-haired freak with all your crazy ideas thriving in her head. You've ruined your life, but you didn't succeed in ruining mine and you won't ruin hers. You and your stage-struck notions that never got you anywhere. She's going home where she belongs!"

She could hardly breathe for keeping down the rising tide of her terror, but her eyes were always cold for him.

"Your daughter has a lyric-soprano voice, and however little that may mean to you she is going to delight the world with it some day. One of the great masters of the world has made her his protegee. She is preparing for her audition--her hearing--in the fall, and it is even possible she may be singing in grand opera next season. You cannot--"

"I'll see her dead first. You were an opera bird, too. I'll see her dead first before I let her make a zero mark out of her life as her crazy mother did before her."

"Albert, can't you see! Zoe's the wine. You, mamma--papa--the vine. I don't count. I--I'm sort of the grape--that fermented--you see! She's me--plus. Her arm is long enough to touch what she wants. Mine wasn't. I saw it, but I couldn't reach. I was one generation too underdone. You cannot have Zoe. I cannot. She doesn't belong to you or me. She belongs to life. She's not mine. She is only my success; she--"

"She--goes--home!"

"No!"

"Why in God's name did you get me on here? You don't expect to see me stand by and countenance your craziness?"

"Why! Why! I've asked it ever since the moment I sent the wire. Why! I had to do it somehow--a fear of--something--war--life--death--but you shall not have her. Not unless she decides it that way. No. Never!"

"I'm a slow thinker! And slower to act. That's been my trouble. But this time the bit is between my teeth. I've a family now and family obligations. Don't be so sure yet that I'm on my way overseas. There is a way around every situation if you look for it hard enough. My place is here now. Home! My daughter goes home!"

She could see in profile the heavy jaw clamp upward, and more and more that wooden stodginess became terrible to her. In a flash-back she could see those seventeen years of beefsteak suppers; his temples at-their trick of working. Seventeen years all cluttered up with bed casters, bathtub stoppers, and poultry wiring. That party back there at Flora's. The lotto and tiddledywinks tables laid out. Page Avenue on a summer's day with the venders hawking down it--ap-ples--twenty cents a peck--ap-ples. Zoe--caught!

She closed over his wrists with a little predatory grip.

"Albert, don't do that! Don't take her back. She'll claw you like a wild eagle in a cage--out there. She belongs to the world. In the fall she sings for Auchinloss. It may lead to anything! Albert--you ask why I sent for you. Let her be. Let her stay here with Mrs. Blair--a friend--a dear--good friend of mine. Her education--Take me, Albert. Take *me* home--Albert."

At her hand on his wrist something raced over him like the lick of a flame; he pressed against her with the entire length of his body and his lips were moist.

"Lilly," he said, very darkly red and trying to clasp her about the waist, "I'll take you! I oughtn't, but I will. Come back, Lilly, and make it up to me for all these years. Being near you makes me forget everything except that--you are near me. I've missed you all these years--I guess--but never so much as this minute. You've gotten so handsome with the years. Something--Come home, Lilly--make it up to me. Give me--your--your lips!"

She kept retreating before the dark red and the moist lips which he wet more and more with his tongue.

"Will you leave her be--then--Albert? Here?"

"Lilly--your lips--give me."

"Will you, Albert--leave her here--Zoe?"

She could feel the scald of his breathing.

"Yes--if you come."

"You promise?"

"Yes, Lilly. Your lips--let me."

Suddenly he had her to him, there in the light darkness of the deserted square of reservoir, kissing her so that his mouth smeared over toward her ear.

She was not quick enough entirely to avert her face, and in the embrace his Adam's apple was against her throat so that she could feel it beat, and with her nails biting into her palm to keep her from screaming, she was shrieking over and over to herself at his nearness: "Ugh! Ugh! Ugh!"

CHAPTER X

Albert did not sail.

A certain depression seemed to settle over him the evening following, after they had dined at a Broadway restaurant and were spending the interim before theater in the lobby of the Hotel Astor, where Mrs. Becker never tired of observing and commenting upon the transient swirl and peacockery.

"Look at that tight skirt, will you! It's a shame for any self-respecting woman to have to look at, much less wear it."

"Tippy dear, not so loud."

"Look at that low-cut back, will you! And white hair, too. I wouldn't live in this town if you gave it to me! Sixty cents for string beans the menu read to-night. I can buy a bushel at home for that. If I had been alone I know what I would have done. Walked out. It's only for millionaires here. The rest have to live in back rooms so they can put everything on their backs. You should thank your stars you have a home to go to, Lilly, instead of you and Zoe crying over each other all day. If I had my say she would go, too. Education! St. Louis education is good enough for anybody. Ben, I want you to look! If I was to ask you to buy me a chiffon cape like that you would drop in your tracks."

"Now, old lady, do I ever refuse you anything?"

"No, because I never ask for anything."

"I think we had better be going," said Lilly, leaning forward to tilt Zoe's hat farther down over her face. "I don't want you to miss the first act."

There was to be a box for "Who Did It?" and a visit behind scenes between acts.

"I want to get a look-in on what goes on behind there," specified Mrs. Becker through a sniff. "Fine mess!"

From where he sat with crossed knees and his nicely polished shoes far out so that passers-by were forced to a small detour, Albert looked suddenly across at his mother-in-law, rather scaredly white.

"Mother," he said, "I've got a pain in my chest."

On the instant her rosiness blanched.

"Albert, one of your colds coming on? They never start on your chest. It's influenza; the papers are full of it. They say next winter we're going to have it in a terrible epidemic. Albert, what hurts?"

He inserted two fingers into the front pleat of his shirt.

"It hurts here," he said.

"Albert," cried Mrs. Becker, instantly taken with panic, "let me feel if you have any fever!"

"Now, now, Carrie, don't create a scene here in the lobby. You've nursed him through enough colds not to be alarmed."

"But, Ben, in his chest! It's a symptom, I tell you; the papers are full of it!"

"Nonsense, Carrie! It's probably a little indigestion. You will insist upon those table d'hotes. On the way to the theater we'll stop in at a drug store."

"Theater! Don't even mention the word. Come upstairs, Albert. Luckily I put a pair of your flannelette pajamas in the trunk. Ben, you rush over to the drug store for some camphorated oil. Albert, do you feel achy?"

Lilly laid out a quietly firm hand on his arm.

"Mamma, please let Albert get a word in."

"I know that boy like a book. He looks feverish."

"Albert," said Lilly, holding to the sedative quality in her voice, "do you feel ill?"

"I've a pain in my chest," he persisted, doggedly and with the drawn look about his mouth whitening.

They put him to bed. By nine o'clock a slight flush lay on Albert's cheek and he kept feeling of his brow.

"I think I have fever," he said once, always in scared white manner. "Look in the paper and see if dry lips is one of the symptoms."

Then Zoe was dispatched home and the house physician called in, Mrs. Becker, as usual, tempestuous with instantaneous hysteria and conjuring to Lilly another sick room from out the hinterland of her childhood.

"Doctor, is it the Spanish influenza? Has he fever? He's always subject to colds, Doctor. He's not as strong as he looks. I've sat up many a night with his quincy sore throats. Many is the time, before we got the auto, that I rode down for him in the street car with his rubbers, if a rain came up. Doctor, do you think it could be that Spanish influenza? O God! if he should take sick away from home! Our doctor at home understands his system. My boy--my son--"

With a frozen sense of her alienism, Lilly sat, as it were, outside the situation, proffering herself almost with a sense of intrusion.

The doctor would not pronounce, but left with instructions and the promise of a midnight return. Into that Mrs. Becker read darkly.

"He's a sick man or one of these busy New York doctors wouldn't be returning again to-night. My boy is a sick man."

Meanwhile Albert had fallen into a light sleep. They sat beside his bedside watching his lips puff out, sometimes in bubbles.

The silence of midnight descended over the transient formality of the hotel room.

Undoubtedly Albert had a fever which seemed to be rising. He moistened his lips now constantly and threw himself about beneath the coverings, and then Mrs. Becker, not to be restrained, would lean forward to brush backward from his brow, as if there were hair.

At midnight the doctor returned and at one o'clock Albert was removed to Murray Hill Hospital.

He was ill three days, slipping off almost from the beginning into a state of coma from which he did not emerge.

With a celerity that was presently to race it through the country, this strange malady laid low its victim with what might have been pneumonia, except for certain complications that baffled and alarmed an already thoroughly aroused medical world.

The second day a sort of dark rash broke out over Albert's chest, so that his nurses entered the room in gauze masks, and finally, in spite of Lilly's protestations and Mrs. Becker's most violent hysterics, no admittance to the sick room was granted them.

And now comes a tide in the affairs of Lilly Penny which, being too true life, is not sufficiently true to fiction.

On the day that was to have been Zoe's formal graduation from High School, so that the pearl-embroidered slippers were never worn and her diploma brought home to her by a classmate, Albert Penny died, with no more furor than he had lived.

Stupor enveloped Lilly. She moved through days incredibly crowded with detail, and yet, somehow, so withdrawn into the very nub of herself that it was the shell of her seemed to compete with the passing time. Certainly it was this shell of her followed Albert in that strangest of little processions, to his cremation.

There had been an effort to travel west with the remains, but quarantine conditions forbade, and it was just as well so.

Four times on that ride through a warm summer rain to the crematory Mrs. Becker went off into light faints, sobbing herself back into consciousness. It frightened Lilly to look at her father; his face had dropped into hollows and the roundness of his back was suddenly a decided hump. And he had fallen into a silence. A sort of hollow urn of it that not even the outbursts of his wife could rouse to his usual soothing chirpings. He merely sat stroking her hand and staring into a silence which he seemed to see.

A very quiet and very frightened Zoe had been packed off to Ida Blair's, through it all Lilly's stupor persisting.

Mrs. Becker's state became cause for concern. Once back at the hotel, with Albert's room locked off, and once more thrown open to the impersonal feet of transiency, she would only moan and wind her hands and go off into the light states of unconsciousness.

"I haven't my son any more! Why did we come? It might not have happened at home. Our daughter wronged him, but, thank God, we tried to make it up to him. My boy. He was so steady--so careful. I can't realize he's gone--without me. The way he used to come home. Never a habit--evening after evening his newspaper and bed. Thank God, I don't think he ever missed her going as he might have. It hurt at first. He wanted to resign his Bible class, and that day we broke up the house--he kept twitching with his eyes. You remember, Ben. And that bed caster. Funny to have twitched over that. It seems he brought it home the night she left--it came over him all of a sudden, it wouldn't ever have to be fitted in. That's it! O

God! all these years without knowing his own child. He was so steady--a good boy if God ever grew one. Ben, Ben, how can we go home without him? How can we go home without our boy?"

"Carrie, it is God's will."

"It is nobody's will. God couldn't will it that way. Just as he had got a little happiness in his way. To think he was willing to take her back. I don't care for myself, we're on in years, Ben--we're done--and now we've lost our--all--nothing to live for--"

"Mamma, mamma, don't talk that way. Let me try to make up to you for--"

"I can't face going home. He was my life, that boy. He made up for what we suffered through our own. He was a son to us. I can't face going home without him. Albert--where are you? Albert!"

"Mamma, mamma, won't you let me try to make up, dear, for what I have failed you?"

"Albert--can't you hear me--Albert--"

"Carrie, we've got our daughter back. Isn't that something to be--"

"I want my son, I tell you."

"Mamma darling, you're killing me. Let me make it up to you--even a little--the--"

"No, no; you're not a daughter to me. I want my son. Our way was his way."

"Mamma, please--take me home in his place. I'll make it up to you. Let me go back, dear, in Albert's place. I want to pay up--to you. I'm finished--here, dear. I'm ready--ready--"

Suddenly Mrs. Becker seemed to experience one of her cyclonic shifts. Tears came raining down her face, her sobbing cleft with great racking gulps. Then she dropped to her knees beside her daughter, and, before Lilly could prevent, reached up to drag down her face against her own tear-drenched one.

"Don't leave us, Lilly. Don't ever. Come home with us. We're getting old, Lilly. Don't ever leave us, me and papa. Promise me, Lilly. Promise."

"Of course I promise, mamma darling. Of course I promise."

CHAPTER XI

For a full week after Albert's strangely curtailed obsequies, a gray blanket of woolly humidity hung with July unseemliness over the city in a clinging fog that feathered the throat.

The morning that Lilly returned to the office electric lights were burning and electric fans were whirring into it.

The unassailed normality of the machine whose functioning depended upon its parts! How easily even the most component of those parts could be replaced! The rows of stenographers, in her but two weeks' absence, new faces among them, outlined against windows of space and East River. The hinged little mahogany gates swinging to their goings and comings. Her own office with its glazed pane of door glass and outlook over city roofs and tug-specked band of river.

It was as if the tide of life were once more licking at her feet. She hung up her hat, patting at her hair in the little square of mirror above the stationary washstand, looking back at herself out of eyes a bit dreggy with tiredness, but her skin so deep in its whiteness that it was almost as if its creamy quality had congealed of mere richness.

She rubbed her cheeks to pinken and quicken them, and rang for an office boy, turning her back on the pile of letters and her reports on the desk and her eagerness to be at them.

"Ask Mr. Bruce Visigoth if he can see me."

The message came back on the instant. He could.

She turned the knob to his office door so slowly that she saved the slightest squeak, and stood there with her silhouette against the ground glass for a long moment. When she did enter, from the center of the room where he had been watching her silhouette against the pane, Bruce advanced to meet her.

He took her hand and on the instant she felt her eyes fill, burningly.

He was in summer and office negligee, an unlined blue-serge coat, a white-silk shirt which lay lightly to his body flexuosity, and above the soft collar he had taken on enough outdoor tan to make his smile whiter. She could have bitten her lips for their trembling, and tried to smile with her tortured eyes.

"Lilly," he said, topping her hand with his, "why didn't you let me know sooner? Your letter an hour ago came out of a clear sky. You see, I didn't even know he--he was here."

"It was all so--so quick!"

"Jove! I don't seem to take it in yet."

"Nor I," she said, quiescently and letting him lead her to a chair. "He--You see, he was only ill three days."

"There doesn't seem much for me to say, does there, Lilly?"

"No," she said, "that's it, there's nothing to say."

"I can't bear to think of your having been exposed to it."

"That was the least. He died--afraid. That is so terrible to me, somehow. I wouldn't mind all of the horrible rest if only he hadn't died--afraid. I wonder if you know what I mean. He lived so--so meekly to have died--that way. Afraid."

"Yes," he said, "I think I do know." He wanted to keep his gaze away from her and to keep it cool, but somehow each time their eyes met a flame leaped up out of embers, a fiery new consciousness that kept dancing.

"He and--and my parents--you see, they--Well, I told you everything in the letter."

"Are your parents returning home?"

"Yes. That's what I've come to say. You see--they--we--we've decided to remain here two months. Until September--up in my little apartment, all of us. In September Zoe is to have her audition with Auchinloss. So much depends on that. We've such hopes, her teacher and I. She's pure lyric soprano. We think grand-opera brand. And now with the war on, more and more the American girl is getting her chance. That's why my parents have finally consented to wait here with me until then. After that, Zoe is to stay with Ida Blair and we three--my parents and I--are going home--together. That is what I have come to tell you. I'll be giving up my work with you in--September. I'm going home--with them."

He regarded her, his flush going down perceptibly.

"You're fooling."

"No," she said, trying to smile. "I suppose it's about the most solemn job I have left to do in life--going home."

"Why, you--you can't go back there."

"I can," she said, her voice held calm.

"I--we can't let you go."

"Why? Zoe--my big job's done."

"Lilly, I tell you we need you here more than ever. My brother arrives this morning from Seattle. We've completed the cross-country chain. I'm free now to branch out. I'm counting on you. I'm full of an idea for that community opera scheme and I'm ready to do the play from the Russian on your say-so. Lilly--you cannot go now--"

"I can--must," she said, scraping back her chair. "You must work out your dreams--alone--with some one else. I--must--go." And then withdrawing from what she saw: "No! No! Bruce! No! No!"

But just the same they were in each other's arms with the irresistibility of tide for moon and moon for tide. Press him back with her palms as she would when his lips found hers, it was as if something etheric had flowed into her brain. She wanted to resist him and instead her hands met in a clasp about his neck. "No, no." And yet as he kissed her eyelids and down against the satinness of her hair, it seemed to her that toward this moment all the poor blind years had been directed.

"Lilly--darling."

She tried to shake off her enchantment.

"You hurt!"

"I want to."

"My--love."

"My love."

"So this--this is it?"

"What?"

"Love."

"Love. Love."

"How beautiful--sex."

"I want to kiss those stars out of your eyes. I want to wind you in moonlight."

"Bruce, I think I must be mad. Crazily--deliciously mad."

"Me too. I'm as deliciously, as crazily mad as any young Leander. I want to swim a thousand Hellesponts for you. I want--"

"No--no--no, Bruce, you don't understand--my love--"

"I do understand. That I have you now to love and adore, to marry--"

The door opened then, quite abruptly. It was Robert Visigoth. He had a straw hat in one hand and an alligator traveling bag in the other. The latter he set down rather abruptly.

So instantaneous was their springing apart and so ready the mind to believe what the heart denied, that it was almost conceivable that he had not seen. There was not even a pause, and through the perfunctory greetings of these two men of strangest relation, Lilly found herself somehow back at her desk, little prickles out all over her body and particularly against her face, like the bite of sleet, something like this running behind her lips:

"Please, God, don't let him tell. He promised! Please! God, I'll never give in again. Bruce--my darling--don't let him tell you. He promised he wouldn't. Don't tell him, Robert. Bruce, don't let him. Please, God--don't let him."

After a while, burning with the fever in her blood, she plunged, for the sedative of it, into the work before her. The first of a stack of reports on her desk was from the Adelphi Theater, Akron, Ohio.

"Three Melodious Sisters."   12 minutes. Well received. Wardrobe worn.
"Whistling Bicyclers."   14 minutes. Skillful. Comedy weak.
"Please, God--don't let him--"
"Shenck and Bent."   9 minutes. 3 laughs.
"Sylvia King & Co."   9 minutes. Weak patter but finished strong.
"Musical Gypsies."   10 minutes. Fair. Good opening number.
"Please, God, don't let him tell."

After what might have been minutes or hours, then, the door opened and without preamble Robert Visigoth walked in, and in the wide-kneed fashion forced upon him by corpulency seated himself beside her desk.

"How long has this thing been going on?" he said, looking at her from under beetling brows that had grown bushy with the years. Time had done just that to

Robert Visigoth. Beetled him. His years overhung him. He carried them massively. It was not so much that he had lost his waistline, but he had settled into himself. That was it! Robert Visigoth had settled rather appallingly into himself.

For a second Lilly's eyes moved from the two fifty-cent cigars protruding from his waistcoat pocket to a lodge button at his lapel, and then, finally trapped, met his.

"How long? I said."

"You've told him?" she asked, leaning forward to hear through the buzzing in her ears.

"Whether I do or not depends upon you."

She tried not to let him see how the room was rocking around and around, how suddenly the buzzing had lifted until she felt light-headed. She could have shouted, danced, wept, or fainted her relief. Nothing mattered, not even the squatty person sitting there with little diabetic puffs beneath his eyes.

"How long has this thing been going on?" he repeated, his voice a rising gale.

"Are you your brother's keeper?"

"From your kind, yes."

"There has been nothing between us."

"That's a lie."

Through the scorch of her humiliation it was a second before she could command her lips.

"I swear to God."

"Bah!" he almost spat out, "after what I walked in on!"

"Yes," she said, biting off the words with a clip, "after what you walked in on."

He leaned forward with a thrust of face that was unpleasantly close.

"All I have to say is, hands off there."

"There has been nothing between us. I tell you it's true."

"I'm not concerned whether it is or not. What has been has been. But now, hands off. You can't land my brother. I heard the word. Marry. The cheek--you-- my brother! You must be crazy."

"You're wrong. You're wrong," she managed to insist, her throat rising and falling like a sea.

"My eyes aren't wrong. They saw what I stumbled in on."

"I know. I know. It's difficult--impossible to explain away an--an occurrence like that. How well I know the futility of trying to convince your kind of man that there are more than two kinds of women in the world. Good and bad. The woman you marry and the woman you ruin. I'm bad. Have it your way. Bad. Bad. Bad. But for what was your sin as much as mine you are free in your man-made society to go your way, fulfilling your life, and then you dare to come here and sit judgment on my fulfilling mine. When are women going to venture from *behind* the man-made throne to sit beside, and make you men move over?"

"I'm not here to discuss the double code with you. I don't know and don't care how you have lived since. It is not my business. For sixteen years you have given this firm fine satisfaction for which we, in turn, have tried to express our appreciation. You know that. We know that. Your morals are none of my business except when they touch me! A man's a man. I don't know how you've lived. For my part, I think you've gone pretty straight, but that doesn't change matters. I know what I know, and a man's a man. What are you going to do about it? You know, too, that there is no love lost between me and my brother in the little things. We go our ways. But when it comes to the big--he's my brother. Blood. Get me? Whatever I am can't change me here inside. He's my brother. You're--you!"

"You're right. I wouldn't. I couldn't. I must have been mad--this morning. I--somehow--it got all beyond me in a moment. I swear to you for the first time! Do you think I'd muss up one hour of his life? Even if I dared? Even if you were to come to me, on your knees, begging me to--to--marry him? To begin with, I'm older--only a year in time, it's true, but he--he's just beginning. I'm beginning over. What is my life compared to his? He's on the brink of a thousand realizations. And I--oh, I'm not whining. I'd do it all over again, loathing you as you must know I loathed you--that night. But my child got her chance. You sold it to me and I paid for it in the basest coin of the realm. But I'd do it again--knowing what I know now, I'd do it again. You hear! Do you hear!"

"That's past now--"

"No. For you, yes, but I'm still paying. Paying at this moment with my--my heart's blood. But if I hadn't done it--gone with you--something would have been lost that night that was worth every cent I paid. They'd have got her back. I don't care. I've won. I've won if I've lost."

She was on her feet now, her eyes, like blue wells that were filling with ink, plunging beyond his with a Testament defiance that seemed to shout, "I am fearfully and wonderfully made."

"Yes, I love him. You can't take that from me. That is why he is so safe from me. I love him too much for him to know. And yet I think--I believe--I know that even if he did know, in the end it wouldn't matter--"

"You must be crazy. Once let your idealist wake up and there is no more dreaming for him."

"He mustn't ever wake up--for his sake! Promise. Promise me that you won't ever wake him!"

"Whether I do or not is up to you."

"What do you want?" she said, tiredly.

"I suppose the black and white of it is that you must quit."

"That is easy. I'm resigning anyway the fifteenth of September to go West to live."

He took on the half-conciliatory graciousness of one who has gained his advantage with unsuspected ease.

"I'd give a great deal not to have had this happen, but, after all, a man is a man and life is life."

She let her gaze bore into his like gimlets burning for center.

"I think you've explained that before."

He began to back out before her immobility.

"I am remaining East two months. I hope your resignation will allow us that much time to attempt to fill your place."

"I leave that to you. It can be either immediate or take effect in September."

"By all means the latter. Will you--can you believe me when I say if there is anything I can do--letters--an opening with a Western firm--"

"Please," she said, turning him a shoulder in high distaste.

"I have your word--then?"

"My word," she said, looking past his hand toward the door.

He backed out in the somewhat ludicrous crab fashion and then she sat down, swinging around on her swivel chair toward the desk. The stack of reports lay facing her. She caught up the next in order.

People's Playhouse. Tulsa, Oklahoma.

For the next half hour she must have sat there trying to co-ordinate out of chaos by staring at the heading and repeating over and over again: "*People's Playhouse. Tulsa, Oklahoma. People's Playhouse. Tulsa, Oklahoma.*"

*   *   *   *   *

Whistles were blasting through the noonday fog when Bruce finally and without preamble burst into her office.

It struck her even on the gale of his entrance how young he was that his hair should show the nervous plowing of five fingers, and how sensitive his profile and ready to flare at the nostrils. His tie, too, burnt orange, from a soft collar and badly knotted! She wanted to jerk up his chin and putter at remaking the four-in-hand.

"Lilly--sweetheart--"

She sat regarding him over the top of People's Playhouse, Tulsa, Oklahoma.

"Sweetheart, let us call it a day. I want to drive you out to Tarrytown to--"

"Don't," she said, frowning.

"Don't what?" Her immobility an ineffectual stop to his exuberance.

"Come now," wanting to draw her from her chair by the two hands, swinging them wide and then together; "don't let his nibs bouncing in that way throw a damper. We were too quick for him, anyway. Don't believe he saw a thing. And what if he did? He's going to know it anyhow, and pretty quick, too. I want to shout it from the housetops, I want to megaphone it up to the stars. Lilly--Lilly-mine! Sweetheart!"

She crowded back into the chair.

"How dared you!"

He fell back with his gesture still wide.

"Why--what? Dared what? Oh, come now, sweetheart, I could wager he didn't see, and suppose he did? We've nothing to conceal. I'm for telling him to-day!"

"No. No. No. You played unfair. You took me--unawares. You misunderstood me horribly--most horribly."

"You mean--"

"Why, you--you **boy!** What has happened cannot make any difference between you and me. It was outrageous of you--silly *boy* you--to--to take advantage. After all that has passed--all these years--it is unthinkable that you didn't understand. Why, you--you *boy!*"

She saw his jaw fall and the sense of his ridiculousness set in.

"What has merely been absurd all along you have suddenly made intolerant. You make more imperative my resignation. You must understand--Mr. Visigoth--under what conditions I will consent to remain here these few weeks."

The words were so stilted that she had the sensation of throwing metal disks on a stone floor and waiting for their tinny clatter. She could see the high red drain out of his face and then rush up again as if he had been slapped.

"Lilly, for God's sake, you--you cannot be serious!"

"No mock heroics--please."

His ears tipped with flame; he straightened back from her.

"No more mock heroics," he said, in a voice suddenly quieted down like vichy gone stale. "Forgive an old--fool--a young--fool--and forget it. Thank you for jerking me up."

He raised her limp hand, bowing over it until his lips hovered but did not touch.

"My solemn word on it this time--no more--mock--heroics." And still Lilly, on the click of the door after him, could not clear her brain of the running threnody of nonsense:

People's Playhouse. Tulsa, Oklahoma. People's Playhouse. Tulsa, Oklahoma.

CHAPTER XII

Time flies or does not, according to the eyes of the beholder. As the days began to lengthen into the longest spokes of the cycle, and parlors and magazines to don summer covers, it seemed to Lilly that somewhere an interim too subtle for mortal eyes must have occurred, because suddenly there came a very torrid day in September, the fourteenth, to be exact, when the little apartment in West End Avenue stood denuded, stripped to a few huddled trunks, and Zoe's dressing table, chair, piano, and desk ready to be carted out to the little sea-view room that awaited her in Ida Blair's Long Island bungalow.

They were a group diverse of emotion and perilous to one another's nerves this last morning.

MRS. BECKER: "I think I'd better write my girl another postal to be sure and have supper ready when we get home Thursday night. There is some canned salmon in the grocery closet, I forgot to mention, and she can borrow a few potatoes from the Shriners for frying, until I get a chance to lay in supplies when I get home. Poor Albert! How he loved creamed salmon and fried potatoes! Ben, help me to realize what has happened. O God, I--"

MR. BECKER: "Now, Carrie."

MRS. BECKER: "The Shriners are nice neighbors, Lilly. They are the only ones besides us on the block who stuck after the street began to go down. You'll like Edna Shriner. You remember her? Pock-marked. She used to be in your dancing-school class. She never married, but how she keeps that little home for her old father! Kitchen floor! You could eat off it. And as handy a body with the needle as ever lived. Her French knots. The guest-towels that girl has French-knotted."

LILLY (to herself): "Salmon and fried potatoes. Page Avenue. Shriners. Funny!--O God!--Why--Oh!--Oh!--Funny!--"

ZOE: "Lilly, feel my heart, how it beats."

It was as if Lilly could not take her eyes from off her daughter.

"Remember what Triest said, dearest, let your nerves be so many violin strings, tightening but not quivering."

"It's your going, Lilly--I--I can't seem quite to grasp it. You will come back to me soon--in two months--one--I couldn't stand it longer!"

"Yes, and, Zoe, you will write every day. Every little single thing. Your work--your life--your friends--every tiny success--"

"Lilly, Lilly--don't go! It's madness. Stay, darling. I feel like a pig--all that money--his fortune. If you are not entitled to touch it, I am not--"

"You are his child and the only wrong you ever did him was through me."

"Lilly--don't go, darling--"

"Zoe, don't tear me to pieces."

"I'll work, darling, as I've never worked before."

"Zoe, Zoe, go straight to your mark."

"I--I can't realize it, Lilly. To-day! He's going to hear me to-day--this very afternoon. I--I feel as nervous at the prospect of singing before you as before him. I--I think I'm the luckiest girl in the world. Lilly, sometimes I--I--think life has--has sort of cleared the way for me to walk in its lovely places--you have cleared the way. But what--what if he doesn't think I've the voice *maestro* thinks I have? I couldn't stand that, Lilly--the way you stood it."

"But he will," said Lilly, a memory shaping itself. "Remember your power begins where mine left off. You heard Du Gass the year before she died, but you were too young to remember. Your voice is so much--so infinitely bigger, Zoe, and your knowledge and defiance of life and of the Auchinlosses--makes me so unafraid for you--"

"Kiss me, Lilly. I'm frightened--not of Auchinloss--or life--but of--Oh, I don't know--frightened of silliness, I guess."

"I'm not."

"But you're trembling."

"Of hope."

At eleven Lilly went down to her office. Leon Greenberg already had her desk. It was largely a matter now of sliding in the new prop before sliding out the old.

There were several farewell offerings from various of the older girls. The immemorial trifles that women exchange. A bottle of eau de cologne. The inevitable six handkerchiefs. A silver bodkin for running ribbon through lingerie. And from the booking department, a silk umbrella suitably engraved. She cried a little.

By noon the top of her desk was bare and the drawers empty.

She sat looking out over the waves of roofs of a city that had beaten her back at every turn, lashed her, and yet with the mysterious counterflow of oceans had carried her out a foot for every ten it flung her back.

She felt full of sobs, but quiet. Strangely quiet, as if the champing machinery of her life had stopped suddenly, leaving an hiatus that made her heart ache of passivity.

At two o'clock, by appointment, came Zoe ... like a blaze of light. Her eyes with her mother's trick of iris, full of inner glow, and her blond hair so daringly boxed, set off with a droop of tam-o'-shanter.

There had been a new frock of heavy white crepe with a wide white hat for this occasion. Instead, with last-moment decision, she had come in one of the straight blue frocks, the wide patent-leather belt, a knot of orange and blue ribbon, representing her active membership in a local canteen service, at her throat. She came glowing through the daring simplicity, flamboyantly and to the nth power of Lilly's slower personality, her mother's child.

"Hurry, darling, I've a taxi waiting. We're to meet *maestro* at the Opera House."

"Zoe, I'm glad you wore this instead. Did your grandmother feel badly that you didn't wear the one she gave you?"

"I wasn't myself in it. No--room."

In the corridor, going out, Bruce stepped suddenly out of his office into their path.

Zoe's hand had shot out.

"Hello, you!" she said.

He looked at her through a slow smile.

"Well, I'll be hanged! The youngster! Good Lord! What have they done! Who elongated you? Where are the knee dresses and the corkscrews?"

She withdrew a highly haughty hand.

"You poor, misguided Rip Van Winkle. When did you return from the

Catskills?"

"When did it happen?" he asked Lilly, trying to keep his eyes from crinkling.

It was the first time in this last brace of weeks that there had been more than the merest perfunctory word between them, and she tried to thaw her cold lips into a smile.

"You forget that you haven't seen her since last Christmas. Six inches more of skirt and a few hairpins did it."

"Well, I'll be hanged!" he kept reiterating. "Zoe grown up!"

"Is it true you are going to try for the aviation? Ida Blair says you are."

"Looks that way."

"You're too old."

"Well, then, I'll have to come down to earth. You and your mother have different ideas regarding my age. I'm rather dizzy about it this minute, myself. Either time is putting one over on me or you have caught up. By Jove! that's it! You've caught up! You're immense!"

She was suddenly, and to Lilly's amazement, a creature of flashes and quirks, of self and sex consciousness.

"Don't like to be--immense!"

"Gorgeous, then."

"Better."

"Don't go. Let me look at you."

"Come with us. Dare you."

"Zoe!"

"Where?"

"I'm singing this afternoon for Auchinloss. My audition at the Opera House."

"The deuce you say!"

"I've a cab waiting," she said, challenging him with a flash of eyes to their corners.

"Wait," he said, darting into his office.

"Zoe, how dared you?"

"Lilly--he's thrilling! I want him along; I feel keyed up now. The way I want to feel! Edgy!"

Before her persistently cold lips would reply he rejoined them and presently they were all three in the cab.

His contemplation of Zoe became a stare.

"So the little Zoe grew up."

"I'm eighteen. You used to be old enough to be my father. Not any more. Now you are old enough to be my--anything."

"Zoe!"

"Good Lord!" he said. "Fact."

Suddenly her nervousness came flowing back over her.

"Lilly, look at me every second while I'm singing, darling. You too," leaning toward him and placing cold fingers on each of their wrists.

"Delightful and easy task."

She made him a *moue*, prettily pouty.

"You'll be sorry, when I'm famous, that you didn't take me seriously."

"How can I take you at all when you've taken me off my feet?"

"You've never heard me sing, have you?"

"No."

"Wait."

"I palpitate."

"I'm going to be all alone now, you know," she said, looking at him with her brilliant eyes filling.

"More's the pity," he said, feeling rather than seeing the downward brush of Lilly's lashes.

"I'll be out at Ida Blair's until--for a while."

"May I come out and play with you, now that you are caught up and I can be your--anything?"

"You may."

Laughter.

With the stopping of the cab such a javelin of nervousness shot through Lilly that it was as if it had pierced her heart.

A lovely pallor was out over Zoe, enlarging the dark pools of her eyes.

"Sit out in the house, center aisle, and look at me, dears--so I can feel you there--"

To the magic of a bit of cardboard Lilly and Bruce were in the vast fantastic hinterland of the Opera House, and, stumbling through various degrees of black-ness, were presently down in the colossal maw of the auditorium, finding out seats in the great pit of darkness.

They sat in silence, except that for Lilly the beating of her heart seemed to re-cord like a clapper against her brain.

"Don't be nervous," he said once.

"I'm not," she lied.

There was a bunch light on the stage, a dirty backdrop of Corinthian pillars and esplanade and no wings, one or two stage hands moving about, and finally a concert grand piano dragged down.

Suddenly Lilly recognized Auchinloss. He was standing just outside the pool of light that flowed over the piano, the unforgetable outline of his shaggy head, joined by two little peninsulas of sideburns to the heavy spade of beard, gray now and not the sooty black she remembered.

The odor of that little room up on Amsterdam Avenue came winding back. Millie du Gass, the supreme soprano of two continents--dead now, of heartbreak, some said; Alma, in her plaid-silk waist and the bookkeeper's curve to her back. That walk across the parlor floor--

"There's Auchinloss now," said Bruce.

She did not reply, but sat with her handkerchief against her mouth and crowd-ed breathing.

There were three auditions.

A high-bosomed young woman with a powerful mezzo soprano that pulled her mouth to a rhomboid sang Santuzza's famous aria from "Cavalleria Rusticana," stopping suddenly to some unseen signal.

"Fine, strong voice of resonant tin," said Visigoth, under his breath.

A throaty young tenor sang "Ride, Ride, Pagliacci," through to the sob, antici-pating it with a violent throw of body.

Then Trieste took the piano, running downward an avalanche of quick chords, the sepia-outlined head of Auchinloss gone meanwhile from the stage and down somewhere in the sea of dimness that rolled through the auditorium. Lilly could see his profile etched into the twilight.

Very suddenly Zoe was downstage, and through the cymbals hitting into Lilly's consciousness the voice finally came through to her, flowing so easily on the beautiful, the tried old theme of Michaela's aria that she had the feeling of great bolts of every color ribbon, winding about and not even half un-flung as they struck the topmost places.

How true her flight!

With each fluty mount how like a bird, the line of her throat, as her chin went up, throbbing slightly of its warbling, and from where she stood her gaze seeming to plumb them out.

She sang through without interruption, so that when she had finished, the timbre lay like a singing wire on the silence.

Somewhere between the ecstasy of the elbow that pressed against hers, and the ecstasy of her child's voice still trilling on the black silence, Lilly was conscious of movement. The gray silhouette marching down the aisle of gloom. A group up about the piano. Another chord struck out. Zoe's voice skipping upward in grace notes.

Vague, indeterminate passings of figures through a fluid of unreality, like submarine life behind glass.

Then somehow they were out again into the gloom of wings and then on to the white, incredible humdrum of the side street, standing there beside the little door marked "Private," Bruce at her side, rather quivery at the flanges and mopping constantly at the damp rim of his hair.

"Lilly, you've won!"

She felt sillily inclined to laugh.

"I seem to have, don't I?" she said, turning her face under pretense of adjusting her hat, but really for fear that even a smile would induce the threatening laughter which she knew, once let go, would slip up beyond her control.

"She's a flute. She's a lark. She's a dream. I--I don't believe I seem to take it in."

"Nor--I."

Later, Zoe joined them, an air of assumed composure belied by the flaming brilliancy of her eyes and cheeks.

"Why didn't you come up afterward?" she said, forcing a commonplace, and to Bruce, "Hail a cab, Pretty-please."

He did, helping them in and poking his head in after.

"Where?"

"Anywhere. Let it be the Park for a while, Lilly?"

She nodded.

"Is three a crowd?"

For answer she drew him in by the sleeve and on the jouncing off of the cab was in her mother's arms, covering her cheeks with close-pressed, audible kisses, and, after the inexplicable manner of women, both of them crying.

"He--he didn't say much, Lilly. Kissed my hands. Told me to live beautifully and work endlessly. Asked me if I loved poetry and painting and sunrises and spring--a lot of stuff about the awakening of spring. And kissed my hands again. I'm going back to-morrow. They're discussing things now--he and *maestro*--something about a five-year contract--but a great deal of red tape first--board meeting. I'm to be a secret until next season, *maestro* cried--and Auchinloss--Lilly, you need never be afraid for me--you hear--you hear--never! We measured each other--he called me wonder-child. Me--Zoe. Lilly--it's happened ... and you--did it. Lilly, kiss me."

"You darling. You're like a queen. All the little lives that go into the making of your cloth of gold, yet each proud to be ever so humble a party to it!"

"Lilly, you're sad! On *my* day you're sad."

"Glad! You're the meaning of everything. The road had to lead somewhere. Everything is so clear now. You're the lovely meaning, Zoe, behind all the circumstances that went to weave you."

Only half plumbed, Zoe sprang from her mood, flashing with all the amazing coquetry that was so new to Lilly, around toward Bruce.

"Well--what?"

"On the very day I've found you I've lost you."

"To whom?"

"Fame."

"Nonsense!" she cried. "Don't forget the awakening of spring." And buried her face against her mother because she had been outrageous.

Persiflage rose.

"Skylark, when I become more coherent I'll tell you how wonderful you are."

"Zoe dear, hadn't we better drive home?"

"Lark. Lark. I cannot go home now, Lilly. Let's have a lark!"

Suddenly Bruce caught her by the dancing hands.

"Let's celebrate."

"Let's!"

"We'll dine at Sherry's, dance at the Bilt--"

"Lovely! Lovely! I've never been to either!"

"No, no, Zoe. Please! Your grandparents at home. Besides, it's war time."

"Nonsense! Laugh while we may. Next month this time I'll probably be in the thick of it myself. Let's laugh to-day. Vote her down, Zoe!"

"Pl-ease, Lilly."

"Your grandparents, Zoe, they don't even know the news yet--"

"Lilly, this once. Tippy and Dapples aren't going to be thrilled. They think the whole business rather low, anyway. Besides--there's time--it's my day--Lilly--"

"Not Sherry's, then, Zoe--a quieter--"

"Immense! I have it! Tarrytown. An opportunity to show you the place before you go. We'll drop this taxi and pick up my car at the garage. How's that, dinner at Tarrytown? Perfect, I'll say."

"What a duck of an idea! Oh, la, la, la, la!"

And so, quite dumbly, Lilly acquiesced and by easy shift to the tan-upholstered car that ironed out all jolts, and a stiff breeze from the Hudson whirring softly against their faces, they were whirling out along quiet stretches, dusk coming down like a veil.

Seated between them, Zoe fell to singing, trilling highly and softly, her head bared to the wind, her tam-o'-shanter on Bruce's lap, and Lilly sitting silently by with lids down against hot eyeballs, and fighting a sense of cross grain.

Presently lights began to come out along the river, like the gold eyes of cats.

"How cool your fingers are, Zoe. Like the petals of something."

"Lilly, naughty man is holding back one of my hands on me."

"Lovely hands."

"Naughty man."

Silence.

"Oh dear."

"Oh dearest."

"That wasn't for you. That was a sigh."

"But I stole it."

"Cheeky."

Giggles.

Silence again and they turned off a macadamized road that was prematurely dark with trees and into a lariat of driveway that elicited from Zoe a squeal of enthrallment.

Even to Lilly, though she had figured in its purchase, there was something startling in the vast classic whiteness and formal Italian chastity of the house as they flanked it, drawing up under a porte-cochere of Corinthian columns. Through a double row of cypresses turning black, that inclosed a sunken garden, Dante and Virgil might have moved, and yet, Lilly, aching with the analogy which could not conjure, could only call up rather foolishly the three-color magazine advertisement of a low-streamline motor car, drawn up before just such Renaissance magnificence.

Three sheer and cunningly landscaped terraces dropped down from what was actually the rear of the house, but which overhung the river, so that, stepping out of the car, an unsuspected, breath-taking panorama of river wound itself, at that moment the Albany boat moving upstream, light-studded.

ZOE (out at a bound): "Oh! Oh! Oh! Isolde's garden. Tristan, where are you?"

"Here."

"I want to kiss a star--that luscious one up there."

"Let me be proxy."

"Lilly, chastise him!"

She smiled at him with her tortured eyes.

"Like it?" he said, smiling back at her with something impersonal in his eyes that deadened her. "All this formality is hardly my choice; it's Pauline's idea."

They were met by Pauline--known to Zoe and her mother through perfunctory office meetings. She was exceedingly petite, rather appealingly so in her widowhood, and of her younger brother's rather Spanish darkness, except for a graying coiffure worn high and flatteringly.

There were seventeen years between them and yet her shoulders were deeply white, and rose, quite unwithered, out of a jetted evening gown; and her profile, also with the heat lightning of a scarcely perceptible nervous quiver to it, entirely without the sag of tired flesh.

A certain petulance lent to her exceedingly well-bred diction quite a charm, and she was playful and adoring enough to pinch each cheek of her brother's as she tiptoed to kiss him.

"Nice boy to bring home charming people and save me from the boredom of dining alone. How's my handsome brother? Naughty boy! It's the first time you've looked yourself in weeks. They work him too hard down there, Mrs. Penny. I tell my fat brother he's become little more than an ornamental gargoyle. It's too sordid for this boy, and now you running away from him just when I had hoped the time was ripe for him to dabble in some of the things he's set his heart on. The kind of plays he reads all night until I have to turn his lights out. Shame on you for running away!"

Her twitter, from topical bough to topical bough, hardly demanded reply. She exclaimed over Zoe, admiring her extravagantly, insisted upon kissing away a purely imaginary look of headache from her brother's brow, and led the way quite tinily regal, her running line of comment unbroken.

In a soft boudoir of French grays, French doors, cerulean blues, and a litter of every extravagant requisite of the toilet, Lilly faced herself in a cunningly triplicated mirror.

"We're not dressed. We shouldn't have come," trying to ride down her sense of misery.

"I'm dressed in all the cloth of gold you have woven for me," quoth Zoe, in mock grandiloquence, still pitched to her exultant key and in all her youthful capacity for it, full of self.

There were enamel-backed brushes with deep bristles that plowed her hair out into dust of gold, and a finely wrought amber comb which she ran through the fluff, striking an attitude.

"She walks in splendor like the night--"

"Zoe, you're losing your head."

"Splendor! This is me. Marble--terraces--rugs that slide--only I want peacocks--that strut--and tails that open like fans and--starlight--him--"

"Who?"

"Silly darling--nobody--the world--life."

There was no restraining her. She smoothed her mother's hair only to kiss it awry again. She fluffed a fragrant cloud of powder along her neck. Trilled at a drowsy canary in a wicker cage. Stretched herself in the conscious pose of a Reca-mier on the lacy mound of a chaise-longue, and finally followed her mother into the drawing-room, entirely at ease in the straight blue frock.

It was a room almost the width of the house, with a balcony at one end hung in a shah's silk prayer rug, and a stone fireplace, out of the Davanziti palace, opposite. Three sets of leaded doors opened out on to a flagged parapet that overlooked the Hudson and beyond the deep purple of perfect September.

They met in a little group at one of these doors, and Lilly noticed gratefully that Mrs. Enlow had thrown a net wrap over the formality of her evening gown and that Bruce had merely changed to flannels.

He smiled at her with that impersonal sort of kindness which could cause such a gush of blood to her heart, and spread himself in a playful salaam before Zoe.

"Princess."

She held out her hand to be kissed, which he did five times, finger by finger.

"These terraces," said Lilly, trying not to be heavy, "are like the setting for an Aegean romance."

He smiled back at her again through the new film across his eyes.

"Write it and I'll produce it."

"Close the doors, Dicky; it's growing chilly," said Mrs. Enlow.

"Yes," said Lilly, shivering a bit, "chilly."

"And I'm burning, Dicky, Tickey Tavey," cried Zoe, applying the name auda-ciously. "How can anyone be chilly on such a night as this?"

"Come, Princess, and I'll show you some stars."

"Don't wander too far before dinner, children. Mrs. Penny and I will sit in-doors. Only youth can risk swollen joints."

"Yes," said Lilly, feeling herself rather terrifiedly past the fiercer rush of life, "only youth."

They sat on a great overstuffed divan that faced the parapet, lighted softly at each end by the first lamps of evening.

"Why, you poor child, you're shivering of chill! It's the damp. Let me get you a wrap."

In the thickening silence Lilly sat alone looking out through the glass doors.

Bruce and Zoe were silhouetted out there against a fathomless evening sky that was brilliantly pointed with a few big stars. But they were not gazing out. Her face was up to his like a flower about to be plucked, and, looking down into it, his whole body seemed to sway to its sweetness.

Suddenly the ache in Lilly's heart was laid. With all of her old capacity for the incongruous, but without any of her usual pump of terror, she thought suddenly of her father, two nights hence, sitting down to the creamed salmon and fried potatoes on Page Avenue, hanging his napkin with the patent fasteners about his neck. Edna Shriner must teach her that French-knot stitch for Zoe's gowns--in case--heigh-ho!--in case--

With her gaze on those two etched and eloquent profiles, a piercing sense of achievement seemed to flow with a warm rush of blood, curing her of chill.

Her heart beat high with what even might have been fulfillment.

The Codes Of Hammurabi And Moses
W. W. Davies

The discovery of the Hammurabi Code is one of the greatest achievements of archaeology, and is of paramount interest, not only to the student of the Bible, but also to all those interested in ancient history...

QTY

Religion   **ISBN:** *1-59462-338-4*   **Pages:132**
MSRP $12.95

The Theory of Moral Sentiments
Adam Smith

This work from 1749. contains original theories of conscience amd moral judgment and it is the foundation for systemof morals.

QTY

Philosophy ISBN: *1-59462-777-0*   **Pages:536**
MSRP $19.95

Jessica's First Prayer
Hesba Stretton

In a screened and secluded corner of one of the many railway-bridges which span the streets of London there could be seen a few years ago, from five o'clock every morning until half past eight, a tidily set-out coffee-stall, consisting of a trestle and board, upon which stood two large tin cans, with a small fire of charcoal burning under each so as to keep the coffee boiling during the early hours of the morning when the work-people were thronging into the city on their way to their daily toil...

QTY

Pages:84

Childrens   ISBN: *1-59462-373-2*   **MSRP $9.95**

My Life and Work
Henry Ford

Henry Ford revolutionized the world with his implementation of mass production for the Model T automobile. Gain valuable business insight into his life and work with his own auto-biography... "We have only started on our development of our country we have not as yet, with all our talk of wonderful progress, done more than scratch the surface. The progress has been wonderful enough but..."

QTY

Pages:300

Biographies/   ISBN: *1-59462-198-5*   **MSRP $21.95**

The Art of Cross-Examination
Francis Wellman

QTY

I presume it is the experience of every author, after his first book is published upon an important subject, to be almost overwhelmed with a wealth of ideas and illustrations which could readily have been included in his book, and which to his own mind, at least, seem to make a second edition inevitable. Such certainly was the case with me; and when the first edition had reached its sixth impression in five months, I rejoiced to learn that it seemed to my publishers that the book had met with a sufficiently favorable reception to justify a second and considerably enlarged edition. ..

Pages:412

Reference   ISBN: *1-59462-647-2*   *MSRP $19.95*

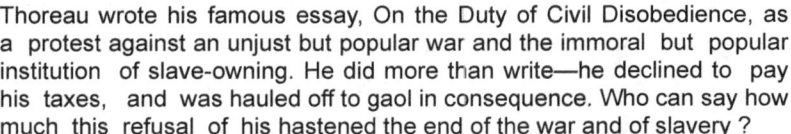

On the Duty of Civil Disobedience
Henry David Thoreau

QTY

Thoreau wrote his famous essay, On the Duty of Civil Disobedience, as a protest against an unjust but popular war and the immoral but popular institution of slave-owning. He did more than write—he declined to pay his taxes, and was hauled off to gaol in consequence. Who can say how much this refusal of his hastened the end of the war and of slavery ?

Law   ISBN: *1-59462-747-9*   **Pages:48**

MSRP $7.45

Dream Psychology Psychoanalysis for Beginners
Sigmund Freud

QTY

Sigmund Freud, born Sigismund Schlomo Freud (May 6, 1856 - September 23, 1939), was a Jewish-Austrian neurologist and psychiatrist who co-founded the psychoanalytic school of psychology. Freud is best known for his theories of the unconscious mind, especially involving the mechanism of repression; his redefinition of sexual desire as mobile and directed towards a wide variety of objects; and his therapeutic techniques, especially his understanding of transference in the therapeutic relationship and the presumed value of dreams as sources of insight into unconscious desires.

Dream Psychology
Psychoanalysis for Beginners

Sigmund Freud

Pages:196

Psychology   ISBN: *1-59462-905-6*   *MSRP $15.45*

The Miracle of Right Thought
Orison Swett Marden

QTY

Believe with all of your heart that you will do what you were made to do. When the mind has once formed the habit of holding cheerful, happy, prosperous pictures, it will not be easy to form the opposite habit. It does not matter how improbable or how far away this realization may see, or how dark the prospects may be, if we visualize them as best we can, as vividly as possible, hold tenaciously to them and vigorously struggle to attain them, they will gradually become actualized, realized in the life. But a desire, a longing without endeavor, a yearning abandoned or held indifferently will vanish without realization.

Pages:360

Self Help   ISBN: *1-59462-644-8*   *MSRP $25.45*

www.bookjungle.com *email: sales@bookjungle.com fax: 630-214-0564 mail: Book Jungle PO Box 2226 Champaign, IL 61825*

QTY

The Rosicrucian Cosmo-Conception Mystic Christianity *by Max Heindel*   ISBN: *1-59462-188-8*   **$38.95**
The Rosicrucian Cosmo-conception is not dogmatic, neither does it appeal to any other authority than the reason of the student. It is: not controversial, but is: sent forth in the, hope that it may help to clear...   New Age/Religion Pages 646

Abandonment To Divine Providence *by Jean-Pierre de Caussade*   ISBN: *1-59462-228-0*   **$25.95**
"The Rev. Jean Pierre de Caussade was one of the most remarkable spiritual writers of the Society of Jesus in France in the 18th Century. His death took place at Toulouse in 1751. His works have gone through many editions and have been republished...   Inspirational/Religion Pages 400

Mental Chemistry *by Charles Haanel*   ISBN: *1-59462-192-6*   **$23.95**
Mental Chemistry allows the change of material conditions by combining and appropriately utilizing the power of the mind. Much like applied chemistry creates something new and unique out of careful combinations of chemicals the mastery of mental chemistry...   New Age Pages 354

The Letters of Robert Browning and Elizabeth Barret Barrett 1845-1846 vol II   ISBN: *1-59462-193-4*   **$35.95**
by Robert Browning and Elizabeth Barrett
Biographies Pages 596

Gleanings In Genesis (volume I) *by Arthur W. Pink*   ISBN: *1-59462-130-6*   **$27.45**
Appropriately has Genesis been termed "the seed plot of the Bible" for in it we have, in germ form, almost all of the great doctrines which are afterwards fully developed in the books of Scripture which follow...   Religion/Inspirational Pages 420

The Master Key *by L. W. de Laurence*   ISBN: *1-59462-001-6*   **$30.95**
In no branch of human knowledge has there been a more lively increase of the spirit of research during the past few years than in the study of Psychology, Concentration and Mental Discipline. The requests for authentic lessons in Thought Control, Mental Discipline and...   New Age/Business Pages 422

The Lesser Key Of Solomon Goetia *by L. W. de Laurence*   ISBN: *1-59462-092-X*   **$9.95**
This translation of the first book of the "Lemegton" which is now for the first time made accessible to students of Talismanic Magic was done, after careful collation and edition, from numerous Ancient Manuscripts in Hebrew, Latin, and French...   New Age/Occult Pages 92

Rubaiyat Of Omar Khayyam *by Edward Fitzgerald*   ISBN:*1-59462-332-5*   **$13.95**
Edward Fitzgerald, whom the world has already learned, in spite of his own efforts to remain within the shadow of anonymity, to look upon as one of the rarest poets of the century, was born at Bredfield, in Suffolk, on the 31st of March, 1809. He was the third son of John Purcell...   Music Pages 172

Ancient Law *by Henry Maine*   ISBN: *1-59462-128-4*   **$29.95**
The chief object of the following pages is to indicate some of the earliest ideas of mankind, as they are reflected in Ancient Law, and to point out the relation of those ideas to modern thought.   Religiom/History Pages 452

Far-Away Stories *by William J. Locke*   ISBN: *1-59462-129-2*   **$19.45**
"Good wine needs no bush, but a collection of mixed vintages does. And this book is just such a collection. Some of the stories I do not want to remain buried for ever in the museum files of dead magazine-numbers an author's not unpardonable vanity..."   Fiction Pages 272

Life of David Crockett *by David Crockett*   ISBN: *1-59462-250-7*   **$27.45**
"Colonel David Crockett was one of the most remarkable men of the times in which he lived. Born in humble life, but gifted with a strong will, an indomitable courage, and unremitting perseverance...   Biographies/New Age Pages 424

Lip-Reading *by Edward Nitchie*   ISBN: *1-59462-206-X*   **$25.95**
Edward B. Nitchie, founder of the New York School for the Hard of Hearing, now the Nitchie School of Lip-Reading, Inc, wrote "LIP-READING Principles and Practice". The development and perfecting of this meritorious work on lip-reading was an undertaking...   How-to Pages 400

A Handbook of Suggestive Therapeutics, Applied Hypnotism, Psychic Science   ISBN: *1-59462-214-0*   **$24.95**
by Henry Munro   Health/New Age/Health/Self-help Pages 376

A Doll's House: and Two Other Plays *by Henrik Ibsen*   ISBN: *1-59462-112-8*   **$19.95**
Henrik Ibsen created this classic when in revolutionary 1848 Rome. Introducing some striking concepts in playwriting for the realist genre, this play has been studied the world over.   Fiction/Classics/Plays 308

The Light of Asia *by sir Edwin Arnold*   ISBN: *1-59462-204-3*   **$13.95**
In this poetic masterpiece, Edwin Arnold describes the life and teachings of Buddha. The man who was to become known as Buddha to the world was born as Prince Gautama of India but he rejected the worldly riches and abandoned the reigns of power when...   Religion/History/Biographies Pages 170

The Complete Works of Guy de Maupassant *by Guy de Maupassant*   ISBN: *1-59462-157-8*   **$16.95**
"For days and days, nights and nights, I had dreamed of that first kiss which was to consecrate our engagement, and I knew not on what spot I should put my lips..."   Fiction/Classics Pages 240

The Art of Cross-Examination *by Francis L. Wellman*   ISBN: *1-59462-309-0*   **$26.95**
Written by a renowned trial lawyer, Wellman imparts his experience and uses case studies to explain how to use psychology to extract desired information through questioning.   How-to/Science/Reference Pages 408

Answered or Unanswered? *by Louisa Vaughan*   ISBN: *1-59462-248-5*   **$10.95**
Miracles of Faith in China   Religion Pages 112

The Edinburgh Lectures on Mental Science (1909) *by Thomas*   ISBN: *1-59462-008-3*   **$11.95**
This book contains the substance of a course of lectures recently given by the writer in the Queen Street Hall, Edinburgh. Its purpose is to indicate the Natural Principles governing the relation between Mental Action and Material Conditions...   New Age/Psychology Pages 148

Ayesha *by H. Rider Haggard*   ISBN: *1-59462-301-5*   **$24.95**
Verily and indeed it is the unexpected that happens! Probably if there was one person upon the earth from whom the Editor of this, and of a certain previous history, did not expect to hear again...   Classics Pages 380

Ayala's Angel *by Anthony Trollope*   ISBN: *1-59462-352-X*   **$29.95**
The two girls were both pretty, but Lucy who was twenty-one who supposed to be simple and comparatively unattractive, whereas Ayala was credited, as her Bombwhat romantic name might show, with poetic charm and a taste for romance. Ayala when her father died was nineteen...   Fiction Pages 484

The American Commonwealth *by James Bryce*   ISBN: *1-59462-286-8*   **$34.45**
An interpretation of American democratic political theory. It examines political mechanics and society from the perspective of Scotsman James Bryce   Politics Pages 572

Stories of the Pilgrims *by Margaret P. Pumphrey*   ISBN: *1-59462-116-0*   **$17.95**
This book explores pilgrims religious oppression in England as well as their escape to Holland and eventual crossing to America on the Mayflower, and their early days in New England...   History Pages 268

QTY

The Fasting Cure *by Sinclair Upton*   ISBN: *1-59462-222-1*   **$13.95**
In the Cosmopolitan Magazine for May, 1910, and in the Contemporary Review (London) for April, 1910, I published an article dealing with my experi-ences in fasting. I have written a great many magazine articles, but never one which attracted so much attention... New Age/Self Help/Health Pages 164

Hebrew Astrology *by Sepharial*   ISBN: *1-59462-308-2*   **$13.45**
In these days of advanced thinking it is a matter of common observation that we have left many of the old landmarks behind and that we are now pressing forward to greater heights and to a wider horizon than that which represented the mind-content of our progenitors... Astrology Pages 144

Thought Vibration or The Law of Attraction in the Thought World   ISBN: *1-59462-127-6*   **$12.95**
by William Walker Atkinson   Psychology/Religion Pages 144

Optimism *by Helen Keller*   ISBN: *1-59462-108-X*   **$15.95**
Helen Keller was blind, deaf, and mute since 19 months old, yet famously learned how to overcome these handicaps, communicate with the world, and spread her lectures promoting optimism. An inspiring read for everyone... Biographies/Inspirational Pages 84

Sara Crewe *by Frances Burnett*   ISBN: *1-59462-360-0*   **$9.45**
In the first place, Miss Minchin lived in London. Her home was a large, dull, tall one, in a large, dull square, where all the houses were alike, and all the sparrows were alike, and where all the door-knockers made the same heavy sound... Childrens/Classic Pages 88

The Autobiography of Benjamin Franklin *by Benjamin Franklin*   ISBN: *1-59462-135-7*   **$24.95**
The Autobiography of Benjamin Franklin has probably been more extensively read than any other American historical work, and no other book of its kind has had such ups and downs of fortune. Franklin lived for many years in England, where he was agent... Biographies/History Pages 332

Name	
Email	
Telephone	
Address	
City, State ZIP	

☐ **Credit Card**   ☐ **Check / Money Order**

Credit Card Number	
Expiration Date	
Signature	

Please Mail to: Book Jungle
PO Box 2226
Champaign, IL 61825
or Fax to: 630-214-0564

ORDERING INFORMATION

web*: www.bookjungle.com*
email*: sales@bookjungle.com*
fax*: 630-214-0564*
mail*: Book Jungle PO Box 2226 Champaign, IL 61825*
or PayPal *to sales@bookjungle.com*

Please contact us for bulk discounts

DIRECT-ORDER TERMS

20% Discount if You Order Two or More Books
Free Domestic Shipping!
Accepted: Master Card, Visa, Discover, American Express

www.ingramcontent.com/pod-product-compliance
Lightning Source LLC
Chambersburg PA
CBHW081143020726
47504CB00009B/1978